Ransome's Quest

KAYE DACUS

HARVEST HOUSE PUBLISHERS

EUGENE, OREGON

Scripture quotations are taken from the King James Version of the Bible.

The author is represented by MacGregor Literary.

Cover by Left Coast Design, Portland, Oregon

Cover photos © Konrad Bak / Shutterstock; iStockphoto / jgroup

This is a work of fiction. Names, characters, places, and incidents are products of the author's imagination or are used fictitiously. Any resemblance to actual persons, living or dead, or to events or locales, is entirely coincidental.

RANSOME'S QUEST
Copyright © 2011 by Kaye Dacus
Published by Harvest House Publishers
Eugene, Oregon 97402
www.harvesthousepublishers.com

Library of Congress Cataloging-in-Publication Data
    Dacus, Kaye,
    Ransome's quest / Kaye Dacus.
        p. cm.—(The ransome trilogy ; bk. 3)
    ISBN 978-0-7369-2755-0 (pbk.)
    ISBN 978-0-7369-4166-2 (eBook)
    1. Kidnapping—Fiction.   2. Ship captains—Fiction.   3. Pirates—Fiction.   4. Caribbean Area—Fiction. I. Title.
    PS3604.A25R38 2011
    813'.6—dc22

                                                                2010051821

Printed in the United States of America

11 12 13 14 15 16 17 18 19 / DP-NI / 10 9 8 7 6 5 4 3 2 1

"I must endeavour to subdue
my mind to my fortune.
I must learn to brook
being happier than I deserve."

Captain Frederick Wentworth
from Jane Austen's *Persuasion*

Tierra Dulce Plantation
St. Catherine's Parish, Jamaica
September 1814

No moon. Wispy clouds hid most of the stars. He could not have asked for a more perfect night. Before him, the house glowed like a lantern atop the hill. Behind him, his men waited for his command.

Julia Witherington was back in Jamaica. Finally. The pirate paused a moment, trying to count the years—the ages, the epochs—he had been on the quest to strike back at Admiral Sir Edward Witherington.

Julia was married, and she had brought her husband here with her. The inimitable Commodore William Ransome. The admiral's favorite; the man he'd taken publicly in hand as a son long before Ransome married the admiral's daughter. The one man in the world the pirate hated almost as much as the admiral.

He smiled. The commodore would ensure word reached Sir Edward of his daughter's abduction.

Movement caught his attention and honed his focus on the house. He turned, maintaining his crouched position. "Remember, men, no killing—especially the navy officer. The woman is mine. No one is to harm her. Is that understood?"

"Aye, Cap'n," his men whispered back.

The pirate turned to face the house again. It seemed he had awaited this moment his entire life. The rules of engagement were about to change.

⊛⊛⊛⊛⊛

"There is one thing you are forgetting."

Ned Cochrane pressed himself farther into the shadows at the man's voice. He didn't mean to eavesdrop. He meant only to protect the reputation—and person—of Charlotte Ransome.

"What is that?" Charlotte's voice fluttered toward him on the breeze.

"This."

At her slight whimper of protest, Ned stepped forward. Henry Winchester, steward of the Tierra Dulce sugar plantation, held Charlotte by the shoulders, his mouth crushed against hers. She was unsuccessfully pushing against the man's chest.

But before Ned could make his presence known, Charlotte stopped struggling. Winchester's grasp loosened. Charlotte brought her heel down on Winchester's foot and then sent her fist into his midsection.

Winchester groaned and staggered back, arms around his stomach, hopping on one foot. "What was that for?"

Charlotte swiped the back of her hand across her mouth. "For taking liberties that are not yours to take."

Ned took that as his cue to step into the situation. He fought to keep his expression stern and his tone serious, wanting to smile over Charlotte's ability to handle herself in any situation. "Is everything all right here?"

The dim light coming down the wide porch that circumnavigated the large house illuminated Charlotte's face. She smiled broadly at him. "Aye—yes, Captain Cochrane. Mr. Winchester and I were clearing up a little misunderstanding." She stepped toward Henry Winchester. "I am going to take you up on your promise to release me from our engagement, Mr. Winchester. I have had a change of heart." She glanced over her shoulder at Ned. "In fact, I love someone else and wish to marry him."

Ned's heart swelled in his chest, filling his throat and pounding into his head. Charlotte loved him. She wanted to marry him. It was all he could do not to break into the jig the sailing master aboard *Audacious* demonstrated every evening during the crew's free time.

Winchester stopped groaning and hopping. His expression hardened as he looked first at Ned and then back at Charlotte. "We shall see about that. You agreed to marry me, Miss Ransome, which means your legacy is mine for the claiming."

Charlotte rubbed her lips together and then cocked her head. "You are more than welcome to take your case to my brother. It is he who controls my dowry, and it is he who never had knowledge of nor gave permission for our ill-advised engagement. I am certain he will be happy to come to terms with you. But, pray, do not plague me with your attentions any longer. I know you do not love me and want only my money. Therefore, we have nothing further to say to each other."

Henry gave them one more malevolent look and then stalked off into the darkness.

"Now I understand." Ned leaned against the porch railing and crossed his arms. As she was the one backlit, Ned could not make out her expression. He tried to keep his own face neutral, inscrutable—the way her brother, his commanding officer, did so well. He was almost certain he failed at it.

"Understand what?" Charlotte moved closer, tension radiating from the set of her shoulders and her twisting hands.

"How you made an enemy of Midshipman Kent and lived to tell the tale." He shook his head and stood, wanting to both shake her and embrace her. "Have you *no* common sense? Do you not know better than to taunt a hungry shark?"

She settled her hands on her hips. "It is the shark who should not taunt *me*. Have I not proven I am capable of surviving anything that comes my way? Have I not shown that I can do what a man can do as well as a man can do it? Have I not demonstrated—"

Unable to resist her any longer, he kissed her, reveling in the softness of her lips. She grabbed the lapels of his coat and swayed as if about to swoon. He supported her weight with one arm around the small of her back. With the other, he pulled off her mobcap and caressed the back of her head.

He ended the kiss and held Charlotte close, his fingers stroking her short, silky hair. "Aye, you have proven all those things."

"I was a good midshipman, was I not?"

After everything she'd been through, he could not believe she doubted her adequacy as a midshipman. "Yes. One of the best I have had the pleasure to serve with. But it makes me worry."

She pushed against his chest to look into his eyes. "Worry?"

Fear—not worry—nearly clogged his throat. But had she not said...? "Aye. Will you be content to give up your prospects for further promotion in the navy to become merely the wife of an officer?"

Charlotte swallowed before answering. "Aye, sir. It would make me most content to be the wife of Captain Ned Cochrane."

He kissed her again, joy making his legs weak and nearly capsizing both of them. "You have made me the happiest of men." He once again tucked her into his embrace, resting his cheek against the top of her head.

She stiffened. "What was that? Did you hear—"

He shushed her. Then the hairs at the back of his neck tingled. He released her, wishing he'd thought to bring his pistol with him when he had followed Charlotte and Winchester out here.

The noise came again. Not quite a rustling, not quite a scratching. More like the shuffling-scraping sound made by sailors' bare feet on a ship's deck.

"Stay behind me," Ned whispered, pulling Charlotte behind his back. "We'd best go inside."

"I concur, wholeheartedly." Her hands settled on his waist.

Without turning, he walked backward toward the warm glow of light from the open windows and doors at the other end of the too-long porch. Why hadn't he taken Charlotte inside immediately after Winchester's departure?

A thud behind them. Charlotte gasped and her hands dropped away from his waist.

Ned turned—and the side of his head exploded with a searing, bright white pain before contracting into darkness. More pain shot through his legs as his knees hit the porch decking.

Rustling noises...sounds of a struggle? Ned tried to stay upright, but he needed to lie down—no, he needed to help Charlotte. Where was she?

He rubbed his eyes against the darkness. His left hand came away wet, sticky. The side of his head throbbed.

"Ned!"

Panic drove him to his feet. "Ch—"

Fresh pain at the back of his head. Stars bloomed before his eyes and he fell forward, knees, chest, and chin hitting the floor. He rolled to his back.

A dark figure crouched over him. "Tell Admiral Sir Edward Witherington it is time for him to pay for the sins of his past. Until he does, the woman's survival depends on the mercy of a pirate."

Ned reached for the man's throat, desperate for any means to stop him, but the pirate shoved his hands aside. Ned tried to pull himself up, but darkness swirled around him, drowning him. He fell back to the porch.

When he opened his eyes, all was silent. No movement, no rustle, no harsh breathing.

His head ached and spun. Something warm trickled down his cheek.

He pushed himself into a kneeling position. Taking hold of the porch railing, he hoisted himself up, no better than a hulled ship bobbing in a stormy sea. After a few wobbly steps, he found his sea legs.

"Charlotte?" He could muster only a whisper. No response came.

Finding the nearest open door, he staggered into the house, not knowing whose bedroom he entered. In the hallway, he turned around three times before taking a deep breath and getting his bearings. There, two doors down.

He barreled into his bedroom and ran right into the bench at the end of the bed. On it was his small traveling bag, as yet unpacked. He rummaged in it and finally wrapped his hand around the smooth butt of his pistol.

The door scraped farther open, and light flooded the room. Ned leveled the pistol at it.

"Sir, it's me! Jeremiah." The dark-skinned man held the lantern high, near his face. "I heard a commotion—"

"Come, I need your help." Ned snatched the candle-filled lantern from the plantation's overseer and hurried from the house. At the back he carefully descended the steps to the wide expanse of grassy lawn.

No moon. Almost complete blackness. He crossed the lawn toward the cane fields that surrounded the house. He'd seen a cut-through somewhere in this direction which appeared to lead to the inlet far below the hilltop-set house.

Rustling. Footsteps.

Ned stopped, raising the pistol. "Who goes there?"

"Commodore William Ransome. Identify yourself."

"Captain Ned Cochrane." He nearly collapsed with relief—and dread. He stopped and leaned over, his head pounding.

Jeremiah took the lantern from him.

"Jeremiah? What—?" Julia Ransome appeared from behind her husband's back.

Ned straightened. He had to tell the commodore and his wife about Charlotte.

Mrs. Ransome gasped and rushed forward, pressing a handkerchief to Ned's left temple. "What happened?"

Wincing at the pressure she put on the injury, he took the cloth from her and wiped the worst of the blood from his face.

"Pirates." He spat the word. "They attacked me from behind. The blow disoriented me. By the time I could see straight, they were gone."

Ned locked eyes with William. "They took Charlotte."

I t is too dangerous."

William Ransome snapped his cutlass into its scabbard and turned to face his wife. "The longer I delay, the farther away they take Charlotte."

Dread froze his lungs, his stomach, his heart. Charlotte. His sister. Taken. "If anything happens to her…"

Julia wrapped her arms around her abdomen and leaned against one of the heavy posts at the end of the bed. "Why the message to my father? What has he to do with Charlotte?"

William double-checked the load of his pistol and tucked it under his belt. "Your father has publicly vowed—more than once—to rid the Caribbean of pirates and privateers for good. Charlotte was likely a target of opportunity, not purpose."

"But if the man's argument is with my father, it should have been me taken, not Charlotte."

William could not disagree with her. Nor could he agree, as the very idea of Julia's being taken by pirates nearly ripped his heart from his chest. "I should have put her on that ship in Barbados returning to England. If I had followed my conscience"—instead of listening to Julia's and Charlotte's emotional arguments—"she would have been well out of harm's way by now."

They both startled at a knock on the door.

"Come."

The door opened at his command, revealing Jeremiah. "The horses are ready, Commodore."

"Very good." William took up his case and hat and moved toward the door.

Julia stepped in front of him, expression imploring. "Please, William, wait until dawn. The roads are treacherous enough in the full light of day. At night…and you do not know where you are going. What good will it do Charlotte if you become lost or…or something else happens to you or the horse? Or what if the pirates have laid a trap and done this to lure you from the safety of the house?"

A mirthless laugh expanded in his throat, but he stifled it. Safety of the house? Was the house safe when the brigands had snatched Charlotte from the porch almost directly outside this very room?

"I am sending Asher with him, Miss Julia," Jeremiah said. "He knows the roads 'twixt here and Kingston better than anyone I know."

William tore his gaze away from Julia's anxious face. "Jeremiah, I am depending on you to protect Mrs. Ransome and ensure no harm comes to her while I am away."

"I will protect her with my life, sir."

He stepped around Julia and handed his bag and hat to Jeremiah. "Thank you. I shall join you in a moment."

As he hoped, Jeremiah understood the dismissal. He gave a slight bow and left the room, closing the door behind him.

William took Julia by the shoulders and directed her to the chaise positioned at the end of their bed. He had to apply more pressure than he liked to make her sit. "You are to stay at Tierra Dulce. You will keep an escort with you at all times. I want armed guards posted near the house."

She nodded, never blinking or breaking eye contact. "Yes, William."

"If you hear any word from Charlotte or receive"—his voice caught in his throat—"a ransom demand from the pirate, you will send a messenger to Fort Charles. They will get word to me."

"Yes, William."

Heart tearing asunder at the necessity of leaving Julia behind, he bent over and pressed his forehead to hers. "Pray for Charlotte."

Julia's hands slid around behind his neck, her fingers twining in his hair. She angled her head and kissed him. "I promise. I will pray for you also, my love."

He kissed her again and then tore himself away from her embrace. "I must go. I promise I will return—and I *will* bring Charlotte with me."

Determined to not look back, he made for the door. He opened it and then hesitated. Without turning around, he said the words he needed to say, just in case they were the last he ever said to his wife. "I love you."

"I love you, William." Though softly spoken, her words acted as the command that loosed him from his mooring. He stepped through the door and closed it, leaving her on the other side.

Ned Cochrane paced the drive below the porch steps when William exited the house. He barely spared his former first officer a glance. Intellectually, he knew Ned had done his best, having been taken by surprise and set upon by several men. However, in his heart, he wanted to rail at the younger man for failing to protect Charlotte.

Though a horse was his least favorite mode of transportation, William easily swung himself up into the saddle. Once he was settled—and Ned appeared to be also—William nodded at Asher to lead the way.

Darkness enveloped them. Behind, the light from the house acted as a siren's call, beckoning him to turn, to look, to regret his decision to leave in the dead of night and wish he had taken Julia's advice and waited until dawn.

His neck ached from the effort of keeping his face forward instead of giving in to temptation and taking one last look at the house, hoping to catch a final glimpse of Julia.

He focused on the bumpy motion of the animal underneath him. He must leave all thoughts of—all worries about—Julia behind, just as he now left her home behind. Jeremiah had known Julia most of her life. He had been as much of a substitute father for Julia as her father, Admiral Witherington, had been for William.

No, he could not worry about Julia and her safety. Rescuing Charlotte must be his only focus, his only thought.

The monotonous rhythm of the horses' hooves, at a walk over the dark, deeply rutted dirt roads, along with the necessity of keeping his eyes trained on the light shirt stretched across Asher's broad back, lulled William into a stupor.

Ahead lay his ship. The thought of boarding *Alexandra* and getting under sail chipped away at his anxiety. As soon as he was on the water, as soon as he stood on the quarterdeck and issued the command to weigh anchor, he would be that much closer to finding Charlotte and bringing her home.

The road widened, and Ned pulled up beside him.

"You are certain the man did not identify himself?"

"No, sir. He did not give his name. He only said her safety depended on the mercy of a pirate." Ned's voice came across flat and hoarse.

"What were you doing out on the porch, alone with her in the dark?" Even as William asked this, he reminded himself Ned was not at fault. But if Charlotte had been inside, perhaps...

"I followed them—Miss Ransome and Winchester—when they went for their walk. I did not trust Mrs. Ransome's steward to behave honorably." He paused. "I need not have worried. Char—Miss Ransome handled the situation admirably and dispatched Winchester, and their engagement, with aplomb."

"Winchester was with you when she was taken? Why did you not tell me this before?"

"No, sir. Miss Ransome dismissed him. He had been gone for... several minutes."

Could Winchester be involved? Dread sank like a cannonball in William's gut. Julia already suspected the steward of embezzling money from the plantation. And William had left her there with that man—

"I asked her to marry me."

If Winchester were involved, and this was a ploy to get William away from Tierra—he yanked the reins. The horse voiced its protest and jerked and swerved, nearly unseating William. "I beg your pardon?"

"After Charlotte broke her engagement with Winchester, we talked about our mutual regard. I proposed marriage to her, and she accepted."

Ned's words barely rose above the sounds of the horses' hooves on the hard-packed earth.

From a sinking ship into shark-infested waters. Could Charlotte not have waited even a full day after breaking one engagement before forming another—again, without her family's knowledge? "And if I refuse my permission?"

"Then we shall wait. We'll wait until you think I am worthy to marry her, sir."

Worthy to marry her. William did not have to think hard to remember standing before Julia's father twelve years ago and saying the same words. Sir Edward had graciously given him—a poor, threadbare lieutenant with no prospects and nothing to recommend him as husband or son-in-law—a father's blessing for William and Julia to marry based on nothing other than their love for each other. William had been the one to deem himself unworthy of her affections, and he had almost lost her forever.

"We shall discuss this after we return Charlotte home."

"I pray that will be soon, sir."

"So do I, Ned. So do I."

୧୧୧୨୨

Charlotte awoke with a gasp. Wooden planks formed the low ceiling above her. A canvas hammock conformed to her body and swung with the heave and haw of the ocean beneath the ship.

A ship?

Not possible. They had made port, hadn't they?

She stared at the underside of the deck above, trying to clear the haziness from her brain. Yes. They had made port. Left *Alexandra* and ridden in carriage across those horrible, rutted roads to Tierra Dulce, Julia's sugar plantation. The low, sprawling white house with the deep porch that wrapped all the way around and the white draperies billowing through the open windows.

The porch. She blinked rapidly. The porch. At night. In the dark. Henry Winchester and…and Ned.

She bolted upright and then flung her torso over the side of the hammock as her stomach heaved.

Why should she be sick? She hadn't experienced a moment of seasickness on the crossing from England to Jamaica. She climbed out of the hammock, skirt and petticoats hindering her progress until she hoisted them above her knees, and made for the small table with a glass and pitcher.

Wan light from the stern windows sparkled through the glass, revealing a residue of white powder in the bottom of it. She set the glass back on the stand. Last night the pirate had made her drink from the glass, and then everything had gone hazy. But before that…

She buried her face in her hands. Being torn away from Ned. She prayed they had not killed him. She'd heard no gunshot, but as their raid had been one of stealth, they would more likely have used a blade to end Ned's life.

A sob ripped at her throat, but she forced it to stay contained. She would not give the pirates the satisfaction of seeing her upset. And she must, and would, find a means of escape.

Thirst got the better of her, and she lifted the china pitcher of water and rinsed her mouth before drinking deeply the brackish liquid. She then turned and surveyed the cabin. Obviously the pirate captain's quarters. Though smaller than Ned's aboard *Audacious*, which was in turn smaller than William's aboard *Alexandra*, the room was neatly kept, with serviceable furnishings, whitewashed walls and ceiling, and plain floors. Nothing to exhibit the extravagance or wealth she'd expected to see in a pirate's private lair.

The desk. Perhaps something there would tell her more about her captor. She crossed to it, rather surprised by the empty work surface. No stacks of the papers or books like the ones resting on William's or Ned's worktables. Her fingers itched to open the drawer under the desktop and the small doors and drawers along the high back of it, but Mama had taught her better than that.

Two miniatures hanging above the desk caught her eye. One showed a woman, probably a few years older than Charlotte, with dark hair and angular features. Too plain to be called pretty, but not ugly either. The green backdrop of the second painting contrasted vividly with the reddish-brown hair of a pretty girl and matched her vibrant green eyes.

Mahogany hair and green eyes—just like Julia. Why would a pirate have a portrait of Julia hanging in his cabin? But, she corrected herself, the painting was of a girl no older than thirteen or fourteen. Surely the resemblance to Julia was merely coincidental.

"She was lovely, was she not?"

Charlotte gasped and whirled. A dark-haired man dressed in a blue coat that resembled a commodore's or admiral's—complete with prodigious amounts of gold braid about the cuffs, collar, and lapels—stood in the doorway of the cabin.

He tossed a bicorne hat—also similar to a navy officer's—onto the oblong table in the middle of the cabin, clasped his hands behind his back, and sauntered toward her, his eyes on the portrait.

"What do you want with me?"

"I am sorry for the manner of your coming here, Miss…?" He cocked one eyebrow at her.

"Ransome. Charlotte Ransome. My brother is Commodore William Ransome. He will hunt you down. And when he finds you—"

"When he finds me," the pirate said, sighing, "I am certain the encounter shall be quite violent and bloody. Is that what you were going to say?"

Charlotte ground her teeth together. The man stood there, serene as a vicar on the Sabbath, acting as if they stood in a drawing room in Liverpool discussing the weather. "What do you want with me?"

"With you? Nothing." He flicked an invisible speck of dust from the oval frame. "My business is with her."

"With her?" Charlotte nodded toward the painting. "Is that…?"

"Julia Witherington—or Julia Ransome, as I have lately learned. Empress of the Tierra Dulce sugar empire."

The strange lilt in his voice when he said Julia's name sent a chill down Charlotte's spine. "Yes, she is married. To my brother."

"The famous Commodore Ransome." The pirate turned and ambled toward the dining table. "His reputation precedes him."

Worry riddled Charlotte at the pirate's lack of worry over the thought of William's hunting him down and blowing him and his crew out of the water. After Charlotte escaped, naturally.

"You were not part of my plan, little Charlotte Ransome." He turned, leaned against the edge of the table, and crossed his arms. The coat pulled across his broad chest and muscular shoulders. A lock of dark hair fell over his forehead, softening the way his heavy black brows hooded his eyes. His nose had been aquiline once, but now it sported a bump about halfway down from whence the rest of the appendage angled slightly to his left. A scar stretched across his forehead and down into his left eyebrow. On first sight he could have passed for Spanish, but his accent marked him as an Englishman.

If he weren't a no-good, dastardly, cowardly, kidnapping pirate, she might consider him handsome.

"Did you kill him?" The question squeezed past her throat unbidden.

"Him?"

"Ned—Captain Cochrane. The man with me on the porch." She schooled her emotions as best she could, pretending the man stand-ing before her was none other than Kent, her nemesis during her days aboard *Audacious* as a midshipman.

"If he is dead, it is through no work of me or my men. We do not kill for sport, only for defense."

"Ha!" The mirthless laugh popped out before she could stop it. "Morality from a *pirate*? Someone who spends his life pillaging and thieving and destroying and killing and…and…" Heat flooded her face.

"And?" The pirate stood and stalked toward her, an odd gleam in his dark eyes. "And ravishing young women? Is that what you were going to say?"

Charlotte backed away, right into the edge of the desk. She gripped it hard. "N-no."

The pirate leaned over her, hands on either side of her atop the desk, trapping her. "Do not try to lie to me, little Charlotte Ransome. You have no talent for it."

Stays digging into her waist, she bent as far back as she could. "Yes, then. Ravishing." Not that he would get a chance to ravish her. A fork. A penknife. Anything with a sharp edge or point. Once she had something like that in her possession, she would be able to defend herself against him.

Up close, the pirate's brown eyes held chips of gold and green. A hint of dark whiskers lay just beneath the skin of his jaw and above his upper lip.

He blinked when someone knocked on the door but didn't move. "Come!"

"Captain, Lau and Declan are back."

"Very good. I shall meet with them in the wheelhouse momentarily to hear their report. Dismissed."

Charlotte wanted to cry out to stop the other man from leaving, but she knew she deluded herself. She was no safer with any man on this ship than with their captain.

Would Ned still want her—even be able to look at her—after the pirates were finished with her?

"What's this?" The pirate reached up and touched Charlotte's cheek. "Tears?"

She shook her head, more to dislodge his hand than in denial.

With another sigh he straightened and then handed her a hand-kerchief. "Calm yourself, Miss Ransome. I have no intention of ravishing you. Nor of allowing anyone else to ravish you. While you are aboard my ship, you are under my protection."

He crossed to the table and retrieved his hat. "You, however, must stay to this cabin at all times. Though my men know my rules of conduct, a few of them might give in to the temptation of their baser desires should they see you about on deck."

Charlotte leaned heavily against the desk. The handkerchief in her hand was of the finest lawn, embroidered white-on-white with a

Greek-key design around the edge. She frowned at the bit of cloth. Why would a pirate carry something so delicate?

He settled the bicorne on his dark head, points fore-and-aft, the same way the officers of the Royal Navy wore theirs.

"Who are you?"

He touched the fore tip of the hat and then flourished a bow. "I am called El Salvador, and you are aboard my ship, *Vengeance*. Welcome to my home, Miss Ransome."

Chapter Two

El Salvador de los Esclavos. The Savior of the Slaves. He'd adopted the epithet many years ago, when he heard it chanted over and over by the dark-skinned men and women bound in chains on a ship he liberated. His reputation, if not his real name, had preceded him.

El Salvador de los Esclavos. The pirate who had kidnapped a young woman—and the wrong young woman at that. What would his reputation be now?

Salvador closed the cabin door softly behind himself and joined his five most trusted men on the quarterdeck.

"Who is she, Cap'n?" Declan, his first mate, preferred meetings on the deck rather than in the captain's cabin. At six-and-a-half feet, he was too tall to be a sailor. But he was one of the finest men Salvador had ever sailed with.

He had to be honest with these five—the men he trusted with his very life. "She is Charlotte Ransome, sister of Commodore William Ransome."

"Ransome?" Picaro ran his fingers through his ginger curls. The second mate—who'd been known as Simon Donnelley before he turned pirate—had been part of the crew the shortest amount of time, only five years; but his knowledge of the Royal Navy proved time and again to be vital. "Ransome. The man has quite the reputation. He's never engaged in a battle he didn't win."

"Then we must make certain he does not find us, so he cannot engage us in battle." Salvador crossed his arms.

"He's going to have a powerful need to get his sister back." Jean Baptiste, the sailing master, whose tone was as dark as his skin, did not take his hands from the wheel or remove his eyes from the horizon beyond the bow of the frigate.

For the first time in his life—his life as a pirate—Salvador feared he'd done something he might come to regret. "The plan worked. We simply ended up with the wrong woman."

"Think we can still get the admiral to pay? And if we can get that kind of swag from snatching girls, why haven't we done it before?" Picaro asked.

"It ain't what we do." Declan leaned on the railing that separated the elevated quarterdeck from the waist of the ship and scowled at Salvador. "I'll say it again. I don't think it's right to go around snatching young women from their families. It ain't what we do."

"The captain has his reasons for taking this action." Lau, the boatswain, could always be counted on to defend Salvador, even if in this case his actions might not be worthy of defense.

Salvador raised his hands. "There is no point in further discussion of the merits or disadvantages of taking the girl. It is done. Now I must decide what action comes next."

"Give her back. Put her in one of the boats with some food and water and set her adrift." Declan stood, towering over everyone else. "We're still close enough to land that someone should come upon her before nightfall."

"Someone?" Salvador cocked his head. "What if that someone happens to be Shaw?"

The first mate's lips pressed into a tight pucker. "Unless I'm disremembering, Shaw's the reason we set out on this fool's errand to begin with. Something about how he'd been bragging he was going to snatch Julia Witherington if ever she came back to Jamaica. And you decided to snatch her first. But now"—Declan raised his left arm and pointed downward, presumably toward Salvador's cabin below them—"you've got the wrong girl, and you've dragged Commodore Ransome away from Tierra Dulce, where he could have provided some protection against Shaw for the Witherington woman."

Salvador's stomach churned at Declan's precise explanation of how he'd managed to bungle the whole affair. "Other than casting the girl adrift, which is not going to happen, what do you suggest?"

"Well, we certainly can't go back for the Witherington woman now. Not with Ransome on our tail." Declan glared at him.

"We lead them astray and then double back and take the other woman," Lau suggested. "Plant a few false leads to send Ransome far afield—up to Cuba or over to Hispaniola. Then we come back around and take the Witherington woman now no one's there to protect her."

"*Two* Royal Navy ships docked at Kingston, if you will recall." Picaro kept his voice even and calm. "Ransome could order the second ship to protect the inlet. We would have to go overland, which would take far too long."

"Captain." A soft voice edged out the others for Salvador's attention.

"What is it, Suresh?" Salvador glanced at his steward.

The young, reed-thin East Indian nodded toward the raised skylight behind them.

Salvador turned, and his breath caught in his throat. Charlotte Ransome's blue eyes widened and then disappeared from the windows at the front of the raised box that provided extra light for his cabin.

Just what he needed. A prisoner who did not know her place, which was cowering in a corner and fretting over all of the horrible things that could happen to her aboard his ship. He went down the companionway to the half deck and shoved his cabin door open.

Charlotte Ransome stood near the stern, hands clasped behind her back, looking out the windows. The door slammed with more force than he'd intended.

Miss Ransome turned at the sound. "Captain El Salvador." She curtsied, somehow maintaining her balance against the swaying of the ship.

The name sounded ridiculous coming from her. "It is simply Salvador."

"I must call you by your proper rank, sir."

He sighed. "Captain Salvador."

She reached her right hand up and then dropped it. The motion had been familiar—like a naval officer about to touch his hat in salute to a superior. But it must have been his imagination. She was a woman.

"Why were you spying on me and my men?"

Miss Ransome stood with her feet shoulder-width apart and clasped her hands behind her back again. "It is my duty as a captive to learn whatever I can about my abductors and devise a means of escape, is it not, sir?"

He scoffed. "You, a slip of a girl, escape my ship?"

She squared her shoulders. "I will have you know that I spent two months—" Her face flamed and she dropped her gaze to the floor.

Intrigued, he moved closer. "You spent two months doing what?"

"It is none of your concern." She looked up at him again, this time with a coquettish smile. "I simply wanted to find out why you have brought me here."

"And what did you learn by listening at the window like a scullery maid?"

"That you took me by mistake. That you intended to take my sister instead."

"She is not your sister, she is—" Heat flooded Salvador's face, and he turned on his heel. He had never come so close to revealing what he knew about the Witherington family to anyone. But now Julia Witherington was so near, almost within reach...

"She is what?"

"It is none of your concern." He composed himself and faced his captive once again. "Yes, you were taken in error. I meant to take Julia Witherington—Julia Ransome, that is—before another pirate could snatch her."

"Shaw?" Miss Ransome's voice cracked, hollow and weak.

"Shaw."

"Is he as vile as the stories make him out to be?"

"Worse." Salvador dropped into one of the chairs at the heavy oaken table in the center of the small cabin.

"Then what does that make you, wanting to take Julia before he could?" Miss Ransome's fists settled onto her narrow hips.

He could take the hot coals of guilt from Declan, but not from a girl. He rose and stalked toward her, pleased—and ashamed—when her eyes widened and she drew back until the edge of the window seat took her legs out from under her. She sank onto the bench, grabbing the leather-padded edge.

The fear that flickered in her blue eyes made him pull away. "You know nothing of my motivations, Miss Ransome. You will do well not to speculate as to my intentions."

"If you would explain them to me, then I would not need to speculate."

He stared at her in astonishment. One moment she could not hide a flash of fear, and the next she spoke boldly, as if this were her sitting room and he an uninvited guest. "You listened to our conversation. You must know all."

"I heard that you intended on ransoming Julia, on getting Sir Edward to pay money for her release. What would you do if he refused to pay? Kill her? Turn her over to someone like Shaw if you found you had not the stomach for it yourself?"

Salvador whirled to face her, fist raised.

Miss Ransome did not flinch. Instead, she rose from her seat and stood before him. The light from the windows that stretched across the stern of the cabin illuminated the left side of her face—and the scars beside her eye and down her cheek. Scars that could not be more than several weeks old.

He dropped his fist, his anger over her opinion of him dissipating. "What happened to your face?"

She reached up and touched the red lines. "The ship I sailed here on came under attack on the voyage. I was…hit in the face by flying debris."

Something in her tone indicated she lied—or did not tell the entire truth. But now was not the time to demand the telling. "You believe I intended to kill Julia if Sir Edward did not pay the ransom, and yet you stand there, bold as brass, with no concern for your own life."

"W-would you?" She lowered herself onto the window seat again.

He now clasped his hands behind his back. "If you must know, I did not plan to bring any harm to Mrs. Ransome. And extorting money from Sir Edward, while an added benefit, is not my main priority."

Miss Ransome's eyes narrowed. "So, why?"

"I wanted to take her before Shaw did."

"That still doesn't explain—"

"I wanted to take her before Shaw did to protect her from him."

∞∞∞

The chaos on *Audacious's* quarterdeck matched the surprise with which Commodore Ransome and Captain Ned Cochrane's sudden appearance had been met at Fort Charles four hours ago.

Ned railed internally at the necessary delays in getting under sail. He understood the need to review the charts and the information in the files they had on the pirates active in the waters around Jamaica so they could determine a course of action, but the general inefficiency at the fort in responding to Commodore Ransome's orders to resupply the ships with water and food put them even farther behind the brigands who had taken Charlotte.

He paused in his pacing of the quarterdeck at the change in activity of the crew. Yes, the boatswain had finally given the order to clear the tackle and return the grates to the hatches.

"Cap'n Cochrane, sir." Boatswain Parr scurried over and stopped in front of Ned, crooking his forefinger and touching the side of the knuckle to his forehead in salute. Like the rest of the crew, Parr looked fit to burst with curiosity about Ned's reappearance—and the bruising and new scars on his face. "All supplies are laid in, and the supply boats have cleared away."

"Very good." Ned turned and motioned the closest officer over. "Lieutenant Hamilton, signal to *Alexandra* that we are ready to make sail."

"Aye, aye, sir." The acting fourth lieutenant touched the fore point of his hat in salute and took the stairs up to the poop deck in three bounds, Midshipman Jamison on his heels to record the signal and the reply in his journal, no doubt.

Ned's heart twisted at the sight of the teen in the midshipman's uniform. Oh, to go back to the days when the biggest worry he had was trying to figure out a way to ensure no one aboard *Audacious* learned one of their mids was none other than Charlotte Ransome in disguise.

Her presence had made his first few weeks of command miserable—living in constant fear she would be found out or that he would accidentally reveal the truth himself. At least she had been here, with him. Safe. Not held captive by a pirate and being…being…

A cry of agony almost escaped his throat, but he stopped it. *Dear Lord, please keep her under Your protection.*

"Sir, reply from lead ship. 'Weigh anchor and execute your orders.'"

Ned nodded at Lieutenant Hamilton and called for his first officer. Lieutenant Gardiner immediately appeared. "Mr. Gardiner, weigh anchor and take us out of the harbor. Then set course for Black River."

A center for logging and the rum and slave trades, the town of Black River was also a target of pirates—as well as a gateway to some of their inland hideouts, according to the information Commodore Ransome had.

"Aye, aye, sir." Gardiner turned and relayed Ned's orders. The chaos of moments before became well-orchestrated action as sailors manned the capstan to raise the anchor and others flowed up the masts and out along the yardarms to release the sails as soon as the order was given.

Ned took what felt like his first breath since last night as soon as he gave the order to loose the headsails. The white sheets of canvas flapped and then, as soon as they caught the wind, billowed forth and stretched taught, propelling the ship forward.

Navigating Kingston Harbor took a little more skill than leaving Portsmouth and sailing out of Spithead, but the inexperienced first officer and experienced sailing master managed it well together.

Once they put the harbor behind them and Ned had conferred with the sailing master on the course to be followed, he passed word for all of the lieutenants to join him in his cabin.

A couple of minutes later, once all had convened around the long dining table in the antechamber to Ned's living quarters, he fought a building anxiety looking at the men surrounding the table. After losing *Audacious's* captain and first and second lieutenants in an attack on the crossing from England, the three remaining lieutenants had taken over the senior positions, with two midshipmen—Hamilton and Martin—receiving field promotions to acting lieutenant to fill the void. Ned eyed all five men critically. Their combined time of service as lieutenants exceeded his own tenure at the rank by mere months.

If they found the pirate ship and engaged in battle...Ned shuddered at the only outcome he could imagine.

"Gentlemen, I thank you for your patience in waiting to hear the explanation behind my sudden reappearance and the urgency in setting sail." Ned clasped his hands atop the table and leaned forward. "A little more than twelve hours ago, Commodore Ransome's sister was abducted by pirates."

Murmured expressions of shock and astonishment flew around the table, as expected.

"The commodore has decided the course of action we are now following. We are sailing west; he is sailing east. He has intelligence on locations pirates in this area frequent, and we are beginning at one of those—Black River. Once we are there, I will go ashore with a small party and meet with a contact, a man who passes along information on pirates to the Royal Navy. What he tells us will determine our next course of action."

Lieutenant Gardiner glanced around the circle of his peers, as if seeking consensus, before speaking. "Sir, you know we will do our uttermost to fulfill the commodore's orders and to hunt down the pirate who took his sister."

Ned nodded at his first officer. "I know you will, Mr. Gardiner." He looked around the circle too. "We must be on highest alert at all times, as if we were back in the war again chasing Frogs through the Channel. Eyes and ears open, lookouts at all points during every watch."

When Ned first received the news of the voyage to the Caribbean and their assignment of ridding the waters of pirates, it had been with the excitement of a lieutenant serving under an experienced and decorated commander. But even though Commodore Ransome still held the position of Ned's commanding officer, Ned now stood in the position of captain—a post he never wanted—with the lives of more than six hundred sailors hanging on his decisions.

The situation he had dreaded for ten years, ever since a decision directly resulted in the deaths of two sailors under his command, now fell upon him. Around the table eager and anxious young lieutenants all looked to him for their orders...and their security and safety. The only face Ned could see, though, was that of Charlotte Ransome.

Determination to rescue her drove away any lingering traces of fear or doubt in his crew's, or his own, experience and abilities.

He pressed his hands flat on the table. "Men, we may be young, and we may lack the years of experience of the commodore's crew, but those things do not matter. A woman's life is at stake. We must save her, at all costs."

He made eye contact with each of the five men, pleased at the kindling gleams of resolve in their eyes.

"And if we happen to take down a notorious pirate in the process of rescuing Miss Ransome, all the better for us."

Chapter Three

Julia stared through the window over the grassy tops of the cane to the sapphire waters of the lagoon beyond. For more than a year she had dreamed of nothing else than coming home to Jamaica, home to Tierra Dulce. Now that she was here, it felt strange—foreign. Almost as if she no longer quite belonged here.

She flinched at the knock on the door that split asunder the silence of the office. "Enter."

"You asked to see me, ma'am?"

For a moment, standing there staring out at the water, she thought she could almost feel the roll and pitch of the waves under her feet. But, no. William's place was at sea; hers was at Tierra Dulce. Julia turned and walked back to the chair behind the large ornate desk.

"Please be seated, Mr. Winchester." She motioned him toward one of the chairs on the other side of the desk. "As I am certain you are aware, Jeremiah sent me the second copy of each of the plantation's ledgers. Over the past few months, I have taken the time to review each ledger line by line. I grew concerned when I discovered discrepancies in the arithmetic in one of the ledgers particularly."

Julia watched the steward closely, trying to catch any hint in his expression to confirm her suspicions that the discrepancies were not mere miscalculations, but rather the purposeful action of a person of ill intent.

However, Henry Winchester betrayed no guilt or panic over having been found out. "Discrepancies, you say? I do not see how that can be possible. I check through my calculations scrupulously. Did Sir Edward find the same discrepancies?"

If he meant to insult her by hinting the problem lay not in his faulty ledgers but in her mathematics skills, he succeeded. But rather than give in to the quick temper she inherited from her father, she chose instead to imitate her husband's unflappable calmness. "My father did not need to review the ledgers for himself. That is a task he has trusted me to do for the past ten years."

Winchester splayed his hands before him in a gesture of supplication. "I assure you, ma'am, if any errors are in the accounting, they happened purely by mistake. I will look into the matter as soon as time allows."

Julia allowed her brows to rise as the only expression of her surprise. "As soon as time allows? Pray tell, what could be more urgent than the accurate reporting of the plantation's income and debt? I must insist this issue be addressed immediately."

Winchester's jaw worked back and forth as if grinding unsavory words between his teeth. Julia shifted in her chair to mask her shudder of revulsion. That he was a handsome man, she could not deny. So had been her cousin Drake Pembroke. The two men were cut from the same unsavory cloth. What had she seen in Henry Winchester to convince her to hire him? Worse yet, what had Charlotte seen in him to make her not only agree to a secret engagement, but also disguise herself as a boy and sign on to *Audacious* as a midshipman to come to Jamaica to marry him without her family's knowledge or approval?

"It will take a few days for me to gather the required documents for an audit of the ledgers," Winchester said.

Today being Thursday, with calls to make and receive tomorrow and Saturday, and church Sunday, Julia knew she would not be able to get back to town to visit her banker and solicitor before Monday, and she needed time to review the most recent account records too. "Very well. We shall meet again in one week—Thursday next—to audit the ledgers."

Winchester did not hide his relief adequately. "I shall inform Jeremiah to turn over his books—"

"Jeremiah will be joining us. Three sets of eyes are better than two for uncovering any errors or oversights."

The steward inclined his head, but not soon enough to keep her from seeing the glint of resentment in his eyes. "Yes, ma'am."

"Please bring me the current books so I can review them before we meet."

His jaw started the grinding motion again. "Yes, ma'am. Is that all, ma'am?"

With what remained of her waning strength and energy, Julia did her best to appear relaxed and unconcerned. But she was not. "Mr. Winchester, I want to assure you Commodore Ransome will do whatever he must to bring Charlotte home safely."

Winchester's long, straight nose wrinkled and he muttered something.

She sat forward. "I am sorry. I did not hear you clearly."

"I am certain the Ransome family will be happy to have her returned. But I…well, all I can say is I am gratified she broke our engagement before she was taken and her reputation—and virtue—ruined." He snorted. "As if I would have married her after the manner of her coming here. Living among sailors, doing everything she could to assure her reputation would be in tatters long before she revealed her secret engagement to her family."

Julia stood and pressed her fists against the desktop, leaning toward him. "You will say no more to impugn the reputation of my sister." She took a steadying breath. "You have one week to gather all of the necessary documents for the audit. Once the audit has been completed, you will be advanced two months' pay and provided transportation into town. Your services will no longer be required at Tierra Dulce."

This time Winchester did not bother to hide his disdain. "As if I would stay at a plantation run by a *woman*."

"Jeremiah." Julia spoke the name in a tone raised only a little above normal.

The plantation overseer entered through the side door. "Yes, Mrs. Ransome?"

"Please assist Mr. Winchester in gathering everything necessary for a full audit of the ledgers. You will supervise his work for the remainder of the time he is here."

Winchester shot from his chair. "You're going to put a ni—"

"You will keep a civil tongue as long as you are on my property, Mr. Winchester." The fury that gurgled in her stomach reminded her she was her father's daughter through and through. She struggled to maintain a calm facade. "Jeremiah, please escort this man from my sight."

"Yes, Mrs. Ransome." Jeremiah's dark eyes twinkled, but Julia was not in the mood to respond to his ever-present good humor. He ushered Winchester out the main door of the room, closing it behind them.

Too furious to sit and return to her work, Julia paced the room. But it was too confining; the remnants of Winchester's foul insinuations lingered in the air.

She flung the door open and left the office building to return to the house. A young man with brown hair that appeared the same texture as lamb's wool turned when she stepped out onto the stoop, a musket cradled in his arms.

He touched the wide brim of his hat. "Ma'am. Mr. Goodland said I was to escort you to the house."

Jeremiah would follow William's instructions to the letter. "Thank you. I appreciate your effort to keep everyone here safe."

Rather than walk beside her, he trailed a few paces behind. She felt like a prisoner being marched to the gallows at gunpoint. When she reached the steps to the porch, she turned and thanked him again.

He touched his hat and returned to the office building. Julia shook her head. She'd best get used to it. Jeremiah would ensure she never went anywhere alone until William returned.

The man standing guard at the entrance leading into the bedroom-wing of the house inclined his head as she walked past him through the open door.

So many new faces she did not recognize. But she had time to learn their names and get to know them now she was home for good.

Without realizing it she passed the bedroom she had taken for William and herself and found herself standing before the closed door to another chamber. She pushed the door open and walked in.

Everything about the room was just as she remembered it. The quilt on the bed—handmade by the women of Tierra Dulce. A book of poetry lay on the seat of the tall-backed wooden chair beside the bed, a ribbon marking the last page read. A white lawn dressing gown was draped like a sleeping ghost across the chaise near the fireplace. And on the dressing table, a stack of folded handkerchiefs with sprigs of dried lavender between them.

Julia picked up the top handkerchief and held it to her nose, breathing deeply. Tears swam in her eyes. The only thing different about this room was her mother's absence. She crossed to the chair beside the bed and, after picking up the book, sank onto the hard seat.

Here she'd sat, morning and evening, those long, terrible weeks as her mother's health had declined. Not even the promise of Papa's imminent arrival had given her enough strength to hold on. If only he'd arrived on schedule, he would have been able to say goodbye instead of arriving in port to the news his wife had passed away two days before.

She reached out and touched the place where her mother had lain. "Mama, please forgive me," she whispered. "I did not understand you, did not understand the powerful hold love holds over a woman when her husband is gone. I resented you for loving him more than you loved me, but I would do anything if I could have only a few minutes with you again, to tell you how much I love you and miss you."

Leaning forward, she rested her cheek on the quilt, dabbing her tears with her mother's lavender-scented handkerchief. *Almighty God, please keep William safe.*

She startled out of slumber at a touch on her shoulder. Sitting up, she regretted having fallen asleep leaning over in such a manner. Her back protested, and pain shot down the side of her neck when she straightened it.

"Jerusha?"

The older woman pushed Julia's flattened curls back from her face. "I came to find you for tea. When I saw the door open to this room, I knew you must be in here."

Tears welled in Julia's eyes. "My mother deserved a better daughter than me."

"Now what makes you say a foolish thing like that?" Jerusha placed her fists on her hips. "No daughter could have been more devoted to her mother than you were, especially there at the end."

"I didn't love her the way I should have. I resented her for pining for my father. I thought her foolish and overly sentimental. If I'd truly loved her, I would have understood how deep her love for my father was and respected her for that."

Jerusha caressed Julia's cheek. "This is how it happens when a loved one dies. The person who survives remembers the one who passed on as a saint and sees herself as a sinner." The housekeeper leaned against the high mattress. "Now, you know I loved your mama like she was my own sister, but she was a trial. She seemed to take pleasure in being miserable, no matter if it was the heat, the rain, your father's absence, your brother's insistence on joining the navy, or your insistence in learning to run the plantation. If Eleanor Witherington did not have something to be aggrieved over, she manufactured something. And you—your patience and caring and perseverance with your mother's carrying-on amazed me. You might not believe me, but there were times you loved your mother more than she deserved."

Julia gasped.

"I don't mean to speak ill of the dead. But you have nothing for which you should feel ashamed when it comes to your mother. She loved you dearly. And she was proud of you."

New tears pooled in Julia's eyes. "She was embarrassed by me and my headstrong ways. She wanted me to marry, to give her grandchildren."

"She may never have told you, but every person who set foot in this house knew how proud your mother was of you—because she told them, repeatedly. You were her pride and joy, dear Miss Julia.

You were the kind of strong, capable woman she'd always wanted to be herself." Jerusha nodded at Julia's look of incredulity. "She told me so. She wanted nothing to hold you back from doing what made you happy. But she worried you would suffer from her example."

"Suffer?"

"She feared you would hold yourself back from finding love—that you would shy away from it in fear of becoming like her."

Shame flooded Julia's face with heat. "She was right to fear that. I believed love to be a distraction, marriage merely a necessity."

"But you are stronger than your mother."

"I do not feel stronger." Julia slumped forward, arms wrapped around her midsection. "I want to go crawl into my bed and stay there until William returns. I want to insist he take me with him wherever he goes, no matter how dangerous. I want him to choose me over the navy—to choose to resign his commission and stay here with me forever. And then I know I'm a horrible wife, wanting him to give up what makes him happy to make me happy."

Jerusha chuckled and rested her hand on the top of Julia's head. "You aren't a horrible wife for *thinking* those things. The fact that you realize you cannot ask him to *do* those things proves you are a woman who truly loves her husband. But you are a new wife. Have patience. You will learn that your husband's happiness will bring you more joy than bending him to your will."

Julia stood and hugged her friend and second mother. "Thank you." She stepped back and encompassed the room with a sweeping gesture. "And thank you for this. For not changing anything about Mama's room."

"I was of two minds about it, worried you would not want to see your mother's belongings still laid out, and worried if I put them away you would be hurt that I'd done so."

Julia turned to the vanity and ran her fingers down the engraved silver spine of her mother's comb. She sank onto the low stool and stared at herself in the mirror. Dark-circled eyes filled with anxiety and exhaustion stared back at her. With a sigh, she ran her hand over her creased forehead.

"You should go lie down, Miss Julia. You of anybody need to be well rested."

Julia turned to face Jerusha. "I of anybody?"

"Yes, if you are going to be fit to receive our neighbors over the next few days, all while trying to determine how badly Master Winchester has cheated you." Jerusha raised thin eyebrows.

Julia shook her head. "Jeremiah told you his suspicions."

Jerusha nodded. "We've been together for nigh on forty years, since I was all of fifteen years old. We share everything."

Julia's mind drifted as the only housekeeper Tierra Dulce had known since Julia's father purchased the plantation twenty years ago extolled her husband's virtues.

Would she and William ever come to a point where they shared everything with each other? That would be hard to do with him at sea most of the time.

She once again prayed for his safety. Auditing the accounts would be tedious, but it would keep her mind occupied and her worries at bay. Of course, it would mean spending more time with Winchester—

"Jerusha, did you call the steward *Master* Winchester?"

Startled at the sudden interruption, it took the housekeeper a moment to answer. "Yes. Master Winchester insisted that because he's a white man and rightfully in sovereignty over us, we're to call him *Master* Winchester."

"That ends now." Julia clenched her teeth and closed her eyes. The supposition of the man! She could think of a few choice things to call Winchester, but saying them aloud would only scandalize Jerusha and debase herself. Where was Dawling when she needed a good epithet spoken aloud? The sailor who served as William's manservant aboard *Alexandra* had only mastered the art of censoring himself a few weeks before they made port in Kingston Harbor.

A smile—an expression that recalled countless pleasant childhood memories for Julia—played about Jerusha's full, rosy lips. "I will pass the word to the rest of the staff. Now, off to your room with you. I shall fetch you in an hour or so."

Julia ducked her chin and raised her brows. "Make it an hour. Your *or so* could be much longer than I should be resting."

"You always were a stubborn child." Jerusha left the room, muttering under her breath, the smile still dancing about her mouth.

Finding a smile of her own, Julia rose and started for the door—but something on the nightstand on the opposite side of Mama's bed caught her eye. She rounded the bed and picked up the top volume of a stack of the well-worn leather journals. It easily opened in her hands. The yellowing pages were filled with Mama's compact handwriting.

Julia had seen her mother write in books like this every day of her life. Her gaze fell onto the page on the right side.

> *My darling Edward,*
>
> *It is thirty-six days since "Indomitable" left Kingston. Michael fell from his pony this morning and hit his head. Blood everywhere. I became faint at the sight, fearful his injury was grave. But Julia, my strong, brave girl, doctored her brother as if she had been plying the trade for years instead of being a child of thirteen...*

Julia remembered that day. When Malachi, Jeremiah and Jerusha's oldest son, had shouted for help, Julia dropped the petticoat she'd been embroidering and ran to see what had happened. All she'd done to "doctor" her brother was to press her handkerchief against the cut over his ear to quell the bleeding. Jerusha was the one who had stitched the wound closed and made an herb poultice to help it heal faster.

She flipped a few pages further back in the journal. The whole book was filled with letters to her father, letters recounting the everyday events of life at Tierra Dulce—most of it about Michael and Julia.

She opened the second and then the third. All the same—filled with daily letters to her father from her mother. Had he ever read these? Did he know of their existence—evidence of how her mother pined for him?

The cover of the fourth journal was newer, stiffer, the paper inside still a pale ivory. Only a quarter of the pages were filled. The loose scrawl, the uneven lines indicated Mama's weakness as she wrote.

Julia turned to the last page.

> *My darling Edward,*
>
> *I fear my time has come. Julia tells me there has been word your ship is delayed a week or more. I wanted to see you one last time, but I have not the strength to linger.*
>
> *Comfort Julia as best you can. She deserved a better mother than I, someone who matched her in strength and wit. Encourage her to marry, to find love, as I did. For though I have spent these many years longing for your presence, I lived a life of splendid fulfillment because I loved you.*
>
> *I go now to be with Michael. We shall await you in heaven.*
>
> > *All my love,*
> > *Eleanor*

Julia dashed at the tears creeping down her cheeks. All these years she had believed herself a disappointment to her mother—while Mama believed just the opposite. Oh, to have five minutes more, to say things left unsaid.

Guilt creeping in from reading private thoughts meant only for Papa's eyes, Julia stacked the journals together and laid them in the chest at the foot of the bed. She wanted to know her mother better, but if Mama had wanted her to read them, she would have let her know that.

Reluctantly, she left Mama's room and returned to her own. She crossed to her desk, opened a drawer, and pulled out a similar, but newer, journal—the one she'd purchased in Portsmouth to write in on the Atlantic crossing. Yet it had stayed in the drawer the entire journey, untouched.

She sat, uncorked her ink bottle, and picked up a quill. She spread the book open to the first page.

My darling William,

    To carry on a tradition started by my mother, I am writing these letters not only to recount the daily events at Tierra Dulce but also as an expression of my deep love for you. As a way of holding you near to my heart while duty keeps you far away...

Chapter Four

M an—no, *woman* overboard!"

At the lookout's cry, Salvador dropped the compass and bolted for the quarterdeck, taking the steps in one stride. "Where away?"

"Directly astern, sir. There." The young man pointed to the churning waters behind the ship. "She jumped through the window in your cabin."

Fighting the urge to release a string of oaths—cursing being heavily fined on *Vengeance*—Salvador ripped off his coat and waistcoat, flinging the garments at his steward. "Lau, man a boat and stand by to launch if necessary."

"Aye, Captain." The boatswain practically flew down to the main deck, calling men's names and giving orders.

Salvador dropped his belt and hat to the deck, took the end of a rope handed him by Picaro, and tied it around his waist.

"Trim sail." He climbed atop the balustrade, took a deep breath, and dived into the sea.

He kicked and fought the wake, trying to propel himself away from the ship and toward the surface. Finally, the pull lessened, and he managed to get his head above the water. Orienting himself to the back of the ship, he turned to swim in the direction he'd last seen the billowing fabric of Charlotte Ransome's dress.

"Two points to larboard, Captain." Picaro's voice skittered over the water.

Salvador adjusted his bearing right—hoping his second mate meant the larboard side of the ship, not to Salvador's left. When no correction came, Salvador poured all his strength into his stroke. As he crested each wave, he paused, looking for the girl.

There, only a few dozen yards ahead. He gulped air—and a bit of water—and plunged forward, arms and lungs burning from the added drag of the rope and his boots.

The thrashing quality of Miss Ransome's swimming told Salvador he'd reached her with little time to spare.

"No, no, no!" Charlotte increased her effort, but Salvador slipped his arm around her waist. She tried to push him away, but he squeezed until she squealed, "Enough!"

Obviously, the words *I surrender* were not in her vocabulary. The faint cheers of his men prepared him for the increased pressure of the rope around his waist. He pulled Charlotte's back tightly to his chest and grabbed the rope with this other hand, guiding it close to hers.

"Hold on to the rope. My men will pull us to safety."

Her small hands joined his on the line.

"Would you care to explain yourself?"

"I told you. My duty as a captive is to find a means of escape."

Salvador wasn't certain if his nausea was from the pressure of the rope around his gut or what he'd just heard. "There is no land within swimming distance, no ships in view. You would have drowned before you found rescue. Am I to infer you find death preferable to the hospitality I have shown you?"

"Hospitality? You abducted me! Attacked my fia—" A wave from the ship's wake interrupted her derisive statement when it slapped over them. She coughed and sputtered.

"Attacked your…were you going to say *fiancé*, Miss Ransome?"

"Yes. Not that it is any of your concern. He had only just proposed when you and your nefarious crew of villains came upon us."

"Then may I be the first to wish you joy?"

"You may not."

He sighed. "Must you rebuff all my overtures of civility?"

"Yes."

"Very well." He dropped all effort at conversation.

Picaro directed the men to pull Salvador and Miss Ransome around to the larboard accommodation ladder. Before allowing his captive to climb the side of the ship, though, Salvador called for his steward.

Suresh's dark face appeared over the bulwark—along with most of the crew, who lined the side of the ship. "Yes, Captain?"

"Retrieve my dressing gown from my cabin."

"Yes, Captain."

Charlotte struggled against him.

"Be still."

"I want to get out of the water."

"You should have thought of that before you jumped into it."

"Is this some kind of punishment, keeping me down here?"

"No—but the decision does have merit." He untied the rope from his waist and looped it around hers before securing it with a knot she would never be able to untie. "We are waiting until Suresh returns— ah, there he is. You will come up behind me."

ⴱⵆⵆⴱ

Charlotte gawked at the man. He was making her wait down here, being knocked against the side of the ship by the waves until his manservant returned with his dressing gown? Of all the—she hadn't expected him to be so dandified that he could not walk the few yards from the waist entry port to his cabin in wet clothes.

As soon as he turned his attention from her to the shallow notches in the side of the ship, Charlotte turned hers to the rope. He thought a simple knot like this would confound her?

"Do not dawdle, Miss Ransome."

Under the water, the knot came loose and the rope fell away. "Coming, Captain Salvador."

She fit her toes and fingers into the notches—but her skirt and petticoat, molded to her body, wrapped around her legs. She couldn't climb the side of the ship one-handed while holding up her dress.

She dropped back into the water.

"Is there a problem? Did you not understand my command?" Salvador leaned over the railing beside the open entry port.

"My skirt impedes me from climbing."

Salvador sighed loud enough for her to hear. "Pull her up with the rope."

The burly sailor beside Salvador braced himself. He pulled the rope—and staggered back when the line gave way easily.

Before it whipped away from her, Charlotte grabbed the end of the rope and twined it around her arm. Finding the ladder slots with her toes, she bundled her skirts in her free hand and, with the burly sailor's assistance, climbed up to the deck.

Her head had hardly cleared the edge of the deck when someone grabbed her, yanked her up, and tried to smother her.

Remembering the suffocating feeling of the burlap sack thrown over her head the night before, Charlotte panicked. She swung her fists and elbows, a few grunts telling her she'd connected.

She cried out when someone wrapped his arms around her from behind, trapping her in the cloth.

"Be still." Salvador's hot breath on her ear made her shiver. "Believe it or not, I am trying to protect you, not hurt you. In case you have not noticed—for certainly my men will if given a chance—the water has made your dress almost transparent."

She stilled and then clutched the dry fabric close around her. Salvador's dressing gown. The one he'd sent his steward for before they came out of the water.

As soon as Salvador released her, she turned to look at him. Who was this man? Concerned about her modesty? But he was a pirate, a black-hearted villain.

"Come." He stalked toward his cabin.

Head hung, avoiding the curious stares of the crew, Charlotte followed him.

Suresh stood at the cabin door, which he closed after Charlotte entered. The steward had already laid out a change of clothes for

Salvador. The pirate scooped them up and took them to the quarter gallery—his private privy—to change.

Suresh handed Charlotte a towel.

"Thank you."

The East Indian man, probably not much older than Charlotte herself, inclined his head but did not speak.

She rubbed her hair vigorously, grateful for its shortness. It would dry quickly, unlike her clothing. She had not given her plan much forethought, especially this scenario: Ending up right back where she started—only now with every piece of clothing she possessed soaked with seawater.

Salvador came out of the quarter gallery in fawn breeches and a billowing white shirt that exposed quite a bit of his chest before he pulled the laces closed.

"You owe me a pair of boots, Miss Ransome." He tossed the water-logged ones back into the privy. Suresh bustled about him, helping the captain don fresh hose and boots, a neckcloth, waistcoat, and his gold braid–adorned coat.

Charlotte did not dare move throughout the proceeding. Once Salvador again resembled a Royal Navy commodore, he crossed to exit the cabin. But before he did, he turned and looked at her.

Here it came. The rebuke for her action. Would he yell? Be deadly calm like William?

"In that trunk there"—he pointed to an ornate chest under the hammock she'd slept in—"you will find clothing you can borrow until yours dry." He left the cabin, Suresh his silent shadow.

Strange man.

Charlotte wrapped her arms around her middle and shivered. Jumping out the stern window had not been wise. She'd realized that as soon as she struck the water and almost drowned in the ship's churning wake. But the opportunity had been there.

Unsure of when the pirate captain or his steward might return, Charlotte flung away the pirate's dressing gown, peeled off her wet dress, and crossed to kneel before the trunk.

She lifted the lid, and the delicate perfume of roses met her nose.

Closing her eyes, she inhaled the scent, picturing herself in Lady Dalrymple's garden again. Dressed in…

Not a wet chemise and petticoats, certainly. With a sigh, she opened her eyes. Inside the chest lay gowns that rivaled those she'd left behind in Portsmouth—silks and satins in shades from palest pink to deep rose, yellows and greens, and the blues, greens, and grays of the sea. Half a dozen fine dresses, petticoats and undergarments, stockings, and even two pairs of softest kid dancing slippers.

She lifted each layer carefully, impressed by the richness of the fabrics and the exquisite tailoring of each of the garments. She lifted the last layer and her finger caught on something hard. She peered over the edge of the trunk. Two large, leather-bound books lay in the bottom of the trunk. She lifted the top one out and opened it.

A ledger. She carried it to the window seat for better lighting. Columns of dates, ship names, cargo, and amounts of money filled each page written in a fine hand. Dates, ships, cargo, and money—a reckoning of everything Salvador had ever taken?

Noise beyond the door startled her. If Salvador learned she had discovered his account books, he would not be pleased. She returned the ledger to the trunk and layered the garments in on top of it again. She put aside the plainest garment she could find and requisite foundation garments and finished repacking everything else.

Charlotte removed the remainder of her wet garments and gratefully slipped into dry underpinnings, and then she held the dress she'd chosen up to her chest. Dark blue with white trim around the square neck and a white sash. She could no longer wear her midshipman's uniform, but this dress served as a good reminder of her experiences aboard *Audacious*. She slipped it on—grateful it was a round gown that buttoned at the left side instead of lacing or buttoning up the back—and wrapped the white ribbon sash tightly around her ribs twice before tying it in the back to address the fact the gown had been made for someone quite a bit larger. She'd have to remember to pick up the skirt before walking to keep from tripping over the several inches of extra length.

She wished Salvador had a full-length mirror in his cabin, but the man defied all descriptions she'd ever heard of pirates being self-centered and concerned only with accumulation of wealth and their own appearance.

The indigo silk swished with a soft hiss when she moved. She lifted the skirts and executed the opening steps of an allemande. If only Ned could see her in this gown.

But Ned couldn't see her in this dress. Reality doused any sense of joy she took in the fine garment with the same force she'd hit the water with less than an hour ago, bringing with it a different, but equally frightening, sensation of drowning.

She closed the trunk lid. The light from the windows glittered across gold letters painted in fine scrollwork in the center. *SD*.

Who was SD, and why was her trunk full of dresses aboard a pirate's ship?

Charlotte staggered back and sank into Salvador's desk chair. A trunk of clothing like this meant only one thing: She wasn't Salvador's first female "guest."

Would her fate be the same as the woman whose gown she now wore?

❧❧❧

William slammed his hand on the table, making his charting instruments clank. Though showing Ned and his own crew nothing but confidence they would quickly find the pirate ship and rescue Charlotte, here, alone in his cabin, fear and doubt reigned. His prayers seemed to bounce off the ceiling.

Where was God? How had He allowed this to happen?

"Everything all right, Com'dore?"

William squeezed his hands into fists. "Everything is fine, Dawling."

"Your supper's ready, sir."

"Any sightings?"

"No, sir. Not yet. But it'll be soon, sir. I feel it."

Of course there had been no sightings. He would have been notified at the least hint of a sail in the distance. "That will be all, Dawling."

"Aye, sir." The steward left as quietly as he entered.

William stood, turning his back on the charts and reports showing the most recent pirate activity in the waters near Jamaica.

Emptiness filled the large day cabin. Before, this had been his place of refuge, of peace, of retreat from the crush and cacophony created by the almost eight hundred men aboard. Now, something was missing.

No, not something. Someone. Much as it pained him to admit, he wanted—needed—his wife. Less than two months married, and she'd managed to twine herself around his heart and soul. Without her, he foundered like a sinking ship in shallow shoals.

Eating supper alone at the long, empty dining table did not help his frame of mind. More from necessity than hunger, he bolted down the food and then retreated to the quarterdeck, hoping the crew's activity and noise would help drive away his doubts and self-recrimination, even if only for a short while.

"Commodore, request permission to beat to quarters for evening inspection." O'Rourke saluted, shifting from foot to foot.

"Granted." Perhaps he should have had the crew practicing at the guns all afternoon. After all, it had been months since their last engagement. They were bound to need the refresher.

The boatswain's whistle and the shouted orders of the officers, midshipmen, and masters temporarily drowned out William's thoughts. As soon as the men were at their stations, William started his inspection, O'Rourke trailing behind.

William forced himself to focus on the men's dispositions, giving a word of praise or correction where warranted. On the main gun deck, O'Rourke went before him, a lighted lantern held aloft.

Kennedy snapped to attention when William paused to review the senior midshipman's gun crews. The eighteen-year-old would be standing for his lieutenancy examination soon, and William resolved to spend time preparing him—

"Sail, oh!"

William's heart jumped, as did most of the crew, at the shout from the lookout high above. He dashed up the nearest companion stairs.

"Where away?" he called, craning his neck to see the sailor on the mainmast top.

"Two points off the starboard bow."

William grabbed his spyglass from Dawling, who panted and puffed from his haste to bring it from the cabin. William scanned to the right side of the bow.

There. Definitely sails.

"Alter course to intercept."

"Aye, aye, sir." O'Rourke ran to the wheelhouse to relay the order to the sailing master.

Anticipation vibrated through William's limbs. He tamped down his hope of finding Charlotte so quickly. And if it were the pirate ship and battle ensued, he could put his sister's life in jeopardy. But she'd survived the attack on *Audacious* on the voyage from England. He prayed she would be able to protect herself now.

He paced the quarterdeck, checking the position of the other ship every few minutes through the telescope. The setting sun made seeing the details of the other vessel harder.

"Sir, she sails under the British ensign," the lookout called.

Disappointment weighed on William's shoulders, threatening to drag him to the deck. He collapsed the glass and strode to the wheelhouse. "Close with them. We shall find out if they have seen anything."

"Aye, aye, Commodore." The sailing master knuckled his forehead.

William turned to his first officer. "Release the crew to duty stations. I will be in my cabin."

O'Rourke saluted. "Aye, aye, sir."

William returned to the day cabin, but again his quarters failed to provide the respite he sought.

Dawling entered and lit the candles in the wall sconces and hanging lanterns. "Aught I can do for you, Com'dore?" He hesitated near the door separating the main cabin from the dining cabin.

"No. That will be all." William did not look up from the charts— the charts he'd been staring at but not seeing since returning here half an hour ago.

"Aye, sir." Dawling disappeared. Time, however, made its presence quite clear—and it seemed to want to stay stationary, the periods between the bells stretching longer than thirty minutes.

To conserve the candles, William allowed Dawling to believe he would retire for the night a few hours later, but he dismissed the steward before Dawling could help him undress. After Dawling doused all the candles and retreated to his own bed, William sat at the round table in the middle of the cabin, staring out the bank of windows at the sea and stars.

If Julia were here, she would have kept vigil with him.

His body tensed, as if by straining he could make the bells marking five o'clock in the morning come any faster. Instead of bells, however, he leaped to his feet at the sounds of scuffling and voices out on deck. He flung the door to the wheelhouse open and then jumped back to avoid getting knocked on the forehead.

"Report."

Flustered, Lieutenant Jackson staggered back a few steps and stammered briefly before recovering himself. "Sir, we are within range of the other ship. They just cleared for action."

Anticipation roiled in William's chest. Could it be they had stumbled upon the pirate ship flying under false colors?

Without bothering to put his waistcoat and jacket back on, William charged out onto the quarterdeck. He braced himself against the ship's rolling and took a deep breath, to put all the power he could behind his voice.

"All hands! All hands to battle stations. Clear for action."

Chapter Five

William shrugged into his coat but shooed away Dawling's attempts to button it for him. He snatched his telescope from where Dawling had it tucked up under his arm.

"Lieutenant Blakeley, signal the other ship our identity and tell them to stand down."

"Aye, aye, sir."

In the predawn gloom, William could not make out much detail of the other ship, save that it was smaller—with only one gun deck to *Alexandra's* two.

The fifth lieutenant scampered up the shrouds to the foremast top, the long handle of the signaling lantern over his shoulder. William forced himself to stand still, though the urge to pace the quarterdeck made his legs twitch.

The other five lieutenants had not the same restraint. Though not all chose to discharge their anxiety through pacing, none stood still.

"Sir, they're standing down," Lieutenant Campbell called from the forecastle.

Muscles still as tight as a sail in a stiff wind, William buttoned his coat and donned his hat. "Bring us abreast of the other ship, Master Ingleby."

From his position at the wheel, the sailing master saluted. "Aye, aye, sir."

William craned his neck and turned his face toward the foremast top. "Mr. Blakeley, signal to the other ship that their captain is to report to me in person within the hour. Lieutenant O'Rourke." He waited until his first officer stood beside him. "Stand the men down but keep them on alert until we know precisely who is on the other ship."

"Aye, aye, sir." O'Rourke touched the fore tip of his hat and set about implementing William's order.

Blakeley scuttled down the shrouds and dropped lightly to the deck, signal lantern swinging from his arm. "Commodore, the other ship signaled they received your orders and their captain will comply."

"Very good. Report to Lieutenant O'Rourke." William returned to his cabin to prepare it and himself to receive the captain of the other ship. While waiting, he updated the log entry he'd start last night, recording the facts and details of the long night's vigil while keeping his doubts, misgivings, and fears to himself.

Out on deck the bell chimed, marking six o'clock in the morning. The other captain had but a few minutes to present himself. Shouts from the quarterdeck marked the arrival.

William set his journal by, stood, changed his plain frock coat for the formal one, and stepped into the dining cabin. He went around to stand behind his chair at the head of the table.

The expected knock came. "Enter."

A man in a post captain's uniform entered the room and stood at attention. "Captain James—" The man's voice choked off. "William?"

The familiar voice acted like a sudden wind in the doldrums on William's soul. He rounded the table to get a better look at the other man. As soon as he did, he grabbed the captain by the shoulders as if afraid he were an apparition that might just as suddenly disappear.

"James! How…? Last I heard, you were on your way to India."

"I had orders to India, but then the Peace came, and I was reassigned to Jamaica station." He eyed the gold adornment on William's jacket. "You seem to have come up in the world since last we met. Commodore? Or did they just skip you ahead to Admiral of the Red? I assume Sir Edward has managed to raise himself into a position to make such a promotion possible."

William dropped his hands back to his side, surprised by the edge of bitterness in James's voice. "It is commodore. I have been put in command of a division out of Fort Charles."

James took a turn about the dining cabin, eyeing each detail with a critical expression. "As Admiral Witherington sent you here, I would imagine you have been tasked with hunting down the few remaining pirates and privateers of these waters."

"You say that as if it were a bad thing." William returned to the head of the table. He crossed his arms and watched the other man, trying to see him objectively, as just another fellow officer. "I was given proof less than forty-eight hours after my arrival of how important it is to rid these waters of these desperate and vile criminals."

James snorted in derision. "Oh yes? Did you witness one of them steal your beloved admiral's sugar shipment again?"

William worked to keep his anger contained. Why was James behaving thusly? "No. They decided to take Charlotte instead."

James stilled, all vestiges of cynicism leaving his expression. "Charlotte?"

"Charlotte Ransome. Surely you remember her. After all, she is the only sister we have."

William's brother faced him from the opposite end of the table. "Having spent more time at home with our family, I can assure you I know her better than you. How did this happen? What was she doing in Jamaica?"

William pulled out his chair and sank into it. "It was not my choice, believe me. Charlotte, apparently, began a secret correspondence with a young man Mother deemed inappropriate. The young man came to Jamaica to make his fortune working as a steward for a sugar plantation—my wife's sugar plantation, in fact."

"Your...wife?" James snorted with laughter. "Now I know you are telling tales."

Clamping his back teeth together, William tried to maintain a calm countenance. "I have been married these seven weeks."

James made a derisive sound in the back of his throat. "Who—no, do not tell me. I know already. You married Sir Edward's daughter.

Does the man's patronage never end? He saw you raised through the ranks faster than any other officer of your age, put you on a third-class ship of the line—the youngest captain to have command of one—assigned you to such actions as would ensure you the quick accumulation of wealth, promoted you to commodore, and gave you his daughter and her inheritance in the bargain—or did he make you his legal heir, as well?"

William stared at his brother. Though the man leaning over the other end of the table resembled William so greatly they could have been twins, he no longer recognized him. Two years younger than William, James had been set up for patronage by their father under another captain their father had served as sailing master. Phillip had been sent to the captain their father served before signing on to the ship that took him away from their family forever. Neither of his brothers' captains gained wealth, recognition, or promotion as Julia's father had done; therefore, neither of his brothers had achieved promotion as quickly nor wealth as readily as William.

And that was no fault of William's. "Yes, I married Julia Witherington. But that is not the issue. The issue is that Charlotte has been taken by pirates."

"Ah, yes, Charlotte and the secret correspondence." James straightened and paced the other end of the cabin.

"And she made the ill-judged decision to disguise herself as a midshipman and run away to Jamaica on a ship in the convoy I led here. We learned of her presence only when she fell ill to yellow fever and had to be cared for aboard my ship."

"You did not put her on the first ship back to England?" James's voice bounced off the thick oaken joists overhead like thunder. "If she had been in my care—"

"You would have known there was no other course of action to take." William rose and braced his fists on the tabletop. "Was I to turn her over to a captain I didn't know, to make the return voyage surrounded by strangers who cared nothing for her virtue or well-being?"

James seemed to contemplate this, and William worked to control his fury. He'd always imagined that his reunion with his brothers once the war ended would be a far more pleasant experience.

"I have contacts in Port Antonio on the northeast point of the island. I will make sail for Fort George and start the search for her there."

"No."

"From Fort George, I can go on to Brunswick. Aye, the mayor owes me a favor."

William straightened. "Captain Ransome, I said no. You are not to divert from your previous orders. I am attending to this matter."

"She is my sister, Commodore Ransome, and you need all the help you can get. Otherwise, she never would have been taken."

The temptation to let his boiling anger explode the way his father-in-law did proved almost greater than William could bear, but he mustered all the strength he still possessed to speak calmly. "She may be your sister, but I am your superior officer. If you divert from your commanding officer's orders, I will have you relieved of command and sent back to Kingston to face a court-martial for mutinous insurrection."

"You...William, you would do that to your own brother?"

"In this instance I cannot allow our familial bond to sway my command decisions. You are under orders from someone other than me. For me to allow you to join the hunt for Charlotte's abductors would be no better than if I commandeered your ship. We would both face courts-martial, James. Surely you can see that." He would not put himself in the same position as Admiral Witherington found himself when he learned his son's ship had been attacked by pirates and the crew either killed or held for ransom. If Sir Edward had not captured a notorious pirate and several privateers in the futile attempt to save his son, he would have lost everything instead of being promoted to commodore and, three years afterward, knighted for his actions during the war.

James glared at William through narrowed eyes. "Aye, rank, patronage, and promotion were always of greater importance to you than your family."

William clenched and unclenched his fists. "Leave my ship."

James slapped his hat onto his head. "Gladly." The cabin door slammed behind him, and William was fairly certain he heard one of the panes of glass crack in the windows beside the solid door.

His entire body trembled from the effort of containing his anger at his brother. What had happened to make James so bitter, so cynical, so resentful toward William and the blessings Providence—and Sir Edward—had given him?

He took a few deep breaths and returned to the quarterdeck just in time to see the top of his brother's hat disappear at the accommodation ladder. He turned back to the wheelhouse. "Lieutenant O'Rourke, Master Ingleby, resume course for Port Morant."

"Aye, aye, Commodore." The first officer and sailing master immediately set to work—O'Rourke shouting orders to put the crew in motion to stretch canvas and find the wind, and Ingleby to set the heading.

William glanced at the stern of his brother's ship. HMS *Insolent*. He averted his gaze and refused to look as *Alexandra* pulled away from the thirty-eight gun frigate. A vessel with a more apt name could not have been assigned to James Ransome. William prayed he would not have to follow through on his threats and charge his brother with mutiny. He worried how his mother had endured Charlotte's disappearance. To have to inform Mother he'd had James arrested and court-martialed would be more than she could bear.

In truth, it would be more than he could bear.

෧෨෪෨෯

Compared to the plain dress of everyone who lived and worked at Tierra Dulce, Julia felt more out of place now than she had her first weeks in Portsmouth. She smoothed her hands over the green day dress and touched one of the loose, long curls at the nape of her neck. The women of the house, from Jerusha to Julia's lady's maid to the chambermaids, had been thrilled at the stack of fashion magazines she'd brought back with her.

Julia would have been much more comfortable in one of her plain cotton work dresses.

She took a deep breath and left the sanctuary of the bedroom for the receiving room, but she stopped in the doorway. Here, Mama had received callers, had pretended she enjoyed the company of the "locals," as she called them.

Julia grimaced. For the daughter of a baronet who had spent and gambled away his fortune and almost landed his family in the poorhouse, her mother had sometimes thought a little too highly of rank and birth for Julia's liking. While now wealthy and moving amongst the best society in Jamaica, many of their neighbors had been no better than shopkeepers, farmers, or menial laborers back in England—or younger sons of nobles. The latter had been the families to whom Mama had tried to connect Julia through marriage.

The sounds of a carriage arriving clopped and jangled and rattled through the open windows and doors. Julia steeled herself for a long day.

Though the tedium of telling the same story again and again—of her life in Portsmouth and of marrying William—began to wear as the day dragged by, Julia reveled in the familiar faces and voices of the neighbors she had known most of her life. And her neighbors did not ask much of her. The women wanted to admire her fashionable dress and the beautiful emerald ring William had slipped onto her finger less than two months ago at their wedding, and the men enjoyed Julia's description of William's ship and the voyage from England to Jamaica. It rather surprised her that none of her neighbors mentioned Charlotte's abduction. She hoped the news would stay secret and remain only a family matter. The less known about Charlotte and how she came to be here, the less damage would be done to her reputation.

"We were concerned after your dear mother's passing that the admiral would decide to sell Tierra Dulce." The owner of the plantation neighboring Tierra Dulce to the north tried to look sincere.

Julia kept her smile to herself. The only thing he had been afraid of was that her father would sell the plantation to somebody else.

"Nay, my father knows how much I love this place, and how I enjoy the running of it."

The older man across from her shifted uneasily on the light blue damask chair. "Yes, yes. But it goes without saying, of course, that when you run into problems I'm ready and able to assist you and set things to right."

Perhaps Julia should have included an accounting of her escape from the sinister designs of her aunts and cousin back in England along with the anecdotes she'd related about the year she had been away. And she kept her opinion to herself that her neighbor was the one more likely to find himself in need of help running a plantation than she.

The man's wife, an angular, severe-looking woman, gazed down the bridge of her long nose at Julia. "And should you need someone to talk to about, well, more delicate matters, such as wifely duties and behaviors, I will be more than happy to step into the place left void by your dear mama."

Because she wanted to laugh at the preposterous idea of going to this woman for wifely advice, Julia had no trouble smiling at her. "I will keep that in mind, thank you. It is wonderful to have neighbors who care so much."

As if sensing Julia would be unable to withstand more of these neighbors, Jerusha appeared in the doorway.

"Will we see you at church Sunday?"

Julia did not miss the pointed implication behind the question. "As I did before my mother died, I will attend services in the chapel here at Tierra Dulce tomorrow."

The look the older couple exchanged made Julia glad for the years she had spent watching her mother paste a smile on her face and be pleasant to people she did not like. Julia did the same now. She stood and paid her farewell courtesy, keeping the smile on her face until her visitors disappeared out the door. She sank back into her chair rubbing her forehead. "Who is here now?"

"No one. But Jeremiah needs to see you out in the office."

Julia snapped her gaze up to the housekeeper, surprised to find grim lines framing Jerusha's usually smiling lips. "What is it? What's wrong?"

Jerusha shook her head. "I'm not sure, Miss Julia. Jeremiah just said send for you as soon as you could come."

Julia jumped up from her chair and hurried toward the door. She paused when she reached Jerusha. "Should anyone else arrive—"

"I shall tell them you are much indisposed with business and cannot take any more callers today."

Julia considered Jerusha's suggestion a moment. "Why scandalize the neighbors more than necessary? Tell them I am indisposed from the long voyage but will repay their kindness with a call as soon as I can."

Jerusha chuckled. "Yes, Miss Julia."

"Thank you." Julia squeezed the housekeeper's arm before hurrying through the house and out the door at the end of the bedroom corridor. The bright blue sky, the delicious heat of the afternoon, and the salty breeze blowing off the bay wiped away the previous two hours' tribulation so much so that she did not mind the armed guard who trotted along behind her as she hurried to the plantation office.

The square white building sat at the edge of the cane field. With a deep porch that ran around the outside of the building, it could have made a very pretty little house. All the doors and windows were open to catch the cooling sea breeze; but unlike the main house, there were no gauzy white drapes to catch the current and wave in welcome. Julia paused as soon as she stepped into the central hall to let her eyes adjust from the brightness outside. Three of the building's four rooms were used as offices; the fourth room with a large table in it made a good place to work in a group. Upstairs were the living quarters for the plantation steward.

Julia passed the stairs with a glance upward and clenched her teeth. She would find out what Henry Winchester had been up to if it was the last thing she did. Bypassing her own office on the front left corner, she went to the room behind it, but Jeremiah was not in his office. A scuffing sound drew her attention, and she crossed the hall and stepped through the open doorway into the steward's office.

Jeremiah sat at Henry Winchester's desk rifling through the drawers. Julia stepped further into the room. "Jeremiah? What are you doing? Where's Winchester?"

"That's why I sent for you, Miss Julia. That thieving scoundrel is gone."

Chapter Six

The savory aroma of the roasted chicken was enough to make Charlotte cry, but she had survived worse in her weeks aboard *Audacious*. She could survive this. Never before had she seen such sumptuous fare served aboard a ship at sea, but Captain Salvador—though his tastes in furnishings seemed simple—enjoyed elaborate dining. And his steward had presented his captain with meals even Lady Fairfax would have been proud to serve.

Of course, Charlotte could not vouch for the tastiness of the food, not having eaten any herself. She averted her eyes to keep from seeing the chicken's juices running down the meat as Salvador cut into it. Her stomach groaned with hunger, and she swallowed against a wave of nausea. How could he do this to her?

Onto a plate with a succulent chicken breast, Salvador piled vegetables and fruits Charlotte had never seen—all of which served only to pique her curiosity as to what they would taste like and feel like in her mouth, which watered ferociously.

Must he make her sit at the table during meals? It was bad enough that the smell of the food filled the entire small cabin three times a day. She closed her eyes and squeezed her hands together in her lap. She'd never thought there would come a time when she would long for the stringy, greasy mutton that had been the staple of the midshipmen's diet aboard *Audacious*.

Salvador looked at her for a long moment before he started eating.

Charlotte closed her eyes and turned her face away from him. She could survive this.

"Marvelous chicken. Suresh has outdone himself once again," Salvador said between bites. "He has a way of combining spices to make even this mean chicken into a delicacy. And the vegetables…I would imagine there's not a table in Jamaica that could boast better, not even the vaunted Tierra Dulce."

A tear trickled out of the corner of Charlotte's right eye before she could stop it. How could he be so cruel? Couldn't he see how hungry she was?

When silence fell, Charlotte opened her eyes and looked at her captor. She turned her head away again quickly, not wanting to witness the scrutiny in his gaze. But that he watched her for any sign of weakness, she had no doubt.

Salvador grunted and returned to eating. "Just as jumping overboard and trying to drown yourself did not work, I do not know why you believe that starving yourself will avail you in securing your freedom. Besides," he waved his fork at her, "if you truly mean to escape, you will need your strength. Being faint with hunger is not going to allow you to get very far before we recapture you."

Charlotte crossed her arms. "You, sir, are decidedly not a gentleman."

"You, miss, possess the uncanny knack of stating the obvious."

At the sound of fine china scraping across the table, Charlotte canted her eyes to see what he was doing. Salvador pulled her plate of food toward him and cut a small piece of chicken. He held the fork toward her.

"Please do not make me feed you by force." Salvador's dark eyes bored into her like a weevil through a biscuit.

Arms still folded but unable to ignore the demands of her stomach any longer, Charlotte leaned forward and scraped the piece of meat off the fork with her teeth. The promise of the aroma of herbs and spices filling the room had not prepared her for the richness of flavor she now experienced.

Salvador smiled. "Did not I tell you? Suresh is a master with spices."

Unwilling to concede further, and hoping the steward could not hear her, Charlotte said, "Perhaps he is, or perhaps even your boot leather would be tasty to someone who has not eaten in more than a day."

Salvador's smile faded. Charlotte reached for her plate, but instead of letting her have it Salvador pulled it closer to himself and proceeded to cut the large piece of chicken into small bits. He then began to mash the vegetables with the back of his fork.

"What are you doing?" Charlotte snatched the plate away from him. Several pieces of something round and orange slid off the plate. Charlotte grabbed them with her fingers and put them back, surprised at their soft, spongy texture.

"You are acting like a child; therefore, I assumed you need your food cut up for you as a child would." Salvador returned his energies to his own plate. "And you cannot be that hungry. If I recall correctly, you ate everything on your plate and some of what was left on mine yesterday evening after our little swim. I do not believe skipping today's breakfast and midday meal constitutes not having eaten for a full day. But I suppose you are practicing for when—if—you are returned to your family. Telling them the black-hearted pirate starved you for days to punish you for trying to escape will sound much better than telling them about your childish attempt at a hunger strike."

Charlotte jerked her fork at Salvador's insult. The spongy orange vegetable landed with a splat against the palm of her hand.

"Be careful. That dress is a gift, and I would like it to be unspoilt when the recipient sees it."

Charlotte scraped the mushy orange stuff off of her hand. "The gowns...they are gifts? For whom? I assumed they were left behind by a previous guest."

"Which is why you helped yourself to a second gown today, even though your own clothing is now dry?" Salvador arched his scarred left brow at her, but he didn't look angry.

Charlotte pushed the orange stuff around on her plate, trying to figure out what it was. "My dress was still damp this morning." She scooped up some of the mush and put it in her mouth. The odd combination of soft, fibrous texture and sweet, earthy flavor almost made her stomach revolt. She managed to swallow the small amount and then reached for her glass of wine to wash away the flavor, even though she knew the wine would not be to her taste either.

"That is disgusting. What is it so I can be certain never to eat it again?" She wiped her mouth, but would rather have wiped her tongue.

Salvador laughed heartily. "It is called a yam. Roasted yams are very common on tables throughout the Caribbean. You'd best accustom yourself to them. Occasionally, when we cannot put in somewhere to resupply, all we have to eat are yams."

"Then you'd best leave me ashore next time you put in to resupply because I am *not* eating that again." She speared several of the small chunks of chicken with her fork and ate those instead. "For whom did you buy these dresses?"

Salvador carved the back quarter of the side of the chicken facing him and added it to his plate. "They are for my fiancée."

"You are betrothed?" Charlotte looked down at the beautifully worked pink silk dress. Modest and tasteful, it did not strike her as the type of gown a woman who would marry a pirate would wear. She returned her gaze to Salvador and tried to see him objectively. Dark hair that glinted with hints of red in the direct sunlight, brown eyes with flecks of gold and green, broad shoulders, and well-tailored clothing that showed him to be a fine physical specimen. Yes, she supposed he could be considered quite handsome—when he wasn't abducting innocent young women.

"Does she know, your fiancée, who you are? What you do, I mean? Does she know the gifts you bring her are purchased with ill-gotten gains?"

"She knows what I have told her, and that is enough."

CRASPD

If Salvador had known telling Charlotte Ransome he was engaged to be married would result in such a drastic change in her demeanor, he would have revealed that fact within hours of bringing her aboard *Vengeance*. She did not speak for the remainder of the meal, a contemplative frown etched between her delicate eyebrows.

The consternation had no effect on her appetite, however. She consumed almost half the chicken on her own, in addition to the few vegetables she ate. He liked a woman with a hearty appetite; though having felt nearly every bone in Charlotte Ransome's body when he carried her away from Tierra Dulce and again yesterday in the water, he wondered if this appetite was newly discovered. She couldn't weigh more than a couple of cannonballs together, even when she had been fully clothed and soaking wet.

Not like Serena. No, it would have taken more than one man to haul a sodden Serena up the side of the ship yesterday. Holding Charlotte Ransome against the pull of the rope, he'd been concerned he might crush her delicate ribs. If she had not told him she also was engaged to be married, with her bobbed hair and her boyish frame he would not have guessed her age to be more than fourteen or fifteen. And Serena's dresses on her gave her more the air of a child than her immature and illogical words and actions could do.

Yet there was something about Charlotte Ransome to make Salvador believe she had been through experiences no woman should have to face. After all, even when he had been his most threatening, with fear sparkling in her eyes, she had held her ground against him. And she felled Picaro and nearly managed to escape before they subdued her at Tierra Dulce.

After the dishes were cleared, Salvador dismissed Suresh. Charlotte moved to the leather-upholstered bench below the stern windows and stared out at the darkening horizon. Salvador leaned back in his chair, fingers laced over his sated stomach.

Such an odd contradiction of a girl-woman, at times seeming to be no more than a child and then surprising him with her maturity and grit.

She rose from the window seat and paced the short distance between the stern and the door.

He should have entertained her for dinner formally with his officers. He'd developed the habit of eating with them rather than alone so the empty table wouldn't remind him of just how alone he truly was. Though, no matter how much he believed he could trust his men, he must keep his distance in order to maintain his position of command.

But need he keep the same distance with Miss Ransome? Here, perchance, was a kindred spirit. Someone who might help him through the grueling loneliness that held him clenched in its grip since the moment he'd bade Serena farewell on the dock in Philadelphia nine months ago.

"Miss Ransome—"

Without warning—or knocking—a hulking figure burst into the cabin. Charlotte squeaked and tried to back away, but the gown cut for Serena's taller frame caught under her feet. She waved her arms, apparently trying to find something to break her fall.

Salvador jumped to his feet, but he wasn't near enough.

Declan reached out one long arm and wrapped it around Charlotte's waist. Stooped over to keep from hitting his head on the ceiling, he turned toward Salvador.

"Ship sighted, Cap'n. Off the starboard stern and closing. Lookout said he caught sight of the British ensign."

Salvador tried to ignore the fact his first mate's arm was still around Charlotte's waist. Her head was lolled all the way back as she stared up at Declan, her lips slightly parted, eyes widened in astonishment.

"Loose all sheets and increase the distance between us. It's possible the ship is headed toward Black River also and not purposely following us. To be safe, run up the Dutch pennant."

"Aye, aye, Cap'n." Declan grinned at Charlotte. "Miss."

Charlotte reeled backward when Declan released her before leaving the cabin. Regaining her balance, she turned on Salvador. "How could you let that...that...Goliath take such liberties upon my person in that way?"

And then there were times when that girl-woman sounded more like Shakespeare's shrew. Salvador arranged his expression into one of mild unconcern. "My first mate, Declan, holds claim to a greater share of any spoils this ship takes—other than mine, of course. Seems only fitting he should have as much opportunity as I to take liberties upon your person in that way." That, and the fact he was Serena's brother and the only person other than Suresh to whom Salvador could entrust Charlotte's safety.

He bowed to her before taking up his hat and spyglass. At the door he paused. "Please do not jump from the window. I am down to my last pair of boots and would be very displeased if I had to ruin them by jumping in to save you—again."

Charlotte crossed her arms, closed her eyes, pursed her lips, and turned her head away from him.

He laughed and let the door slam behind him.

◈◈◈◈

"Report."

"Lookout saw a ship off the larboard bow, but it's disappeared into the gloaming, sir." Second Lieutenant Wallis ducked into the sheltered wheelhouse. "Midshipman Jamison identified it as a frigate—likely fifth rate, about thirty-eight or forty-two guns. Believes he saw a Dutch pennant before we lost sight of her, sir."

While Ned had tried to keep his hope from rising, the swell of disappointment told him he had not succeeded. "Keep on this tack. The charts of the harbor at Black River are less than two months old. We will dock in a few hours, and I will go ashore and begin conducting my investigation."

Wallis and First Lieutenant Gardiner exchanged a glance. "Sir, we should go with you, just in case there is trouble."

Ned regarded the two young lieutenants. He imagined neither of them had ever set foot into the types of establishment in which he'd been told to find his contact. He gritted his teeth against the irony. *He* had never been into an establishment like that. Having men he could trust guarding his back would probably be wise.

"Fine. Wallis, pick a crew for the boat." He leaned in closer. "Some of the larger men, those skilled in hand-to-hand combat. I pray it will not be necessary, but we do not know into what we are sailing other than its reputation as a hive for piracy and villainy. It is wise to err on the side of caution."

"Aye, aye, sir." Both lieutenants saluted and rushed off.

Ned returned to his cabin, but he could not return to the meal he had abandoned minutes earlier. At the cry from the lookout, he had clearly seen himself taking the other ship by surprise, finding it to be the pirates, and rescuing Charlotte. But with hundreds of ships in these waters at any given time, finding one—and one for which he did not know the name or who captained her—might prove impossible.

William believed in miracles. Ned tried to.

He stood at the round table in the center of the day cabin. Spread out in front of him were reports from other officers detailing their experiences with the pirates and privateers still operating in and around Jamaica. Other than rereading these again, he had no idea how to prepare himself for what he might face when he landed ashore in Black River tonight.

He certainly did not expect a brisk knock on the door less than an hour after returning to his quarters. He stood, turned his back to the table, and faced the door. "Enter."

Lieutenant Gardiner did not come far into the room. "Sir, I hate to disturb you, but there is a disciplinary matter which requires your attention."

Ned clasped his hands behind his back. "I am available to listen to this matter now."

"Thank you, sir." Gardiner entered, and two young men followed him into the room, both wearing stormy expressions.

Ned's jaw tightened. Kent and Jamison were the two most senior midshipmen, captains of their watches and sharing command of the cockpit where the midshipmen berthed. Kent's presence did not surprise Ned. After all, on the voyage over from England, Kent had been at the center of most of the mischief amongst the junior officers, as he had taken quite a dislike to Midshipman Charles Lott.

Perhaps there were such things as miracles. Had not God arranged a way to get Charlotte off the ship before her identity became known?

Kent and Jamison took up positions on either side of Lieutenant Gardiner, facing Ned.

"Report, Mr. Gardiner."

"Captain, sir, Midshipman Kent and Midshipman Jamison had a disagreement. But rather than resolving it as gentleman, as future officers should do, the disagreement came to blows in the cockpit in front of the other midshipmen not currently on duty."

Ned squinted against the dimness of the cabin. Yes, now he could see that both teens looked sure to sport a few bruises on their faces tomorrow. While Ned fully understood the frustration that could build after a long crossing and the cancellation of promised shore leave, as officers in training Kent and Jamison had certain expectations they must meet if they ever hoped to gain promotion.

He gave them the fiercest frown he could muster. Not trusting Kent to tell the whole truth, Ned turned to Jamison first. "Explain, Mr. Jamison."

The ginger-haired boy cleared his throat. "Captain, I know how wrong it was to allow the disagreement to escalate into a fight. However, it was a matter of honor."

Ned could not stop his eyebrows from rising. "A matter of honor? Whose?"

"It was a matter of honoring the memory of one who is no longer with us, sir. Mr. Kent was making disparaging remarks about Midshipman Lott, God rest his soul, sir."

Ned's stomach heaved as the ship hawed. How was it possible that, more than a month after she left the ship, Charlotte could still be causing problems? He sighed. "I understand it's hard to listen to somebody else speak ill of a friend after they are…gone, but that is no reason to ignore the rules of decorum and behave as bad or worse than ordinary seamen."

"But, sir, you did not hear what he was saying. He said Midshipman Lott was…was…*a woman*." The last two words came out as a harsh whisper.

Ned caught Kent's smirk from the corner of his eye but would not look at the other midshipman lest he betray more than he ought.

Jamison continued speaking. "Sir, he said he found something in Lott's sea chest—something that proved Lott was an interloper, someone who was deceiving us."

With his reactions now back under control, Ned looked at Kent. "What is this evidence?"

A gleam of what appeared to be malevolence sparkled in Kent's pale blue eyes. He reached behind his back and under his jacket and withdrew something that he then held forward toward Ned.

Ned gaze down at the bundle of folded muslin cloths, momentarily confused.

"Sir, I found these hidden in the bottom of Lott's sea chest. They're... well, sir, of course you know what they are."

Having spent his childhood and all of his leave time from the navy with only his mother and sister in a small house with little privacy... Ned swallowed hard. Kent was right. Ned did know what those were. Why had he not thought to send for Charlotte's trunk when she ended up on *Alexandra*? Oh yes, because he had been out of his mind with yellow fever. "That is quite an assumption to make, Mr. Kent, from nothing other than a few pieces of cloth. While aboard this ship, Midshipman Lott served with distinction. Let nothing more be said—no more assumptions, no more accusations. Is that understood?"

"Aye, sir," both boys answered, though Kent's response sounded somewhat grudging.

"And there is to be no more fighting. For the crew to be united, the officers must be seen as united. Any further incidents of fighting will be met with the severest punishment. Do I make myself clear?"

"Aye, sir."

"Midshipman Jamison, Midshipman Kent, you are hereby on continuous watch for the next twenty-four hours. Dismissed."

Gardiner turned to leave with the boys.

"Lieutenant Gardiner, a moment."

The first officer closed the door behind the boys and turned to face Ned again. "Aye, sir?"

"Have Lott's sea chest brought to my quarters. I will see to the dispatch of any personal items and disposal of the rest once we return to Kingston." And keep anything else that might point to Charles Lott's true identity out of the hands of anyone who might want to expose her. "That is all, Mr. Gardiner."

"Aye, aye, sir."

After his first officer's departure, Ned sank into the closest chair at the table. He pressed the heels of his hands against his brows. Kent had no doubt made his accusations in front of at least a dozen midshipmen. With many of the boys still loyal to *Audacious*'s previous captain, and therefore to Kent, the rumor that Midshipman Charles Lott had been a woman in disguise would spread like fire in the powder magazine. And if Ned were the one to rescue her and bring her aboard, she would be recognized—and the steps he and Commodore Ransome had taken to protect her reputation, as well as their own careers, would be for naught.

Chapter Seven

He sat with his back to the wall. The public house crawled with naval officers—some in uniform, some not—out spending their month's wages on ale and wenches. He sipped his port and leaned his chair back until it rested against the stones.

When a particularly comely lady of the profession walked by, he responded to the invitation in her intense gaze with a slight raise of his chin, a squint of his eyes, and a half smile—a full smile was enough to make women swoon. The dark-haired vixen responded with a half smile of her own, her eyes lowering to rest on the triangle of skin exposed by his shirt that hung loosely open to the middle of his chest. With one last lock of their gazes, she strolled away, rejoining the boisterous crowd near the front of the alehouse.

Yes, he would find her later. Assuming his man did not keep him waiting so long she gave up and accepted someone else's business.

There, through the crowd. A tall man with light hair and angular features.

He let his chair down slowly until all four legs were once again firmly on the floor. The two men flanking the table moved farther away as the newcomer sat down.

"Well?"

"She knows."

"She made an accusation?" He slowly swirled the blood-red wine in his glass.

"No, but she insisted on reviewing the accounts. Everything."

"When?"

"Five days from now. Thursday."

He glared at the other man, narrowing his eyes. "I should hang you from the yardarm for such a foolish action. She is an intelligent woman who looks into everything. I warned you she would notice what you were doing. And you decided to add more suspicions to those she already has by running away. Do you not think your absence will be noted?"

"I am certain it has been already, but I can be of more use to you free from the constant vigil of the armed guards set about the place since the abduction of the Ransome girl."

He leaned his chair back again, taking a sip of the sweet, fortified wine. Ah, yes. The abduction of the Ransome girl that took the two biggest obstacles out of his way—*Alexandra* and *Audacious*. He silently thanked whoever had done him such a favor. "And our other man on the inside?"

"Well placed and not suspected at all."

Grudgingly, he had to agree with the overall assessment and actions taken so far. "Armed guards around the house?"

"Day and night. All men well known and trusted by the overseer. Not a chance of bribing a single one. She goes nowhere without one following along behind."

"Getting to her will be difficult."

A sly smirk formed on the other man's face. "She will be leaving the plantation Monday morning to make the drive here, into Kingston, to visit her banker."

"And our man?"

"Will be with her."

He allowed himself the luxury of a smile. "You've done well, brother."

Henry Winchester returned his brother's expression. "Soon, everything you've suffered these last twenty years will be repaid in kind."

Arthur Winchester motioned for a barmaid to serve his brother a drink. Yes, soon everyone in the Caribbean—and England—would know that he was a better man than either Admiral Sir Edward

Witherington or Commodore William Ransome. The two men responsible for ruining his career and destroying his family. Watching as he did the same to them would make the two decades' wait for revenge worthwhile.

⁂

Charlotte Ransome's nearly endless chatter was enough to drive Salvador insane. But her silence for the past hour—since *Vengeance* entered the harbor at the mouth of the Black River—worried him. He took an extreme risk docking here at all. Going into town and seeking out a messenger willing to make the journey back to Kingston added to the probability that what he had done and whom he had aboard his ship would be discovered. But that was nothing compared to the fear Charlotte would attempt escape again.

He could say nothing to her that he had not already articulated. Threats of what he would do to her if she tried to escape again were met with disdainful laughter; entreaties to think of her own personal safety answered with a pitying shake of her head. So, with one last look meant to remind her of all he'd said, Salvador left the cabin and joined his men on the main deck, grateful the moonless night added a layer of protection.

"Leave the Dutch pennant up. The navy ship will be looking for it."

A half dozen ships of varying sizes, ages, and repair lay at anchor in the harbor. If the ship coming in behind *Vengeance* was indeed a Royal Navy vessel, the variety already gathered in the harbor would provide good camouflage for the frigate, which Salvador kept in much better repair than many of his counterparts. Of course, he was more successful at avoiding being fired upon than many of his counterparts as well. No one ever suspected *Vengeance* was a pirate ship until it was too late to rectify that mistake.

"Declan," he said, pulling his first mate aside, "you must stay here. Stay here and guard Miss Ransome."

"No one on this ship would dare—"

"It is not the men from whom she needs protecting. It is from herself. I cannot believe that someone who would jump from a ship out in the middle of the sea would not attempt to escape this close to land."

"Aye, Cap'n." But Declan looked anything but acquiescent to Salvador's command. "And if the English captain should decide to come alongside and question us?"

"Picaro speaks Dutch. I'm leaving him here with you, as well. Have him tell them your captain has taken men into town to negotiate for supplies."

A commotion near the waist port drew Salvador's attention. He strode over in time to see his boatswain, Lau, pull two young men apart—both of whom were smaller than the quiet man from the deep reaches of the Orient.

"What seems to be the trouble?" Salvador planted his fists on his hips.

Declan came up beside him and crossed his arms, towering over all of them.

"No trouble, Captain." Lau gave the two teens a good shake before releasing their shirt collars. "Just one too many for the boat crew to row you ashore."

"Who was winning?" Declan asked.

"This one." Lau nodded toward the young man on his left. The scrawny lad wore a round hat pulled down almost to his eyes, and what the hat did not obscure, the darkness did.

Declan grunted in approval. "Good. The captain may need someone who can hold his own in a fight. You, boy—"

"Martin, sir."

"Martin, the boat is waiting." Declan waved toward the open port.

"Aye, sir." Martin scurried down the side of the ship to the boat waiting below.

Salvador hesitated briefly. Too many new faces had come aboard *Vengeance* in the past few weeks, and he'd had no time to get to know them, but now that would have to wait for another day. He pulled Declan away from the waist port. "Remember, she's unpredictable and likely to do something idiotic and unexpected. Be on your guard."

"Aye, Cap'n."

Salvador crossed to the gap in the bulwark, ready to go ashore and complete his business. The sooner he got away from here and the possibility of crossing paths with the captain or officers of the ship coming up behind them, the better. But he was forgetting something.

He paused and patted all his pockets. Of course.

The darkness in the cabin surprised him when he arrived back there, as it had been full of lamplight when he'd left it less than half an hour ago. He lit a candle and held it aloft.

Charlotte must have decided to turn in early. Her figure did not make much bulk in the hammock hung in a corner of the room, but the outline was unmistakable. And, he knew, even if she weren't already asleep, she would pretend to be if he tried to talk to her.

He moved quietly to his desk on the opposite side of the room and retrieved the letter he'd written earlier, which he slid into his coat pocket. Turning back toward the door, he could see movement in the hammock.

"Goodnight, Miss Ransome."

A slight, muffled sound was all the response he received in return.

Chuckling, he made his way to the boat waiting to row him to the town of Black River. While he regretted the outcome of his action, Charlotte amused him as no one had in a very long time. He wished Serena were here. He had a feeling the two of them would be great friends in no time.

The men made the oars whisper through the water—all, that was, except for Martin. But Lau addressed the matter, and within a few strokes the new lad maneuvered his oar as quietly as the other eleven men.

As soon as the boat scraped the wooden dock, Salvador jumped out. "Lau, new boy—Martin—you're with me. The rest of you stay here and be ready to leave as soon as we return. This should not take long."

✂✂✂

Charlotte had no idea what had come over her, but the moment the giant of a first mate had turned his attention to her, Lieutenant Martin's name was the first one to pop into her mind. Even though Salvador had not known her as Charles Lott, the name was too close to her own, and he was too clever by half. She hadn't meant to start the fight on deck, just to slip down onto the boat and come ashore. But she hadn't accounted for the loose manners aboard a pirate ship.

And now Salvador wanted her to accompany him on whatever nefarious mission he undertook.

She fell in step with the small Oriental man called Lau a few paces behind Salvador. He headed for the town—the seedy end of the high street, from the sounds and number of well-lit buildings. Her heart raced. She must make her escape before they reached the lights of the taverns, for Salvador would surely recognize her.

Where would she go? She strained her eyes against the darkness. There, in the distance to her left. That looked like a church bell tower. Yes, she would go to the church and seek refuge. They would protect her.

As soon as they entered the crowded high street—

But Salvador turned, ducking into a darkened alley rather than heading for one of the taverns. A few more turns down a few more narrow, dark streets, and Charlotte wasn't certain she could remember which way was which. And the closeness of the buildings blocked her view of any landmarks that would lead her to the church. Best to stick with Salvador and Lau for the moment.

The pirate finally stopped and banged on the door to a house that looked as if it were held up by the owner's sheer willpower. He had to knock three times, increasing the pressure and volume each time.

The sounds of scraping were heard inside and then the door flew open. "What d'you want in the middle of the ni—Salvador?" The rough-looking man framed in the door held aloft a lantern. "It is you, m'boy! Come in, come in. What can ol' Dandy do for you?"

Charlotte hung back and waited until the man—Dandy—had moved far enough into the room that she was assured of deep shadows in which to hide upon entering.

Salvador reached into his coat pocket and pulled out something—a letter. "I need to get this on the next ship to Kingston."

Kingston? Charlotte started to step forward to see what Salvador handed over to the other man, and then she remembered the need to stay out of the circle of light from the lantern.

Dandy took the letter from the pirate and angled it toward the light to read the address. "Tierra Dulce plantation, eh? You picked off another one of their ships and want to taunt them with your success?"

"Something like that. How soon will this get there?"

"I'm sailing a packet out in about four hours. We'll be in Kingston by midday Monday, then another several hours for the messenger to get out to the plantation." He tapped the letter against his grizzled chin. "I hear the mistress of Tierra Dulce is returning."

"She arrived two days ago, along with her husband and sister-in-law."

"Husband, you say? Had to be some money riding on that one somewhere. Thought for sure that old maid would stay that way. Never saw the chit myself, but a woman who couldn't find anyone to marry her before she was nigh thirty years old cannot be that much to look at."

Anger rose in the back of Charlotte's throat. How dare they speak of Julia in such an insolent manner. She ought to—

"Julia Witherington is a fine-looking woman. That was not the issue with her not marrying." Salvador clasped his hands behind his back.

Did he always wear shirts with those fancy lace cuffs and she hadn't noticed them, or had he dressed specially for tonight—showing his wealth and finery ashore differently than he did on his ship?

"How much do I owe you for carrying the letter for me?"

Dandy mouthed to himself as he counted something on his fingers. "One guinea."

Salvador dipped his fingers into a pocket and then flicked a gold coin toward the other man. "Thank you." With a nod toward Charlotte and Lau, he turned and made toward the door.

"And where will you be, should there be any reply?"

Salvador paused. "The messenger need not wait for a reply." He inclined his head again, and strode out the door.

This time, Charlotte did not wait for Lau to go ahead of her. She had no desire to be left behind alone, even if just for a moment. Something about that man frightened her in a way the two pirates she was with did not.

A few twists and turns away from the house, Salvador broke the silence. "While I'm here I must stop at the Crown and Sword to see what I can learn about Shaw and his movements." He made a right turn and then, a few steps later, they walked out onto the broad high street.

Charlotte stopped to orient herself. The church tower rose above the other buildings to her left. To her right, lights and noise from the taverns. Now was her chance, but she wanted to find out what Salvador learned about Shaw. If she ran now, she would not know if Julia was in jeopardy.

She hurried to catch up with Salvador and Lau, pulling the hat she'd taken from the boy she'd fought with lower over her eyebrows.

It only took one whiff of the stench inside the public house to make Charlotte regret her decision to stay with Salvador. The smell of alcohol would not be so bad on its own, but combined with the stench of unwashed bodies, tobacco smoke, and other odors she did not care to distinguish, it made her stomach churn.

The noise dimmed momentarily upon Salvador's entrance. He stood tall and straight, surveying the dark, dank room as if he were the proprietor. But the novelty of his entrance did not hold the patrons' attention long, and soon the cacophony returned to deafening levels.

Salvador cut through the room toward the back. Charlotte's skin crawled, and she jumped at every touch, bump, and jostle until she remembered that no one here saw her as a woman. Calling upon everything she learned aboard *Audacious*, she lifted her chin and squared her shoulders, pushing through the men and women in Salvador's wake.

At the back of the room Salvador paused briefly, and then he pushed through a heavy black curtain and disappeared.

Charlotte stopped, but Lau nudged her forward.

The back room contained one large table around which sat six men, with several others standing around the perimeter. All stared at Salvador.

"Come to play or to knock heads?" A portly man with tufts of dark hair growing irregularly from his shiny head laid his cards facedown on the table and dropped his hands to his sides.

"Neither. I came for information." Salvador reached into a pocket and withdrew a leather pouch. He tossed it onto the middle of the table with a loud clank of coins. "What hear you of Shaw?"

"Still on about that'un, are you?" The tufty man spat toward a brass receptacle, and missed with a wet splat against the rough wood floor.

Charlotte turned her face away to keep from gagging. When Salvador did not immediately answer, she turned to look at him.

He stood still, arms hanging at his sides, but he was not relaxed. She could almost feel the tension radiating from him.

"Shaw."

Tufty eyed the pouch of coins in the middle of the table atop those that had been wagered on the game in progress. "He was here, nigh on a week ago. Talking about how sommat was being delivered for him in Kingston and how, soon as it arrived, everyone would know his name back in Merry England."

"And was he taking both of his ships?"

Shaw had *two* ships? Charlotte reeled, catching herself against the wall.

"Nay, said his pickup in Kingston would be easy. I reckon he sent *Sister Mary* to the bay to wait it out."

Charlotte frowned. Sister Mary? Was the second ship captained by a nun? Shaw's sister?

"So he definitely sailed *Sister Elizabeth* to Kingston?"

Oh. *Sister Mary* and *Sister Elizabeth* were the ships' names. Strange.

"Aye. If you're wanting to ask more questions, I'm going to need to see another one of those." Tufty nodded toward the money pouch.

"That is all I need to know." Salvador gave a stiff bow, and Charlotte was happy to follow him out of the tavern.

He slowed his pace once back out on the high street. Lau walked beside him, but Charlotte hung back, ready to break away and run but wanting to hear Salvador's thoughts and plans.

"He could be making his move against Julia—Miss Withering—Mrs. Ransome right now." He barked a mirthless laugh. "He may have already taken her."

"We stand no chance against both ships together." Lau's soft voice betrayed no emotion.

"No. And it is unlikely we will easily come upon *Sister Elizabeth* if he has already left Kingston."

"He would have to come back this direction to rejoin *Sister Mary.*"

"Aye." Salvador's pace slowed more. "And there are many good moorings near the bay that would shelter us from view of a ship coming from Kingston if we could make it past the mouth of the bay without being seen."

The two pirates began discussing strategy. Charlotte trudged along behind them, her own mind whirling. If only she could get this information to Ned or William. They needed to go after Shaw instead of chasing Salvador.

She bumped into something solid and looked up, her hat falling to the street.

Salvador glanced over his shoulder with a frown. And then his expression changed. "Why, you—"

Taking advantage of his shock, Charlotte bolted around him and ran as fast as she could toward the church on the opposite end of the street—the very, very long street—praying with each slap of her foot against the hard-packed earth that she could outrun both Lau and Salvador.

Chapter Eight

At the sound of shouts and pounding feet, Ned stopped. Two men were running after a slighter figure—no doubt one of them had just been pick-pocketed or otherwise offended by a street urchin. He hoped they caught the scamp.

"What do you suppose that was about?" Lieutenant Wallis stopped beside him.

"Nothing to concern us." Ned nodded toward the shoddy building ahead of them. Light, noise, and a foul stench were pouring from it. "The Crown and Sword. This is where we're supposed to be able to get information."

Wallis looked at the public house with disdain. "Best have done with it, then, sir."

"Agreed." Ned straightened his plain brown waistcoat, wishing he could have worn his uniform. But the reports indicated the informant did not respond well to having men in Royal Navy uniforms enter his establishment.

The smell and noise inside the building made Ned's head reel. He could swim underwater for quite a while, but he wouldn't be able to hold his breath for as long as this would take.

He shoved his way through drunken men and drunker women toward the bar, ignoring the attempts of a few barmaids to get him *sommat*.

The dark-skinned man pouring something from a dust-covered bottle into an equally dirty glass eyed Ned suspiciously.

"I need to speak with Mr. Lynch."

"Why's he going to want to speak with you?" the barman grunted.

Ned pulled a small bag from his pocket and shook it so the coins inside jangled.

The barman jerked his head toward a doorway obscured by a thick black curtain. "He's in the back."

Ned nodded his thanks and headed for the curtain. He hesitated in front of it momentarily, remembering all too well the sight that met Emily St. Aubert when she lifted the black veil. He almost laughed at himself. If only his sister had not secretly tucked *The Mysteries of Udolpho* in his traveling bag before he'd left Plymouth. With no money to purchase books before setting sail, he'd turned to the ridiculous romance the first week to keep from running mad with boredom during his off-duty hours. He'd meant to pass it on to Charlotte once they arrived at Tierra Dulce.

Feeling quite stupid for his thoughts running in such a direction, Ned pushed the curtain aside and stepped into the room. Five men sat at a round table playing cards, with several more standing around looking on. None but the one sitting directly across from the door did more than glance around at Ned's entrance before returning their attention to the game.

"Who are you, and what do you want?" The thick man with hair growing in odd patches over his head puffed on a thin cigar.

"Are you Lynch?" Ned's voice hadn't cracked at all…or very much, anyway.

The man paused before nodding.

"I'm Ned Cochrane, captain of…of the ship *Audacious*. I'm searching for someone, and I've been told you might have useful information for me." Ned tossed the coin purse on the table.

Lynch grabbed the bag and opened it, peering into its depths for a moment before tightening the strings again and tucking it into his already burgeoning waistcoat pocket. "Who's it you're looking for?"

"A pirate. I don't know which one, but he came to Kingston—to the Tierra Dulce sugar plantation—and abducted a young woman. I have been tasked with returning her to her family." And to himself so they could get married. But Lynch didn't need to know that.

An odd glint entered Lynch's small, piggish eyes. "Very interesting. Just had someone else in here asking about the same thing."

"Who?"

"Never you mind about who came asking. I'll tell you what I told him. Shaw was in here a week ago bragging on how he was going to make himself famous and saying there was sommat being delivered for him to pick up in Kingston."

Ned's stomach turned. It was as they feared. Shaw had taken Charlotte. Reading reports of the rare survivors from ships the pirate attacked had given Ned nightmares. He prayed for Charlotte's safety. "What was this thing being delivered?"

Lynch took a few draws on the cigar before answering. "Not a thing. A person. Ever heard of a woman called Julia Witherington?"

Julia? "Aye—yes, I know of her."

Lynch nodded as if he'd given a complete answer.

"You mean to say that Shaw went to Tierra Dulce for the express purpose of taking Mrs. Ransome?"

"Ransome, eh? Heard the bird got married. Aye, he holds some grudge against her and her father, the esteemed admiral." But from the sneer in Lynch's voice, it was obvious he didn't esteem Sir Edward much at all.

"Did he take both of his ships to Kingston?"

"Don't believe so."

"Where would the second ship have been while Shaw made this... pickup in Kingston?"

"Ah, now that'd be premium information, lad."

Of course. Ned reached into his back pocket and withdrew a larger, heavier bag. He let it swing from his fingers rather than tossing it onto the table. "Where?"

"There's a bay near the point at Negril where Shaw's been known to lay up and count his gold. But you'd best not try to take even one of his ships on by yourself, boy. Even with a sixty-four-gun man-o'-war under your command."

So much for not wearing his uniform to keep Lynch from knowing who he really was. "Thank you for the information." He flung the second purse at the man, turned on his heel, and marched out of the place as fast as he could.

He didn't slow or speak until he was almost at the dock.

Shaw. Shaw had Charlotte. If he'd meant to take Julia, what would the man whose depravity and cruelty were whispered about from one end of the Caribbean to the other do when he learned he'd taken the wrong woman?

Back in the boat, Wallis looked as though he wished Ned would confide his thoughts to him, but Ned wasn't certain yet what he was thinking. All he knew was that he needed to get Charlotte out of that pirate's hands as soon as possible, no matter what consequences befell his own career once his crew recognized her as Charles Lott.

William even now was sailing in the opposite direction. He'd determined that if whoever took Charlotte was serious about collecting a ransom, he would stay within a few days' sail of Kingston. He'd created a plan for the two of them to circumnavigate the island and meet on the north side by midweek, gathering as much intelligence along the way as they could.

If Shaw had indeed taken Charlotte, the more than half-day lead he had on them meant he could already be docking in this protected bay doing…no, he wouldn't allow himself to imagine what the pirate might be doing to Charlotte.

Dreadful determination descended into the pit of Ned's gut. He had no choice. He must sail for the secret bay and engage Shaw.

⸎

Salvador glowered at Charlotte Ransome, looking for all the world like a lad in baggy breeches and a voluminous white shirt under a too-large waistcoat. His shoulder ached from landing on it when he'd tackled Charlotte only a few feet from the churchyard.

He hated to admit it, but she was more ingenious—and faster—than he'd suspected. At least his threat that he would take her back to the Crown and Sword, reveal her true identity, and leave her at the pub patrons' mercy had gained her cooperation.

But how had she gotten out of the cabin? And who had been in her hammock when he'd returned for the letter just before leaving?

Charlotte rowed with the rest until the boat bumped up against *Vengeance*'s side.

"You, boy—Martin—you go up first." Salvador waited until she'd gone halfway up before following her. Though she hadn't been able to climb up the day they had gone for a nice long swim in the ocean, she had no trouble scaling the side of his ship tonight as if she'd been born to it.

Once on deck he grabbed her upper arm—his fingers and thumb meeting easily around the scrawny yet firm limb—and dragged her toward his cabin, ignoring the questioning looks from the crew still about on deck.

The half deck was lit by a lantern hanging over Declan's shoulder where he sat outside the door to Salvador's quarters.

"Welcome back, Cap'n. Get what you needed out of ol' Lynch?"

"Aye."

Declan looked up from the piece of wood he was whittling, frowning at the hard tone in Salvador's voice. "What went wrong?"

By way of answer, Salvador reached up and swiped the hat from Charlotte's head.

Declan dropped the figurine and the knife. "How—?" He jumped from his chair, his head crashing against the deck above with the sound of a cannon. The giant dropped to his knees, clutching the top of his head and groaning.

"Serves you right." Salvador skirted around him and stormed into the main cabin. "Suresh. Suresh!"

"He's not—" But Charlotte's words died at the look of warning Salvador shot her.

He returned to the half deck and carried the still-groaning Declan's lantern back with him. He crossed to the hammock and held the light over it before yanking the thin sheet off the writhing figure.

Lying on his side, hands and feet tied and his mouth gagged with what looked like Salvador's silk neckcloths, Suresh's dark eyes implored Salvador to release him.

Salvador lowered the gag and then began freeing his steward from his bindings.

"Captain, I am so sorry. It is my fault, solely mine. I do not know what happened, only that I was struck from behind. I woke up here and have been unable to escape." Upon closer inspection, Salvador saw that Suresh's feet were tied to the hammock's ropes, and with his hands behind his back, it was obvious why he'd been unable to free himself.

After he was finished with the neckcloths, Salvador turned to Charlotte, who stood in the middle of the cabin toying with the bottom button of her waistcoat. "Explain."

"You should have known I would try to escape."

He sighed. "Yes, I did. But I obviously underestimated just how devious and hurtful to others you can be."

Were those tears welling in her eyes? Surely over her failed escape attempt and not over his reprimand.

"I did not want to hurt Mr. Suresh,"—she stepped forward and looked around Salvador to the steward—"but I couldn't be this close to land without trying to get away." Her blue eyes snapped back to Salvador's. "I waited until you left the cabin the first time, and as Mr. Suresh was leaving to follow you, I knocked him on the head with the heavy pewter candlestick from your desk. I tied him up and, though it took some doing, managed to get him into the hammock by letting one end of it down first, tying his feet to the other end, and then hoisting the head back up again."

He had underestimated not only her cunning but her physical strength as well.

She again looked at Suresh. "I borrowed some of your clothing, Mr. Suresh, and I am sorry to report that when Captain Salvador unceremoniously threw me to the street, he tore the sleeve. I am very good with a needle. I can mend it for you."

Suresh, as usual, said nothing.

Charlotte returned her gaze to Salvador. "After I was dressed in Mr. Suresh's clothing, I exited from his cabin and made my way to the quarterdeck. And I did not mean to start that fight—please do not punish the other boy. He was fighting me because I took his hat."

Salvador turned and paced the cabin—so that Charlotte would not see his expression. If she weren't related to the officer tasked with hunting him down and putting him out of business, and if she weren't a woman, he would offer her a place aboard *Vengeance*.

However, as things now stood, he could not risk another escape attempt.

"Suresh, go tell Declan to join us." He did not bother to turn around to make sure his steward obeyed the order.

Moments later the steward and first officer returned together, Declan bent over to save his head from another encounter with the beams above until he stood under the skylight, where he could straighten to his full height.

Salvador leaned against the edge of the table and took a long moment to study each of the three people in the room. Charlotte Ransome, looking like a bedraggled boy in Suresh's clothes, sat in one of the chairs, chewing the inside of her cheek. Suresh, trying to hide in the shadows, shame flowing from him in tidal waves. And Declan, the man who'd spent the last few hours guarding the wrong captive.

This was all Charlotte Ransome's fault. Before she set foot on his ship, he'd controlled everything that happened on *Vengeance*. He supposed this was his punishment for doing something he shouldn't have done in the first place.

He took a deep breath, steeling himself for the next wrong thing he was about to do.

"Captain Salvador, what are we going to do about Shaw's taking Julia? Do you think he'll really do it, or was he merely bragging about it?" Charlotte gnawed the tip of her thumb.

Her question knocked the wind from his sails. He'd been trying to figure out how best to tell Charlotte she would spend the rest of her time here tied to a chair, and she'd been worrying about the true problem.

Declan rested his hands on the table and leaned over it—close enough to Charlotte that, should she shift to her right, her shoulder would touch his arm. "You got confirmation, then? Shaw is taking the Witherington woman?"

Salvador sighed and ran his fingers through his hair. "Aye. Lynch said Shaw was here not a week ago talking about a package being delivered for him in Kingston. He knows Julia—Mrs. Ransome—is back in Jamaica, and he plans to exact his revenge upon Admiral Witherington and Commodore Ransome." He shook his head. "And I, in my idiocy, made it possible for him to get to her more easily."

"What?" Charlotte jumped from her chair. "You helped him? What would you do that for?"

"My dear Miss Ransome, by taking you and not your sister-in-law, I drew away the best protection my...Mrs. Ransome had: your brother's ship and the other Royal Navy ship that arrived with him. I can only pray that the commodore had the good sense to set guards about Tierra Dulce to protect Julia before he left to search for you...for me."

"How did he know she was coming?" Declan asked.

"Obviously, he had someone inside Tierra Dulce, just as we do." Salvador ignored the way Charlotte gaped at him at that admission. "I never thought that new steward looked at all trustworthy."

"The new—you mean Henry Winchester?" Charlotte dropped back into her chair.

"You met him, did you?" Salvador pulled out a chair and sat, pressing his knuckles against his temple and leaning his elbow on the table-top. "I never met the man myself, but from the reports I heard of him, and from seeing him in Kingston, I am certain he is a blackguard."

"Met him? He's the reason I came to Jamaica. I thought I was going to marry the man. Now you say he's dishonest and could be working with a pirate?" Charlotte's voice increased in volume and shrillness with each statement. "We have to do something! We must warn

Julia. She needs to know her steward cannot be trusted. Can we get back to Kingston in time? Do you think Shaw has made his move yet? Are we well armed enough to take his ships?"

Salvador chuckled at Charlotte's sudden defection to his crew—and her forgetting he was also a pirate. He was glad she no longer thought of him as cut from the same cloth as Shaw.

"I would like nothing better than to protect Mrs. Ransome, but I fear by the time we could return to Kingston, it would be too late. Shaw will take advantage of the absence of your brother and his ships and move in to put his plot into action soon, if he has not already done so. And, no—we are not well enough armed to take down even one of Shaw's ships, much less both of them."

"You said he wanted to exact revenge against Admiral Withering-ton and my brother. Why? What did they ever do to him?"

"I do not know precisely what happened, but from what I've learned, it all stems from something that happened twenty years ago when Admiral Witherington first brought his family over from England."

"William was on that ship. That's when he and Julia met for the first time. She said she went out on deck dressed in her brother's clothes and climbed to the mast top to see a French ship." The smile from Char-lotte's memory faded. "Are you saying Shaw was on that ship too?"

Salvador leaned forward, elbows braced against his knees, plagued by his own memories. "He isn't on the Navy List. No one by the name of Shaw served on *Indomitable* on that voyage."

"But if we don't know what happened twenty years ago, we don't know what kind of revenge he's seeking now." Charlotte looked from Salvador to Declan to Suresh and then back to Salvador. "Do we?"

Salvador dropped his head into his hands. "I wanted to protect her. But instead I made it possible for him to get to her."

Declan's fist slammed onto the table, making them all jump. "We might not be able to catch him coming out of Kingston with her, but we know where he'll head."

"Negril." Suresh's soft voice came from the shadows.

"We can make it there and find a good place to hide and wait for

him to show up. Soon as he does, we'll have the element of surprise."
Declan paused.

Salvador stared at the rope jammed into the crack between the deck boards under his feet. If anything happened to Julia because of what he'd done—

"So we go to Negril."

Salvador looked up at Charlotte's emphatic statement. "We?"

She crossed her arms, glaring at him. "Aye, *we*. What choice do I have? I am not foolish enough to believe I'll be able to escape—and even if I did, it would only serve to distract from the mission to rescue Julia. In for a penny, in for a pound, I say."

"Meaning you will help us rather than hinder us?" Salvador straightened in his chair.

"Aye—especially if you'll let me work out on deck."

"No."

"But I was a senior midshipman—captain of a watch—on *Audacious*. I've seen the young men on this ship. They need someone to set an example for them."

"No."

"You need me as part of your crew."

In two strides, Salvador reached Charlotte and grabbed her by the bony shoulders. "I said no."

"Not even assisting the sailing master by keeping logs?"

"No."

"Jean Baptiste has been complaining that no one has been able to do a decent job of it since his last mate died of dysentery," Declan added. "Besides, it will keep her busy and out of trouble."

Salvador swung his gaze to his first officer and future brother-in-law. "Et tu Brute?"

Charlotte looked up at the giant of a man and smiled at him, turning Declan a shade of red Salvador had never seen. Wonderful. Now not only did he have to worry about rescuing Julia from Shaw, he also had to worry about Declan's infatuation with Charlotte.

When God said vengeance was His, the Bible should have gone

on to warn about dire consequences for anyone who decided to take his own revenge. For this was surely Salvador's punishment for thinking he could take the task out of God's hands. He prayed Shaw's punishment was even worse.

Chapter Nine

Julia's back ached from sitting on the narrow wooden bench for so long, but her heart soared at the sounds of the voices raised in song around her. Here, in Tierra Dulce's chapel, there was little formality and no inhibition when it came to exclaiming joy and praise and pain and vulnerability.

And hearing Jeremiah preach again…The only thing that would have made this day more perfect would have been for William to be experiencing it with her.

Absent was the prayer book and its prescribed readings and canticles murmured by the congregation in a disinterested monotone. Instead, everyone joined in singing hymns that carried Julia back to her childhood with their familiar lyrics and tunes, made even more meaningful by the beautiful harmonies and the cadences not unlike the waves washing against her beach.

What came after the service, however, was what Julia had been looking forward to for days. The men quickly set up boards and carpentry braces and set the benches from the church along the long table lining the wide, hard-packed dirt avenue that ran between the neat, well-kept white houses.

Out of each house came dish after dish of food. When Julia tried to help, everyone waved her off, including Jerusha, who insisted she take a seat and allow everyone else to do their work.

"I do not want to be treated like a guest. I want to be part of the family again."

"Let them treat you special this one day, Miss Julia. It's their way of showing you how happy they are you're home and that Master... Mr. Winchester is gone." Jerusha leaned over and put a dish of rice and peas in the middle of the table. The aroma of coconut milk coming from it made Julia ache to taste it. "Mr. Winchester thought such a gathering like this was disrespectful on the Lord's day. This is the first time since you left that we've gathered for dinner after church."

"He would have stopped us from gathering for church if he could have." Jeremiah hefted a large platter of roasted goat meat onto the table. "I believe he feared if he let us get together and start talking amongst ourselves, we would be talking 'bout him and speculating 'bout what he might be up to."

Julia's heart wept for her people. She had done this to them by hiring Winchester.

"Now, don't you go feeling bad, missus." Jeremiah patted her shoulder. "Your mama had just passed on. You had to make the best of a bad predicament."

"But I did not have to return to England. I should have stayed and seen to my duty here."

"No, you needed to spend that time with your father." The words came out in an almost wistful tone from the man who had been the proxy for her father most of her life.

"And you needed to retrieve that husband of yours." Jerusha winked at her.

"Winchester didn't do any permanent damage. He may have stolen a vasty sum, but this year's crop is the best we've ever had. And sugar prices keep on rising, especially now we can trade with France and Spain again."

"No talk of cane or trading on Sunday." Jerusha admonished her husband with a severe look that set both him and Julia to laughing. "This is a day for celebrating our family coming back together." Joining in their laughter, she put her arm around Julia's shoulders and gave her a quick squeeze.

The past twelvemonth faded into distant memory over the next few hours as Julia lost herself in becoming reacquainted with those who lived and worked at Tierra Dulce, holding new babies, and receiving dirty, sticky hugs and kisses from older children who remembered her, even after so long a separation.

Thunderclouds rolling in brought an end to the afternoon's merriment. Once again, no one would let Julia help with any of the work, and she finally obeyed Jerusha and returned to the main house just as the rain started.

The quiet oppressed her after weeks aboard *Alexandra* and the chaos of the last few days. She wandered from empty room to empty room, wondering how she had endured the stillness of the house and the long, empty days of inactivity she'd known in England.

England—yes, that was just what she needed. She returned to the study, sat at the desk William had been so good to make room for in their cabin aboard *Alexandra*, and pulled out a stack of stationery. First, she wrote a long letter to her dear friend Susan Yates, explaining everything that had happened since they bade each other farewell in Portsmouth two months ago. Then, a letter to her father.

Nightfall extinguished what little light remained in the rain-obscured sky, and she had to light another lamp to increase the brightness in the room. Fighting fatigue, she wrote a letter to Lady Dalrymple, apologizing to her for any inconvenience or worry Charlotte's departure had caused.

She should not have stayed up so late writing, but she could post these from town tomorrow. She carried all three letters and one of the lamps with her to her room and tucked her correspondence into the satchel holding the account book and papers she wished to review with her banker.

Dark, disconnected images disturbed her sleep, and when she turned out from bed as the sun rose, she almost felt poorly enough to put the trip into town off one more day.

But that would be pure sloth.

She drank her coffee—a good, strong, dark coffee from a neighboring plantation—while her maid arranged her hair. The dark blue damask dress conveyed the level of seriousness Julia desired.

In the kitchen Jeremiah rose to greet her. Julia joined him at the table in the middle of the large room, separated from the house by a breeze-way. And this morning's breeze promised a hot day full of sunshine.

"Roads are muddy but clear." Jeremiah pushed the platter of sausages toward her. Cook set a plate containing two fried eggs, sausages, and ackee and saltfish down in front of her.

Julia smiled at the combination of the English eggs and sausage and the traditional Jamaican dish—dried fish soaked in water and then cooked with ackee fruit, onions, peppers, and tomatoes.

A young man Julia wasn't certain she'd met yet entered the kitchen and swiped his hat from his head. "Ma'am, the carriage stands ready for you at the front of the big house."

"Thank you," Julia said, smiling her thanks at the boy no older than Charlotte, who blushed under his deep complexion and backed out of the room. She turned to Jeremiah. "New groom?"

"Stable hand." He speared another sausage. "He is the Martinezes's boy."

"Not the quiet one who always hid around corners watching everyone?"

"The very same. Are you going to finish that?" The overseer pointed at Julia's ackee and saltfish with his knife.

Julia parried it away with her fork. "Yes, I intend to eat every bite."

Once her stomach was sated, Julia exited the front door to find the carriage driver waiting for her, a smile splitting his dark face.

"'Tis good to have you home, Miss Julia."

"Thank you, Levi." She queried the man about his family, having known all of them for as long as she could remember. After getting a report on each child and grandchild, she turned to the two younger men standing beyond Levi. "Ruben, it is good to see you again."

The footman, the middle of Levi's three sons, bowed his head. "Ma'am."

"And…Asher?" Julia marveled at the changes a year had made in the maturity of Levi's youngest son. Asher held a musket and had two pistols tucked under his belt. "Thank you for looking after my safety."

"Yes, mum."

"Very good, then. Jeremiah," she turned to the overseer, "I believe we can get underway."

"I'll see to things here." Jeremiah stepped out of the way as Ruben came forward to assist Julia into the carriage. "I have everyone on the lookout for Winchester."

Julia settled onto her seat and adjusted the brim of her hat to shade her eyes from the sun. "What will you do if he comes back?"

"Hold him in the smokehouse until you return and we can fig-ure out what to do." Though his expression remained deadly serious, Jeremiah's voice held a lilt of amusement. "As I said, I'll take care of things here. No need for you to fret. You have enough to worry about regarding the task you're undertaking now."

"Thank you. I should return by midday tomorrow, and by then we will know how much damage Mr. Winchester has done to Tierra Dulce."

Levi climbed up onto the driver's seat, and his two sons clambered up onto their perch in the rear. Jeremiah backed up a few paces and raised his hand in a farewell salute. Julia returned the wave and then pulled out the novel she'd brought to pass the time on the long drive into town.

Less than half an hour after leaving Tierra Dulce, Julia resolved to request a meeting with the parish magistrate to discuss the condi-tion of the road with him. With many miles yet to go, she was already tired of being bounced and jostled. But not even that could keep her fatigue at bay. After staring at the same page without taking in any of the words printed upon it for too long, she finally gave up, closed the book, and shut her eyes.

She dozed intermittently, coming back to wakefulness at the worst of the holes and ruts in the road. Two hours into the trip, she consid-ered telling Levi to turn the carriage around and take her back home. She should have waited until tomorrow, until she was better rested and in a better frame of mind, for the meeting that awaited her on the end of this trip. But they had come this far. She would just have to inure herself to further discomfort and displeasure and console herself with the anticipation of returning to Tierra Dulce tomorrow.

The explosive blast of a gun sounded from somewhere nearby, followed only seconds later by the screaming shrill of the left-side carriage horse. It reared, throwing the barouche off balance and tossing Julia from her seat onto the floor. Behind her, Ruben and Asher shouted as the conveyance tipped toward the right. She hoped they had time to jump free.

Grasping for something, anything, to give her anchorage, an image of William's face—the way he had looked at her at their wedding—filled her mind.

Men's voices. Gunshots. The shrill cries of the injured horse. Falling.

Sharp pain exploded in Julia's side when the open-top carriage tipped over, and she landed half on the door and half on the ground. Her chest refused to expand and fill with air. Blackness crept in around the edges of her vision, but she struggled against it. Men in dirty, ragged clothes darted here and there, in and out of her narrowing field of vision. More yells from Levi and Ruben and Asher. No not Ruben. The brigands dragged Levi and Asher around the horses and forced them to kneel, pressing pistols to their heads. Another man worked to free the uninjured horse from its now-moaning partner and the twisted harnesses.

Julia took short, shallow breaths hoping the pain in her side would ease once she got herself upright again, but before she had a chance to try sitting up on her own, rough hands grabbed her and yanked her up. A cry of agony burst from her throat before she could stop it. Her knees buckled and would not support her weight. Throbbing pain wrapped around her chest like the anchor rope around the capstan.

Another gunshot and the horse's moaning stopped. Julia prayed the men—highwaymen, pirates, whoever they were—would not use the same means to ease her pain.

She found her footing and gained her balance, and so long as she did not move either arm or take deep breaths, the pain subsided to a throbbing ache.

Blood trickled from Levi's nose, and Asher's left eye was almost swollen shut. Where was Ruben?

"Have you got her?"

Julia gasped at the familiarity of the voice coming from behind her—and immediately regretted it when fire bolted through her chest. The hand squeezing her upper arm yanked her around.

Julia clamped her teeth together to keep from betraying her continued pain.

Henry Winchester—dressed in breeches, tall black boots, and an open-necked white shirt—stood before her, feet braced wide apart, fists on his hips.

"It's her, Master Winchester."

Julia whipped her head around to discover that her captor was none other than Ruben. "How could you do this?"

Ruben's strong jaw worked back and forth, and he would not look at her. "Because I am no more than a slave at the plantation. Master Winchester showed me that. He showed me how I could make my fortune and not have to work for the likes of you and yours."

"Slave? Boy, you know nothing about what it's like to be a slave," Levi yelled. A grunt followed this outburst.

Ruben winced at the word *boy*. But he would not look at his father either. "I'm not going to be like you, Pa, toiling my life away for somebody else. I'm going to be my own man."

"What should we do with these two?"

Winchester looked past Julia and Ruben. "We only need one of them to return to the plantation and spread the news. The boy can go faster. Kill the old man."

"No—" Julia lost her balance when Ruben released her arm and the support he offered her.

"That was never part of the arrangement." The nineteen-year-old grabbed the front of Winchester's shirt as if to shake him.

Three more brigands stepped forward, pistols aimed at Ruben's heart.

"I would back away if I were you, boy." Winchester stepped toward Ruben. "Unless you want to be the one dying today."

Ruben released him and held his hands out in front of him before dropping them to his sides.

Winchester took his time straightening the front of his shirt. He stepped around Ruben to speak to the man holding the gun to the back of Levi's head. "The boy will be the messenger. Shoot the old man in the leg."

"No! I won't let you." Julia turned, thinking to put herself between Levi and the man intent on doing him harm, but in her injured state she could not move fast enough. Winchester's hand whipped out and grabbed her arm, yanking her back and causing enough pain to bring tears to her eyes.

"Shoot me! Shoot me!" Asher struggled against his captor, trying to gain his feet and knock the man standing over his father away. But his position on his knees put him at a disadvantage, and Winchester's man easily subdued him.

Julia closed her eyes and braced herself, but her legs still gave way at the report of the pistol. Her knees hit the ground hard, the impact taking her breath away once more. Left hand pressed to her aching ribs, Julia opened her eyes. Levi lay on his side, clutching his bleeding thigh with both hands. Winchester stalked over and lifted a trembling Asher by the lapels of his red livery coat.

"Take the spare horse and ride back to Tierra Dulce fast as you can. You tell them their mistress has been taken. Tell that overseer that if he wants his mistress to live, he'd best send for her husband. My brother would like a word with him."

"My father—"

"Will stay here and bleed to death if you aren't fast enough." Winchester pulled a sealed letter out of the top of his boot and handed it to Asher. "You give this to Jeremiah. It tells him everything else he needs to know. Now"—he motioned for someone beyond the boy to come forward—"get on this horse and ride for Tierra Dulce as if your father's life depends on it. Because it does."

Julia's heart broke for the young man as he dashed his sleeve over his eyes before mounting the horse.

"I'll be back, Pa. I'll bring help." He turned the horse back the direction they came and kicked it into a run.

Julia tore a long, wide strip from one of her petticoats and, taking advantage of Winchester's momentary lapse of focus on her, went to Levi and began to bandage his leg.

"Saint Julia to the rescue." Winchester sneered, grabbing her arm to yank her away from the groaning man. But he did not order the bandage to be taken from Levi, who managed to sit up and begin wrapping the strip of linen tightly around his wound.

"Come. The commodore does not like to be kept waiting." He dragged her toward the treeline a few yards from the edge of the road.

"Who is the commodore?"

Winchester's smile was anything but pleasant. "You'll see. I believe he would be angry with me if I spoiled the surprise."

"Why are you doing this?" She struggled to free her arm from his injurious grip.

He tightened his hold. "Because it's time your family and the Ransomes pay for what they did to us."

Confused, Julia stopped struggling. "Did to you? What do you mean?"

He whipped around and leaned his face into hers. "You ruined our lives. All of you. The whole lot of you Witheringtons and Ransomes." He straightened, as if remembering himself. "But I will let the commodore explain it. After all, he was the one directly involved. Now, get on the horse."

"I think I may have broken a few ribs when the carriage overturned."

"And why is that a concern of mine?" Winchester grabbed her around the waist and lifted her off the ground. Perhaps he meant to throw her up onto the horse's back, but he did not have the strength. She grabbed onto the saddle, and though it sent fresh spasms of agony through her torso, pulled herself up into a sidesaddle position on the regular saddle.

"Give me your hands."

She held her hands out in front of her. Winchester tied them together and then secured the other end of the long rope and the horse's reins to the saddle on his mount.

Rather than take the road, Winchester and his men headed for the grove of trees. Julia clung to her horse's mane, terrified of falling off and being dragged behind Winchester. Riding was not something she counted among her accomplishments. And without a proper side-saddle, the prospect of sliding off the leather seat below her was all the more real.

Pain became her constant companion for the next hour. Julia stopped trying to figure out where they were going, as thinking interfered with her ability to try to ignore the pounding ache in her right side. Closing her eyes made her feel the way she did the first few days out at sea.

At long last Winchester stopped and dismounted. He placed his hands on Julia's waist and helped her slide down from the tall mount. Several men came out of the underbrush surrounding them.

"Weren't followed, Mr. Winchester."

"Boat's ready and waiting for us."

"You got the bird? Commodore'll be mightily perturbed if you don't have the right one."

She did not recognize the beach or cove. Asher's ride to Tierra Dulce would have taken too long for her to have even a faint hope that men from the plantation would come crashing down the side of the bluff and rescue her. Her only recourse was to pray word would reach William quickly.

No matter what position she found herself in, sitting or standing, as long as she did not move overly much, the ache in her side remained bearable. Winchester positioned her in the middle of the jolly boat. She stared ahead at the ship looming ever larger ahead of them in the secluded bay. They could not be far from Kingston Harbor. She tried to hold on to the hope that this ship would be spotted and stopped before they could take her away.

She held her breath on the ride up the side of the ship on the bosun's swing, fearful each moment their rough handling of the rope would result in dumping her into the water. With her hands still bound together, she eased herself off the board seat and stumbled before finding her balance.

Fear gripped her innards at the mangy, fierce collection of men who surrounded her on the deck. She turned toward the stern, intent on marching to the captain's cabin and demanding an explanation. But before she got three steps, the crowd parted for a solitary figure coming toward her.

Squaring her shoulders, she wiped her expression of all fear, pain, and fatigue. The man, obviously the commodore to whom Winchester referred, stopped about five feet from her. A tall man—taller than William—his shoulder-length, straight hair had been bleached by the sun, contrasting with the dark whiskers across his jaw as if he had not shaven in several days. He glared at her through narrowed blue eyes and crossed thick arms over a muscular chest.

"I demand to know why I have been brought here against my will." At least with her hands bound, he could not see them trembling.

"You *demand*?" The man laughed, showing dimples in his cheeks. How could someone so despicable have dimples like that?

He closed the distance between them, grabbed the rope dangling from her hands, and jerked it. She stumbled toward him.

"You are in no position to make demands, Mrs. Ransome."

"You…you have me at a disadvantage, sir." Her stomach churned and her heart pounded.

He dropped the rope, stepped back, and flourished a bow. "Well, do forgive me, madam. Allow me to introduce myself. I am Commodore Arthur Winchester. But mostly, I am simply known as the pirate Shaw. This is my flagship, *Sister Elizabeth*."

She could not disgrace herself by giving in to the sudden weakness in her legs. "What do you want from me?"

"From you?" He laughed again, but his blue eyes remained cold. "You are nothing but a pawn, the instrument with which I intend to exact justice on the men who ruined my life. Welcome to your new home, Mrs. Ransome. It will probably be your last."

Chapter Ten

I'm going with you."

Salvador turned to see Charlotte exit his quarter gallery privy once again dressed in Suresh's trousers and shirt. For the past two days, she'd been cooperative—overly so—and he had been waiting for her next outrageous action.

"No. You will stay here, where it is safe."

"Are you saying I'm not safe with you?"

He closed his eyes and sighed. Heaven help Captain Ned Cochrane in marrying this woman. "You will be safer here. 'Tis a dangerous climb to the top of the bluff, and I need not tell you the consequences if someone from *Sister Mary* spots us. Lau assured me he took care of all of the lookouts on this side of the bay, but there may be others."

She mimicked his cross-armed stance. "Would you rather I tie up Suresh again and sneak onto the boat, or would you rather I jump overboard after you leave and swim to shore?"

"I vote for jumping overboard," Suresh mumbled from his position behind Salvador.

Salvador fought to maintain his stern expression. "Have you been this difficult all your life?"

Charlotte cocked her head, as if considering. "No. I kept this to myself most of my life. I did not want to do anything that might upset Mama." She shrugged. "I have a lot of years of holding it all in to make up for."

At least she was honest about it. "Do you think yourself capable of making the climb in quick order?"

"You would be surprised to find out what I am capable of."

"Oh, yes, your month's experience as a midshipman." His own experience his first months aboard a ship reminded him how quickly the job must be learned.

"Almost two months. And I was promoted—"

"Yes, yes, promoted to watch captain above boys with more seniority." When this was all over, he would sit Ned Cochrane down and find out exactly what the man had been thinking to not immediately turn Charlotte over to her brother. For surely the man had recognized her as soon as he saw her, disguised or not.

Just as he himself had recognized her when first seeing her dressed as a boy? He shook his head over his own folly.

"So?"

"So?"

"Can I go with you?"

He wouldn't put it past her to find some way to follow him ashore, and Declan and Suresh would lead the mutiny and maroon both him and Charlotte on a deserted island should her scheme involve either of them again.

"Yes, you can come. You will need stouter boots than that. Suresh—"

The steward bumped him out of the way and motioned Charlotte to sit on the sofa so he could replace the shoes she wore with a pair of his own sturdy boots. Once he finished that, he handed her a pair of thick leather gloves and a straw hat.

"Wear these to protect your hands when you climb. This will keep the sun from your face. When you tire in climbing, rest and catch your breath before continuing."

Charlotte nodded at each piece of advice. "Thank you, Mr. Suresh."

Suresh offered his hand to assist her to her feet. "Do be careful, miss."

"I will." She turned to Salvador. "I'm ready."

With a curt nod, Salvador led the way out onto the deck. Rather than acknowledge his captain, Declan, standing watch on the quarterdeck, tipped his hat to Charlotte. Lau bowed to her and motioned for her to precede him down the accommodation ladder. The sailors manning the launch made a space for her in the middle.

Salvador chewed the inside corner of his bottom lip. Good thing he would soon be giving up the pirate trade, settling his debts, and moving on to a life as a respectable merchant ship captain. After this experience, he wasn't certain his crew would ever be the same.

As soon as the boat scraped the sand, Salvador leaped out onto the beach. He turned to assist Charlotte, but before he could raise his hands to catch her around the waist, she bounded over the side and landed lightly beside him. Lau followed immediately behind.

"When you see us begin our descent, man the boat and prepare to return to the ship upon our return."

"Aye, aye, Captain." Picaro touched the brim of his hat. While having Picaro commanding the boat crew was not the best use of his second mate's abilities, the friction between the Irishman and Declan made Salvador want to find ways to keep them separated, especially when he was not there to mediate and diffuse the situation.

The ascent up the side of the mountain began easily enough. Though no trail existed, by choosing a diagonal path they could walk almost upright.

"Captain Salvador, how did you know of this hiding place? If Shaw uses this bay often enough that you knew of its existence, how has he never been caught? Surely it would be a matter of simple tactics for the Royal Navy to wait until both ships are docked here, block off the entrance, and fire upon the ships until he surrenders."

He glanced over his shoulder at Charlotte. Already winded himself, her sprightly step and long speech betrayed no sign of her tiring or feeling the physical strain. He took a deep, burning breath and continued up the ever-steepening slope. "It has been tried. Why do you think there was an opening for your brother to take command of a squadron of ships on this station? Shaw is too cunning to allow himself to be trapped in an inescapable position. And even when outgunned by three Royal Navy ships of the line, he was more willing than they to sacrifice everything."

"He took down three ships of the line?"

Salvador paused and then almost lost his balance when Charlotte bumped into him. She braced her hands against his back to keep him from toppling over on her. The dirt and scrubby brush gave way to what looked like sheer rock face in front of him.

"In concert, his ships dealt mortal blows to two of the Royal Navy ships—hulling them below the waterline too severely for them to be salvaged. The third—the former commodore's flagship—he put out of commission by taking down her masts and having his snipers relieve the officers of command."

Spying his first foot- and handholds in the rock face, Salvador took a deep breath and began the climb.

"I have heard rumors of him. Of what he has done to people, to the women and children he has taken captive from the ships he attacks... ghastly, unmentionable things that will surely condemn his soul. Are... are they true? The rumors?" Charlotte clung to the side of the bluff with no evidence of effort.

Salvador's entire body protested the unfamiliar physical strain. "I would imagine what you have heard is true. And worse yet. For I doubt the true nature of his black heart would be spoken of before a gentlewoman."

Charlotte began mumbling under her breath.

"What is that?" Salvador took the opportunity to pause and try to catch his wind. "I did not understand you."

"I was praying for Julia. I am no expert at entreating God for help, but if she has indeed fallen into Shaw's hands, the only one who can help her now is the Almighty."

Teachings from his youth—along with the preaching he allowed Jean Baptiste to do aboard *Vengeance* each Sunday—rang through Salvador's head. He had turned his back on God when his father turned his back on him, leaving him at the mercy of the pirates who captured him. Yet it was to those teachings he owed his decision to leave that ship and set out on his own, doing what good he could in liberating slave ships—and the occasional ship from a particularly wealthy and successful sugar plantation.

The rest of the climb was accomplished in silence. At the top Salvador gratefully hoisted himself over the edge onto the almost flat top, a few well-placed boulders providing cover. He lay still, gasping for breath.

Charlotte climbed over the edge and, crouching, stepped over him, pulling out a small telescope and propping it on the lowest rock to look down into the bay below.

"Captain Salvador," she hissed, "another ship is coming."

Heart pounding—from the climb, mostly—he pushed himself up and pulled out his own spyglass. Indeed, over the mountain hemming in the opposite side of the bay, he could make out the topsails of a ship—a large one, from the spacing of the masts. And...

"It's flying a British pennant!" Joy echoed in Charlotte's voice. "We should find a way to signal them—we should have brought the box of flags with us—and tell them to join us on this side so we can come up with a plan together."

"We cannot signal them without giving away our position to *Sister Mary*." Salvador turned his glass downward to observe Shaw's secondary ship. "Hopefully, the ship will continue on her way without taking note of the bay or its inhabitant."

"And *Vengeance*?"

"She is well hidden from any passersby." Or should be, unless the naval ship's captain decided to search the inlet north of the bay, blockaded from the open sea by this bluff. He swung the glass up again. The British ship slowed as it neared the mouth of the bay. Men reefed the topsails.

Cold lead poured through Salvador's innards and sank his soul. He could not intervene without risking his own ship and crew. But could he sit by and do nothing, knowing the fate the naval ship faced?

◌⬥◌

The closer the British ship came to the mouth of the bay, the harder Charlotte's heart pounded. If she had a more powerful spyglass, she might be able to see the individuals on deck and see if she recognized any of them.

Before losing the protection of the bluff on the other side of the bay, the ship stopped. Salvador's mouth drew into a grim line.

"Is there no way we can warn them?" she asked.

He shook his head. "No. And *Sister Mary* will know of their arrival. They will have lookouts on that bluff, as well."

She swung her glass around to sight the pirate ship once more. Activity on the deck, followed by the opening of the gun hatches, affirmed Salvador's statement.

Outside the bay, the British ship lowered one of their gigs into the water.

"I need to borrow your glass, Captain Salvador. I need to know…"

He handed over the larger telescope and she pressed it to her eye. Yes, she could see faces now. Her stomach climbed into her throat. A thin figure with white blond hair climbed down the accommodation ladder to the small launch. "Kent."

Sitting up, she frantically searched the deck. There—with Lieutenants Wallis, Duncan, Hamilton, and Martin flanking him—stood Ned. She choked on her own breath.

Salvador grabbed the telescope from her and pushed her down behind the rock.

"It's Ned! It's HMS *Audacious*. We have to stop them." Her voice rasped against her fear. "We have to find a way to keep him from sending the boat in."

"We cannot." Salvador put the spyglass to his eye again. "The boat has raised the white flag. He is sending them in for parlay. If you truly believe in the efficacy of prayer, Miss Ransome, you had better pray for the men on that boat."

Steadying her breathing, Charlotte raised her own glass and focused on the gig. Kent sat in the bow with another midshipman, while Midshipman Jamison sat in the stern with Lieutenant Gardiner. A white flag flew from the gig's foremast, raised solely for that purpose as the two dozen sailors rowed into the bay.

She prayed as she had never prayed before, though for the most part her prayer consisted mainly of *Please, Lord, keep them safe*.

The boat drew even with *Sister Mary*, though with many yards between them. A man in a gold-bedecked red coat stepped to the waist of *Sister Mary*, in the middle of a row of men with pistols and muskets aimed at the small boat. Gardiner stood up in the stern of the launch and touched the fore point of his hat.

Charlotte wished their voices carried up here. What did Ned know about Julia? Had she been taken?

Something bright flashed from the top of the bluff on the other side of the bay. Charlotte raised her head and glanced toward it—and then crackling booms split the stillness.

Stifling a cry, she lifted her telescope and scanned the water below. Smoke obscured the scene, but the yells and screams echoing along with the report of the gunfire told her clearly enough what had happened.

Where was Gardiner? Jamison? Kent?

"They're going to attack *Audacious*. Lau, signal the ship that we're coming." Salvador crept toward the edge of the bluff.

The smoke below began to clear. The water around *Audacious*'s boat churned with men swimming away. Most wore sailors' clothes, not the dark woolen officers' uniforms. There, taking cover on the far side of the gig from the ship—was that Jamison's red hair?

The crew of *Sister Mary* hoisted a few men out of the water—one of them in an indigo coat and tan pants with pale blond hair. Kent. Shaw's men had Kent.

"Charlotte, we must leave now!"

Salvador's voice broke through her panic. Yes, she could do nothing to help her shipmates from here. She must return with Salvador to his ship so they could go help Ned.

Tucking her spyglass under her belt, she slid over the edge of the cliff and started down, outpacing Salvador and Lau and making it back to the beach well before either. Picaro had the men ready at the oars and had the boat pushed out as Salvador and Lau ran toward them. Charlotte grabbed the side of the bow and flung herself into the boat—and barely had time to roll out of the way before Lau and then Salvador did the same.

At *Vengeance*, Charlotte hurried up the ladder on Salvador's heels. "Declan, set course northwest. Put some distance between us and the bay before *Sister Mary* leaves it."

Charlotte stopped. "What? No! We have to go help Ned, help *Audacious*. He doesn't know what he's facing."

Salvador turned and grabbed her by the shirt collar. "*Never* question my orders on the deck of my ship."

Charlotte called upon all of her internal fortitude to keep from surrendering to fear. "Not even when you're acting the coward?"

Salvador shoved her away from him, anger turning his eyes black. "Picaro, have the prisoner bound and gagged and then get her off my quarterdeck."

The second mate took Charlotte by the arm but did not otherwise give evidence he intended to follow Salvador's orders. "What happened? We heard gunfire."

As Salvador seemed fit only for seething, Charlotte quickly filled in his crew on what they had witnessed.

When she finished, Declan faced his captain. "She's right, sir, and you know it. We must render assistance to the navy ship or else *Sister Mary* will destroy them."

"And in case you've forgotten," Charlotte stepped forward, pulling her arm free from Picaro's loose grip, "the only reason *Audacious* is out here and sent that boat into the bay is because they are looking for *me*. Because they don't know it's *you* and not Shaw who took me."

Salvador's jaw worked back and forth, as if grinding up his words before spitting them out. "Have you considered *Audacious* is just as likely to fire upon us as they are to accept our assistance?"

"Have you considered that helping them could be your way of showing your regret over the mistake you made?" Charlotte softened her voice but not her stance.

Surprise filled his expression at her words.

She took another step toward him, uncrossing her arms and dropping them to her sides. "Yes, Captain Salvador, I know you regret the action you took. This is not who you are. You are a good man. I've seen it in the way you treat your men, in the way they respect your leadership. In the account books I found in your cabin showing how much money you have taken over the years and from whom, because I assume you mean to pay it back somehow. In the fact you set out on this folly because of your desire to protect Julia."

Julia's name acted like a lit match to beeswax. Salvador's tension melted. "Declan, set course to render assistance to the British ship."

"Aye, aye, Cap'n." The giant American turned and bellowed orders to the crew.

Charlotte closed the rest of the distance between herself and Salvador. "Let me help."

"You've already been enough help. Go to my cabin and change back into your gown. Stay away from the windows and keep your head down. If something were to happen to you while we're fighting to save your fiancé and his ship, he would hang me from the nearest yardarm. And he'd be right to do so." Salvador gave her a tight smile and then squeezed her shoulder. "Go, now."

She nodded and made her way through the crew scurrying about the deck to his cabin. Once Suresh learned what had happened, he left her alone in the cabin to go help on deck.

Charlotte closed the door behind him and finally allowed herself to notice the weakness in her legs. She sank to the floor and curled up in a ball on her side. But she would not give in to the fear. She refused to. There had to be a reason why Ned came while Salvador and his ship were here. God must have meant for Salvador to help Ned, to protect him from falling to the other pirate's ship.

He must have meant for Ned to rescue her now so that together they could rescue Julia.

Chapter Eleven

N ed came out of the quarter gallery and immediately crossed to the sideboard to grab the pitcher of water to rinse out his mouth.

Again. He'd done it again. Made a bad decision and sent his men to their deaths. So many opportunities to not be in this position again lost, just like the lives of the men he'd sent into the bay.

Audacious rumbled with footfalls and officers' voices yelling orders to prepare the ship to sail while also preparing her for battle.

His stomach threatened to upend itself again.

The cabin door banged open and his steward entered, with Lieutenant Wallis on his heels.

"Captain Cochrane, there's another ship coming toward us—from the other side of the bay. It isn't flying any flag of identification but is signaling they are coming to render assistance." Wallis's thin chest heaved with his labored breathing, as if he'd run the length of the ship to share this news.

Could it be Shaw's other ship luring them into a trap? Ned would not put his crew at further risk, yet could he risk ignoring the offer of assistance?

More pounding footfalls and the midshipman of the forecastle burst into the room. "Captain, you have to come see this—the message from the ship coming toward us."

Rather than panicked, the boy appeared excited—along with a little confused.

Ned could not let his men see him as indecisive. He slapped his hat back on his head and followed the midshipman to the forecastle. Raising his glass, he looked at the row of small, colorful flags flying at the bow of the ship rounding the mountain on the other side of the bay's mouth.

He blinked, shook his head, and looked again. Rather than flags corresponding to standard words, the typical way of sending messages from ship to ship, the vessel coming toward them had used flags to spell something.

C-H-A-R-L-E-S-L-O-T-T.

He spelled it to himself three times. *Charles Lott.* Charlotte. Hope took anchorage in his chest. Could it be? Was she not only aboard that ship, but safe enough to send a message meant to make him trust the other ship to be on his side?

"What does it mean, sir? Charles Lott. He died of yellow fever in Barbados." The midshipman lowered his glass.

"It means…" Ned took a deep breath and prayed what he was about to say was true. "It means help is on the way. Signal the unidentified ship that we welcome their assistance."

Ned returned to the quarterdeck, but his eyes stayed trained on the yet unidentified ship. Above him, the unfurled sails caught the wind and *Audacious* lumbered out of its hiding place, just as the bow of the pirate's ship came into sight.

The stranger's ship slipped toward the mouth of the bay, their larboard guns run out. Spyglass to eye, Ned searched the deck of the ship, looking for a familiar and beloved figure. But he recognized no one, not even the dark-haired man in what appeared to be a naval officer's uniform standing on the quarterdeck issuing orders.

A deafening boom rent the air and smoke billowed from their protector's side as all of the cannon let loose together.

Ned could not head to open water until he knew his benefactor to be safe. He ran to the forecastle. From here, the cannons had a good line of sight to the pirate ship.

"Fire as you bear!"

Audacious rocked with the recoil of the half-dozen forward cannons that fired. As soon as the smoke cleared, Ned allowed himself a moment of relief. The pirate ship's figurehead no longer had a head, and smoke billowed from the ship's forecastle.

Their partner in the attack tacked toward open water.

"Loose sheets, set course for open water!" Ned's officers relayed his orders to the crew, and with a shuddering turn, *Audacious* caught a good wind and made for the horizon, following their mysterious friend.

The frigate pulled ahead of *Audacious*, and Ned finally got a look at her stern.

Vengeance.

The gold-painted lettering struck a memory, but Ned could not quite grasp it. He returned to his cabin and searched through the stack of papers on his desk. Ah, that's the page he remembered. He pulled out the list of known pirates and their ships. He skimmed it until he found *Vengeance.*

"El Salvador de los Esclavos," he read aloud. Strange name for a pirate. If his limited knowledge of Spanish did not fail him, *El Salvador* meant *the savior*. And *Esclavos* meant *slaves*. A pirate who was known as the Savior of the Slaves?

He returned to the quarterdeck. El Salvador's ship had pulled even farther away from them on a southward bearing. "Don't let them get away from us—loose tops'ls and make chase."

"Aye, aye, Captain." His officers and crew hurried to follow his command. Just as the men who'd died in the bay had done. And just as the men who'd followed the first orders he'd given as a callow young acting lieutenant had done. And they had paid the price for his foolishness. How many more men would die following his commands?

He shook himself out of such thoughts. He could not allow doubts to rule him now. Not when Charlotte's life could be at stake.

"Sir, they're running."

Ned did not need Wallis's statement to verify what his own eyes told him. *Vengeance*, smaller and lighter, cut through the waves more efficiently and quicker than *Audacious*. But with more canvas spread than the frigate could raise, *Audacious* gained speed and began closing the gap between them.

"Signal *Vengeance* our identity and that they are commanded, by order of King George, to surrender and prepare to be boarded."

Wallis's eyes flashed with apprehension and, perhaps, an idea of exacting some justice for his fellow crewmembers. He ran to the forecastle to oversee the midshipman with the flags.

Ned watched the stern of *Vengeance* as they raised their flags to answer.

"They're refusing to stop," Lieutenant Duncan hissed through clenched teeth, lowering his spyglass.

"Fire a warning shot across their stern."

"Aye, aye, sir." Duncan snapped his telescope closed and ran to the bow, stopping by the crew manning the forward most cannon. After taking careful aim, Duncan's yell of "Fire!" echoed up the deck.

The cannonball gouged a chunk of wood from the top corner of the larboard quarter gallery, shattering the windows below it.

Ned flinched and stifled a groan.

Duncan rushed back to him. "I'm sorry, sir. I thought the aim was better—I did not mean to hit the ship, sir."

"It is minor damage and—" Ned raised his glass again, "they are reefing sails."

A new set of flags rose at the stern end of *Vengeance*.

"No surrender, but they will agree to parlay, sir." Wallis joined them, wiping sweat from his face with a handkerchief. "They have invited you and two officers to come aboard for talks." His eager expression told Ned he hoped to be one of the officers.

"*First* Lieutenant Wallis, you will have command while I am gone." Ned prayed Wallis's position as senior-most of the lieutenants would be short lived—that Gardiner was still alive and would resume his role as first officer soon. "Lieutenants Duncan and Hamilton—"

The two young men snapped to attention beside him.

"Get the jolly boat ready. Sailors are to be armed with pistols and dirks. You are both to carry two pistols and your cutlasses." He called for the marine sergeant next. "Have your men line the side, with muskets at the ready."

"Aye, sir."

Ned's steward brought his cutlass and strapped the scabbard so the sword hilt lay at Ned's left hip, but Ned waved off the pistols. There was protection, and then there was antagonism.

His heart leaped into his throat as he descended *Audacious's* side into the launch, and it remained lodged there several minutes later as he climbed the accommodation ladder up the side of *Vengeance* behind Lieutenant Duncan.

The pirate crew stood in eerie silence. Ned pushed Duncan forward when he attained the top of the ladder, and then he saw what had frozen the young man in place.

Standing only yards from the ship's entry port was the tallest, fiercest-looking man Ned had ever seen. Wind conformed the man's open-necked shirt to his body, showing him to be as solidly built as a first-rate man-of-war. The grim set of his face let Ned know he, Duncan, and Hamilton—who drew in a deep breath beside him—were not welcome.

"Cap'n Salvador is waiting for you in his cabin." The giant had a strange accent to his English, possibly American.

Ned nodded and then followed the giant through the column of men gathered on the main deck. He recognized the build of this ship, a Dutch frigate. Dutch...could this be the ship they had followed into Black River?

The giant stopped at the door to the companionway leading down to the half deck. At the bottom of the stairs, a ginger-haired man met them. "This way, Captain."

An East Indian opened the door to the captain's cabin at the red-haired man's knock and motioned Ned, Duncan, and Hamilton to enter.

Whatever Ned had expected to see, it wasn't this—a cabin he might see on any Royal Navy ship. No extravagance, no outward signs of wealth.

The dark-haired man Ned had seen through his spyglass stood in the center of the room, arms crossed, wearing a fully adorned admiral's coat. Duncan and Hamilton flanked Ned, both with their right hands resting on the hilts of their cutlasses.

"Captain Cochrane, welcome aboard *Vengeance*. I am El Salvador de los Esclavos, known to most as Captain Salvador." Salvador inclined his head. Rather than having a Spanish accent, as his name would indicate, Salvador's accent marked him as originating from the south of England.

Ned pressed his lips together to keep from showing any change of expression over Salvador's use of his name before he introduced himself. "By order of King George the Third, I command you to surrender your ship and yourself under charge of piracy."

With a slight smile, Salvador shook his head. "From what I have heard of you, I would have expected the niceties to be observed before business is discussed."

Heat rose up the back of Ned's neck at the rebuke from a pirate about etiquette. "My apologies, Captain Salvador. Thank you for your assistance with the ship in the bay."

"An honor, Captain Cochrane. My condolences on the loss of your men."

Ned's stomach lurched, but he'd already emptied it twice; there should be nothing left to come up. He mimicked Salvador's crossed-arm stance. "I pray they are taken, not killed."

Salvador's smile disappeared. "Given what I know of the men on *Sister Mary*, you might do better to pray they died in the attack rather than being captured."

"So that was Shaw's secondary ship." Ned rubbed his cheek with the palm of his left hand. "Where is *Sister Elizabeth*?"

Salvador relaxed his stance somewhat, moving his arms to clasp his hands behind his back. "I was told in Black River that Shaw sailed to Kingston to…I believe the exact words were 'retrieve a package' there."

Ned snorted in derision. "Only a black-hearted scoundrel would speak of a gentlewoman in that way."

Salvador cocked his head to the side. "I happen to agree with you, Captain Cochrane. Women should be treated with respect and reserve, not as means for exacting revenge."

Narrowing his eyes, Ned leaned his weight forward. "Yet I have a strong suspicion you do not always live by that belief, Captain Salvador."

"What makes you say that?" Salvador's expression did not change.

"Charles Lott." Beside him, Ned could sense his lieutenants' break in composure at the name of the supposedly dead midshipman. "Duncan, Hamilton, wait for me on deck."

"Sir?" Duncan's gaze swung from Ned to Salvador and back.

"Now, Lieutenant."

"Aye, aye, sir." Both young men reluctantly left the cabin.

As soon as the door closed behind them, Ned dropped his arms to his sides. "Where is she?"

Salvador raised one dark brow, its thickness interrupted by a scar, in response. "She?"

"Charlotte Ransome. Her presence aboard this ship is the only explanation for the use of the name Charles Lott. Do you know what the penalty for taking her will be?"

"Only if the captain who discovers her aboard this ship decides to let others know he found her here—and that I was not merely providing her safe passage home." Salvador looked beyond Ned. "Suresh, bring in our guest."

Ned glanced over his shoulder in time to see the East Indian man exit the cabin. He could not breathe for fear of what he would see when the steward returned.

∽∾∿∾∿

Charlotte paced the length of the infirmary—not a long distance—and twisted her mobcap in her hands.

"Your Captain Cochrane is young to be a full captain. And somewhat short, as well."

She paused at Declan's words. Perched on a barrel, the American first mate was still taller than Charlotte. In the light streaming in from the forward windows, she could well see Declan's flirtatious grin.

"He is no more than a year or two younger than Captain Salvador.

As for his height, at least he is not in constant danger of cracking his skull against the decking. How is your head feeling?"

Declan rubbed the top of his head. "I am well recovered. Thank you for your concern, Miss Ransome."

She sighed and returned to her pacing—only to be stopped again, this time by the door swinging open to admit Suresh.

"He is ready for you, Miss Ransome."

Her heart pounded its way up into her throat, and she moved toward the door.

Suresh stepped past her and leaned over to pick something up from the floor. "You decided against the cap?"

Charlotte glanced toward the mobcap—the one she'd been wearing when Salvador took her—which she'd just dropped. "Yes…no…yes…"

Suresh handed it to her. "Take it with you. You may not be allowed to return and retrieve it."

Charlotte took the cap from him and wadded it in one hand. She stopped him from exiting with a touch on his arm. "If I do not get the chance to say it later, thank you for everything you've done for me during my time here. You've made my stay as pleasant as possible, and for that I'll always be grateful."

"What about me?"

She turned to find Declan standing behind her, hunched over as usual. Though she railed internally against the delay, she could not be rude to him. "Thank you, Mr. Declan, for making my time here… more interesting."

"You're welcome, Miss Ransome. Though I'm thinking the captain might put up a fight rather than to let go of his only bargaining chip."

"Yet I believe Captain Salvador is more of a gentleman than you give him credit for, Mr. Declan."

He had the audacity to grin at her again. "We shall see, shan't we?"

"Miss Ransome, he is waiting."

Grateful for Suresh's soft reminder, Charlotte whisked out of the infirmary and hurried down the length of the main deck toward the stern. She almost greeted Hamilton and Duncan at the door to the companionway to the half deck, but she remembered in time that she was no longer Charles Lott and they should not recognize her, so she ducked her head as she rushed past them.

Her heart nearly burst when she entered the cabin. Before he turned completely around, Charlotte launched herself at Ned, throwing her arms around his neck. She whispered his name over and over, twining her fingers through his hair. He wrapped his arms around her waist and lifted her from the floor. She could hardly breathe from the crush of his embrace, but what did breathing matter?

After a forever that did not last long enough, Ned set her on the floor again and, keeping one arm around her, turned to face Salvador.

"You will face charges of kidnapping and assault, Captain Salvador. Miss Ransome's presence here is all the proof I need."

Charlotte pulled away from Ned and placed herself between him and Captain Salvador, facing Ned. "But you cannot—we need his help. He has been nothing but courtesy itself since I have been here."

"Charlotte, he is a pirate. The mere fact he has been pleasant toward you in the few days you have been here does not atone for years of criminal activity." Ned settled his hands on her shoulders. "I expect the trauma you have experienced is muddling your reason at the present. I must execute my duty as an officer of His Majesty's Royal Navy."

Charlotte shrugged his hands off but tried to maintain a serene expression so Salvador could not see how Ned's patronizing tone infuriated her. "My reason is *not* muddled. I can think rationally and clearly as I always have. I understand that Captain Salvador is on the list of pirates you are supposed to hunt down and arrest but…" He would not believe her unless she showed him. She would ask Salvador's forgiveness later.

She crossed to the trunk full of the clothing for Salvador's fiancée, knelt before it, and lifted the lid.

"Miss Ransome, what are you—?" Salvador took a few steps toward her and then hesitated when she dug her arms down under the gowns and undergarments and fabrics meant for his future bride.

Her fingers jammed up against the hard edge she sought. With great effort she extricated the large ledgers and then carried them over to the table. "Unless I am mistaken, Captain Salvador has kept an accounting of every ship from which he has ever taken anything. These"— she pointed at the items that had been struck through—"appear to be those which he has already repaid in some manner. In this book," she opened the second ledger, "he has kept an accounting of the slave ships he has liberated. Now, what kind of pirate repays those from whom he steals and liberates slaves at no profit to himself?"

Ned leaned over the first book and thumbed through several pages. "There seem to be quite a number of entries for ships from Tierra Dulce which have not been crossed out." He straightened and looked at Salvador. "What is your connection with that plantation?"

Salvador's expression did not change, but his posture stiffened. Charlotte moved around Ned so she was between them again, this time facing Salvador. Now she would finally find out why Salvador seemed so concerned about Julia and her safety.

Chapter Twelve

William returned the salute of the lieutenant who met the jolly boat at the dock. Fort George was nothing compared to Fort Charles in Port Royal, but it was a Royal Navy outpost, and for that William was grateful.

"Commodore William Ransome of His Majesty's Ship *Alexandra*. I need to speak with the fort's commanding officer."

"Commodore Ransome. We've been anticipating your arrival, sir."

William frowned but did not question the younger officer as he followed him up the dock to the low stone building.

The lieutenant announced William as soon as they entered. The captain sitting at a small desk stood and saluted.

"Commodore, a messenger arrived in the middle of the night looking for you. I sent him into Port Antonio to secure lodging, as we did not know when you would arrive."

"A messenger?" William's heart stuttered. He had informed Jeremiah to send word to him here if anything…"Did he leave his name?"

"No, sir. 'Twas an older black man, though, if that makes a difference."

William reeled. Jeremiah had come himself? He was not certain how to interpret that—but he hoped it was because Charlotte had been recovered. "Take me where you sent him."

"No need, Commodore."

William whirled at Jeremiah's gasping voice. Julia's overseer stood in the doorway doubled over, hands braced on knees, panting for breath.

Though not spry to begin with, Jeremiah's haggard appearance alerted William the man had traveled hard and fast to arrive here. He prayed it was with good news.

When the lieutenant, still standing near the door, eyed Jeremiah with distaste, William ushered the overseer into the room and onto a chair facing the captain's desk. "Water."

At least the lieutenant knew better than to disobey William's order. He poured water into a tin cup from the pitcher on the stand behind the captain and handed it to William.

Jeremiah gulped down the liquid, wiping a few loose drops from his chin with the back of his hand. "I ran all the way back from town when I heard a Royal Navy ship arrived."

William's hope drowned in the severe expression in Jeremiah's dark eyes. "What has happened?"

"Yesterday morning Miss Julia set out for Kingston to meet with the banker. I sent trusted men with her—Levi, the driver, and two of his sons, Ruben and Asher. A few hours later, Asher came riding back to the plantation with his horse in a lather to tell us Miss Julia had been taken and his father lay shot and dying on the road. He gave me this, sir." Jeremiah rummaged in his pockets and withdrew a crumpled letter.

William almost tore the parchment in his haste to unfold it.

> IN SEVEN DAYS JULIA WITHERINGTON RANSOME WILL BE EXECUTED FOR THE CRIMES PERPETRATED BY HER FATHER, ADMIRAL SIR EDWARD WITHERINGTON, AND HER HUSBAND, COMMODORE WILLIAM RANSOME.
>
> SHAW

William's knees buckled, and he had to grab the edge of the desk to keep from toppling to the floor. How could Shaw have Julia when he'd taken Charlotte?

"Before I could leave to bring you this message, another messenger arrived with this." Jeremiah handed him another letter.

William opened it, apprehension numbing his fingers.

Charlotte Ransome is safe and well and will remain so if negotiations for her return can be made under the flag of parlay.

Further information forthcoming.

El Salvador de los Esclavos

Shaw had Julia; Salvador had Charlotte. William's chest felt as if it were collapsing. He could not go after both his wife and his sister. And while what he knew of Salvador led William to believe the pirate was interested only in ransom, he still could not endanger Charlotte by leaving her in the hands of a pirate while he hunted down Shaw to save Julia's life.

The close heat and humidity in the room turned frigid.

"I rode through the night to get here, sir. Asher said he thought he heard one of the pirates say something about Negril." Jeremiah set the cup on the desk.

William stared at the water remaining at the bottom of the cup. Julia or Charlotte? Charlotte or Julia? A prayer formed in his mind, but his anxiety blocked him from articulating it. How could he be expected to make such a choice?

If only he had not sent James away. He could send his brother after Charlotte and focus all his energy on finding Julia. But he could not...

A thought poked through the anxious haze clouding his mind. Ned Cochrane. Ned could continue the search for Charlotte, allowing William to set his sights on Shaw. "I need a map."

Moments later William leaned over a chart. If he continued on around the north side of the island, with full canvas spread and a good wind, he could be at Negril in less than a day—and if Ned had stayed on course, William could probably intercept him near Negril, as they were not supposed to meet at Falmouth for two more days.

He straightened and adjusted his waistcoat with a tug at the hem. "Should anyone need to know, I shall be sailing *Alexandra* for Negril." He looked at each of the three men with him. "Thank you for your assistance." He gave a brief nod and turned to leave. The sooner he could get *Alexandra* underway, the sooner he could start the search for Julia.

"Commodore—wait."

He paused in the doorway at Jeremiah's entreaty and turned to look at Julia's overseer.

Jeremiah launched himself from the chair. "I want to go with you."

William shook his head. "No. I need you to return to Tierra Dulce to see that everything continues to operate efficiently, as Mrs. Ransome would expect. She will be very put out with both of us if she comes back to find the plantation had foundered in her absence."

"Yes, sir." Jeremiah ran his fingers along the wide brim of his woven grass hat. "Bring her home, Commodore."

William's heart echoed the pain in Jeremiah's voice. "I will."

He sent the words to God as a vow. Because life would not be worth continuing without Julia.

☙❧

Shaw knocked his brother's feet off the lacquer table, one of his favorite pieces in his cabin. "I spent two years—*two years*—getting you the training and job postings necessary to secure you the position of steward at the Witherington plantation."

"And I spent months...weeks courting the Ransome girl and making her fall in love with me so she'd agree to marry me. I'd say you had the easier task." Henry swiped his blond hair from his eyes and tilted his chair back on two legs.

Unable to control his rage any longer, Shaw grabbed his brother's throat and pushed him back. He crouched over him, hand tightening until the smirk left Henry's face. "If you were not my brother, I would have already killed you for disobeying me."

Henry grabbed Shaw's wrist, trying to ease the chokehold, but Shaw's anger had not yet abated. "All you had to do was continue following the plan. Work the plantation. Court the Ransome girl. Listen. Watch. And make sure you were in position when the opportunity came."

He held Henry's throat a moment longer to drive his point home. As soon as he released his grip, Henry gasped and coughed, doubling over before rolling off the upturned chair.

Shaw returned to gazing out the stern windows. "If you disobey me again, I will forget you and I share the same blood."

Henry grabbed the edge of the table and pulled himself up. "When are you going to admit that what I did turned out to work for our advantage?"

"I fail to see how that's true."

"It got her away from the house. With the protection her husband and that overseer set up after the Ransome girl was abducted, your men might not have been able to get to Julia Witherington—Mrs. Ransome—anywhere but away from the plantation." Henry opened the casket holding his brother's remaining few cigars.

Shaw snapped the lid shut before his brother could take one. "Do not mistake mere coincidence for a successful plan. Your greediness could have ruined everything."

Henry shrugged. "I could have taken the Ransome girl myself. If only I'd recognized her when she first came to speak to me," he muttered to himself. "She'd never have broken off the engagement."

Shaw laughed, though he felt no mirth. "Even in that you failed. How could Charlotte Ransome be the one woman in the whole of Jamaica who didn't fall for your supposed charms?"

"If I'd had more time, I could have wooed her back to me. I made her fall in love with me once. I could have done it again." Henry rubbed at the red marks around his throat.

"I find that highly unlikely."

Shaw turned at the soft female voice. Near his feet Julia Ransome pushed herself up into a sitting posture from her prone position on the floor and lifted her bound hands to feel her right cheek.

"So good of you to rejoin us, Mrs. Ransome." Shaw leaned over and grabbed her jaw, yanking her head to such an angle that the light from the windows fell over the side of her face, showing that her cheek and eye were already swelling under the red mark that would, in a few hours, turn purple. "However, it seems you did not learn your lesson. Unless you want to feel the back of my hand again, you will keep your thoughts and opinions behind your teeth."

⚘

Julia worked hard at focusing on Shaw and his words through the throbbing of her cheek and the searing pain in her side. After a night locked in a windowless, airless compartment barely large enough for her to sit and stretch her legs out in front of her, she'd made the mistake of once again demanding an explanation as to why she'd been brought here when dragged to Shaw's cabin earlier.

She'd been in the middle of her statement when Shaw smashed the back of his fist into her cheek, knocking her unconscious. Now, in addition to cracked ribs, she had a bruised cheek and an eye swollen nearly shut.

Shaw jerked her jaw upward, and Julia struggled to gain her feet rather than let him cause her further injury. After another long moment of the painful grip, Shaw pushed her backward with a sinister smile. Julia took a few steps to keep from falling to the floor again.

"Why not just kill her now and be done with it? Ransome will never know the difference." Henry Winchester seemed to take a measure of cheer in the thought of killing her, given his tone of voice.

"No ransom will be paid if I am dead."

Shaw raised his fist, but Julia refused to cringe.

"Ransom?" Henry laughed. "You think we took you for money? Did you not discover already that I could take as much as I wanted from your coffers without that slave of yours realizing it?"

"Had it not been for Jeremiah's careful calculations, I might never have caught the false entries." Julia refused to rise to Winchester's bait about Jeremiah's status as a freeman.

"But if he—"

"Enough." Shaw slammed his fist on the Chinese lacquer table, startling both Winchester and Julia.

"If you did not take me to hold for ransom, why did you take me?" She tensed, waiting for Shaw's blow. After all, the last time she asked, he had knocked her senseless.

"Revenge has a value far greater than gold." He traced the edge of the table with one finger. "Your father and husband will learn what it feels like to have their family taken away from them one person at a time until no one is left. Then they will know my pain."

Julia shook her head—which reminded her she was on a ship under sail. Whether from Shaw's blow or the motion of the sea beneath her feet, her stomach threatened revolt. "But you have not lost your family. I heard you say Mr. Winchester is your brother."

Shaw took a step toward her, brows in a straight, angry line. "I lost everything because of your father and your husband. When I learned of my mother's and sisters' deaths, I vowed I would exact revenge on the men responsible."

Papa and William were accountable for the deaths of Henry and Shaw's mother and sisters? Not possible. "Tell me why you blame them for the loss of your family."

"'Twas because of that upstart Ransome. At seventeen I was pressed into the navy. A year later I was assigned to *Indomitable* under the command of Captain Witherington, bound for Jamaica. We had been promised we would make our fortunes in the Caribbean, hunting pirates and privateers. The night we reached Barbados, we celebrated." Shaw glared at her as if demanding her agreement that celebrating was the appropriate thing to do.

"I still fail to see—"

"I'm not finished yet," he snapped. "The purser was stingy, so my mess mates and I subdued him and took the key to the stores to liberate what remained of the grog. Midshipman Ransome came down to act the little king and order us to be quiet, as we were disturbing the captain's family with our revelry."

"And that's why—" Julia swallowed her question at Shaw's menacing step toward her.

"The purser revived and told Ransome I was the one who had hit him. Ransome tried to arrest me. So I hit him. A few times."

"Oh." Julia covered her mouth with her bound hands.

"Captain Witherington sentenced me to be executed upon reaching Jamaica, but I escaped. I signed on to a French privateer, which was then taken by pirates. After weeks of imprisonment and torture, they made me part of their crew. I knew the Royal Navy would never stop hunting for Arthur Winchester, so I took the name Shaw—my mother's family name." Shaw dropped onto a velvet settee in the corner of the cabin and sprawled on it.

"I came looking for him several years later," Henry took up the story.

Julia shuffled around until the backs of her legs touched the seat under the stern windows—where she could see both Shaw and Winchester.

"When Arthur was sentenced—and then escaped—the navy stopped his payments. Our mother and sisters and I ended up in the poorhouse. Mother, Elizabeth, and Mary fell ill and died after just a few weeks. I escaped by agreeing to sign on as crew on a supply ship sailing to the West Indies. Arthur had managed to get one letter through to us, to let us know he was still alive and still in the Caribbean. It took me a year to find him. By then he had seized command of the pirate ship."

Julia twisted her wrists, trying to alleviate the raw, burning sensation under the ropes binding them together. "Your mother and sisters died of illness in the poorhouse. How can that be the fault of anyone?"

This time it was Henry rather than Shaw who attacked. He bolted from his chair and grabbed Julia by the throat, pushing her down onto the bench and knocking the back of her head against the windowsill. "Your father and husband interfered with my brother—sentenced him to execution, branded him dishonorable—and my mother was unable to bear the humiliation of the reports in the London newspapers of my brother's supposed misdeeds."

Black spots danced in Julia's peripheral vision. She clawed at Winchester's hand, trying to get him to let go or loosen his grip.

"Release her, Henry. A quick death is too good for her. Besides, I want her husband to witness the deed."

Fear pounded through Julia's body with the deep gulps of breath she took. She wasn't sure what to pray for. The sooner William caught up with them, the shorter her life expectancy; but though she hoped he would find her quickly, the longer she stayed on this ship, the more opportunities she might have for escape.

"Henry, take the launch back to Kingston. Spread the word that the pirate Shaw has taken Julia Witherington Ransome of the Tierra Dulce plantation and that it is because of a debt of honor Commodore Ransome owes me." Shaw rose and came to lean over Julia, putting his face only inches from hers. "Because when I complete my mission, I want everyone to know it was Shaw who killed William and Julia Ransome."

Chapter Thirteen

Charlotte flung her head to the side, making her short hair flip. "I will not go back with you."

Ned stared, openmouthed, at her. "You must return with me, Charlotte. You cannot stay on a pirate's ship, no matter how noble and courteous you believe him to be." He paced Salvador's cabin. "And for all his explanations that he targeted Tierra Dulce's ships because he knew them to be the richest, I do not believe him. He is hiding something."

She drummed her fingers on the dark tabletop. "And I told you it is not because of him that I refuse to return to *Audacious*. Ned, my reputation is already ruined. Even if we tell others that Salvador rescued me from another pirate and was bringing me home, you cannot take the time to return me to Kingston—not when finding Julia is of utmost importance. I cannot stay on *Vengeance*, but I cannot go with you on *Audacious*, either."

"We can put you ashore at Negril and secure overland transportation back to Kingston."

Charlotte snorted a laugh. "And how, exactly, do you believe that will be safer for me?"

Ned wanted to tear his hair in frustration. Instead, he stopped at the end of the table and wrapped his hands around the finials of the chair in front of him. "I surrender. What is your solution?"

"Salvador's sailing master." Charlotte smiled sweetly at him.

Ned thought about shaking her until she gave a straight answer but settled for increasing his grip on the chair. "What about him?"

"Jean Baptiste had his own church in New Orleans before he ran away for fear of being captured and put into slavery." She raised her eyebrows and nodded her head.

The chair started rattling against the floor under Ned's grip. "And what has that to do with you and where you will deign to go?"

Charlotte sighed and rolled her eyes. "Ned, he is a minister. That means he can marry us."

The chair stopped rattling with a thump as Ned released his grip. "Marry us?"

"Yes. If I return to *Audacious* as your wife, none of the crew will question my presence there, as we have already determined you cannot turn me out on land. And it ameliorates any blight on my reputation. After all, you would not marry me if I were a woman with a soiled reputation."

Oh, he would marry her no matter how soiled her reputation. But marry her now? To even entertain the idea was foolish. William had not given his consent when Ned told him he'd asked Charlotte to be his wife.

"No. I cannot." He crossed his arms, clinging to that decision.

"You mean...you no longer wish to marry me?" Charlotte's voice turned reedy and high pitched. "It *is* because of my reputation. You believe my honor to be too damaged and that it will reflect poorly on you." She stood so quickly her chair fell backward. "I never thought you would—"

Ned rounded the table and grabbed her by the shoulders, kissing her before she could accuse him of anything horrible. Her soft lips, and the way her body melted into his, added wind to the sails of his confusion. Before he lost all his senses, he pulled back.

"I still want to marry you. Never doubt that. But without your brother's blessing, it would not be right to do so." He tucked her head under his chin so he did not have to see the disappointment in her face.

"William will understand. I am certain there is no one else he would rather see me marry than you."

Pride expanded in Ned's chest. *Pride goeth before a fall.* The memory of the Scripture deflated him.

"And it is a matter of honor, Ned. If you do not marry me, no one else will. After all, it is partially your responsibility that I lived in the cockpit aboard *Audacious* for so many weeks. You could have turned me over to William when we docked in Madeira."

He growled in the back of his throat. Again, he wanted to shake her, but this time settled for increasing the pressure of his embrace until she squeaked. He loosened his hold, kissed the top of her head, and then held her at arm's length.

"All right. We will ask this Jean Baptiste to marry us. But when we return to *Audacious*, I will hang my hammock in Lieutenant Gardiner's berth until he is rescued"—*Lord, please let him still be alive*—"and for now the marriage will be in name only, for the protection of your reputation and identity. Then, if your brother disapproves, we can have the marriage annulled."

"But—"

"Those are my terms. It is that, or I put you ashore in a carriage bound for Kingston." Ned searched her blue eyes, half hoping she'd choose the carriage to Kingston rather than his terms.

"Very well. A marriage in name only. For now."

The joy reflected in Charlotte's face renewed Ned's questions as to the wisdom of this decision. Once bound in the eyes of God, would he be able to keep to his own terms? "Come, let us go speak to Captain Salvador of our decision."

He led Charlotte from the cabin and up to the quarterdeck. Salvador stood on the starboard side and inclined his head to them as they joined him. A hint of a smile played around his mouth. Ned glanced behind the pirate at the raised skylight—the raised skylight with the upright panes open to catch the breeze. No wonder Salvador had been so accommodating in granting Ned's request for a private conversation with Charlotte. He'd known he would be able to hear every word.

He at least did them the courtesy of listening to Ned's full explanation of the decision they had made.

"I cannot speak for Jean Baptiste, but you are more than welcome to put your request directly to him." Salvador motioned to someone over Ned's shoulder.

He looked around and tried to hide his surprise. He should have listened to Charlotte's explanation of why the man had left New Orleans more carefully. In addition to having the darkest skin Ned had ever seen, Jean Baptiste's shaved head and hooded eyes gave him a sinister look Ned found incongruent with a minister.

Charlotte stepped forward. "Jean Baptiste, I would like to introduce you to Captain Ned Cochrane, my fiancé."

Jean Baptiste inclined his head to Ned, who touched the fore point of his hat.

"Captain Cochrane and I would like for you to marry us before we return to his ship."

The sailing master turned his intense eyes on Ned, who grew uncomfortable under the scrutiny.

"Are you certain you want to marry the likes of him, Miss Charlotte?"

Ned stepped forward, about to remind the pirate of just who he was, but he stopped when Charlotte laughed.

"Yes, I am certain I want to marry him." She slipped her hand through Ned's elbow and squeezed his arm. "Captain Salvador, will you give me away? I think it is only fitting, given that I am your captive."

Salvador grinned at her, indulgent as a brother. Well, perhaps not William, but possibly as indulgent as one of her other brothers might have been under these unusual circumstances. "Aye, Miss Charlotte, I will hand you over if that is what you wish."

"Cap'n, I need pen and paper to draw up the certificate." Rather than a request for permission to leave the deck, Jean Baptiste's words were apparently a declaration of his intent to go below and do what he needed to do.

"Miss Ransome, you cannot be married in such a state." Salvador frowned at her crumpled, saltwater-stained gown. "Go below, choose a gown from Serena's trunk, and dress for your wedding. Suresh will be more than happy to assist you, I am certain."

Releasing Ned's arm, Charlotte stood on tiptoe to kiss the pirate on the cheek. "Thank you, Captain Salvador."

As soon as she disappeared below deck, Salvador pulled Ned forward, away from the skylight. "I believe there is something else you wish to speak to me about."

Ned clasped his hands behind his back. "Aye. There is a matter of trust in this venture."

"Ah, yes. You are a captain in the Royal Navy. Therefore, I cannot trust you not to arrest me." Salvador smirked at him.

"Something like that. Though I was thinking more that you're a pirate, caught with a kidnapping victim on your ship, and as soon as Miss Ransome and I leave your ship—"

"But she'll be Mrs. Cochrane when you leave my ship."

Ned ignored the interruption. "As soon as Charlotte and I leave your ship, I do not trust that you will keep to your end of our bargain and not run as soon as we part company."

Salvador tapped his forefinger against his chin. "That is a dilemma. Whatever can we do?"

That the pirate was not taking this discussion seriously infuriated Ned, though he did his best to hide his reaction. Making him angry was obviously Salvador's goal. "We will exchange first officers."

The smile faded from Salvador's face. "Exchange first officers? Do you have enough officers remaining to spare even a midshipman?"

Ned's confidence in his superior position collapsed at Salvador's reminder of his failure, of the lives lost or in jeopardy because of his folly.

Salvador's demeanor changed from mocking to serious. "I know my word does not mean anything to you. I will send my first mate, Declan, back with you to *Audacious*, and I swear I will abide by the terms of the agreement without anyone from your ship here to ensure it."

"How can I be sure you will not leave your man behind?"

Salvador's lips twitched at the corners. "Because he is my fiancée's brother. And I am more afraid of what Serena will do to me if I lose him than of anything you could do to me."

⁘

Too many years of building his image, of creating a reputation as a ne'er-do-well pirate had given Salvador the ability to mask his true feelings with sarcasm. Never before today had it felt truly wrong— wrong for him to be mocking Ned Cochrane's genuine concern over hunting down Shaw and saving Julia when Salvador's own conscience thundered at him to get on with the search.

He'd almost told Cochrane he himself would go to *Audacious* instead of sending Declan, so great was his desire to see Julia rescued. But though he trusted Declan to follow his orders in his absence, he could not be certain the rest of the crew—led by Picaro, no doubt—would not mutiny against Declan, take *Vengeance*, and run.

Coming to the bottom of the stairs, he did something he had not done since taking command of a ship ten years ago. He knocked on the door to the captain's cabin.

Suresh opened it.

"Is she ready?"

"She awaits you within." Suresh stepped back to allow Salvador to enter.

Charlotte stood in the center of the little bit of open space between the table and her hammock and the trunk. Late afternoon light bathed her in a warm glow. The ivory brocade dress she'd donned was far too big for her, but somehow she and Suresh had made it fit.

Salvador took her hand and lifted it to her lips. "You look lovely, Charlotte."

"Thank you." She seemed in no hurry to leave the cabin.

"Nervous?"

"No. Just locking everything into my memory. This will be a tale my grandchildren will never tire of hearing."

"Of how your handsome sea captain rescued you from a black-hearted pirate?"

"Of how a good-hearted man made a mistake, which led to my discovery of something no one else except he knows."

He arched a brow, challenging her conclusion. "And what is that?"

She leaned toward him, adjusting the folds of his neckcloth. "I know who you really are, Captain Salvador."

His heart jumped, as if his foot missed a ratline coming down from the shrouds. "And whom do you think I really am?"

"The pieces all fit. You were in the Royal Navy as a boy, a midshipman."

"I never told you that."

"No—but your adherence to naval regulations and schedules betrayed you." She flashed an apologetic smile. "You were around fifteen when you first served on a pirate ship."

"Many lads run away from home at that age to see adventure and fortune." The room grew uncomfortably hot.

"Your conscience bothered you at the bad things those pirates did, so as soon as you could, you struck out on your own. You liberate slave ships and you raid plantations that hold slaves, taking as many with you as you can to send to freedom. And occasionally, you relieve a Tierra Dulce ship of its gold. Is that how you pay back the other plantations you raid?"

"I do not reimburse anyone for the loss of their slaves. Human beings should not be bought and sold like pigs and horses." He started to relax. So far, her deductions were mostly correct, but that did not mean she knew his real name. The name he had not used in more than ten years, except with Serena.

"So the entries crossed out in the journal?"

"Are plantations that have set their slaves free or have not gained any additional slaves since the last time I went there on a liberation raid."

Charlotte nodded, as if fitting this new piece of information in with her existing conclusions. "I should have known when first I saw you who you are. The eyes and hair are slightly different—darker. But otherwise, it is so obvious."

"What is?"

"That you are m—"

Salvador pressed his hand over Charlotte's mouth, heart pounding. He wasn't certain he wanted her to know the truth. He absolutely did not want anyone who might be listening at the skylight—or Suresh, standing near the door—to know his identity.

Charlotte's eyes twinkled and she nodded at him. He slowly lowered his hand.

"You are my captor and a good man, El Salvador de los Esclavos." She lifted bunches of skirt in both hands. "Now, you promised you would hand me over to my fiancé. Shall we go?"

Salvador followed her up the stairs, stopping twice as she paused to readjust her grip on the excess fabric so she wouldn't trip. At the top of the companion stairs, he offered his arm, but Charlotte shook her head, turning to take the three steps up to the quarterdeck with the material still secured.

Ned stood with Jean Baptiste, along with the two lieutenants from *Audacious*.

The two young men scrutinized Charlotte and then exchanged a questioning look. But if they recognized her as their former shipmate Charles Lotte, they hid it well when they turned their gazes back toward her.

Salvador waited while Charlotte straightened her gown and then offered the crook of his arm to walk her several feet to where the others stood waiting for them.

Declan bounded up onto the quarterdeck. Charlotte glanced over her shoulder.

"He's got two standing up with him. You should have two standing up with you also."

Salvador shook his head, certain when he informed Declan he would accompany Ned and Charlotte to *Audacious* that his future brother-in-law would be delighted.

"Dearly beloved," Jean Baptiste looked beyond Charlotte, Ned, and Salvador to the main deck below, "and everyone else witnessing this blessed event, we gather here in the sight of God Almighty to join this man and this woman in holy matrimony."

Never having attended a wedding in his life, Salvador listened carefully to the words Jean Baptiste spoke, preparing himself for the day when he and Serena would be joined.

Charlotte nudged his side.

"Who gives this woman to be married?" Jean Baptiste repeated, his dark eyes boring into Salvador.

"Oh. I hereby relinquish her to the care of Captain Cochrane." He took Charlotte's hand from his arm and placed it in Ned's outstretched hand.

With her free hand and shoulder, Charlotte nudged and pushed Salvador until he realized she wanted him to step to the side so she and Ned could move closer together.

"If anyone can show just cause why these two should not be joined together, let him speak now or forever hold his peace."

"She's our'n!"

"She belongs to the captain!"

"Who's he think he is, coming in here and taking our gal?"

The sailors on the main deck a few feet below waved their fists—some even waved their cutlasses and dirks—as they yelled their displeasure at the idea of Ned marrying Charlotte.

Salvador stepped to the railing that kept men from falling off the raised quarterdeck. He held one hand aloft and the shouts stopped. "Miss Ransome was spoken for by Captain Cochrane before she came as a guest aboard *Vengeance*. It is her choice to marry him."

"But she's your woman!" shouted a man aloft the larboard mainmast shroud.

"No. Remember when we were up north, the pretty who came to the beach to bid me farewell?"

After a moment's thought, most of the sailors nodded.

"She is my woman."

Several men still looked confused. "But she's up north. Why can't ye have one there and one here?"

Yes, it was time he gave up this life. "Because I am content with just one woman. Now, if that is all?"

"Aye, go ahead and let them get married. Bad luck to have a woman aboard anyway."

Salvador returned to his spot and looked at Charlotte to see how she'd taken the interruption to her wedding.

If her smile grew any wider, her head would split asunder.

The rest of the ceremony went quickly. Ned and Charlotte repeated vows to each other and listened to Jean Baptiste tell them what marriage meant.

"Do you have a ring?"

Panic flickered in Ned's face. "No, I—"

Salvador turned. "Suresh!"

The steward hurried through the door from the stairs and up onto the quarterdeck. Rather than stop at Salvador, who had called for him, he went straight to Ned and held something out to him between two fingers.

Salvador hoped it was not the ruby ring he planned to put on Serena's finger the day they married. He had taken plenty of jewelry off the crew of slave ships over the years, and though most went toward paying his men, he'd kept a few nice pieces. Serena's ring, however, he'd purchased. He did not want any taint on the emblem of their undying love.

Ned slipped a plain gold band onto a finger on Charlotte's left hand.

"In the eyes of God and this company, I hereby declare that you be husband and wife. What God has joined together, let no man split asunder."

Ned slipped his hand around the back of Charlotte's neck and kissed her—thoroughly.

Serena once said she always cried at weddings, because they reminded her of what she was missing. Salvador had laughed at her. In his next letter he would apologize, for he understood how she felt.

As soon as they rescued Julia, there would be no more Salvador. No more *Vengeance*.

Vengeance is mine...saith the Lord.

And the Lord was more than welcome to her.

Chapter Fourteen

Charlotte tucked the bundle Suresh had handed her more securely under her feet and positioned her left hand on her lap so the ring on her finger glinted in the starlight. It wasn't a large, sparkling emerald, like Julia's wedding ring, but it was a wedding ring. *Her* wedding ring.

Charlotte Cochrane. Delight shivered down her spine. She had come to Jamaica to get married without her family's permission. A twinge of guilt invaded her pleasure. Ned's arguments in favor of waiting until they rescued Julia and then seeking William's blessing nibbled at the back of her mind.

She looked up—and caught Declan's humor-filled expression before he turned to face forward again. Given her knowledge of Salvador's true identity, the need for Ned to bring one of his crew on *Audacious* seemed ridiculous, although she had made her argument for it to be Suresh. The only thing that kept Suresh from being the perfect lady's maid was his gender.

The jolly boat scraped up against *Audacious*'s hull. From his position behind her, Ned called for the bosun's chair. She turned to argue—to insist she could climb the accommodation ladder—but the look on her husband's face when their eyes met stilled her tongue.

So many familiar faces gazed over the bulwark along the quarterdeck. Charlotte adjusted the straw bonnet Salvador had given her so the brim shadowed her entire face. His generosity had not extended to giving her one of the gowns meant for Serena, but Suresh had managed to get her own dress back to a clean and wearable, if some-what crumpled, state.

At least sitting on the wooden swing didn't threaten to pull her shoulder out of joint the way being hauled up the side of *Vengeance* with a rope wrapped around her arm had. She clutched Suresh's bun-dle to her chest as the seat swung her up and over the side of the ship.

Having been aboard *Vengeance* for a week, Charlotte reveled in the size of Ned's ship. Though the frigate had the advantage of speed and maneuverability over the man-of-war, on *Audacious* the decks were wider and longer, the masts taller, and the crew more respectful and disciplined. They cut Declan a wide berth as he lumbered up onto the deck, obviously in awe of his size.

She tugged at the brim of her bonnet again, aware of the attention she also drew from the men. According to Ned, they knew she was William Ransome's younger sister, but should any of them recognize her as Charles Lott…she did not want to imagine what might happen.

Ned joined her on deck and ushered her toward the overhang shad-ing the wheelhouse. His steward stepped forward from the darkness. He looked from Ned to Charlotte to their clasped hands. Ned imme-diately released her. "Please see to Miss…Mrs. Cochrane's comfort."

Charlotte handed the canvas-wrapped bundle to the steward, but rather than follow his lantern through the darkness of the wheelhouse to Ned's cabin, she caught her husband's arm to stop him from walk-ing away from her. "Are you not going to address your crew to tell them about our marriage and why Declan is here?" She leaned closer and lowered her voice. "Is it not better to do it now, so the darkness can keep anyone from recognizing me?"

His lips pressed into a tight line, but he nodded and motioned to Lieutenant Wallis. "Signal all hands. Mr. Declan, come with us."

Ned took Charlotte's hand again and headed for the steps to the poop deck. The leeward wind tried to dislodge her only means of dis-guise, but she held the bonnet on with her free hand while trying to keep from tripping up the steps to the uppermost deck of the ship—and with Declan close on her heels, she dare not stop.

Whistles and echoed commands hit Charlotte's ears like the finest music in the most beautiful concert hall in the world. Oh, how she had missed this.

When the entire crew of *Audacious* stood looking up at them, lanterns intermittently illuminating the faces of men Charlotte recognized, Ned stepped forward—his hand trembling in hers. Charlotte increased the pressure of her grip just a bit, trying to impart courage and assurance.

He cleared his throat twice. "Officers and crew of His Majesty's Ship *Audacious*, I am honored to introduce to you my wife"—his voice faltered on the word—"Mrs. Cochrane."

The men exchanged confused looks while cheering and applauding.

"And this is Mr. Declan. We will be working with Captain Salvador of *Vengeance* to continue our hunt for the pirate Shaw, and Mr. Declan has agreed to come aboard *Audacious* to assist us." Ned turned and gave Salvador's first mate a challenging look.

Declan nodded. "Put me to work however you see fit."

For that, Charlotte graced him with a smile. She liked Declan. She just did not appreciate the way he insisted on flirting with her constantly.

"Lieutenant Wallis, please dismiss the crew." Ned pulled Charlotte toward the steps, and Wallis took their place to issue the command.

Like a Gargantuan puppy, Declan stayed behind Charlotte, almost on the hem of her skirt. She picked up her pace to keep Ned from dragging her down the steps. He didn't slow until he reached the door of the dining cabin. The marine guard started—Charlotte couldn't blame him, as it was quite dark down here—and opened the door for them.

When they entered the day cabin, Declan let out a low whistle. "Fancy."

"This was the previous captain's decor." Charlotte flexed her hand, now free from Ned's tight grip.

Declan stood under the skylight, where he could extend to his full height, though he'd only had to avoid the support beams of the deck above as they entered.

Ned moved from the paperwork on the round table to his desk

and then back to the table. Assuming her presence added to his agitation, Charlotte picked up her bundle and moved toward Ned's sleeping cabin.

"I believe I will rest for a little while."

Ned gave her no acknowledgement, so she left the main cabin without further words. Exhaustion pressed down on her shoulders. She figured the time to be near midnight. After the wedding, Ned and Captain Salvador's conference to determine their strategy had been quite long.

The sleeping quarters reflected the former captain's taste for luxury as much as the main room. A box bed with embroidered panels—wider than a standard hammock, but not quite as large as William and Julia's double-width bed on *Alexandra*—hung on one side of the narrow chamber, while a standard canvas hammock hung on the other side over a plainly built trunk. She smiled over Ned's preference for the simple rather than the extravagant. A smaller sea chest was wedged into a corner of the cabin—a sea chest that looked familiar.

She set the bundle down in the box bed and pulled a candle out of the wall sconce to better see the chest.

Kneeling before it, she held the candle over the lid. Scratched into the wood, as she hoped—*C. Lott, Midshipman*. Stifling a cry of joy, she opened the lid. While everything inside seemed to be in disarray, her belongings still seemed to be there—from her uniforms to her toiletries to her log book to…why was the bundle of muslin cloths on top of everything else?

Embarrassment flamed her cheeks when the answer came to her. Ned had searched through the chest when he'd realized it was still here. William had allowed her to use one of his smaller sea chests to pack her belongings in—the dresses and underthings Julia had purchased for her in Barbados—for the journey to Tierra Dulce, and she had never thought to see this one again. She hoped that Ned, being the only person aboard who had known she wasn't Charles Lott, was the one to have gone through the trunk.

Hot wax dripped onto her hand, and she stood and returned the candle to its holder. Though Ned would refuse to let her be seen in her midshipman's garb, knowing that she had more clothing to wear should anything happen to her one and only gown was reassuring.

Outside a full moon had risen, sending a bright shaft of light in through the gun port. Charlotte turned her attention to the parcel Suresh had handed her as she left *Vengeance*. She untied the twine, rolling it up and setting it aside, and folded back the corners of the square of canvas.

The silvery light fell across something shimmery and dark with a white square in the center. She picked up the piece of parchment.

Dear Miss Ransome,

I bought this from a merchant in Philadelphia. I thought I might save it for a gift for my bride, but as I have no woman, I can think of no one more deserving than you to receive it.

Yours cordially,
Suresh Bandopadhyay

Charlotte lifted the contents of the bundle, which unfolded to reveal a swath of heavy silk embroidered with silver thread. In the dimness of the room, she could not gauge the design of the embroidery nor the fabric's color, though it looked dark blue or perhaps purple or maybe even burgundy.

After what she had done to Salvador's steward, she deserved no such kindness. She refolded the fabric and wrapped it carefully in the canvas square. Somehow, she would find a way to return it to him. Though, Ned had mentioned that if they received William's blessing for their marriage, Ned would insist on a proper church wedding. The fabric would make a beautiful wedding dress, whether or not she was already married.

❧❦❧

"You will be treated as one of the lieutenants." Ned leaned against the edge of his desk and ignored the oncoming headache.

Declan sat at the worktable, long legs stretched before him, seeming to take up at least half of the cabin. "I will ask Lieutenant Wallis to instruct you on your duties as a naval officer."

Could nothing wipe the grin from the giant's face? "I don't know how different it is in your navy, but in the American Navy, we lieutenants received very good training."

"You were in the American Navy?"

"I served with distinction on USS *Constitution*. Shall I recite for you the list of English ships we captured? There was *Guerrière*"—Declan butchered the pronunciation—"*Java*—"

Ned held up his hand. "No recitation is necessary." How had this man gone from serving in the military to becoming a pirate in only two years? Unless his distinction was that of dishonor rather than honor. "While you will act as a lieutenant, you will not be given command of a watch."

"Don't trust me?"

"No, I do not. You serve at my pleasure. And should your manner of service displease me, I will have no qualms about carrying out the sentence to which all pirates are condemned. Do you understand?"

"Aye, aye, Cap'n." The mocking tone remained in Declan's voice, needling Ned almost to the point of breaking, but he had other issues to deal with at the moment. He crossed to the dining cabin door and called for his steward. "Pass word for Lieutenant Wallis."

In moments the acting first officer arrived. "Show Mr. Declan to the wardroom. Wallis, you are to take Lieutenant Gardiner's berth for now. Make sure Mr. Declan becomes acquainted with the behavior and decorum expected of every man who serves King George. If he does not comply, you have my permission to place him under arrest and bring him to me to carry out his sentence."

"Aye, aye, Captain." Though much thinner than Declan, Wallis stood only a few inches shorter than the tall pirate. He cocked his head to motion Declan to precede him through the door.

As soon as it closed behind them, Ned staggered to a corner of the cabin and sank into the upholstered armchair there, leaning his head back against the cushion and throwing his arm across his eyes. He'd lived three lifetimes since the sun rose. Twelve men dead, captured, or missing because of his folly. An alliance with a known enemy and a pirate serving as an officer aboard his ship. And a wife waiting in his sleeping cabin.

Even as he'd told Wallis to take Gardiner's berth, Ned had seen the flaw in his plan to ensure his marriage to Charlotte could be annulled if her brother objected. With Declan quartered in the wardroom, that left no available space for Ned to sleep down there. Now, even though he did not intend to consummate the marriage, trying to get it annulled would be near impossible, simply because he would have to share quarters with her and no one would believe they slept apart.

A door creaked and soft footsteps shuffled across the floor. He lowered his arm, expecting to see his steward entering to help him prepare for sleeping. Instead, Charlotte stood by the table, fingering a carved pinecone finial atop the back of one of the chairs.

"I know you are not happy that I forced you into a decision aboard *Vengeance*." Her voice came out just above a whisper. "I understand your feelings that we must stay apart until William gives his consent for our marriage, which I know he will do." Charlotte's volume increased a bit to add emphasis to her confident statement. "But I hope that you will not stay angry with me for too long. I would not be able to bear that."

The vulnerability in her voice catapulted him from the chair. He pulled her into his arms, the panic of discovering she'd been taken still fresh in his memory. "How could I be angry with you? I love you." He held her as tightly as he dared, fearing he might damage her yet wanting to keep her as close as possible. "I was so frightened"—he choked on the jumble of words and emotions trying to tumble from his throat—"so frightened that I would never see you again. That you would be…injured. That horrible things would happen to you."

Charlotte raised her head and kissed his chin. "When I was first taken, I was convinced the pirates had done you grievous harm when you tried to protect me. All I could think about was that I needed to get back to you, to make certain you were still alive."

Ned lowered his head and captured her lips with his, feeling, for the first time today, a spark of something other than soul-numbing fear and doubt. He raised his hands to cup Charlotte's face and deepened the kiss.

A soft whimper brought him back to his senses. He pulled away and stepped back, trembling. "I do apologize if I offended your sensibilities."

Charlotte reached for the back of the chair beside her, panting as if she'd overexerted herself. "Offended my...are you mad? Ned, we are married. Though I am a novice at this estate, I do believe it should offend *your* sensibilities if I took offense at that."

He fought the urge to take her in his arms and continue his offense, taking another step away from her. "We agreed our marriage is to be in name only. There can be no more kissing—no, nor even thoughts of kissing. We must behave with decorum, as if we were still courting."

Charlotte made a sound that was half laugh, half sob. "Courting? Decorum?"

"If you do not abide by these terms, I will put you ashore and send you back to Tierra Dulce." He never would, of course, but he needed some measure of control, and threatening her with a consequence was the lifeline he clung to. He clasped his hands behind his back and began to pace. "We must come to an agreement."

Charlotte sighed and sank into the nearest chair. "I thought we already had."

"There will be no more kissing. Nor embraces." He wasn't certain on which of them that edict would be harder. "You may have the sleeping cabin. I will hang my hammock out here."

"Where?"

How could he not have been clear? "In the great cabin."

"I meant how will you hang your hammock in here? There are no hooks from which to hang it." Charlotte swept her arm in a circle to encompass the room.

Ned looked around. "Tomorrow I will have the carpenter install the hooks. Tonight, I will sleep in the chair."

"No. You need your rest. We do not know what tomorrow will bring. Your hammock is already hung in the sleeping cabin. Ned, I shared the cockpit with almost twenty men for more than a month. Do you think if we sleep in the same room, in separate beds for one night, it is going to do my reputation any more damage? Besides, what rumors will start among the crew if the carpenter knows we are not living as husband and wife?"

Ned rubbed the bridge of his nose. Had she baited him into introducing her to the entire crew as his wife with this end in mind? To ensure they shared sleeping quarters? "Fine. We will share the sleeping cabin." He waved his hand toward it. "Go to bed. I need to speak with my steward as to your accommodation."

Charlotte stood and stepped toward him as if for a goodnight kiss, but Ned held out a hand to stop her. "Goodnight, Mrs. Cochrane."

The flickering candlelight reflected off the disappointment in her expression. "Goodnight, Captain Cochrane."

As soon as she disappeared into the other room, he once again sank into the armchair. Beyond the stern windows, the moon hung low over the horizon, bathing the sea in its indifferent light. Miles away, in a rocky bay, men who trusted him lay dead under that silver surface. They would never have the opportunity to see their wives and sweethearts again. And on the same day Ned sent them to their needless deaths, he experienced what should have been the happiest event in his life.

He did not deserve to be happy. He did not deserve to be blessed with Charlotte as his wife, to hold her, to feel the embers of passion her kisses stoked. He did not deserve her love.

Chapter Fifteen

Wi‌lliam scanned the dark waters with his spyglass. Miles farther south than where he should have found *Audacious*, fear gripped his innards that Ned had skirmished with Shaw and the ship had been damaged…or worse. He reminded himself that they could have passed each other in the dark. But the echo of the ships' bells carried far distances over open water—and he'd set Ned's course himself. If Ned had obeyed his orders, they should have come bow to bow hours ago.

To his left the sky began to lighten. Dawn would bring with it a better chance at finding Ned and reassurance that he would not be sacrificing Charlotte by going after Shaw to rescue Julia.

Activity in the forecastle drew William's attention away from the horizon. A midshipman ran aft, skidding to a stop near William's position on the quarterdeck. "Lieutenant Gibson's compliments, sir. The forecastle lookout spotted something, sir."

William barreled past the lad. He composed himself before speaking to the junior-most lieutenant. "Report."

"Sir, the topman reported seeing masts over that ridge."

William eyed the cliffs off the larboard bow. Their height blocked him from seeing anything from the deck. He tucked his spyglass under his belt and heaved himself onto the shroud. Halfway up he remembered it had been many years since he'd been in the practice of climbing the shrouds regularly. But he plucked up his reserve strength and made it to the platform at the mast top. He gathered up as much air in his burning lungs as he could when he gained his feet. "Where away?"

The sailor pointed just beyond the foremost peak of the ridge. William raised his glass. There, against the dusky sky, three upright beams. Masts or something built atop the cliff?

The three upright structures moved. Yes, indeed. Masts. But whose?

William descended the shroud as fast as he dared and then made his way astern to the wheelhouse. "What is our position, Mr. Ingleby?"

The sailing master held his lantern over the chart on his table. "Near Negril, sir."

Negril. A town reported to be one of Shaw's favorite haunts.

"Commodore Ransome, the other ship is setting sheets and braces."

Whoever they were, they were preparing to sail. "Hold position here. Let us find who they are before engaging." The last thing he wanted was to open fire on *Sister Elizabeth*, Shaw's flagship, and have Julia injured during the battle.

The eastern horizon burned with light beyond the tops of the craggy cliffs before the unknown ship sailed out of the inlet beyond. With *Alexandra*'s sails fully furled, William prayed the still-dark sky behind them would provide a measure of camouflage and hide them from the view of the unknown ship.

Their position put them at such a distance away that William needed his largest telescope to make out the lettering on the back end of the frigate. *Sister Mary*. Shaw's secondary vessel. Not the one carrying Julia.

"Loose sheets and set course to intercept."

The officers relayed his commands and the crew of *Alexandra* leaped into action. Moments later she caught the wind and lurched forward.

William kept half of his attention on the smaller ship ahead and the rest split between the wheelhouse and the leadsman measuring the depth of the water below them.

"By the mark, twenty," the leadsman called, indicating the sea's depth to be twenty fathoms, more than one hundred feet. Comfortably deep for *Alexandra*'s twenty-two feet of draught, but that could change quickly this close to land.

"Commodore, she knows we're following," called Lieutenant Blakeley. "She's loosed all sail."

"Then I suggest we do the same, gentlemen. Clear for action and run out the guns."

His lieutenants showed their agreement by going to their areas to relay the necessary command. With the topgallant canvas spread, *Alexandra* leaned into her course like a thoroughbred racing for the next fence in a steeplechase.

"By the mark, seventeen."

William returned to the wheelhouse and leaned over the chart where the sailing master and his mates marked the ship's position.

"Shallow shoals coming up quick, Commodore. Frigate has a shallower draught than we do."

"I am aware of that, Master Ingleby." William traced his finger around the deep water at the edge of the shoals. Though *Alexandra* currently gained on the frigate, *Sister Mary* could put an insurmountable distance between them if she entered the shoals.

William returned to the quarterdeck. "Lieutenant Campbell, are we in firing range?"

"No, sir. A while longer yet."

A while longer and *Alexandra* faced running aground. William's body vibrated with anxiety, making it almost impossible for him to stay in one position.

The sun had risen several degrees above the horizon before Campbell called, "In range, sir!"

"By the mark, eight."

William turned to face the wheelhouse. "Hard to starboard." He spun around to face the left side of the ship as *Alexandra* careened to the right, angling her larboard armament toward the pirate vessel's stern.

"Fire as you bear!"

With *Sister Mary*'s back to *Alexandra*, William had the advantage. The two long-nines mounted on the lead ship's back end could do little damage to *Alexandra*'s thick hull.

Alexandra shuddered with the recoil of dozens of thirty-two pound cannons firing together. *Sister Mary* heeled as it too turned to starboard. Smoke billowed from the aft section where many of *Alexandra*'s cannon had struck, but rather than running for open water, with the advantage of a faster ship and a slight lead on *Alexandra*, the pirate ship turned completely about, coming back toward them, all the guns on its single gun deck run out and ready.

"Starboard battery, fire as you bear. Take cover!" William ducked behind the gunwale bulwark as grapeshot showered the quarterdeck. Below his feet, *Alexandra* rumbled with the firing of her cannons. He ventured a look over the side. Cannonballs from *Alexandra*'s much larger cannons pounded into *Sister Mary*'s hull.

Crouching, William made his way to the starboard carronade cannon on the forecastle. He leaned over and sighted along it. "Chain shot. Raise her ten degrees."

"Aye, aye, Commodore." The gun crew hastened to obey, loading the two cannonballs linked by a chain and working to raise the barrel.

"Gun ready, Commodore!"

"Run 'er out." William sighted along it again and then took the gun lock's lanyard in his hand and moved back, to be out of the way of the cannon's recoil. He pulled the cord and the cannon bellowed, spitting its double shot toward the enemy.

He straightened, watching the shot arc over the water between the two ships. The chain shot found its mark, crashing into *Sister Mary*'s mainmast. With a horrifying crack louder than any cannon blast, the fractured mast snapped under its own weight, heaving the frigate almost onto its side before the mast broke in two.

William's crew cheered.

"Commodore, another ship, coming up fast!" Midshipman Kennedy bolted up the steps to the forecastle.

"Where away?"

"Six points off the larboard bow. Their guns are run out."

"Commodore!" Lieutenant Jackson waved his hat as he ran along the quarterdeck. "Another ship bearing down on us. Four points off the starboard stern. They're cleared for action."

With *Sister Mary* crippled, he could have taken on one additional ship. But two? His pleasure in what looked to be a certain victory sank.

The pirate ship blocked *Alexandra* from tacking for open water, and they could not turn back to larboard for fear of the shoals.

"Make the guns ready. We will give them all we have." His officers scattered to follow his command, formerly smiling faces now set in grim lines.

The smoke from the cannon fire began to clear, allowing William a view of the ship approaching off their bow. He blinked to clear his eyes and ensure he'd seen clearly.

A British ensign was flying from the rear.

He did not have time to ponder the meaning before *Sister Mary's* cannons opened on them again. Hot pain seared his right cheek and left shoulder. He ducked behind the carronade to avoid being grazed—or hit—by any more grapeshot.

William's crew returned fire, the larger cannonballs ripping into the frigate's sides and decks, smoke once again obscuring the scene.

More cannon fire boomed. From the other British ship?

"By the mark, eight," the leadsman's voice pierced the sounds of battle.

Doubled over, William made his way back toward the wheelhouse. Changing course while being fired upon condemned the men aloft to almost certain death or injury. But he could not allow his ship to run aground.

Jackson met him on the quarterdeck. "Sir, the ship approaching from behind—"

"And shallows ahead, Lieutenant. We stand a better chance against that ship than the shoals."

"Aye, sir."

In twenty-two years of service, William had never lost a battle. He gazed around *Alexandra's* deck, thinking about the more than seven hundred men whose lives depended on the decisions he made now.

He needed to capture the captain of the pirate ship to question him about Shaw's plans. He needed to rescue Julia.

But in this moment, he needed to protect the lives of his crew. "Cease firing. All hands aloft to take the sails aback. Move us away from the enemy ships."

Audacious rattled and rocked from the enemy fire. Charlotte tucked a white shirt into tan pants and pulled the belt as tight as it would go. She didn't bother with anything other than a simple knot for the neck-cloth, thrust her arms through the holes in the waistcoat, and threw a coat on over it without bothering to button either.

She could tell by the men's yells that many were injured, and being severely short on officers and midshipmen to oversee the gun crews, Charlotte knew what she needed to do.

With a dirk in its sheath at her side, she exited through the steward's cabin and took the protected companionway in the wheelhouse down to the main gun deck. Though her crew was on the starboard side, currently facing the open sea and not the enemy, Charlotte scanned the crews manning the larboard cannon and saw young Isaac McLellan trying to command five gun crews by himself.

"Reload, quickly now," she yelled, taking a position behind the three cannons closest to her.

The young midshipman turned around, mouth dropped in a shocked *O*. "Ch-Charlie?"

"Mind your gun crews, Isaac."

A cheeky grin replaced the expression of surprise. "Aye, sir!"

The acrid smoke, deafening booms that thundered through her chest and rattled her bones, and yells of "Gun ready, Mr. Lott!" followed by her own yell of "Fire!" resonated in Charlotte's heart like a symphony.

After several rounds Lieutenant Duncan's voice echoed through the deck. "Cease firing. Prepare to board enemy vessel."

Charlotte's pulse pounded. She should return to the cabin. But... Ned. What if he was hurt? She ran up the stairs with everyone else, dirk in hand. The gun crews on the quarterdeck used grappling hooks and lines to reduce the distance between the two vessels, and as soon as they were close enough, lines were readied for the boarders to cross over.

She couldn't see him, couldn't find him. No, wait—Ned's golden hair flashed in the sun on the deck of the other ship. Charlotte sheathed her weapon, grabbed a line, and with a running leap swung over onto the other ship's deck. She landed off balance and fell, but she rolled onto her side to keep from hurting herself. Gaining her feet, she grabbed her dirk, ready to defend herself.

"You, there. Get below and search for prisoners." Declan fought two pirates on his own with seemingly little effort.

Prisoners. Gardiner and Jamison and…Kent. Yes, they might all be here. "Isaac and you two"—she motioned to a pair of burly men from the gun crew she'd commanded moments before—"come with me."

She turned and gasped. Several feet away a pirate leveled a pistol at her. But before he could get off his shot he went down, a red stain blossoming across his dingy shirt. Swallowing against the bile rising in the back of her throat, Charlotte moved forward and forced herself to lean over the dead man and retrieve his pistol. She'd never fired one before, but she might be better with it than with the long knife she carried.

"With me, men." She forged ahead. Fortunately, the smaller ship had a similar design to *Vengeance*. She paused and peered around every corner before venturing forward as they reached the lower levels of the ship. More fighting happening on the main gun deck. No prisoners.

Down to the orlop, then.

She tucked the gun under her belt at the small of her back and grabbed a lantern from a nearby post before continuing down one more level. A stench unlike anything she'd ever breathed met her when she reached the bottom of the companionway. This boat needed a good cleaning.

Everything on this, the ship's lowest level, seemed to be abandoned. The storage area for lines and cables, the food repository, a few dank cabins, the hold for the water barrels. Water swirled around her ankles. One of the ships firing upon *Sister Mary* had damaged her below the waterline. The thick oaken decking blocked out most of the noise of the continuing fight above.

So where was the sound of yelling coming from? Charlotte paused to listen. "Forward. Someone's there." She splashed through the rising water toward the bow of the ship.

"We're here! In the bilge! Officers of His Majesty's Ship *Audacious*."

"Lieutenant Gardiner?" Charlotte used what remained of her voice to respond to the disembodied and familiar voice.

"Yes! Please hurry. The water is rising. He's drowning."

"Keep calling out so we can find you."

"Lieutenant Gardiner, HMS *Audacious*, commission date 16 March 1809. Born in Shropshire, 22 June 1790. First ship, *Hampstead*, served as a volunteer. Second ship, *Valmont*, served as a midshipman..."

Charlotte followed the sound of Gardiner's voice as he continued naming all the ships on which he'd served. She rounded piles of broken down barrels and—

"Oh, thank the Lord."

If it hadn't been for his voice, Charlotte would not have known Gardiner. Both eyes were swollen and his face bore the cuts and bruises of a severe beating. Jamison was in much the same condition, though his red hair glowed in the candlelight. She handed the lantern to Isaac and used her dirk to cut through the ropes binding Gardiner to an upright support beam of the grating holding the scrap wood and metal in place.

"No, help him first." Gardiner nodded toward another support beam. Charlotte took the lantern back from Isaac and raised it. His face half in the rising water, Kent lay slumped over, held partially upright only by the rope binding his hands to the beam. He looked dead, but then the swirling water splashed over his mouth and nose and he sputtered and coughed.

Charlotte motioned to the two sailors who had come with her. She handed the light to one and motioned the other to crouch down beside her. "Hold his head up."

Kent, who had dried blood tracks from his temple and nose, opened his eyes. He blinked several times. "Lott? Am I dead?"

"No, you're not dead. Not yet, anyway." She sawed at the rope.

"But you're dead."

"Not quite." The fibers gave way under the blade, and she reached up to uncoil the rest of the length.

"You're a girl." Kent closed his eyes again.

Isaac and the two sailors stilled and stared at her. Gardiner and Jamison, who probably could not see much through their blackened eyes, turned their faces toward her. "Don't try to speak, Mr. Kent." She glanced over her shoulder, continuing to work at loosening Kent's rope. "Lieutenant Gardiner, where are the rest of the men?"

"The rest?"

"Aye, sir. The other midshipmen and sailors who were with you on the launch."

Gardiner shook his head. "It's my fault. Only a few of us survived the initial assault. They fished us out of the water. I refused to answer the pirate's questions, and he dragged me out on deck where he shot the other four men—two midshipmen, two sailors—right in front of me."

The last loop of rope holding Kent captive came loose. He flung his arm free and knocked Charlotte back. She lost her balance and landed hard on her backside in the water, at least two feet deep now.

"I won't be saved by a girl!" Kent flailed his arms.

Charlotte crab-crawled backward to stay out of the range of Kent's fists. Though still eyeing her suspiciously, the sailor who had held Kent's head up and kept him from drowning subdued him.

She returned to help Isaac finish freeing Gardiner and Jamison.

"Mr. Kent, sir, if you don't be still, I'm going to have to cuff you one to make you still…sir." The big fellow's threat finally quelled Kent.

The second sailor handed the lantern back to Charlotte and then looped Lieutenant Gardiner's arm around his shoulders.

Charlotte and Isaac, both smaller than Jamison, did their best to support him. Thankfully, of the three, Jamison seemed the most ambulatory. By the time they reached the companionway, the water was up to Isaac's chin and Charlotte's chest, making it easier for them to support Jamison but harder to move forward.

"Anyone below?" Wallis's voice ricocheted off the rising water.

"Yes, sir. Coming up with rescued prisoners," Charlotte yelled. "We'll need help getting them up to you."

Wallis, Duncan, and four others appeared through the opening at the top of the stairs. Charlotte, whose arm shook from holding the lantern high enough to keep the water from dousing the candles inside it, gladly relinquished Jamison to one of the sailors.

Duncan held his hand out for her, but as soon as she came into the half light of the gun deck, he loosened his hold on her forearm and she started slipping backward, her hat falling off and floating away in the roiling flood.

He rectified the mistake quickly and hauled her up. He pulled her away from the others, leaning over her, studying her face. "I don't believe it. It isn't possible."

"Please, Lieutenant. No one knows."

"Mrs. Cochrane, why are you here, dressed like this—like Charles Lott? That's why the pirate ship signaled us with that name. *You're* Charles Lott. But you're the captain's wife."

She clapped her hand over his mouth. "Please, don't say anything. Charles Lott is dead. He died at Barbados of yellow fever."

He pulled her hand away but lowered his voice, leaning toward her. "Then how will you explain your presence here? How will you explain to the three men you rescued, and the three who helped, that the person who saved them is dead?"

She shrugged. "A ghost? I've heard stories—"

Duncan snorted. "You know those stories aren't true. And the men aren't stupid." He straightened. "I will take you to Captain Cochrane."

"I'd rather return to *Audacious*."

Duncan pressed his lips together, but before he could respond another yell came from above.

"*Alexandra* is cleared for action and looks to broadside *Vengeance*. All hands, return to *Audacious* and prepare to intercept HMS *Alexandra*!"

In the melee of getting back to *Audacious*, Charlotte managed to lose herself in the crowd. She could not get back into the cabin through the main door. The marine guard would not let her pass unless she identified herself—not a good idea dressed as Charles Lott, soaking wet, and smelling like something left to rot in the gutter from the filthy water in *Sister Mary's* orlop. She would have to enter the same way she exited.

She sneaked through the milling crew to the door into Ned's steward's cabin. She cracked the door open and peeked in. Empty. With a sigh of relief, she slipped in and cut through the small captain's galley to the door of the sleeping cabin.

Pulling off her sodden coat and waistcoat, she pushed the door open—and yelped.

Ned stood in the sleeping cabin, dressed in nothing but his trousers and boots. His shirt and waistcoat, both bloodstained, lay crumpled at his feet. His surprise quickly gave way to suspicion and anger once he realized what she was wearing.

She started to apologize, but he stopped her with a raised hand. "We shall speak of this later. Right now, I have more pressing issues." He pulled a voluminous shirt over his head. "Clean yourself up, put on something more appropriate, and, above all else, *do not leave this cabin again.*" He stomped through the door into the day cabin, calling for his steward.

Charlotte pantomimed touching the brim of her hat, now lost. "Aye, aye, Captain."

But even through her bravado, shame gnawed at her. Not only had she put herself in jeopardy, she had revealed herself to several officers and crewmen. If word got out about Charles Lott's being a woman, Ned's knowing and then marrying her, and then Charlotte's dressing like a midshipman again to participate in an action, Ned could be court-martialed. He could lose his commission or even be discharged from the Royal Navy.

She dropped the coat and waistcoat atop his ruined clothes. Ruined. Yes, she had ruined her reputation by rash and foolish actions. Now she might have ruined Ned's career, his life.

Why couldn't she learn to think before she acted?

Chapter Sixteen

The pirate's delays in obeying William's command to stand down and prepare to be boarded stretched his patience to the breaking point. He stood on the starboard side of the poop deck, trying to discern meaning from the activity aboard *Vengeance*'s quarterdeck. The frigate still had her guns run out, but, unlike the marines lining the side of *Alexandra*, muskets raised and ready to fire, the upper decks of *Vengeance* were mostly empty.

"Commodore, signal from the other ship. It's *Audacious*, sir. They—"

William cut Lieutenant Eastwick off. "Signal *Audacious* to flank the enemy ship and prepare to fire on my signal."

Eastwick hesitated rather than immediately obey William's command. "Sir, the captain of *Audacious* requests permission to come aboard *Alexandra*."

Rather than relay his message through the third lieutenant, William marched to the forecastle himself.

"Signal *Audacious* to flank the enemy ship."

"Aye, aye, sir." The midshipman grabbed the appropriate flags and hoisted them.

Audacious changed tack and moved to take up position on the other side of *Vengeance*.

"Now signal permission for Captain Cochrane to come aboard."

"Aye, aye, sir." The midshipman lowered the first message and raised the second. William returned to the poop deck to keep watch on the pirates.

Half an hour later, Ned approached him.

"Thank you for your assistance with the first ship, Captain Cochrane." William turned to his friend and protégé. "With the second pirate ship coming astern, I do not know if I could have extricated *Alexandra* from this battle."

"It is my honor, sir, to have arrived in time to help. I saw the mast fall. Your handiwork?" Ned tapped his fingers against his legs, a sign of agitation that belied his calm words.

"Aye. What is going on, Ned?"

Ned glanced at *Vengeance* and then back at William. "You cannot fire on her, sir."

"I know I cannot. He has Charlotte, and I cannot put her life in such jeopardy."

"No, sir. Captain Salvador does not have Charlotte."

William pulled the note out of his pocket and thrust it toward Ned. "He *does* have her. I have proof. He will pay for his crime."

Ned turned and motioned to someone behind him. William stepped to the side—and then closed his eyes in blessed relief. Charlotte wrapped her arms around him. He returned the embrace for a moment and then took hold of her upper arms and held her away from him for closer inspection.

"You are well? Not injured?"

Charlotte shrugged his hands away and stepped back toward Ned. "I am quite well, thank you, William."

Her downcast eyes and timid stance, with hands folded demurely in front of her, indicated she was anything but well. "Are you certain? I want you to tell me what the pirate did to you, no matter how indelicate it seems."

Her head snapped up. "He did nothing to harm me. In fact, Captain Salvador saved my life when I…fell overboard and might have drowned. He has been nothing but solicitous and courteous toward me. And all of his crew as well."

William looked at Ned, who kept his gaze conspicuously turned away from Charlotte. Unusual, given their conversation about Ned's wanting to marry her last they talked.

Then Ned began to speak, explaining how he came upon *Vengeance*— or, more precisely, how *Vengeance* had come upon him. William clasped his hands behind his back and let the motion of the ship sway him from side to side.

When he got to the part about taking Charlotte off the pirate's ship, he hesitated.

Charlotte looked up at Ned, down at her hands, and then up at William. She took a deep, unsteady breath. "William, I convinced Ned to marry me to protect what remained of my reputation." She raised her left hand in front of her chest; a thin gold band encircled a finger.

Ned stared over William's shoulder, expression impassive.

"Mr. Cochrane?"

"Aye, sir. It is true. The sailing master aboard *Vengeance* is a minister. He performed the ceremony, before witnesses, and he wrote the certificate of marriage, which we both signed. But, sir, we haven't… the marriage is in name only. I agreed to go through the marriage ceremony and introduce her to my crew as my wife to protect her reputation, but I made her agree that we would behave toward each other in such a manner that, if you disapprove, the marriage could be annulled."

William considered shaking both of them, perhaps knocking their heads together. Such a total and wanton lack of good sense and propriety.

Something in the back of his mind interrupted his outrage. Julia, walking circles around a bench in a garden, explaining to him how she needed him to marry her to protect her inheritance. Her terms had been not only that it would be a marriage in name only, to be annulled after a year, but that William would receive Julia's inheritance even after the annulment.

He turned and stalked to the back of the poop deck. The cliffs around which they had followed *Sister Mary* lay too far away to be seen.

The arrival of Julia's cousin and aunt, who would have used whatever means necessary to get their hands on her fortune, convinced

William to accept her proposition. Julia had turned to him and asked him to be the one to marry her because she trusted him, because she believed he would protect her, because she loved him. And he loved her. Otherwise, he would not have gone through with it.

Charlotte was the same age as Julia had been when William made the mistake of walking away from her instead of proposing to her twelve years ago. And though Ned was a few years older than William had been at the time, William saw much of himself in the young captain.

He returned to his sister and her husband. "You have my blessing. You do realize, of course, that Julia will insist upon a formal wedding ceremony when we return to Tierra Dulce."

Strangely, his statement of approval did not bring the expressions of joy he expected to see on their faces.

"Thank you, Commodore. I will have my steward pack her belongings and deliver them to Dawling to put in your cabin."

William crossed his arms. More than just an illicit marriage plagued these two. And William would not allow himself to be dragged into the middle of it. "Belay that, Mr. Cochrane. She is your wife. Thus she is your responsibility."

"Sir, I cannot have her aboard *Audacious*. She will be…has been… recognized. She—"

Charlotte made an exasperated sound. "What he means, William, is that he doesn't want me on his ship because during the action this morning I dressed in my old uniform and joined in the fight." She moved to stand in front of Ned. "Your ship is shorthanded. A thirteen-year-old boy was trying to command five gun crews by himself."

Ned finally looked at her—right before he grabbed her shoulders and shook her. "That thirteen-year-old boy has more experience serving aboard a ship of the line in battle than you do. Your life was at greater risk than his. Your life is of more value than his."

The tension ebbed from Charlotte's shoulders. "No, Ned, it is not."

"It is to me." He pulled her into his arms. "You could have been killed."

"So could you." Charlotte's words were muffled by Ned's uniform coat.

William cleared his throat. "If I might interrupt, we do have a pirate ship off starboard to which we should be attending."

Ned and Charlotte broke apart. Ned straightened his jacket with a swift tug. "Sir, if I might signal *Vengeance* from here?"

William stepped aside and motioned Ned toward the stern, where a midshipman and lieutenant stood waiting for orders.

Charlotte, her cheeks pink, followed Ned across the poop deck. Moments later, a colorful array of flags raised. C-H-A-R-L-E-S-L-O-T-T. The name his sister had taken in her identity as a midshipman on *Audacious*.

Not only had Ned formed an alliance with the pirate, Charlotte had created such a bond that she felt comfortable sharing secrets with him. William prayed it would not lead to disaster.

☙❧

Salvador climbed the accommodation ladder with trepidation weighing his every step. Forming an alliance with Ned Cochrane had seemed logical, rational. Forming an alliance with William Ransome...Salvador hoped he wasn't about to meet his doom.

The two marines standing sentry on either side of the entry port kept their muskets trained on him, while the several others lining the side kept theirs aimed at his men in the gig below.

He stopped to adjust the lace cuffs of his shirt—Serena's idea and handiwork—and touched the fore point of his hat in return salute to the lieutenant who faced him.

"Commodore Ransome is waiting for you." An Irishman, just like Picaro, save this one had dark hair and a wicked scar running across the right side of his face, from the top of his ear to his chin. It looked like a saber slash, its puckered, rough edges indicating it had been hastily and not neatly stitched back together, probably while the battle continued. Salvador imagined he would enjoy the telling of how the young man received such a badge of honor. For the most part, he found the Irish to be good storytellers.

The eyes of the crew speared him with their distaste for his kind and their displeasure at his presence on their ship. Although a few... he followed their gazes upward to the poop deck.

Charlotte raised her hand in greeting with a tentative smile.

He mustered a smile in return but gave no other outward sign he'd noticed her. Until he knew his own destiny, no need to give the crew any further reason to distrust having a woman aboard.

The officers of the watch in the wheelhouse saluted the Irish lieutenant as they passed by. Only once before had Salvador spent any time on a vessel larger than a frigate with a poop deck that shielded the sailing master and his mates at the wheel from the elements and a big cabin that opened onto the quarterdeck instead of being squirreled-away below it like an afterthought.

He had to give credit to the British shipbuilders. They knew how to design a craft that would create a sense of intimidation.

At the lieutenant's knock, a burly sailor with pockmarked skin opened the door to the dining cabin and motioned him to enter.

The lieutenant stepped aside, and Salvador took that as his cue to go in alone. A long, highly polished mahogany table stretched the width of the room, ten chairs surrounding it. Ned Cochrane stood behind the chair in the center of the table directly opposite the door. Though concerned about his own future, Salvador wondered how the conversation about Charlotte between Ned and Commodore Ransome had gone.

Girding up his courage, Salvador turned to his left, removing his hat.

The man who stood at the head of the table exemplified everything a Royal Navy captain—or in this case, commodore—should be: of good height, but not overly tall, trim of build, and with piercing eyes that announced he would brook no opposition.

Ned made the introduction. "Commodore William Ransome, this is El Salvador de los Esclavos, captain of the frigate *Vengeance*."

"Please have a seat, Captain Salvador."

As soon as all three were seated, Commodore Ransome leaned forward and clasped his hands atop the table. "Captain Cochrane informs me that he has come to an agreement with you. That in exchange for leniency in the charge of abducting Miss"—William closed his eyes a moment and then seemed to regain his composure—"Mrs. Cochrane, you have agreed to assist in hunting down the pirate Shaw to rescue Mrs. Ransome."

"Aye, Commodore. As surety, I sent my first mate aboard *Audacious*."

"Yes, Mr. Cochrane informed me of this as well. And while the explanation that Mr. Declan is your future brother-in-law might be enough to make Captain Cochrane trust you, that is not good enough for me." Commodore Ransome touched the pile of papers near the corner of the table. "I have report here of your misdeeds going back about ten years. So why should I believe you would turn your back on your unscrupulous ways once this alliance ends?"

The time had come. Salvador straightened his coat and rolled his neck. "Commodore Ransome, perhaps I should tell you about myself. At twelve years old, I entered the Royal Navy as a midshipman. My father had great expectations for me and constantly compared my actions, my feats, my successes to someone else, a young man who had become like a son to him. My father seemed to delight in pointing out my failures and explaining how this other young man had done better. So I worked harder. I finally gained promotion to a larger vessel under the command of a captain with a legendary reputation. Once I arrived on his ship, I discovered him to be a cruel taskmaster who played favorites and set his officers against each other."

Salvador shuddered, remembering the beatings and the ridicule he'd received for not being strong enough or fast enough or smart enough. "The captain sent spurious reports of me to my father, who believed him over his own son. My father wrote to me, berating me, and told me to study longer and work harder. He also shared the successes of the young man I know he wished had been born to him rather than me."

He locked his eyes on Commodore Ransome's to judge his reaction to the story. So far, he showed none. "The autumn after I turned fifteen, my ship was tasked with hunting down a notorious pirate. We scoured the coast of Jamaica, Antigua, and Barbuda. In Montserrat, we were told where we could find the pirate, so we set off to find him. I suggested to the first lieutenant that the informant had misrepresented himself and was sending us into a trap. But because the captain did not like me, none of the officers heeded me. A day out from Montserrat, we were set upon by the pirate. Most of the officers were killed in the attack. The sailors were left on the hulled ship as it sank. The rest of us were taken aboard the pirate ship and told our families would be contacted for ransom. If the family could not or would not pay, we would have a choice put before us: death or joining the crew."

William Ransome's expression grew stony. Salvador did not have to guess which choice he would have made. "In the meantime, they put us to work. The captain took a liking to me. For the first time in my life, a man in a position of authority over me encouraged me and showed pride in my accomplishments. When six months had passed and no ransom came from my family, the captain put the choice to me. I do not believe I have to tell you what choice I made."

"That is all very well, but I fail to see how this tale is supposed to convince me to trust you now."

"Though I appreciated the captain's belief in me, I did not agree with his methods. I had to stay with that crew until I had enough money of my own and could gather a crew of like-minded men. I showed the captain how he could ply his trade without all of the killing and mayhem. He took some of my suggestions. But still, I wanted to follow my own path. One day, when I was twenty, we came upon a ship coming out of port. It had just delivered its cargo—hundreds of slaves. I had no problem taking the ship, setting the crew adrift. When my captain began to divide the spoils and talked of burning the ship, I asked him if I could have the ship rather than payment."

Salvador closed his eyes, remembering the dark hulk of a vessel. "It wasn't much to look at, but it had good lines and was sound. A few men went with me and I recruited more. Men who would agree to abide by a strict code of conduct. Who were not after violence and notoriety, but who wanted to be at sea, who wanted to make a little gold, and who wanted to see justice done."

He rolled his head from side to side again, the tension of reliving the past knotting his shoulders. "In the past ten years, we have liberated more than two hundred slave ships—saving thousands of souls from the degradation of human bondage. The slave ships we cannot get to before they deliver their cargo, we take as they come out of port. After all, my crew must be paid and my ship must be kept in repair." And he occasionally liked to buy a new ship when one came on the market, as the current *Vengeance* had two years ago.

"And attacking ships from Tierra Dulce, a plantation that does not hold slaves? How do you justify that?" William Ransome raised a dark brow and pierced Salvador with his icy blue eyes.

"We prefer liberating slave ships before their cargo is delivered. We turn the ship over to the men and women aboard to sail back to Africa or to South America or wherever they wish to go. But they need money for food and to hire a crew if necessary. I give them the money and help them with what they need. This takes a more regular source of gold than raiding ships after they have completed their delivery."

Salvador pulled a small journal—one that he did not keep hidden at the bottom of the trunk he'd bought for Serena—out of his pocket and handed it to the commodore.

William opened the book and slowly turned the pages. After several long minutes, he looked up. "This is a record of Tierra Dulce's annual profits for each year since Sir Edward purchased the plantation, with an estimated net worth figured as well. Who gave you this?"

Salvador would go to his grave before admitting Jeremiah Goodland knew everything and had been passing him information for years. "That is not important. What is important is that I have kept an accounting of every farthing I have taken from the plantation. It equates to the annual income a son might expect from such a legacy."

William snapped the book closed and slid it back down the table toward Salvador. "And why do you believe you are entitled to that? Simply because Sir Edward does not have a son does not mean that money is available for whoever wants to take it."

Salvador rose and, pressing his fists against the tabletop, leaned over it. "Even though you tried to steal his affections away, Commodore Ransome, to ingratiate yourself to such a point he would turn his back on his own offspring, I regret to inform you that Admiral Sir Edward Witherington *does* have a son."

He straightened and pushed his chair out of the way. "I am Michael Witherington."

Chapter Seventeen

With each thunderous boom and recoil, Julia prayed harder that the vessel attacking—or under attack from—*Sister Elizabeth* was not *Alexandra* or *Audacious*. Because Shaw had not come down to retrieve her from her closetlike prison, she hoped that meant it was not William. But she prayed for his safety anyway.

Her side and head ached. The vision in her right eye—when she was not locked in absolute darkness—was blurry. Her stomach churned with each movement of the ship. And, after days—weeks?—of captivity with no water for washing and no change of clothing, she probably smelled like the bilge.

When the battle ended, Julia's ears rang in the silence. She pushed herself up to her feet and pressed her ear to the door of the tiny dungeon, trying to hear anything, but all she could make out were muffled voices and footsteps.

Wait. Those footsteps were coming closer. She backed up until pressed against the opposite wall of the small chamber.

The door swung open, and she shielded her eyes against the light from the lantern. "Commodore wants to see you." The man reached in and grabbed her arm, pulling her along with him, laughing when she stumbled. Smoke filled the gun deck, but from the sounds of the voices this ship had been victorious.

At Shaw's cabin the man pushed Julia inside. She tripped over the torn, soiled hem of her skirt, holding her bound hands out, reaching for anything to help steady her. But then she tripped over something.

She twisted so her shoulder took the brunt of the fall instead of her face. She sat up to search for the obstacle and discovered she'd tripped over a man's legs. Not just any man. A man in a Royal Navy captain's uniform.

Not Ned. The man sprawled face down on Shaw's floor had dark hair like William's, not Ned's light brown.

Apparently her tripping over him was the jolt necessary to bring him back to life. He groaned and rolled over.

Julia gasped. "Wi—" But no. Even though he greatly resembled her husband, there were enough differences to tell he wasn't William. She looked up at Shaw. "What is going on here?"

"You don't recognize him?" The dimples danced in Shaw's cheeks. She was coming to loathe them.

"He resembles my husband."

Shaw let out a laugh that filled the cabin. "How poetic. Well, then, let me introduce you. Julia Ransome, meet Captain James Ransome. Your husband's brother."

Shaw moved over James, grabbed his hair, and pulled his head back so that James had to sit up to keep the pirate from wrenching or even breaking his neck. "Be polite and greet your sister-in-law, Captain Ransome."

"Release me, or I will—"

Shaw went down on one knee, whipped a dagger from his belt, and pressed it across James's cheek, drawing blood. "I told you once already that you do not make demands of me."

Julia grabbed her skirt in her hands and stood. After however long she'd been on this ship, she was becoming quite adept at maneuvering without the benefit of having her hands free. Questions rolled through her mind, but she kept them to herself, not wanting to put James or herself closer to Shaw's rage.

She executed a shallow curtsey. "Captain Ransome, I am pleased to finally make your acquaintance. William, Charlotte, and your mother speak of you often."

James seemed fearful of responding.

Shaw pushed him forward so he was almost doubled over. "You bow and say nice things to your husband's wife. Like how sorry you are that you won't get to spend much more time together."

"M-Mrs. Ransome, I am honored to finally meet you. And may I wish you joy on your marriage to William."

"Thank you."

Shaw stood, pulling James up with him. When both regained their feet, Shaw shoved James toward Julia. She reached her hands out to steady him and keep him from knocking her over. His elbow hit her right side, and she gasped against the pain that shot through her chest.

"I do apologize, ma'am." James wobbled a moment until catching the rhythm of the ship.

"James tells me he attacked my ship because he is looking for his sister. And since the two of you have never met, I have to assume it isn't you he's looking for." Shaw waved the knife in Julia's direction before using it to cut a slice from the apple he'd been eating when she entered. "Now, where can Miss Charlotte Ransome be, if not here?"

"Taken by someone else, apparently." Julia kept her tone mild, observational.

This seemed to amuse Shaw. "Apparently. So James here has lost his ship and his men attacking me for something I don't have." He pulled one of the chairs out from the table and put his foot up on the seat and then leaned forward, resting his elbow on his knee. "His commanding officer is not going to be happy."

James stepped forward, but Julia grabbed his coat sleeve to pull him back. "He's baiting you," she whispered. "Do not retaliate or respond."

"Very good, Mrs. Ransome." Shaw spoke around a wad of partially chewed apple. "You learn quickly."

She pulled James back and then moved until she stood about half a step in front of him. Her stomach rumbled at the sight of the bowl of apples on the table and the plate holding half a biscuit beside it. She could not bring herself to choke down the gruel they occasionally brought her, and even if she could eat it, she did not imagine it would stay down.

"May…may I have that biscuit?" She hated herself for asking, but if she did not have some nourishment soon, she might become gravely ill. She'd seen what starvation did to people.

"This?" Surprised, Shaw lifted the scrap of hardtack from the plate. "Hungry, are you?"

Tears pressed against the corners of her eyes. "Yes, I am."

He carried it toward her and held it out between thumb and forefinger. Julia reached her hands up.

Shaw released it. She lunged, but it was just out of her reach. It hit the floor and broke into four pieces.

"Have it if you want it."

Pride or hunger? The tears pushed past her lids, and she knelt down. The fall had knocked out the remaining weevils, anyway—a few wriggled on the floor underneath when she picked up the pieces. She ate two before she regained her feet. The hard, floury bread absorbed what little moisture she'd had in her mouth, but she choked it down.

She blinked away the remaining vestiges of emotion and tucked the other two pieces of biscuit into her pocket.

Shaw came toward her again. She flinched, but he laughed, lifted her hands, and placed a pewter cup of water in them.

Too thirsty to be suspicious, she drank it. Brackish, but otherwise it tasted like plain water. Besides, she couldn't imagine Shaw poisoning someone.

"Thank you." She handed the cup back to him.

Shaw inclined his head with a half smile. "Of course. I want you to be fully awake and fully aware when I kill dear James."

Julia used her position in front of her brother-in-law to impede his forward movement with her shoulder. "Should I not be presented with a new gown as well?" She looked down at the mess the dark blue damask had become. "Surely you would want me dressed in style to witness his execution."

Shaw threw his head back and laughed, hands planted on his hips. "I like you, Mrs. Ransome. Truly, I do. It will be a pity to have to end your life. But we all have things to which we must attend." He picked the dagger up from the table, wiped its blade on his pants, and resheathed it. "Collier!"

The man who had brought Julia up reappeared. "Aye, Commodore?"

"Please see these two back to the guest suite."

"Aye, aye, sir." Collier grabbed Julia's arm and then reached for James.

"Oh, yes, wait a moment." Shaw glanced over at some coiled rope. "Tie the good captain's hands first—behind his back. We would not want him doing something rash, now would we?"

Julia went along cooperatively with Collier while James struggled and pulled. She could warn him again, but she doubted he'd listen.

She walked straight into the small compartment, turned, pressed her back to the wall, and slid to the floor. Collier needed both hands to shove James in. Once the door closed, she couldn't see him but almost immediately knew where he was.

"I am a"—*thud*—"captain"—*thud*—"in His Majesty's"—*thud*— "Royal"—*thud*—"Navy!"

Julia could picture him ramming his shoulder against the door. Her feet had yet to fully recover from the half hour or more she'd spent kicking at it the first time they locked her in this space.

She rested her roped wrists on her up-bent knees. "You will only injure yourself if you continue," she said when the thudding paused.

"I have no interest in receiving advice from you."

From the way he was moving around, if she stretched out her legs, she could trip him and make him stop that way. But like William and Charlotte, he was most likely stubborn and had to try things for himself before he would believe anything.

Silence fell after a particularly loud thud followed by a grunt and a sliding sound. Something hard hit her hip and elbow—his shoe.

"Sorry." He moved his foot.

"For the kick or for not wanting advice from the likes of me?"

He didn't respond.

"Would you be interested in hearing why we are here?"

Silence.

She sighed. "Fine. I will tell you anyway. It will help pass the time."

She recited Shaw's story of how he became Shaw and why he wanted to take revenge on William and her father.

"So this is your father's fault."

If she had the energy, she would kick him for that. "No, this is Shaw's fault. His fault for the choices he made as a young man and now. He was given the opportunity to adhere to the same code of conduct every sailor in the Royal Navy does. He, however, was more interested in drink and revelry to remember that proprieties needed to be observed. He is a violent, spiteful, angry man with an insatiable thirst for power."

"And how much time have you spent with him to draw such conclusions." James's nasty tone made her glad no light penetrated the small room.

"I am a fast learner, Captain Ransome. It took receiving a fist in my face and being knocked unconscious only once for me to learn not to argue with him or question him or make demands." She touched her still-tender cheek. "You may be strong enough to withstand his blows. I am not."

James stayed silent for a long while. Julia closed her eyes and leaned her head against the wall. More and more, she found sleep lingering just a moment away.

"How long have you been here?"

She dragged her mind back to consciousness. "I am not certain. What is today?"

"Thursday, the sixth of October."

Could she truly have been here so short a time? Only four days? "I was taken Monday, on my way from Tierra Dulce—my family's sugar plantation—into Kingston."

James made a derisive sound.

"We do not hold slaves, if that is the meaning of your scoff. We have not for almost twenty years."

"I do not care about your plantation or slaves."

"Then why do you behave toward me as if I am beneath you?" She once again blessed the darkness. She would not want to see someone who looked so much like William acting the way James did.

"You and your father—and my brother. The lot of you. Holding your honor and esteem and riches over everyone else. 'Twas luck only that saw William signed on to your father's ship and not the captain I fell in with. My father and Admiral Witherington were great friends, you see, so of course the favorite son received Sir Edward's patronage."

"That is unfair. My father was not knighted until many years after William joined the crew of *Indomitable*. When your father made those decisions, there was no method of determining which captain would achieve fame and wealth and which would not. What is more important is that you and Philip and William all lived to see the end of the war."

James snorted. "Oh, yes. So much more important. Of course, it makes no difference to anyone, least of all William, that Sir Edward took him publicly in hand. Practically declared William his son. Tell me, was marrying you part of the bargain so that William could officially become your father's heir?"

Seething silently for a moment, Julia took a few deep, settling breaths. "Did you know I had a twin brother?"

"I heard something about that."

"He was lost at sea when we were fifteen years old. Michael never wanted to join the navy, but he did it to please our father. Father rarely praised Michael. He pushed him to do better with his studies, to make himself stronger physically, to be the first to volunteer to do anything a superior might ask so he could gain patronage and rise swiftly through the ranks. In every letter Michael received, my father touted the successes of someone else—William. But Michael had something William did not. He was his father's son. No matter how close William and my father have become over the years, William could never replace Michael. Nor could my father replace yours in William's heart."

"Reasoned like a woman. You speak of hearts; I speak of fortune and promotion."

Pain spasmed in the back of Julia's left leg. She stretched it out in front of her to alleviate the cramp. "What good does being jealous over what your brother has do you? You sound like a child who has received a beautiful toy as a gift but is unhappy with it because he wants the toy his brother received instead. Be thankful for what you have, not bitter over what someone else has."

James released a weak laugh with a hint that he meant it to sound sardonic. "Thankful for what I have? I've lost my ship, my crew, and am being held captive by a pirate who wants to kill me for something that is no fault of mine."

"You can still be thankful."

"For what?"

Julia rubbed at the twitching, cramping muscles in her leg, wishing she could take a long walk to stretch it out. "You can be thankful you are not already dead. As long as we're alive, there is always the hope of rescue."

⌘

William sat in his desk chair, elbows on knees, head in hands, staring at the deck between his feet. Julia's brother—believed lost at sea at age fifteen—was alive. Not only alive, but a pirate. From a certain point of view, Salvador's…Michael's…explanation of everything he'd done from the time of his capture to now made sense. He had kept careful account of how much money he had taken from Tierra Dulce, considering it a portion of his inheritance.

That a lad of such tender years had the moral fortitude to turn his back on vast amounts of wealth gained through violence spoke to the strength of love and discipline he'd received at home before he went to sea. While William wanted to credit Sir Edward with that, in truth the admiral had been a greater presence in William's younger years than in Julia's and Michael's. Jeremiah was more father figure to Julia than Sir Edward.

Yes, that would explain Michael's desire to free slaves, if Jeremiah had been like a father to him. Again, another reason to understand Michael-Salvador's actions.

But how could Michael Witherington have allowed his family to believe him dead all these years? Julia, especially.

The haze brought on by the shock of Michael's revelation now gone, William rose, straightened his waistcoat and coat, and returned to the dining cabin.

Ned's and Michael's soft voices ceased upon William's appearance. "I do apologize for walking out on you so abruptly." He resumed his place at the head of the table. "Captain Witherington—" he paused. "I no longer see the need for pretense, do you?"

Michael shook his head.

"Good. Tell me why you took Charlotte."

"I meant to take Julia. Her return to Jamaica was well heralded once she was spotted in Barbados. I heard rumors that Shaw intended to grab her. I decided to take her first to protect her from Shaw." Michael, whose face did bear some resemblance to Sir Edward, traced his finger along the edge of the table. "You might not believe me, but over the last ten years, since striking out on my own, I have made a point of checking in on Julia regularly. She has always been under my protection."

He smacked his open palm against the table and then settled himself with a deep breath. "'Twas quite dark that night. I had not seen my sister up close since we were fourteen. And I did not know another young woman had accompanied her home. I saw a woman kissing a man in a Royal Navy uniform on the porch. I made the assumption it was Julia and took her. By the time I realized my mistake, we were too far away to return. The alarm must have already been raised. It was too dangerous to leave Miss Ransome alone and hope she could find her way back to the house. So we had to bring her with us. But I vow nothing untoward happened." He grinned. "Nothing except the escape attempts."

William would wait to hear those stories later. "What did you plan to do after kidnapping Julia?"

"Plant rumors that Shaw had her. Wait for you to subdue him and make sure he was no longer a threat. Then return Julia to Tierra Dulce."

"And then you would go back to pirating?"

"No, sir. Since Parliament abolished the transportation of slaves in British ships seven years ago, I have had to extend my hunting range to include the eastern coast of America. However, they have also since passed laws prohibiting the transatlantic transportation of slaves. Though I could still raid plantations overland and free slaves that way, that plan did not suit my men, who prefer to be at sea. So at the onset of war between America and England, I sailed north and enlisted my ship in the service of the United States as a privateer for two years." He withdrew a folded piece of parchment from his pocket and handed it to William.

William unfolded it, not surprised to see a letter of marque.

"In Philadelphia, a wealthy merchant offered to become my investor. But he insisted his son come aboard and serve as my first mate."

"Declan?" Ned interjected.

"Declan. While *Vengeance* underwent repairs in Mr. Declan's private shipyard, I spent time with the family, including the daughter, Serena. I fell in love with her and she with me. Her father invited me to join the family business when my term of service ended. The first year, we worked mainly along the coast. Nine months ago, when the attacks of American merchant ships coming out of New Orleans increased, we came south—after one last visit to Philadelphia. I asked Serena to marry me. So when this is over, I will return to Philadelphia and marry Serena and join Declan Importing."

"And what about your family? What about the debt you owe Sir Edward?" Sailing off into anonymity in America might have been a good plan before, but William could not allow Michael's offenses against Tierra Dulce and Sir Edward—and Julia—to stand.

"I intend to reunite with my sister. To beg her forgiveness for believing my family abandoned me so many years ago."

William prayed that reunion took place soon. "We shall determine all of the conditions for your release from the charges of piracy later. But there is one condition I must put to you now, because everything else hinges on it."

"And what is that?"

"Once we have subdued Shaw and delivered Julia safely home, you will return to England for Admiral Sir Edward Witherington to adjudicate your fate." William turned his gaze on Ned. "You will travel with Captain Cochrane on *Audacious*." Even though he planned on Ned serving on his station here in the Caribbean, Charlotte needed to go home and explain everything to their mother in person.

"And my ship?"

"I expect you planned to turn out all of your men and sail her back to Philadelphia with only a skeleton crew, newly recruited."

The expression on Michael's face proved William correct in his assumption.

"Then turn her over to your first officer to sail back to Philadelphia. Of course, you will need to rechristen her. Too many Royal Navy ships will be on the lookout for a pirate or privateer vessel named *Vengeance*."

Michael nodded. "I already have a name picked out. One that reflects the next stage of my life."

The slight smile and humored glint in Michael's eyes reminded William far too much of Julia. "And what is that name?"

"*Serenity*."

Chapter Eighteen

I don't care if you just looked. Look again." Shaw aimed his fist at the young man's head, but the teen ducked and bolted up the steps to the poop deck.

"We've waited a full day. Cap'n Iverson's never late—not this late, leastwise. How long are you planning on us staying here?" The first mate stood just beyond Shaw's reach. Wise man.

The little island—a rock with a couple of trees, really—surrounded by the vastness of the Caribbean had served as his meeting place with *Sister Mary* for three years. Captain Iverson knew what would happen to him if he decided to double-cross Shaw and steal away with *Sister Mary*, Shaw's first ship.

The sun edged toward the western horizon. "We'll wait until nightfall. Bring Captain Ransome to my cabin."

The first mate's dark eyes glittered. "Right away, Commodore."

Shaw paced, feeling like the tiger he'd seen at the Royal Menagerie at the Tower of London as a boy. He'd stood transfixed watching the predator rip apart a smaller animal and eat it. Yes, Shaw felt quite like that tiger.

When his first mate arrived with James Ransome, rather than allow him to walk in with dignity, he pushed the naval officer through the door. James's bound hands ensured he lost his balance. His knees hit the deck with a loud crack.

Shaw let him struggle for a while and then walked over, hooked his foot under James's shoulder, and flipped him over onto his back.

Before James could move, Shaw pressed the bottom of his boot to James's throat.

The prisoner's blue eyes bulged.

"Where is my other ship?" He eased up the pressure slightly.

"How should I know?"

Shaw lowered his foot again. "You came upon us in the exact rendezvous spot predetermined between me and my captain. There's no way you could have found us if you hadn't intercepted *Sister Mary* and found out from someone there where we were meeting."

James coughed and gasped for breath when Shaw lifted his foot completely off his throat. He rolled onto his side, to relieve the pressure on his hands. "I found you by my own intelligence and diligent tracking."

Shaw kicked him just below the ribs. James grunted and retched. Shaw liked that.

"Where is my ship?"

"We're on it!" James tried to curl into a ball to protect his gut from more blows.

Wrong answer. Shaw grabbed his dagger and crouched beside the younger man. He grabbed a fistful of dark hair to hold him still and pressed the tip of the blade to his cheek. Years of practice had taught him just how much pressure to exert to achieve the desired results.

James pressed his lips together, screwed his eyes shut, and breathed hard through his nose.

So many men believed a blade to the throat would frighten someone into telling what he knew. But actual pain was the best motivator Shaw had found.

"*Sister Mary.* Where is she?" Shaw put the point of his blade on the other cheek.

"I...do...not...know." Every muscle in James's throat and face tensed, blood vessels popping to the surface and throbbing in rhythm with his heart.

"If you did not attack *Sister Mary* and she is not yet here, that means someone else has intercepted her." Which meant they could probably expect another visitor soon. Shaw grabbed the water basin full of his used wash water and poured it over James's face in a slow, wide stream.

James sputtered and choked, turning his head from side to side, trying to escape the drowning flow.

Shaw shook the last few drops out of the bowl and put it back on the commode. "Collier!"

The steward appeared at once. "Yes?"

"Have Mrs. Ransome join me on the poop. And inform the captain of the," he paused to consider a moment, "starboard mainyard to make preparations. Captain Ransome is going to dance for us."

⬥⬥⬥⬥⬥

Julia pressed her back against the wall when the door opened. Collier filled the opening. "Commodore Shaw wants that you should join him for the entertainment."

The knot of nausea in her stomach grew. Aboard this ship, *entertainment* most likely did not include dancing or a concert. Julia maneuvered herself so that Collier took hold of her left arm instead of her sore right one. Not only did he seem to favor grabbing her right arm, his rough handling of her resulted in his thick knuckles bumping her injured ribs multiple times.

He led her up to the highest deck of the ship. Shaw turned and flourished a bow, a mocking expression on his face when he straightened. "My dear Mrs. Ransome. So kind of you to join me."

"I wish I could say it was my pleasure." The words slipped out before Julia could think better of it. She tensed, waiting for his blow, but his dimples deepened with his smile, though his eyes remained cold.

"You are just in time for the evening's entertainment." He nodded toward the quarterdeck.

Julia turned and swept the deck with her gaze. A larger number of sailors than necessary stood around on deck, and several men were aloft on the lowest yardarm on the starboard side of the mainmast.

"Captain Ransome," Shaw called, looking down into the crowd on deck. The men parted, allowing Julia to see her brother-in-law standing between two men, who held his arms.

Was that a noose around his neck? Julia grabbed Shaw's sleeve. "What are you about to do?"

Shaw pulled his arm away from her. "I warned you both that I would kill him."

"No! You cannot—"

Shaw seized her by the throat, stopping her air. She wrapped her hands around his wrist and tried in vain to pull him off. Pain roared in her ears; tears flooded her eyes. "That sounded like a demand to me, Mrs. Ransome. And we both know what happens when you try making demands."

She managed to nod her head. He let go and she gulped to refill her lungs, her cracked ribs shooting pain through her side.

He pulled her in front of him, his grip painful around her upper arms. "Music!"

At Shaw's command, the men on deck started singing a sea chantey, one Julia had never heard before and hoped she'd never hear again.

"Now, Captain Ransome, dance for us."

Atop the yardarm, three men pulled on a length of rope secured to a block-and-tackle on the yardarm above them. The line running from the block down to the noose around James's throat straightened and pulled tight. Julia turned her head away.

Shaw released her right arm, but then his hand settled over her side. He squeezed, hard.

Julia screamed as the pain of a dozen knives stabbed through her chest. Her stomach heaved, intensifying the pain as all of her muscles contracted.

"I planned this entertainment especially for you, Mrs. Ransome." He held his mouth so close to her ear, bits of spittle landed on her cheek. "You will do me the kindness of watching it."

Shallow, panting breaths were all she could manage. Her head spun, and her dirty, tangled hair stuck to the moisture on her cheeks. Shaw's hand remained on her side.

Below, James gasped and sputtered against the noose tightening around his throat, the toes of his boots still on the deck.

"Make him dance, boys!"

With one coordinated heave, the men hoisted James up into the air. A sob convulsed Julia's chest, generating more pain.

James's face bulged and darkened. His feet flailed, as if trying to find purchase.

How would she ever be able to explain to William that she did nothing but stand by and watch as Shaw murdered his brother? A haze of pain—physical and spiritual—enveloped her. How could the God William loved so dearly and had taught her to trust allow this to happen?

James's kicks slowed until they became mere twitches.

Shaw sighed. He once again pressed his mouth to her ear. "Are you as bored with this as I am?"

Julia made no attempt at a response.

Shaw laughed and raised his head. "Stop the music! Let him down."

The singing ended and the men released the rope, letting James fall several feet to the deck. He coughed, gagged, and gasped, drawing the laughter and ridicule of the sailors surrounding him.

"Collier!"

The steward rushed forward.

"See that our guests are returned to their quarters." With a wink and a flash of his dimples, Shaw left Julia to the tender mercies of his steward.

The horror of what she'd seen and the agony of her body made Julia insensible to everything around her. Collier could have dragged her down the several sets of stairs to her prison for all she knew.

She hit the back wall of the chamber and fell to the floor, her bound wrists preventing her from protecting her side. She longed to lose herself in sobs, but she would not give Collier—still standing in the doorway—the pleasure of reporting such discomposure to Shaw.

Collier moved, letting the wan light from his lantern flow into the little room. Julia scrambled out of the way just in time to keep James's inert form from landing atop her. Before the door closed, she caught sight of blood on his face and down the side of his neck.

He was so still.

Though it increased her agony, she managed to hunch over him and put her cheek close to his nose and mouth. He was breathing.

She pushed herself upright, leaning into the corner for support before losing her last measure of stoicism and letting the shock and terror overwhelm her.

Lord God, if You love William at all, please do not send him into this hell.

⬧⬧⬧⬧⬧

He should have put her ashore in Negril.

Ned tapped his fingers against the sides of his legs and paced another length of the quarterdeck. Never before had the prospect of a coming battle frightened him the way it did now. Because never before had someone he cared for so dearly been aboard his ship.

He should have insisted she stay with William.

Though also headed into the battle, *Alexandra* had the advantage of a full crew. But no matter how shorthanded *Audacious* might be, and no matter that he'd made Charlotte change into her remaining midshipman's uniform—for her own protection, in case something went wrong and they should be overtaken by the pirates—he had made her swear she would not leave the safety of the cabin, giving her the duty of protecting Gardiner, Jamison, and Kent.

At the same moment, everyone on deck seemed to tense and turn toward the wheelhouse. The sailing master's mate stepped forward and put his hand to the bell's clapper, eyes affixed to the large half hour glass beside the bell housing.

The last grains of sand fell into the bottom of the glass and the mate began striking the time.

Ned put all his strength behind his voice. "Loose the heads'ls. Hands aloft to loose the tops'ls."

With hours to review the plan, every officer, midshipman, and master knew his part and executed it admirably.

Still uncertain if it truly worked, Ned mumbled an entreaty for the Almighty's protection for everyone aboard *Audacious*, *Alexandra*, and *Vengeance* and for Mrs. Ransome.

If the man from *Sister Mary* was to be trusted, their three-pronged predawn attack should work, with each ship coming in on a different heading, trapping *Sister Elizabeth* in the middle. Four ships would have been better, but *Alexandra*'s and *Audacious*'s cannons had damaged *Sister Mary* beyond salvation. It was half sunk by the time his crew had returned to *Audacious* with the prisoners. Thankfully, William had insisted on their transfer to *Alexandra*.

He checked his watch, angling it to catch the moonlight. In ten minutes, they would reach the rendezvous point. "Clear for action."

"Captain!" Lieutenant Hamilton came to the back of the forecastle—not part of the plan. "There's debris in the water ahead, sir."

Ned ran to the bow and leaned over the catshead. Chunks of painted wood with splintered edges slapped against the hull. Pieces of another ship.

"Survivors?"

"None so far, sir." But Hamilton and the midshipman of the forecastle continued searching the water with their telescopes.

Something other than wood caught Ned's eye. Something bright atop the dark water. "Look over there. That seems to be fabric."

A sailor used a grappling hook to fish out the item. Ned pulled it off and snapped it open, splattering everyone with water.

A flag. And not just any flag. A British ensign. The concern in his gut showed in the expressions of the men surrounding him.

It could not be *Alexandra*. William was to have taken her on a northward tack and come at *Sister Elizabeth* on the opposite side from *Audacious*.

"Sir, is it…?" Hamilton could not seem to tear his eyes away from the flag.

Ned could not believe this was happening again. But this time he put his entire crew and ship at risk, not just a handful of men while he stood at a distance and watched them die. "It doesn't matter. We stay on course and follow our orders."

He returned to his position on the quarterdeck. This time if everything went wrong, at least he had been following someone else's orders. He only hoped he would not be blaming the failure and loss of life on a dead Commodore Ransome.

⋘⋙

"Man overboard!" Lieutenant Gibson's deep voice bellowed over the din of a ship under full sail preparing for battle.

"Where away?" William called back.

"Starboard, at about three points, sir."

William lifted his telescope and scanned the water. There, face down over a piece of floating debris.

Their mission brooked no delay, but if the man were still alive…

"Make preparations for rescue. Reef sails, pull in one of the boats."

His crew responded even as he called the commands. If only they had come across the man before clearing for action and putting out all the ship's boats filled with the food animals and other items from the ship that could get in the way or become dangerous shrapnel during battle.

Without removing the chicken pens, Gibson and a small group of sailors set out in the launch. With some difficulty they pulled the limp man into the boat and returned to *Alexandra* as fast as they could. As soon as all were on deck and the boat once again tethered to the stern, William gave the commands to get them back underway.

Inert no longer, the survivor coughed and sputtered. At the sight of William, he tried to rise, but William bent over him and pressed his shoulder down. "What ship are you from, Lieutenant?"

"HMS *In-Insolent*, sir. M-m-my name's Carey, sir. S-second lieutenant."

William pressed his hands to the deck to keep from falling over. "*Insolent*? Under command of Captain Ransome?"

"Aye, s-sir." The young man shivered. The officers and sailors standing around all turned worried gazes on William.

He ignored them. "What happened, Mr. Carey?"

Dr. Hawthorne arrived with a blanket and his medical kit. It took only one expressive glance from him to make the onlookers take a step back. "Commodore, it would be better if I took him below."

"In a moment, Doctor." William rebalanced his weight into a crouch. "Mr. Carey, what happened?"

"Captain Ransome heard that the pirate Shaw was sighted coming west, away from Kingston. We searched for three days. Yesterday, we came upon the pirate's ship. We were no match for them—outgunned, outnumbered. After the bombardment, they boarded, killing everyone."

No. Please. Not James. "Your captain?"

"They took him, sir, and then set the powder magazine to blow. I managed to jump overboard before they knew I was still alive."

"Commodore—"

"Yes, Doctor." William stood, his legs unsteady. He looked at the anxious faces around him and said, "Return to your duties."

"Aye, aye, sir." The men scattered to their posts. The doctor and his mates transferred Carey to a litter and took him below deck to the sick berth. William resumed his position on the quarterdeck.

He should have expected that James would disobey his direct order to stay out of this. William moved back toward the wheelhouse. "Lieutenant O'Rourke, inform the boarding party there is another prisoner to find. In addition to rescuing Mrs. Ransome, they are to search for a Royal Navy captain."

"Aye, sir. Do you know his name, sir?"

"Yes. Captain James Ransome. Tell them to search for someone who looks like me."

Chapter Nineteen

I heard you scream." James's voice rasped out of the darkness, startling Julia. She had dozed intermittently since coming back to their closet, so she wasn't certain how long James had been unconscious. Not that time existed here in the absolute dark.

"When Shaw's men ambushed me, they shot one of the horses and the carriage flipped over. I fell onto the edge of the door and, I think, cracked a few ribs. I made the mistake of letting Shaw's men know I was injured. As you well know by now, Shaw finds your every weakness and exploits it to get what he wants."

"How does almost killing me by hanging and then letting me down get him what he wants?" Scraping sounds came from his position, and she imagined him maneuvering himself into a seated position.

"It gains our cooperation." Julia twisted her wrists back and forth. After days of this exercise, she had a greater range of movement under the ropes. She could not keep it up for long, though, before the raw burning of her skin made her stop.

"I'm sorry."

Julia stopped moving, unsure she'd heard the whispered words properly. "Sorry?"

"That he caused you pain to make what I was going through worse. When I heard your scream, all I could think of was how I'd failed you."

"You have not failed me. There was nothing you could have done."

"I failed you by giving Shaw another method of causing you anguish. I saw William a week ago. He ordered me to follow my commodore's orders and not to get involved. But I was so angry at him—and worried about Charlotte—that I disobeyed him and set out after Shaw. I knew his ship was larger than mine, but in my arrogance I believed that with the element of surprise on my side, I could take *Sister Elizabeth*, rescue Charlotte, and gain more fame and fortune than William." His voice gave out at the end of his speech.

"You wanted to rescue your sister. That is an honorable quest."

"Not when it meant sacrificing the lives of more than three hundred men in an action I was not authorized to take. I know if I live that I will be court-martialed, and I will have no excuse to give for my action as the blame lies solely with me. But it is not that sentence I fear." He paused to clear his throat. "It is God's judgment, whether I meet it soon or a long time from now."

James could not have chosen a topic on which Julia felt less adequate to converse. But as Shaw had so vividly proven, neither of them knew how much longer their lives might last. "William has been trying to teach me more about God. I cannot articulate it as well as he, but it is my understanding that God wants us to trust Him entirely so that He can forgive us entirely. If we do not trust Him with everything we do, we will continue to make erroneous choices and do things that go against His will for our lives. Does that make any sense?"

"Some. But the problem lies in what to do when we have gone against His will. Then we will be judged and condemned."

Julia found her first smile since her ordeal began, remembering when she'd put a similar question to her husband in one of their many discussions on this topic. His example had helped her. It should help James. "When you were a child, did you ever disobey your mother?"

"Naturally. All children do."

"What did your mother do?"

"She made me confess, apologize, and promise I would never do it again."

"But did she condemn you? Cast you out?"

James coughed out a laugh. "No. She loved me."

"I have heard and read many Scriptures that say God is our Father and we are His children. So why would He not do the same as your mother: make us confess the wrong we have done, apologize—to Him and to others—and promise to never do it again?"

"But breaking a teacup with a cricket bat and condemning hundreds of men to their deaths are not the same—"

The door suddenly swung open. "Missus, you're to come with me now."

James tried to move between Julia and Collier, but she nudged him out of the way. "No. Rest. Regain your strength."

"I will pray for you, Julia."

"And I for you, James." Julia held her left elbow toward the steward so she could be yanked through the door.

Outside her prison, she was met with a storm of activity. The crew was clearing the ship for action. Her heart raced. Could rescue be at hand?

"James—" She tugged against Collier's grip.

"Commodore Shaw wants to see just you." He yanked her arm, and Julia yelped at the fresh jolt of pain through her chest. She also felt the rope around her wrists give slightly.

The companionway ended in the shade of the wheelhouse, but beyond the edge of the poop deck bright sunlight bathed the quarterdeck. Here, as below, the crew prepared for battle. Collier pulled her out into the sunlight and up the steps to the poop.

She scanned the waters around them. There. A ship off the larboard bow. And another astern. And a *third* to starboard. Three ships?

Shaw did not deign to look at her when Collier pushed her forward to stand beside him. "I see you are as surprised as I to see three ships bearing down on us."

"Are they pirates?" She wanted it to be William but could not think of a third ship he might bring with him.

"In your vernacular, no. In mine, yes. Your husband's ship"—Shaw pointed to the one off the larboard stern—"has already signaled me, demanding my surrender." He turned a wicked smile on Julia. "And you know how I feel about demands."

He took her by the shoulder and led her to the larboard gunwale. "Have a look, Mrs. Ransome. I would be remiss not to offer you the opportunity for one final moment to gaze upon your husband."

She took the spyglass he held out toward her and pressed it to her eye. Though still too far away to be in accurate firing range, the ship came into closer view through the telescope. She scanned each face in the forecastle until—

An involuntary cry leaped from her throat. "William!"

He lowered his spyglass so she could see his face, pressed his left hand to his heart, and then raised the glass again. Julia pressed the telescope and her bound hands to her heart.

Shaw snatched the telescope away from her and called for Collier. "Take her to the bilge. Tie her to a post. And take her across the quarterdeck to the forecastle."

Collier's wide-mouthed grin showed a myriad of missing teeth. "Aye, Commodore."

She gave up trying to struggle when the intensity of the pain in her side became unbearable. Below deck, she trotted to keep up with Collier crossing the length of the ship again. Then down three flights of stairs, finally ending below the orlop in the lowest portion of the ship.

Bilge water lapped at Julia's shoes and tugged the hem of her dress as it sloshed back and forth, following the motion of the ship.

Collier tugged her over to the nearest upright pole—a support beam, as the bases of the masts where they joined the bottom of the ship were enormous down here. He jammed her hands against the beam, as if expecting the rope to split apart to pass around the beam and then stitch itself back together on the other side.

He held his lantern aloft and looked around them. Frowning, he looked down.

"Hold that." He thrust the lantern into her hands and then reached down and untied the rope serving as his belt.

Julia lifted her eyes to the bottom of the deck above, just in case his pants gave way.

He looped the thinner rope down between her wrists, circled it around the beam, and tied the ends in a knot, leaving some slack in the loop.

Collier took the lantern back and splashed back toward the stairs. Julia let her eyes roam down the beam in the fading light. She stifled a gasp, hoping Collier did not hear her sharp intake of breath. He continued up the stairs.

A wan light—not light, really, but a memory of light filtering down through the three decks above—came down the companionway after Collier disappeared. Julia moved around the post so she faced astern. She pressed the sides of her hands against the beam and slowly pushed them upward until her fingers came in contact with something sticking out.

Excitement prickled her skin. The square iron peg wasn't large, just a nail, really, but rather than having a flat end, the end was sharp, as if part of the peg had been sheared away.

She stretched her arms as high as she could reach, panting against the throb in her side, and pulled her hands down until the rope around her wrists caught. She angled her hands to the right and rubbed the rope on the metal peg.

A loud boom shuddered through the ship, which jolted. Sharp-edged iron bit into the tender skin of her wrist. She adjusted the angle of her hands and kept rubbing as fast as she could as blasts and booms filled the air.

⌘⌘⌘⌘

If the pirate El Salvador were hiding prisoners aboard his ship, and if he had no value and respect for human life, where would he put them?

Michael Witherington lowered his spyglass. Why would Julia have been brought up the companionway under the poop deck but led away, once Shaw was assured everyone was watching, down the quarterdeck and through the forecastle? "She's in the aft section, likely the orlop or bilge."

"Sir? How can you be certain?" The sandy-haired lieutenant lowered his glass also.

"Because, Lieutenant Campbell, that's where I would hide her."

William Ransome's second lieutenant startled and then looked scandalized. Again, Michael wondered at Commodore Ransome's choice to send Campbell when a couple of the others had appeared eager at the idea of serving aboard a pirate ship, even if just for a few hours.

But other than trying to think like a pirate—like a vicious, bloodthirsty one—he had work to do now.

The smallest of the four ships now engaged in combat, *Vengeance* could do something *Alexandra* and *Audacious* could not: sidle up to *Sister Elizabeth* through the blinding smoke and dispatch a boarding party. Certainly, the addition of Lieutenant Campbell and several marines to *Vengance* left *Alexandra* shorthanded, because Ned already had no one to spare, and meant quite crowded quarters on *Vengeance*.

The billowing smoke enveloped the frigate, making it impossible to see from one end of the ship to the other.

"Marine guards and sharpshooters, aloft and to the starboard side now," Michael called, keeping his tone low but clear. "Jean Baptiste, take us in."

"Aye, Cap'n."

From their positions on the mast tops and along the yardarms, the sharpshooters—both William's marines and those from Michael's crew—fired down onto the deck of *Sister Elizabeth*.

Michael climbed the mainmast shroud to get a better look. Though the view was clearer from here, smoke still obscured the view. But even with the aid of his telescope, he did not see Shaw anywhere on deck.

Coward.

Beyond *Sister Elizabeth*, the hulking forms of the two Royal Navy ships, each at a forty-five degree angle off the bow and stern of Shaw's ship, looked like phantoms, appearing only briefly through the billows of roiling smoke.

Michael lowered himself to the deck and leaned over the hatch to the gun deck below. "Load chain shot and bar shot. We must put more of their battery out of commission before we draw closer."

"Aye, aye, Captain," Picaro called back.

"Jean Baptiste, lay off here."

"Aye, sir."

Michael returned to the shroud, scanning *Sister Elizabeth*'s deck. He would find Shaw, and when he did, the pirate El Salvador would make one final appearance.

୧୨୧୨

Charlotte sat in the chair directly across the table from the door to the wheelhouse, a loaded pistol on her lap and a cutlass on the table in front of her. Jamison and Gardiner sat to her left and right, similarly armed. Kent, however, paced behind them.

"I'm no child to be cosseted and cared for by a nursery maid. To be in the same room with you is a grievous insult. I will see that Cochrane and Ransome are both drilled out of the service—"

Jamison flew from his seat and pinned Kent to the wall, his forearm across Kent's collarbones. "You will hold your tongue still in your mouth, you ungrateful wretch."

Lieutenant Gardiner stood but made no move to interfere in the midshipmen's quarrel.

Charlotte also rose, not wanting to interfere, but she stepped forward and gently extricated the loaded pistol from Jamison's other hand.

Kent blinked and then squeezed his eyes shut as if trying to clear them of a foreign object. He'd been doing that regularly ever since they returned from *Sister Mary*. And if he happened to be standing at the time, usually wavered and needed to reach out to steady himself. Charlotte hoped for his sake that whatever ailed his vision and balance would correct itself as his other injuries healed.

"You spent five weeks making Charles Lott's life miserable because you were jealous of Lott's skills and knowledge, and perhaps you were frightened Lott would prove you did not deserve to be a watch captain, regardless of your seniority. Charles Lott was one of the finest midshipmen I've ever had the pleasure of serving with. So Charles

Lott turned out to be Charlotte Ransome. Who cares? To me, it makes Charles Lott's accomplishments all the more extraordinary. So still your tongue or I will still it for you." Jamison held Kent there a bit longer and then released him.

"I'll see you're out too, Jamison—"

"That is quite enough, Mr. Kent. You are bordering on insubordination. Now sit down and be quiet. That is an *order* from the first lieutenant of this ship." Lieutenant Gardiner stared at Kent until the younger man looked away.

As Charlotte reached for her chair the ship rocked, throwing her off balance.

"That was a hit for certain." Jamison, whose eyes were still puffy and bruised, squinted toward the door.

"I can't stand this any longer." Kent grabbed his gun and cutlass and ran from the room.

"He's going to get himself—or someone else—killed." Charlotte grabbed her weapons, sheathing the cutlass and tucking the gun under her belt. She ran from the dining cabin and out through the wheelhouse, shading her eyes against the glare of the sun and the sting of the smoke, searching the confusion on deck for the white blond head she'd come to know oh so well during her time as Charles Lott, mainly so she could avoid him.

"Kent! Mr. Kent!" She ducked and wove amongst the sailors and gun crews, her eyes straining against the glare and smoke.

Someone grabbed her arm. "What are you doing here? You swore you would stay to the cabin."

Never had she seen Ned so angry, but this was no longer about her. "It's Kent. He's out here somewhere. I have to find him. His eyes—his balance. He's a danger to everyone, especially to himself."

Ned growled and released her arm. "Find him, fast, and get him back to the main cabin."

"Aye, aye, sir."

Ned disappeared into the fray again. Charlotte raised up on her toes, trying to see over the rest of the crew. Oh, to have Declan's height.

Declan! He could help. She turned, scanning the deck for the giant. There, just a few yards away.

Someone yelled, "Take cover."

Charlotte ducked but kept moving toward Declan. Grapeshot pounded into everything at a certain height above the deck—from masts to rigging to men. Declan disappeared during the barrage, but popped up, bellowing orders as soon as the gun crews on *Sister Elizabeth* stopped to reload.

"Mr. Declan, I need your help—"

"You're not supposed to be out here." Without ceremony he grabbed her around the waist, lifted her off her feet, tucked her under his arm, and started back toward the main cabin.

She slapped and smacked at his arm. "Let me down. I have to find Kent. He's injured. He can't see well. He's out here on deck. You have to find him so I can take him back."

Declan finally set her down. "What's he look like?"

"Tall—well, compared to me, he's tall."

"Everyone is tall compared to you."

"I will laugh at that joke later, I promise." She held her hand up to a height about eight inches above the top of her own head. "About this tall, white blond hair. Sharp features like…like a bird. Wearing a midshipman's uniform."

If Declan held his arms out to the side, he would look like a capstan. He turned slowly around, scanning the crowd. "He's in the forecastle. Want that I should go fetch him?"

"What?" It took her a moment to translate his question. "No. You're needed here. I'll go."

Staying low—which also helped in pushing her way through the sea of bodies crowding the deck—Charlotte reached the forecastle.

"Mr. Kent, return to the big cabin. You are in direct violation of your orders!" Lieutenant Duncan held Kent's wrists, perhaps trying to get the midshipman to drop the short sword and pistol he wielded. "Mr. Lott, get Mr. Kent off the deck."

"Aye, aye, sir." But Kent wasn't going to come back at her request, and she couldn't overpower him. So…"Mr. Kent, you're needed at the cannon in the big cabin. They're making a right mess of it and need someone with your experience."

He turned to look at her. The glazed look in his eyes probably had something to do with why he did not immediately begin hurling insults at her. "Take me to it. I'll show them how it's done. Captain Parker will see. He'll write me the letter of preferment to stand for the lieutenancy early."

Charlotte looked at Duncan, whose face showed the panic she felt. If Kent no longer remembered that Captain Parker was dead, that he had died a week after setting out from England, Kent's mind had gone.

"Take cover!"

Everyone dropped to the deck.

Everyone but Kent.

Charlotte stood to pull him down. Grapeshot and shrapnel whistled past. She wrapped her arms around Kent's middle and twisted, turning her back toward the incoming missiles and crooked her knee into the back of Kent's, making his buckle. They started to go down, but Kent recovered his balance and straightened again, babbling on about taking the lieutenant's examination.

"Mr. Kent, get down!" Duncan crawled toward them and grabbed Kent's wrists and started pulling down.

Charlotte wrapped her arms around his neck from behind and pushed herself off the deck with her feet, putting her entire weight on his back. Finally he started to go down.

Searing pain scorched the back of Charlotte's left arm. Kent fell to his knees and Charlotte rolled off his back and onto the deck. She reached around to feel her left sleeve to see if it was on fire.

No, but it was wet. She pulled her fingers away, covered in blood. Her blood.

She'd had her share of injuries during her service on *Audacious*, but most had been bruises and minor abrasions. Nothing like this.

She floated into the air. No, someone carried her. She blinked to clear her eyes of excess moisture. Declan, a deep scowl on his face, jumped down from the forecastle and started down the companion-way to the main gun deck.

He set her down on one of the tables in the sick berth and then reached one long arm out, grabbed the surgeon's mate's shoulder, and pulled him over. "Fix her."

With that, he left.

Charlotte and the mate stared at each other a moment, both uncertain as to what had just transpired.

"You're bleeding."

"I got shot."

"Probably why." The surgeon's mate smiled at her and set to treating her wound.

Chapter Twenty

Julia continued her awkward, painful, and unrhythmic dance with the post. The shooting pain in her side served to clear her mind of anything but a singular focus: escape. Each volley *Sister Elizabeth* fired and each broadside it received recoiled and rocked the ship. With her hands held over her head as she rubbed the rope over the broken iron peg, every jolt upset her balance.

The bilge water now reached her knees—and she expected every moment that her attempt to free herself would be thwarted by the arrival of the master carpenter and his mates to man the pumps.

After what felt like hours, the rope started to give way. She increased her intensity—and ignored the heat the friction caused.

The loop of rope went lax. Julia lowered her hands and used her teeth to pull at it, and it uncoiled, falling away. In moments she extricated herself from the bindings. She stretched and flexed her hands, arms, and shoulders, delighting in the freedom of movement but was glad of the dark—she did not want to see the truth of the bloody mess her wrists must be, from the nicks and cuts made in the sensitive flesh by the peg.

She struggled against the rising water to get to the stairs. She looked up. No one was standing at the top; at least, not that she could see in the deeper-than-twilight darkness. She cautiously ascended, finding the orlop deserted.

She oriented herself and recognized the passageway leading to the hold. She felt her way along the path between crates of supplies and goods until she reached the walls of the supply rooms.

The second door. Her hands came in contact with the iron bolt, and she slid it back and pulled the door open.

"James?"

No response. She moved into their prison cell, leaning over to feel with her hands in case he lay on the floor.

The space was empty. Frustration pressed painfully against the inside of her head. If James was not here, she could only think of two other places he might be—with Shaw or dead. And if he was with Shaw, James's death would not be far off.

Rather than continue up the stern companionway, she moved forward, to the stairs near the mainmast. This flight led her to the lower gun deck and utter mayhem. Smoke filled the space, shadowy figures churning through it. Voices, orders, screaming, and cannon blasts assaulted her ears.

She crouched under the companionway leading up to the main gun deck, but no one took notice of her. Before they could, she rounded the over-worked stairs and ran up.

Here on the main gun deck, chaos also reigned. Light streaming through the grates covering the hatches above glared off the smoke.

The smoke swirled. Someone ran toward her. She ducked under the stairs, wishing for anything she could use as a weapon.

The pirate stopped and pinned her with an astonished stare. She readied herself to fight him off, but before she could he started running again.

Julia didn't wait any longer. She climbed the last set of steps. Near the top, she paused, peeking over the edge of the opening in the quarterdeck. Smoke and noise and men and bodies and blood…

No. She couldn't focus on that. Climbing up onto the deck, she crouched and ran a few feet to take cover between the rigging brace and the mainmast.

Through the haze of smoke, off *Sister Elizabeth*'s starboard, the smaller unknown vessel looked as if it was trying to get close enough to send a boarding party. Marines—yes, she could see their red coats—were aloft on the yards shooting down into the bedlam about Julia. She could not see more than hints of the two ships at the bow and stern.

Shaw would be somewhere safe, somewhere out of the range of bullets, cannonballs, and shrapnel. His cabin. But he would also want William to be able to see James.

Alexandra was the ship to the stern. Julia rose, scanning the back of the quarterdeck and what she could see of the poop. If Shaw had James on display, he would be somewhere back there, not only visible but vulnerable.

Fire seared her shoulder, and she fell back against the rigging brace. She looked down. A scorch mark marred her sleeve, but, thankfully, the bullet had done no more than graze her.

Fear vibrated through her limbs. Julia took a deep breath, prayed for protection, and stood again.

A bullet thudded into the thick wood of the brace mere inches from her hand. She dropped to the deck. The jolt made something in her side pop, and for a moment, she couldn't breathe. Her head spun and her stomach churned. But then, almost as quickly, the agony started receding. The sharp, stabbing pain she'd had ever since Shaw had compressed her side during James's hanging was gone. She tested herself by moving her arm about. Her side ached and pulled, but she could live with it.

The intensity of the fighting increased along the starboard side of the quarterdeck. The crew of the other ship must be preparing to invade.

She had to find James. She stood—and the world exploded.

❦

Terror ripped through Michael's throat as *Sister Elizabeth*'s mainmast snapped and tipped toward the ship's larboard side.

The exploding shell had landed in the cavity pounded out in the thick wood by constant bombardment. And he'd rejoiced.

Until he saw a flash of long reddish-brown hair and fluttering blue fabric disappear behind the smoke and debris of the explosion.

His crew and the men from *Alexandra* swung over to *Sister Elizabeth*, emptying his ship and beginning the boarding that would be the last act Michael and *Vengeance* would play in this battle.

But he couldn't leave her there. Not if she was hurt—or worse.

Disregarding the agreement he'd made with William Ransome—that he would not take part in boarding the pirate ship—Michael climbed up the mainmast shroud, grabbed a line, and swung over to the deck of the larger ship.

Something hit his back. He grabbed his cutlass and turned. A pirate wielding a canvas bag weighted with what was probably a cannonball staggered a few steps away and then turned. Seeing Michael, he roared and raised the bag over his head, whirling it like a slingshot.

Michael ducked under his arm, and the bag hit the deck. The impact ripped the canvas, and the cannonball rolled harmlessly away. Michael knocked the man in the back of the head with his sword hilt, and the pirate crumpled to the deck.

He dispatched three more men similarly as he fought to get through the fracas.

At the base of the mast, sticking out under a tangle of rigging line, was a small-heeled boot and blue fabric.

Michael sheathed his sword and pulled the ropes away. His sister lay prone, arms over her head, left sleeve torn and bloody at the shoulder. He slid his hand under her torso to lift her.

She groaned.

He shouted with relief. Julia was still alive.

Now he had to keep her that way.

He hoisted her over his shoulder and drew his cutlass again. In the brief time it had taken him to rescue her, the tide of battle on deck had turned—in his favor. He reached the side of the ship with no resistance, found a line, and returned to *Vengeance*.

Jean Baptiste met him and assisted in lowering Julia to the deck.

"We've accomplished our mission. Get us out of here."

"Aye, aye, Cap'n."

Michael crouched over his sister's inert form, pushing her tangled, dirty hair back from her face. He looked up at Lau, who also hovered near. "Light the fires."

"Aye, Cap'n."

William had a surgeon aboard his ship. The idea of having a doctor examine Julia and treat her injuries struck Michael as a good one, but he could not risk that William would refuse to let Michael see her if he turned her over.

He swung her up into his arms and carried her to his cabin, placing her in Charlotte's hammock. "I promise I will make everything right." He kissed her forehead and then returned to deck.

Sailing *Vengeance* with so few men required more of everyone than they were accustomed to. But with the smoke of battle, combined with the heavy black smoke from the pitch and oakum fires burning in strategic points along *Vengeance*'s deck providing cover, they slipped away unnoticed.

With only half the sails unfurled, gaining distance from the battle took time and energy. But the wind cooperated and picked up strength, guiding the frigate away from the thunderous skirmish.

Michael raised his spyglass. *Alexandra* had moved in to try to fill the void left by *Vengeance*'s departure, but *Sister Elizabeth* had sustained enough damage that it would never be able to run away from the two Royal Navy ships.

"Lau, spread all canvas. Jean Baptiste, set course."

The boatswain and sailing master obeyed. Michael closed the telescope and returned to his cabin.

Suresh leaned over the hammock, the washbasin in one hand, a bloodied rag in the other. The steward had managed to remove Julia's dress, leaving her in chemise, corset, and petticoats, which were soiled to the knee with what smelled like bilge water.

"She has many injuries, Captain."

Michael joined him at his sister's side. Her face now clean, he worried at her paleness—and her puffy eye and bruised cheek.

Suresh dropped the rag in the basin and held up one of Julia's arms to reveal inflamed, red rope burns on the outsides of her wrists, and several fresh, shallow, horizontal cuts on the insides.

"Looks like she found something sharp to rub the rope against to release herself." Suresh set her hand down by her side. "When I tried to roll her onto her side so I could check her back for injuries, she cried out when I put pressure here"—he touched the right side of her ribcage—"so she may have broken ribs."

"She woke up?"

"Not completely. She muttered something and then was gone again."

"What did she say?"

Suresh shook his head. "Nothing I understood." He carried the basin to the table and returned with strips of white cloth. "I will bandage her wrists now. I have put water on to heat so you can bathe, Captain."

Michael sat down and began pulling at a boot.

"Is she who I think she is, Captain?"

"Who do you think she is?" He got the first boot off and started on the second.

"Your sister, Julia Ransome."

"Yes, she's who you think she is."

"Why did you take her, Captain? You never said that was part of our mission."

Michael dropped his second boot on the floor with a sigh. "It wasn't. But I could not stand by and watch her die when I was close enough to do something about it."

He stood, collected his boots, and moved toward his sleeping cabin. "This whole nightmare began because I wanted to protect my sister. I could not let it end with her dying only feet away from me."

❧❧❧

The slashing, hacking, deadly blade sent vibrations of rage up Shaw's arm and straight to his heart. He was the greatest pirate to have sailed these waters since Bartholomew Roberts, Henry Morgan, or Black-beard. Men fell silent in fear at the mere mention of his name.

He forced the young officer up the steps to the poop. His ship might be failing, but he would not. He would kill James Ransome and then he would kill Julia. Or maybe he would take her with him and enjoy her company a little longer before killing her. After all, there was so much they had not done together yet.

Terror filled the eyes of the boy on the business end of Shaw's sword. If his men hadn't fallen so easily to the attackers, Shaw would stop this fight now and offer the lad a choice. Death or joining the crew of *Sister Elizabeth*. A vital recruitment strategy. One that had gained Shaw some of his best men over the years.

But this morning, his crew had failed him.

That was fine. He would start over. Start fresh. A new ship. A new crew.

He brought his blade up at an angle and swiped the cutlass from the midshipman's hand. The lad fell back from the force of the blow. Shaw swung his sword around and brought it down hard.

The midshipman rolled out of the way. Shaw turned to follow him and—

Pain—hot, searing, and spreading through his gut. He looked down.

The midshipman still held the smoking pistol pointed toward him. Shaw dropped his sword, the strength ebbing from his arms. His legs went numb and he crumpled to the deck. He clutched his stomach, hot liquid oozing through his fingers.

Gut shot. The best way to kill an enemy. Shoot him in the stomach and watch him die a slow, agonizing death.

This wasn't how it was supposed to end. When he died, it was to be glorious, in battle with an enemy even greater than himself. An enemy he had yet to find.

The fighting continued around him. Did not one of his men care that their captain lay dying? One of the Royal Navy ships should have a good surgeon. They should take him, force him to care for Shaw, and bring him back to health so he could continue his quest to defeat the Ransomes and Witheringtons.

He would rest for just a while.

Lying back on the deck, he thought back to when this battle truly began. Fifteen years ago. He had been a pirate for five years, had worked his way up through the ranks until he was first mate for one of the most notorious pirates of the age—until Shaw had overthrown him and taken that title.

When the survivors from the Royal Navy frigate had been brought aboard to be held for ransom, Shaw discovered Michael Witherington among them. He suggested to the captain that he take the boy under his wing. Convince Michael his family no longer wanted him. Make him turn against them.

And it worked. Shaw dreamed of the day when he had Edward Witherington under his blade and revealed Michael—Shaw's first officer and right hand—to his father. Revealed how Arthur Winchester had been able to take Witherington's son away from him, just as Witherington had taken everything away from Arthur.

But then Michael turned on him. Convinced the captain what they were doing was bad.

Shaw turned his head. Not as many men still fighting. His vision blurred.

But Michael never returned to his father. So Shaw left him alone. Waited for the right time to reveal his existence.

Water. He needed water. He rolled his head the other way. Where was Collier?

A shadow fell over him. He looked up.

Ransome.

"Here's his sword, Commodore." The midshipman who had felled him handed his sword over to Commodore Ransome.

Shaw reached for it. One swift blow, and he could take William Ransome down with him.

"Well done, Midshipman Kennedy. Congratulations. The bounty for bringing down Shaw is a rich one."

"It should be shared by both crews, sir. I was only doing my duty, just like every other man here."

Shaw wanted to laugh at the pious youth, but all that came up was a bloody cough.

"Very good, Mr. Kennedy. Help the others with the prisoners."

Shaw turned his head again. The fighting had stopped. His men had surrendered. He struggled to sit up, but his body would not respond to him.

William Ransome crouched beside him. "Taken down on the deck of his own ship by a sixteen-year-old midshipman. An ignominious end to a bloody and brutal career."

"It…should…have…been you." A hate so cold it stole all the warmth from his body settled over Shaw.

"Yes, I should have been the one to take you down. It is sad when boys are thrust into battle at so young an age. Taking a life is not easily forgotten." William turned the cutlass over in his hands, examining the etching in the silver hilt.

"Tw-twenty years ago…should have killed you."

Ransome frowned. "Twenty years ago?" He seemed to think on it and then shrugged. "If we met then, I do not recall. You do not leave as deep a first impression as you seem to think."

Shaw reached up to choke the smugness out of Ransome's voice, but Ransome batted his hand away.

"Where is my wife?"

"She's…dead. Drowned in the bilge." Shaw laughed, blood filling his mouth, darkness obscuring his vision.

"I see."

Shaw struggled for breath. "Your brother—"

"Yes. We found him, tied to the mizzenmast. My surgeon is even now looking after him. He took two bullets, but his injuries are much less severe than yours." He looked away a moment and then back down at Shaw, a different, almost apologetic expression on his face. "If you ask God to forgive you, He will. And though you cannot make reparations with everyone whom you have wronged, I will forgive you, if you ask."

Cold, stark blackness pressed in around Shaw.

"Don't throw away your afterlife as you've thrown away your life, Arthur."

Too late. It was too late for him.

Chapter Twenty-One

William reached down and closed the pirate's eyes, feeling guilty over having spent so much of Shaw's last minutes of life taunting him over his defeat. He would answer to God for that in the hereafter.

Ned joined him. "Is he…?"

"Dead? Yes."

"Congratulations, sir."

"The honor goes to Mr. Kennedy." He handed Shaw's cutlass to Kennedy, a token of his victory, and then headed for the steps to the quarterdeck. "My brother?"

"Returned to *Alexandra*, and, even now, I am certain, under the care of Dr. Hawthorne."

"And the rest?" On the quarterdeck, William made for the main companionway.

Ned's boots thumped against the deck behind him. "Of *Audacious*, nine dead and more than a hundred injured, ten seriously. Of *Alexandra*, twelve dead and more than a hundred injured, about twenty seriously. *Vengeance* sailed off during the battle. Several men reported seeing thick smoke billowing from her decks—Sir, where are you going?"

"Shaw said she's in the bilge."

"Oh." Ned grabbed two lanterns and handed one to William.

They descended to the bowels of the ship in silence. In the bilge the water reached William's knees.

"Commodore," the master carpenter looked up from his bilge

pump. "Water's down fourteen inches. No major damage that cannot be patched so we can get her back to port, sir."

"Did you find…anyone? I was told a prisoner was being held down here." William held his light high, his eyes searching from end to end.

"Hadn't seen anyone, sir. And we've examined the entire space."

Shaw's words echoed in his head. If she'd drowned, the water was deep enough—but no, the water wasn't *that* deep. William's gut clenched. Shaw had lied to him. Where else would he have kept her?

He turned to Ned. "Have the men stop what they're doing and search the ship for Julia. Go, now. I'll start on the orlop."

"Aye, aye, sir." Ned ran back up the stairs.

William checked every crevice, every corner, every closet and knocked on every crate in the aft section of the orlop. Ned rejoined him, along with Dawling.

They made their way forward, passing several others, and then went up to the lower gun deck. By the time they reached the quarterdeck, the sun had passed its zenith…but William's heart had sunk to the bottom of the sea.

"Commodore Ransome!" A midshipman climbed up onto the quarterdeck from the accommodation ladder and then ran to William, stopping with a salute. "Sir, message from Doc Hawthorne. Your brother is awake and asks to speak with you."

For now, there was nothing more William could do here. He turned to Ned. "Keep searching."

"Aye, aye, sir."

Fear benumbed William, body and soul, and memories of the accounts of those who had survived being held prisoner by Shaw ran through his mind. If, as Michael Witherington had suggested, Shaw had a personal vendetta against William and Sir Edward, Julia had not fared well at his hand. But Shaw had taken effort to show Julia to William—a dirty, bedraggled Julia, but Julia nonetheless—and then sent her below before the battle started. She must be on that ship somewhere.

He entered at the main gun deck entry port instead of climbing all the way up to *Alexandra*'s quarterdeck. The majority of his crew—the ones who hadn't boarded *Sister Elizabeth*—worked on cleaning up and repairing *Alexandra*.

"Commodore on deck!"

All activity stopped as the men turned to pay their respects to their commander—the sailors knuckling their foreheads, midshipmen and lieutenants touching the brims and fore points of their hats. William touched his hat and then made his way forward to the sick berth.

Dr. Hawthorne looked up from the patient on his table and nodded toward the hammocks hung near the open gun port.

James sat in the square hammock closest to the portal, staring out it at the side of *Sister Elizabeth*.

"James."

His brother looked around, and William's chest tightened. How could his brother issue such palpable horror with so vacant an expression? William moved closer and settled his hand on his brother's shoulder. "What happened?"

Red scabs traced cuts across both sides of James's face. Bandages wrapped around his throat, his chest, his wrists, his left thigh. "I disobeyed your orders, Will."

William winced at the gruffness of his brother's voice, a hoarse sound from more than smoke inhalation. "Yes, I realize that."

"I wanted to prove to you that I could be just as cunning, just as bold as you. So I tracked Shaw down. His ships had been seen near this islet before." Under the bandage, James's throat convulsed and he coughed.

William reached around to the barrel behind him and handed a dipper of water to his brother. James took a few sips, grimacing as he swallowed.

"Shaw destroyed my ship. Killed my entire crew."

William took the dipper James handed back to him and returned it to its hook over the barrel. "Not your entire crew. Second Lieutenant Carey survived also. If he did, there may be others as well."

James squeezed his eyes shut, and his face contorted in pain. For all that William had the right to berate him, to lecture him about not following orders and living with the consequences, he knew his brother did not need to hear it. James would punish himself worse than any panel of officers would do at his court-martial.

Haltingly, and taking pauses for water when his voice gave out, James reported what had happened to him while aboard *Sister Elizabeth*.

"She screamed, William. Screamed as if she was being tortured, and there was nothing I could do to help her." Tears streamed from the corners of James's eyes.

Waves of fury wracked William's body. If Shaw were not already dead…

"She said Shaw knew she had broken ribs and squeezed them, that's why she screamed. She was wonderful, afterward, reassuring me and giving me more comfort than I deserved. Then Shaw sent for her and they took her away. I didn't see her again after that. A short while later, they came and got me, tied me to the mizzenmast so you could see me and so, Shaw hoped, I'd be killed in the battle before you could get to me."

"Where did Shaw put her during the battle?"

"I don't know."

Leaning over the portal, William smashed the side of his fist against the gunwale.

"Where is she? I need to thank her." James used the bandages on his wrists to wipe his face.

"We haven't found her yet." William flexed his throbbing hand.

"What do you mean? I saw one of the officers take her off the deck." William turned quickly to face his brother. "Who?"

James shrugged. "Looked like the captain of the frigate that came alongside starboard and sent the first boarding party. He had her over his shoulder, like she might have been unconscious."

Michael Witherington. William should never have trusted the man's declarations that he wanted to turn his back on piracy, wanted to make reparations and reunite with his family. He wasn't supposed to board *Sister Elizabeth*. He was supposed to discharge the boarding party and sail away, making it look as though *Vengeance* were on fire so that the story could be spread that, while trying to assist the Royal Navy in battle, Salvador and his ship had burned.

"William?"

Taking a composing breath, William inclined his head to his brother. "I will pray for a swift recovery, James. We will talk more later."

Leaving his brother sputtering behind him, William climbed to the quarterdeck. "Lieutenant O'Rourke."

The first officer gave the group of sailors around him one final order and then hurried to William with a salute. "Aye, Commodore?"

"How long until we are ready to sail?"

"Another hour. Two at most, sir."

William wanted to leave now. He had a brother-in-law to hunt down and arrest. "Very good. Put together a prize crew, Lieutenant O'Rourke. You will take command of *Sister Elizabeth* and sail her back to Kingston Harbor."

O'Rourke's face twitched with his effort to keep from smiling. "Aye, aye, sir."

"I shall give you written orders shortly. You are to retain command of *Sister Elizabeth* until I join you there. You are not to turn her over to anyone at Fort Charles. Understood?"

"Aye, Commodore."

"She is our prize, and until the new admiral arrives from England, I do not want any question raised as to the possession or disposition of the ship or anything on it." Then, as soon as he returned and could take command of the fort, he would ensure that it ran with the efficiency and honesty it should.

"Aye, sir." O'Rourke saluted again and hurried away, a bounce in his step.

Giving orders, thinking through strategy and tactics, salved William's anxiety. He returned to his cabin to write O'Rourke's orders, as well as a message for the captain at the fort reiterating them. He also wrote a note for Jeremiah Goodland and tucked it in with O'Rourke's orders to have a messenger carry it to Tierra Dulce.

Though he could not attest to Julia's health or well-being, writing the words to assure her friends that she was alive, that Charlotte, too, was rescued, calmed him further.

That was good. He needed to be calm, reasonable even, when he arrested Michael Witherington for abducting Julia.

◈◈◈

Ned splashed water on his face and rubbed it vigorously with his hands. After two nights of little sleep and the exertion and intensity of battle, he wanted nothing more than to climb into his hammock and sleep. But first he must find his wayward bride.

He'd been disappointed, but not surprised, when he returned to *Audacious* to find an empty dining cabin and great cabin.

With a fresh waistcoat and coat, he set out to assess damages and figure out where Charlotte had gotten herself off to.

Lieutenant Gardiner stood on the quarterdeck, directing officers and crew in the cleanup and repair that needed to be done. He reported the progress.

"And Mrs. Cochrane?"

"Never came back after Kent ran off, sir."

"Thank you, Mr. Gardiner." The work progressed apace on the quarterdeck, so Ned headed down to the main gun deck. Lieutenant Wallis gave his report and also said he hadn't seen Charlotte.

Frustrated, Ned moved forward, following voices toward the infirmary.

He stepped into the sick berth and was met with tumult. Declan's broad back blocked most of it from view, but it quickly became apparent what was happening.

"I won't be saved by a girl. She shouldn't be here. I'll have her arrested. They will all be drummed out of the navy."

Ned stepped around Declan. The pirate leaned over a surgery table striving to hold down a struggling Midshipman Kent.

"Mr. Kent, you'll hush your mouth or I'll do it for you." The concern in Declan's face belied his threat.

"What is happening here?"

"Captain Cochrane, sir." The surgeon's mate—the one who had to take over after *Audacious*'s doctor died in the attack the week after leaving England—jumped back and knuckled his forehead. "I don't know what he's on about, sir. But there's something wrong. He's not rational, sir. Has a bump on the head, so I'm wondering if his senses got knocked out. Keeps talking about how Midshipman Lott, here, is a girl and he doesn't want Mr. Lott to touch him."

Charlotte, who had been leaning over someone in one of the hammocks turned, a damp compress in her hand.

"Is there nothing you can do for him?" Ned asked the mate.

"I can give him something to make him sleep, sir, but Doc Hawthorne needs to see him. He's a real doc. He might know something about how to get his senses back, sir." The surgeon's mate wiped his hands nervously on his bloody smock.

"Do it. Mr. Declan, will you help transport Mr. Kent to *Alexandra*'s surgeon?"

"Aye, Cap'n."

Declan had to hold Kent's mouth open so the mate could pour a liquid medication down his throat. Everyone, even the other injured sailors, watched as Kent's struggles lessened before ceasing altogether.

"Very good." Ned locked eyes with Charlotte. "I need to speak with you."

"Aye, Captain." Charlotte bent down, rewet the compress, and then put it on the patient's forehead before following him out of the cabin.

"What happened?" Ned pulled her away from the gun crew working on the cannon just outside the infirmary.

"He's been acting strangely ever since we rescued him. Off balance, blinking like he can't see clearly. Bursts of anger, according to Mr. Jamison. But in the cabin during the battle, he became insensible, yelling about…well, you heard him." She dropped her head, cheeks red.

"And then he ran out of the cabin," Ned prompted.

"Yes, sir. I had to chase him all the way to the forecastle. Lieutenant Duncan was trying to subdue him but couldn't, sir. Kent was armed. He could have hurt someone. We were taking return fire from *Sister Elizabeth*, sir, and so I had to help get him down so that he wouldn't get shot. It took two sailors to get him to the infirmary. I stayed there to help with the wounded, sir. There were so many, extra hands were needed."

Ned nodded, struggling to keep from smiling at the way Charlotte had transformed from young woman to midshipman the longer she spoke. Her stance changed—square shoulders, upheld head—her voice deepened, and even the cadence of her speech changed.

"When we brought him back from *Sister Mary*, he did have a head injury, sir. He may have been concussed, and that could have caused his confusion, sir."

"Thank you for so fine a report, Midshipman Lott."

Charlotte startled at being so addressed, and then she laughed and hugged him.

Oh, how he wanted to hold her, to kiss her. But he took her arms and pushed her back. It would not do for the captain to be seen hugging someone in a midshipman's uniform.

"Oh!" Charlotte pulled her left arm out of his grasp.

"Are you injured?"

"It is nothing. Just a scratch."

He narrowed his eyes at her but took her word for it.

Declan came out of the infirmary, carrying Kent. "Ready, Cap'n."

"What shall I do?" Charlotte asked.

"Stay in the sick berth and help if you are still needed. If not, return to the big cabin. I imagine we will be getting under way soon." He smiled at her, trying not to think about the fact that they were married and that he would like nothing more than to kiss her until the memory of this day was wiped from both of their minds.

"Aye, sir." Charlotte disappeared back into the sick berth.

"She tell you she got shot?" Declan asked.

Ned shoved the infirmary door open. Charlotte turned, startled. "What is it? What's wrong?"

"You got *shot*?" He unbuttoned her coat and pulled it off her left shoulder.

"I told you it is nothing. It had stopped bleeding by the time Declan got me down here."

The full sleeve of her white shirt was stained with dried blood, but the bandage wrapped around her upper arm showed no signs of bleeding. "When did this happen?"

"Whilst saving the life of this ungrateful scoundrel." From the other side of the doorway, Declan indicated Kent with a twitch of his head. "But don't you worry none, sir. I'll make him apologize when he wakes up. You can count on that."

Ned turned back to Charlotte. "We will discuss this later."

Charlotte gave him a sardonic smile. "Aye, sir."

With a final warning look, which she turned her back on, Ned left the infirmary and led Declan up on deck. All of his officers were busy either here or on *Sister Elizabeth*. Ned found several idlers who had finished their tasks and soon commanded a launch across the distance to *Alexandra*.

William had his crew lower the bosun's chair, but because Kent was asleep, someone had to ride up with him. As his commanding officer, Ned offered. By the time he arrived on deck, two surgeon's mates had arrived with a litter to carry him to the infirmary. Ned explained the situation to William and then joined his junior officer in the sick berth, where he described in detail how Kent had been acting before the medicine knocked him out.

Dr. Hawthorne, a man whose ability far outstripped his reputation as a good surgeon, leaned over Kent, looking into his eyes with a magnifying glass. After a long examination, he motioned Ned to step outside of the infirmary with him. "I have a diagnosis and suggestion for treatment, but I need to discuss them with both you and Commodore Ransome."

"He was on the quarterdeck when I came aboard."

They found him, and Dr. Hawthorne asked if they could speak privately. Ned wondered at his severity.

William led them to his dining cabin and invited Hawthorne and Ned to sit.

"Commodore, Captain, the young man, Kent, has sustained a head injury that has caused bleeding in his brain. Though I have not seen his symptoms myself, from what Captain Cochrane described, this is typical when the swelling presses on the brain—imbalance, blurred vision, confusion, uncontrollable anger."

"What is the treatment?" William asked.

"There are two options. The first is to keep him comfortable and sedated, and see if he recovers on his own."

"How long would that take?"

"How long ago did the injury happen?"

Ned thought back. The past week stretched like a year. "At least three days ago and no more than five days ago."

"And he has been acting strangely since?"

"Yes." Or so Charlotte thought. Ned had not seen the young man much since he'd been returned to *Audacious*.

"If his symptoms have changed or if he doesn't go back to acting normally in a day or two, it means the pressure in his skull is not going down. I will have to perform surgery to relieve it."

Ned leaned forward, hands pressed on the table. "You are going to cut open his brain?"

Dr. Hawthorne chuckled. "No, Captain. I would drill a hole where the swelling is and drain off the blood that is causing the pressure."

"But you cannot make this determination if he is kept sedated?" William rubbed the back of his neck. Ned hadn't noticed until now just how tired—how gaunt—his commanding officer looked.

"That is correct, Commodore. And if he is not kept sedated and moves around too much, he could make the problem worse and die."

William leaned back in his chair and released a slow breath. "Ned, I know what I would choose were he a member of my crew. But he isn't. It is your decision to make."

Subject the boy to a dangerous surgery or let him wake up to see if he would heal on his own—all the while yelling about Charlotte for everyone on *Audacious* to hear. "When are we sailing for the bay, sir?"

"Within the hour."

Half a day's sail to return to Shaw's bay to rendezvous with Michael Witherington.

William closed his eyes a long moment. "We should arrive at the bay by dawn. A few hours there, to finish our business with *Serenity*," William gave Ned a significant look, "and then we will return to Kingston."

"I think we should wait to see if Mr. Kent recovers on his own." Ned turned back to the doctor. "I do not mean to impugn your skills, Dr. Hawthorne, but the surgery sounds dangerous, and if there is a chance he could recover without it, I believe we should err on the side of caution."

"I agree, Captain Cochrane. But leave the boy in my care. I can put him in my private quarters. That way he will not disturb those in the care of your sick berth."

"Thank you, Doctor." William stood. "Captain Cochrane, please return to *Audacious* and prepare to sail. We leave at the end of the first dogwatch."

Ned stood. "Thank you, Doctor, Commodore. We will be ready."

Back in the gig Ned silently urged the sailors to row faster. But he kept from giving the order, repeatedly, because he did not want his eagerness to show. But he was eager to get back to *Audacious*. He needed to lecture Charlotte about taking more care, about staying out of danger. And then he might allow himself one kiss. But only one. Until they were married in a proper church, he must stick to his plan of treating Charlotte with decorum.

A kiss could be decorous.

Chapter Twenty-Two

Julia snapped awake and then grabbed for something to stabilize her when the floor shifted beneath her.

No, not a floor. Something soft, cradling her. She reached her hands out and they came in contact with the canvas walls of a hammock. The darkness was not the ultimate black of the compartment in the hold.

The hammock was not her large box bed on William's ship, so he had not rescued her. She lifted her head as much as she dared to peek over the side of the canvas wall.

Moonlight shone through the stern windows, casting its pale glow over a very small cabin. So she was not aboard *Audacious*, either.

A shadow moved. She gasped and then groaned at the twinge of pain in her side.

"Please do not distress yourself, Mrs. Ransome. You are safe."

She heard the sound of a match being struck and then a candle flamed to life. The man who held it aloft was as dark as the night, with thick, curly black hair. A small man; young too, it appeared, not much older than Charlotte. He approached the hammock.

"I am Suresh, and I am here to assist you with whatever you need. I will have a bath ready for you in minutes."

She pushed herself up in the hammock, and when the light blanket fell from her shoulders she realized she wore nothing but her undergarments. She clutched the covering to her chest. "Why have I been disrobed?"

"Your dress was ruined, ma'am, too dirty to launder. I burned it. There are fresh garments waiting for you as soon as you have bathed."

Her head pounded with pain as bad as, yet different from, her sick headaches. She reached up to press her temples and saw the bandages wrapped around her wrists. She looked from them to Suresh.

"I treated your injuries, ma'am. Those I could see. I know you have hurt your side, but I did not try any treatment."

"I..." The last time she'd mentioned to someone that she thought she'd broken her ribs, Shaw had used it against her. "It is just a little sore, that is all."

Suresh turned to put the candle down on the table. "Let me help you down, ma'am."

Getting out of the hammock caused more pain than she would admit to. Until she knew where she was and who held her now, she could not show any more signs of weakness or vulnerability.

Suresh ushered her to a chair before disappearing through a small side door—what was probably the door to the cabin's sleeping quarters—and returning with a small silver tea service and a delicate china cup. And, to Julia's stomach's audible delight, a plate of scones complete with a small jar of what smelled like raspberry preserves.

"I do apologize that there is no cream for the tea or the scones, ma'am. We lost our milking goat and have not found a replacement yet."

Julia stared at the bounty before her, tears pooling in her eyes. "Why am I here?"

Suresh poured tea in the cup and pressed it into Julia's hands. "Eat. Drink tea. I will finish preparations for your bath."

She sipped the tea. The dark bitterness contrasted with something sweet, and she had trouble swallowing it past the tangle of anxiety, relief, pleasure, and pain in her throat. Then, she picked up a scone. She forced herself to break a small piece off one corner. It melted in her mouth with flavors of butter and sugar and spices she could not identify.

Suresh disappeared again and this time reappeared with a large bucket of steaming water, which he poured into the hipbath on the floor opposite the table from the hammock.

"Where are you from, Mr. Suresh?"

"I am from Bombay, in India." He carried in a large kettle of hot water.

Julia started on her second scone and poured more tea. "How did you come to be on a ship in the Caribbean?"

"I was an orphan. When the East India Trading Company advertised posts as cabin boys on their ships, I signed up. But I did not like that so much. When we arrived at Jamaica, I left to make my own way." He left again, with the bucket and kettle, and was gone longer this time.

Julia wondered if that was her signal to begin her bath. She set down the teacup.

Suresh came back, this time with a glass jar. He opened it and sprinkled it over the hot water. A delightful spicy aroma filled the air. Cinnamon and…she breathed in deeply but could not identify the other spices. Not over her own odor.

Embarrassment flamed in her cheeks. How could he bear to be in the same room with her?

He replaced the jar's cork and left it on the table, left, and returned with the bucket and kettle, full of more steaming water. He poured the bucket into the tub, but left the full kettle on the floor beside it.

Moving around behind Julia, he lifted several things off the lid of a trunk. "Here is a towel and a washrag and soap, a sleeping gown, undergarments, and a dress and a comb." He hung the towel over the back of the chair closest to the tub and set the rag and soap on the seat. The clothes and comb, he set on the table. He indicated the kettle. "For rinsing the hair after washing."

He crossed to the cabin's main door and slid a bolt home. "You will want to lock this door behind me when I leave, ma'am. When you are ready for me, simply call my name." He bowed and exited through the side door.

After one last sip of tea, Julia did lock the door. She stripped out of her filthy, foul-smelling clothes, leaving them in a heap in the corner. Unwinding the bandages, she left them on the table with the clean clothes.

The water smelled so good, with the spices floating on top, that she almost did not want to ruin it by getting into it.

Just like the cabin, the tub was small. She had to keep her knees bent, or put her legs out over the end of it to submerse her torso up to her neck. Bathing her entire body took some work—and generated a lot of pain—but the end result was more than worth it. After lathering her hair and body twice, she stood and poured clean water from the kettle over herself to rinse herself clean.

The rocking motion of the ship changed, and footfalls and voices drifted into the cabin. She glanced at the garments draped across the table. While she would love nothing more than to sleep for days, something was happening, so she'd best be as prepared as she could be.

The underthings included a short corset that laced in the front, making it quite easy to dress herself. The dark blue dress with a white ribband fit well, with the exception of being a couple of inches too long. With no shoes, she set the silk stockings aside, not wanting to ruin them. The extra length of the dress hid her bare feet well.

Taking the towel from around her hair, she combed it and plaited it for the first time in…she wasn't sure how long it had been since the morning she left Tierra Dulce.

She tore a thin strip from the end of one of the bandages and used it to secure the end of her braid and then crossed the cabin to unbolt the side door.

"Suresh," she called, a little unsure if calling him back instead of staying behind locked doors was wise.

It did not take long for him to appear. After rebandaging her wrists and then buttoning the sleeves of the dress over them, he lit all of the candles and begin cleaning the cabin—taking away her dirty undergarments, the tub, the kettle, the towel, and the washrag. The soap, he put in a dish beside a washbasin atop a cabinet in the corner.

He even pulled the ticking out of the hammock and turned it over so she would have a clean surface to sleep on. Why was he being so solicitous? What was about to happen to her?

He took the teapot, but a few minutes later, he brought it back, along with a second cup and another plate of scones. "We have arrived at our destination. If you are ready, the captain would like to come in and speak with you."

"Yes. Thank you."

Suresh disappeared again—this time through the main door, after unbolting it.

Julia alternated between sitting and standing—but when she heard footsteps outside the main door, her legs lost their strength, so she sat.

The door opened and the captain entered. He turned to close the door behind him before she caught more than a glimpse at his face.

A face she felt that she should know.

He did not turn around.

In his cabin on his ship? Why should he be hesitant to face her?

His head, covered with wavy dark hair, almost reached the top of the door, and his shoulders were nearly as wide—or so the epaulettes on his uniform coat made it appear.

The captain's hesitancy gave Julia courage. She stood. "Who are you? Why have you brought me here?"

He turned and stepped into the dim light. "I am El Salvador de los Esclavos. This is my ship, *Vengeance*."

Julia's knees gave out on her and she sat again. That voice—though deeper. His face—the jaw squarer now. The deeply set brown eyes. And…"The scar."

Self-consciously, the pirate touched the scar that ran across his forehead and into his eyebrow.

"He was so proud of that scar. Said it made him look like a true sailor." Julia could not breathe, could not think clearly. She closed her eyes against the lie standing before her. "My brother is dead."

At the sound of movement, she opened her eyes. He was kneeling in front of her.

He took her hands in his and pressed the backs of them to his cheek. "I am sorry. I am so sorry, Julia. I can never begin to expect your forgiveness." He lifted his head, his eyes imploring. "It was wrong of me to stay away so long."

Michael. Her twin. The other half of her soul—at least as children.

She pulled her hands out of his and slapped him with all her strength. "How dare you! How dare you come back *now.* Say you're sorry. Tell me how wrong it was to make us believe you were dead for fifteen years. Mama started dying the day we heard your ship had been taken."

Tears filled her brother's—no, the pirate's eyes. "I know. I did not learn about her death until three months after, when I returned from America. I wish I could have been there to say goodbye."

She pushed him away from her, and he offered no resistance, landing on his backside on the deck. He drew his knees up, crossed his arms over them, and hid his face in their circle.

"You *could* have been there to say goodbye. You deserted your family. Became a pirate. You stole from us, Michael! Traitor is too good a name for you." All the years cut off Mama's life because of her grief over the loss of her son. And in pining for her husband.

"I know. I do not deserve your forgiveness."

"Papa was never the same after losing you."

At this Michael's head snapped up. "I suppose he was glad he no longer had to live with the shame of having a son like me."

Julia wanted to slap him again. Instead she stood over him, fists planted on her hips. "He almost lost his commission by taking the two ships under his command out to search for you without permission. He was devastated when they did not find you. He entreated his admiral to let him stay here and continue searching for you."

"Then why did he not pay the ransom?"

The pain in her side, along with the surprise at his question, made her straighten. "What ransom? We never received a ransom letter."

Michael scrambled to his feet. "My captain waited six months. He told me how much gold he requested and that he sent the information to Tierra Dulce and to Father in care of the Admiralty in England. Father did not pay it because he never wanted me as a son."

"Michael, there was no ransom demand. And Papa loved you— loves you still. He told me before I left England." Searching his face, she began to see traces of the fourteen-year-old he'd been when last she saw him.

"What did he tell you?"

The boyish agony in her twin's question, in the longing behind it, chipped away a little of Julia's anger. "He grieved for you. For years he agonized over the hard way he had treated you, that he expected you to be his image, that he tried to force you into a career you never wanted and did not like. He is ashamed for continually comparing you to...someone else."

"William Ransome."

She nodded. And the memory of her own anger toward their father for how he treated Michael, for taunting Michael with William's successes, eased her anger even more. "William Ransome. And he told me he greatly regretted trying to fill the void in his heart your loss left with William."

Hope flashed in Michael's dark eyes but then vanished. "But he does love William Ransome. I read the *Gazette*, I keep up with the rumor mill. He all but declared to the world that William was his son by treating him as such."

Julia touched Michael's cheek—the one she'd slapped moments ago. "William is his protégé. You are his son, his flesh and blood."

"William *is* his son. He is your husband."

Julia sighed and dropped her hand to her side.

Michael picked it up and kissed the back of it. "I knew from the voyage here that you would marry William Ransome someday."

"How did you know? We had not yet reached our tenth birthday."

Michael shrugged. "You are Father's favorite, William is Father's favorite. A perfect match."

"Those are not perfect qualifications for a match. We could have hated each other."

"No, you were meant to be together." Michael stood, moved to the table, and poured tea for both of them. "Suresh does wonderful things with food. I am partial to this—an Indian tea blend sweetened with guava juice."

"I wondered..." Julia took the cup he offered. She settled back on her chair and, after a sip, spread the raspberry preserves on another scone.

Michael pulled his chair closer before sitting. "Are you...I know you have a few physical injuries, but are you well?"

Julia set the scone down untasted. "I wish I could scrub my mind of these past days as easily as I did from my person. I have read novels with characters filled with insensate villainy, but I never imagined such evil could truly exist in a person without rendering him immobile from the weight of it. Shaw hurt us because it gave him pleasure."

"Us?"

"He also captured William's brother James. Though I wish James had not had to experience such agony, I do not know if I would have survived if he had not been there to encourage me, to give me a reason to keep resisting Shaw—in my mind and heart, if not in action." The memory of James being pulled up by the rope—Julia fought her tears and tried to replace the image with something more pleasant. She focused on her brother's face. "How could you turn pirate, Michael?"

"The captain...he treated me well. Like I was smart. Told me I pleased him with my work. That he was proud to have me as part of his crew."

"Everything Papa never said to you." Julia lifted her teacup and held it under her nose for a moment, breathing in the exotic aroma, imagining the steam cleansing her memories.

"He gave me a choice—death or piracy. I did not want to die. I always thought I would come back to you and Mama." Michael circled the rim of his cup with his thumb.

"So once you were on your own, why did you not come back?" Julia picked up the scone, her hunger returning.

"By then I knew what I was, what I'd done. I did not think you would understand. I knew you would not forgive me. I learned what I could about you, about Tierra Dulce. I knew Mama had given up on life. I could see it—"

"See it? How?"

The half smile appeared. The one Michael wore whenever he had a secret. "I came to the plantation. Watched you and Mother. When I saw how frail she had become in just five years, I left, determining she would never know her son had joined a pirate's crew. I thought that would kill her faster than her grief over losing me."

"Why now? How did you come to be in the battle with Shaw's ship?"

Michael set down his teacup and ran his fingers through his hair. "I learned you were coming back to Jamaica, married and without Father. I planned to reveal myself to you after your husband went back to sea. But then, after you were seen in Barbados, word spread throughout the region that you were coming back. Shaw—who was Arthur Winchester, the first mate of the pirate who took me when I first knew him—held a grudge against our family and the Ransomes. He tried to get me to join him when he took over command of that ship. I could see his penchant for savagery even then, so I broke with him and set out on my own."

Could Shaw—Arthur Winchester—have orchestrated the events on the pirate ship to turn Michael against his family as part of the grudge?

"I remembered back to our campaign to convince Father to free Tierra Dulce's slaves. How satisfying it was to secure other people their freedom. Their joy in receiving the news that they had been liberated from oppression. Thousands of slaves were still coming into the Caribbean then, so I decided I would do what I could to free them."

Julia watched her brother's face as he talked about becoming El Salvador de los Esclavos as a way to make up for the bad things he'd done aboard the other pirate's ship, but also because he knew it was the right thing to do. About becoming a privateer for the United States—he laughed at her expression of distaste—and about meeting a wealthy abolitionist in Philadelphia, befriending his son, and falling in love with his daughter.

He stood and reached over the back of his desk and pulled one of the two framed pictures off the wall and handed it to her.

Julia angled it toward the stern windows, warmed by pink dawn light. A handsome woman with strong features smiled demurely at her. "She is lovely."

"Serena and I are to be married as soon as I return to Philadelphia—which will be delayed now. As part of my agreement with your husband for leniency on the charges of piracy and kidnapping, I am to return to England with Captain Cochrane and Charlotte."

Julia's heart leaped. "Charlotte? What know you of her? Is she safe? Where is she?"

"Ah, yes. I was distracted from my telling. When I heard rumors Shaw had been heard bragging he was going to kidnap you, I needed to protect you. The only way I could think of was to take you away until your husband had dealt with Shaw. So after you returned home, I went to Tierra Dulce to abduct you. I planned to leave word in Kingston that Shaw had done it so William would go after him."

The picture became clear. "But you got Charlotte instead."

Michael stretched out a finger and touched it to Julia's hand around the portrait frame. "Serena and her family are Quakers. They have been teaching me about God, about what it means to encounter Him personally, and that the greatest way to experience that encounter is through forgiveness. His forgiveness, and the forgiveness of those we've wronged."

The conversation with James in the hold came back to her. She prayed he was safe and that he found the forgiveness he sought. She looked at her brother, whose brown eyes, almost as familiar to her as her own, implored her with the strength of his love.

"Julia, can you forgive me?"

The cabin door flew open and Suresh burst in. "I apologize for interrupting, Captain, but the other ships have arrived. Both of them are cleared for action."

Michael stood. "Raise the parlay flag." He turned to Julia. "Stay here until it is safe."

"No, I will go with you." She stopped him with a tug on his sleeve. "I can forgive you, Michael, but it may be receiving my husband's forgiveness you should worry about."

Chapter Twenty-Three

William stopped just short of ordering his crew to put a warning shot over the bow of *Vengeance*. They were already giving him odd looks for having ordered both ships to run out the guns as they approached the bay. Michael Witherington had crossed him once; he would not be allowed to do it again.

The bluffs blocked the light from the rising sun, blanketing *Vengeance* in deep shadows as *Alexandra* slipped through the mouth of the bay.

"By the mark, seven," the leadsman called.

Shaw had used this bay as anchorage for both of his ships, and *Sister Elizabeth*, though of French rather than English design, was of a size with *Alexandra*. And the charts he'd taken from Shaw's quarters showed plenty of draught room in the strait. But with barely forty feet of water below them, William worried at the wisdom of entering rather than anchoring outside of it and taking a launch in.

Lights flickered on the deck of *Vengeance*. William lifted his glass. A lantern, carried by Michael Witherington. Another figure moved behind him, followed by a third, also carrying a lantern. The diaphanous, undefined shape of the second figure—and given that Michael appeared about a head taller—gave William a tremor of joyful apprehension. It could be—

James snatched the spyglass from him. "Is it her?"

William took it back, glaring at his brother. "I cannot yet tell." But he hoped.

"Why are your men taking the passage so slowly?" As a child James had had a penchant for whining, and William heard a distant echo of that in his brother's raspy voice now.

"By the mark, six!" A note of anxiety laced the starboard leadsman's voice.

"By the mark eight," the larboard leadsman called.

William let his brother have that as his answer and hardly breathed as *Alexandra* passed through the narrowest part of the strait.

Light crept over the starboard bluff, slowly crawling across the water toward *Vengeance*. The two lantern carriers stood in the forecastle with the other figure between them.

The sun now moved across the water faster than *Alexandra*. A golden line moved across the frigate's side and up onto its deck.

If William's heart could direct the wind, *Alexandra* would have been pushed forward faster than she'd ever traveled, arriving at *Vengeance*'s side instantly. Between Michael and his steward stood Julia, dressed in a dark blue gown, right arm wrapped around her middle, left hand raised, waving.

"Signal *V—Serenity* to prepare to receive me."

"Aye, aye, Commodore." The midshipman of the forecastle bent to open the flag box.

William snapped his telescope closed and handed it to James, who waved back at Julia, and then returned to the quarterdeck. "Lieutenant Jackson, make ready a boat to take me to *Serenity*. Be certain to bring shackles."

The young lieutenant blinked twice, unable to hide his surprise. "Aye, aye, Commodore."

William stayed on deck while the boat was lowered and *Alexandra* continued to drift forward so *Audacious* could enter and take up position on *Serenity*'s other side.

Once they were in position he gave the order to drop anchor and then climbed down the side to the waiting boat. The shackle chains lay at the marine sergeant's feet. William hoped he wouldn't have to use them.

Julia moved from the forecastle to amidships and stood by the entry port, her right arm still pressed against her side and across her waist. He recognized her stance as one of pain, but none of it showed in the beatific smile gracing her face. He kept his own expression neutral. He could not afford to lose his authority with an emotional reaction to seeing his wife—lovely though she was. Her hair was pulled back in a single thick plait, but wispy ringlets fluttered about her cheeks and neck. The dark blue dress accentuated her ivory skin and offset the red tones in her brown hair.

He hoisted himself up from the boat, finding the shallow slots in the frigate's side with his fingers and toes.

Julia stepped back to allow him room to climb up onto the deck. He turned toward her and removed his hat, dropping into a formal bow. "Mrs. Ransome."

Her brows raised. "Commodore Ransome." She started to curtsey but flinched and drew in a sharp breath between her teeth.

Slamming his hat back on his head, he reached forward and cupped her elbows to offer her support. "How may I assist you?"

She took a few deep breaths and then, regaining a smile, looked up at him. "You can greet me properly, as a husband should greet his wife after they have been so grievously torn apart."

And though she smiled, her eyes flooded and two tears fell.

William kissed her—hands leaving her arms to twine his fingers in her hair, not caring that his hat fell to the deck. Her lips, though dry and rough, responded to his with a hunger that tore at his soul and made him forget anything else existed in the world but the two of them.

A loud noise brought him back to his senses and he pulled away from his wife. To their left, William's officers and crew crowded *Alexandra*'s decks cheering and throwing their hats in the air. Heat climbed the back of his neck. Julia, clutching his coat with her left hand, buried her face in his chest with a groan.

"Would that Serena and I were already married so I could greet her in such a manner when I return to Philadelphia."

William stiffened, remembering his other purpose here. Stepping away from Julia, and taking his hat from Michael's steward, William recomposed himself. "Michael Witherington, on charges of piracy and kidnapping, you are hereby placed under arrest. You will be taken to Kingston, where you will stand trial."

Michael's good humor instantly clouded. "You cannot arrest me. We made an agreement. You put it in writing."

"You nullified that agreement when you boarded *Sister Elizabeth* and abducted my wife." No, he should have said *Mrs. Ransome*. This was not personal. This was a matter of justice.

Michael took a step toward him. "I boarded the ship and rescued *my sister* to save her life."

"Just as you abducted Miss Charlotte Ransome to save Mrs. Ransome's life?" William moved forward, his toes nearly touching the pirate's. He needed to punish someone for having taken Julia away from him because he had not had the satisfaction of dispatching Shaw himself. Besides, Michael Witherington's smug self-satisfaction annoyed him.

Julia wedged herself between the two of them and pressed her back against Michael's chest. "That is quite enough from both of you."

William wasn't certain as to whether she was trying to get Michael to back away or to protect her brother from her husband. All he knew was that his wife had come between him and his quarry.

"You will not interfere in matters that do not concern you, Mrs. Ransome." William continued staring over her head at Michael.

She grabbed the lapel of his coat and pushed on his chest. "But this does concern me, Commodore Ransome. You see, I am the concerned party here, not you. I am the one who was injured when my carriage was overturned. I am the one who was taken aboard Shaw's ship. I am the one who took Shaw's fist in my face when I spoke out of turn. I am the one who was almost choked to death by both Shaw and his brother. I am the one who spent days locked in a lightless compartment with little to drink and less to eat and no place to sleep or take care of my personal needs. I am the one who"—her voice broke—"who had to watch as Shaw put a noose around your brother's neck and hang him until he was almost dead and then release him."

William could now not tear his eyes away from the expression of distant horror in his wife's face.

Her breaths came in irregular gulps. "And I am the one who had to free myself from being tied up in the bilge, by my own ingenuity, so that I could try to find James and escape." She sniffed as tears threatened. Her focus slowly returned to William, and some of the terror left her green eyes. "And I am the one who had to do all of that with injured ribs that *still hurt*. So do not tell me that this matter does not concern me!"

She took another gasping breath that sounded more like a sob. "Please excuse me." She slipped past Michael and disappeared down the companionway toward the big cabin, her gait stiff and unnatural.

How could William repair the damage that had been done to his wife? The physical injuries would heal, but the emotional scars…she would carry those with her the rest of her days.

"When the mainmast went down," Michael said, still looking at the door Julia disappeared through, "she was beside it. She was knocked unconscious and buried in rigging that could have suffocated her." He turned to face William again. "*Alexandra* and *Audacious* had not yet started boarding. What else was I to do but step in and rescue her?"

William sighed. "You did what was necessary, and I commend you for the action you took. Our former agreement stands." He pressed his lips together in a tight smile. "Besides, I do not believe she would forgive me if I had you arrested now."

Michael chuckled. "You might be surprised. I recently discovered just how forgiving a heart my sister has." He inclined his head toward the door. "You should go to her."

William nodded his thanks to his brother-in-law and made his way down to the half deck, comprised of the captain's quarters. His first posting as a commander had been aboard a frigate this size. He did not miss it at all.

A young Indian man opened the door at his knock. He stepped back and motioned William into the cabin, seeing himself silently out.

Julia stood beside the round dining/worktable, a cup of tea trembling in her hand. At the sight of her husband, the tears she'd been hold-ing back unleashed and poured down her cheeks. But she did not sob or wail.

He took the cup from her and set it on the table. Gingerly, he placed his arms around her shoulders, cradling the back of her head with one hand. "Can you talk about it?"

"I…feel…so…foolish." She sniffed.

"You have been through an experience no one could comprehend. You need to express your emotions." Her hair smelled of exotic spices which both soothed him and made him want to bury his face in its silky softness.

"It…it is not that." She gasped a breath. "I am c-crying because… my…side hurts. It won't stop. It hurts when I sit down and stand up. It hurts when I try to sleep. It hurts when I breathe…" Julia contin-ued extolling all of the activities that made her side hurt.

William smiled, glad she could not see his face. Of course his wife was weeping over the pain of her broken ribs, not the horrors that transpired over the past seven days. Knowing her, it was the first time she allowed herself to admit just how much pain she was in on a con-tinual basis.

"I am sorry your side hurts. We shall have Dr. Hawthorne exam-ine you when we return to *Alexandra*."

"Thank you, William." She moved her left hand up against his chest and used it to protect her cheek from the rough wool of his coat. "Are you going to arrest Michael?"

"No. I was angry he did what I had set out to do."

"Rescue me?"

"Rescue you." The smell of the spices—in her hair and from the teapot steaming on the table—acted as a soporific compound on Wil-liam. Exhaustion gnawed at his body, his mind.

"All he did was pull me out from under a pile of rope. 'Twas your plan that rescued me."

Bless her for trying to salvage his pride. "No, 'twas your brother who rescued you. Your brother…the pirate."

Julia pushed back against his chest and he loosened his hold so she could look at him. "He's a good pirate, though. He frees slaves."

William ran his finger down the side of her face, freeing the tendrils of hair that had stuck to the moisture on her cheek. "There is no such thing as a good pirate. Michael Witherington bears a letter of marque from the Congress of the United States naming him a privateer. With the renaming of this ship so that his men can sail her back to Philadelphia, the legend of the pirate El Salvador dies with the burning of *Vengeance* as he assisted the Royal Navy to apprehend Shaw. A good ending."

Julia nodded. "A good ending for a good pirate."

William could no longer resist. He bent down and kissed her. Long and soft, trying to convey his love, his devotion, to her.

She raised her arms to embrace him and then gasped, pulling away. "I am sorry, William."

He kissed her forehead. "Do not distress yourself. It will heal."

Julia eased herself into the straight-backed wooden chair with a groan, arms wrapped tightly around her middle. After a moment of easing her spine against the chair's back, she dropped her left arm into her lap. "James is recovering from his injuries?"

"He is almost back to his old ways, meaning he is ornery and discontent with being under my command." William pulled a chair closer so that when he sat, his knee touched hers. He poured a cup of the spicy tea for himself, tasted it, and then, frowning, set it aside.

"You do not like it?"

"I do not like my tea sweet."

"I know, but this is different. Suresh adds guava juice to it."

William was not certain what a *guava* was or why anyone should want to drink its juice, but he did not want to disturb his wife's pleasure in the drink.

"I am thinking about asking him to come work at Tierra Dulce. He could be an under butler. Or he could be your valet."

"I do not need a valet. And if I did, there is Dawling." He pinched a corner off of the toasted brown bread on which someone had spread red jam.

"I appreciate all the work Dawling has done for you, William, but Suresh is…"

"Better? Yes, I agree. But there is loyalty to be considered, and no one has been so loyal to me as Dawling." The sweet tartness of the raspberry preserves awakened William's hunger, and he lifted the entire piece of toast to his mouth.

"While we were waiting for you to board, Michael told me a story of Charlotte and Ned. Is it true?"

He set the toast down, unbitten. "That they had Michael's sailing master marry them?"

She nodded.

"Aye. Charlotte thought it was the only way to protect her identity and preserve what remains of her reputation." He wiped a spot of stickiness from his finger on the cloth under the plate.

"He said his sailing master is a minister and that he had a church in New Orleans. But, William, I do not believe that in the eyes of our church Charlotte and Ned are truly married." Julia worried her bottom lip with her teeth.

"When Michael marries his Serena in an American church, would you consider them not truly married because they were not married in the Church of England?" He picked up the piece of toast and took a large bite.

"No, of course not. But they will be getting married by a minister ordained to do so. We know nothing of this sailing master's qualifications to perform marriages." She set her empty teacup down. "I want Charlotte brought on board *Alexandra* until we reach Kingston. Until they are married by a proper rector, they must behave with propriety, as an unmarried couple."

William finished the last bite of the toast and lifted his cup to wash it down before he thought better of it. He took Julia's empty cup, filled it with water from the pitcher on the table, and tried to wash the cloying sweetness of the tea from his mouth.

"Charlotte is too young to think rationally about this, and as her oldest male relative, it is up to you to make her behave properly." Julia grimaced and pressed her arm tighter against her side as her voice rose.

William refilled his cup with tea and handed it to Julia, keeping hers for water for himself. "Charlotte has been aboard *Audacious* with Ned for four days. He also espoused the idea of waiting until they had a real church wedding before…" Heat crept up the back of William's neck, but not from embarrassment. It was not so long ago that Charlotte had been a child, a baby. So sweet, so innocent, so young. "Yes, I will have Ned bring Charlotte to *Alexandra* as soon as we return."

"What do you think my father will do with Michael?" Julia picked a crumb up from the cloth and put it back on the plate.

"As a naval officer who has served under him most of my life, I believe he will listen to the facts, as Michael presents them and as I will explain in my missive to him, and make an objective judgment." William watched his wife's face.

A smile started at her full bottom lip and danced all the way up to her green eyes, replacing her worry. "And as a daughter who has lived with him, I believe there will be quite a bit of yelling first."

William leaned over and kissed her. "Are you ready to go home, Mrs. Ransome?"

"Quite ready, Commodore Ransome."

He stood and extended his hand to her, letting her take her time in rising, his heart aching to do something, anything, to make her pain stop.

Michael met them at the top of the companionway. "Ah, good. I was coming to get you. Signal from *Alexandra* requesting Captain Cochrane's and your attendance urgently."

Chapter Twenty-Four

Will you please stop mumbling to yourself?" Charlotte tossed the coat and waistcoat into her sea chest and slammed the lid shut. She stepped to the door between the sleeping quarters and the day cabin. "Either speak aloud or keep your thoughts inside your head."

Everything about the cabin, the ship, and even Charlotte annoyed Ned this morning. "What I said was I wish you would have let me know you were planning to stay in the sick berth the entire night." He threw the wardrobe door open hard, and it banged against the wall.

"How was I to know two of the men would become violently ill and I would need to stay?" Had her voice always been so shrill? "At least you were able to get a good night's sleep. I was awake all night cleaning up sick."

Ha! Sleep? Worrying about where she was, about who might be discovering her true identity through the guise of Charles Lott? How was he supposed to sleep? Besides, he'd never even gotten to kiss her last night.

He fought to get his arm through the sleeve of his uniform coat. One of the buttons popped off the cuff, hit the floor with a *thump*, and rolled under the desk. An oath popular amongst the sailors nearly popped out of his mouth, but, with a quick glance at Charlotte, he stifled it and something nonsensical came out under his breath.

She clenched her fists, closed her eyes, and her whole body shook for a brief moment. "Stop doing that!"

Ned bent down to retrieve the button, but his fingers were too thick to reach it.

"Oh, move out of the way." Charlotte pushed his shoulder, knelt down, and easily swiped her finger under the desk to fish out the button. Muttering to herself—it was fine, apparently for her to do it, but not him—she opened the valet drawer in the wardrobe and withdrew needle and thread. Without speaking to him—but continuing to mutter to herself—she grabbed his arm and sewed the button back onto the sleeve while he still wore the coat. She bit the thread off with her teeth and returned the sewing implements to the drawer, which she closed none too softly.

"Now, if that is all, *Captain*, sir, I came back up here hoping to get some sleep finally." She shooed him toward the door with a waving motion of her hands. "So if you will go about your business, I'll be fine here on my own."

He would strangle her. It would stop the ringing in his ears and make him feel much better. "No. Orders from your brother. You are to attend me to *Alexandra*."

Her mouth dropped open. "When?"

"Now."

"Now?"

"Yes. Now."

"But I have not slept all night. I smell like the sick berth, and I have nothing to wear in which I'm fit to be seen."

Ned dug his fingers into his hair and squeezed his temples between the heels of his hands. "I have not slept all night, either. And you are not going to a ball, so put something on. We should have left near half an hour ago. I don't care that he is your brother. Commodore Ransome is my commanding officer and I must obey my orders."

Charlotte looked down at the loose white blouse and indigo trousers she was wearing and then returned to the sleeping cabin.

Ned closed his eyes against the sound of the renewed slamming of her sea chest's lid. He glanced toward the brandy decanter left behind by Captain Parker. Ned had not touched it before now, and only the earliness of the hour kept him from doing so.

Charlotte entered, buttoning her uniform coat. "I lost my hat when I went out on deck to save Kent."

"You will not need it. Let's go." He grabbed her hand and dragged her from the cabin.

In the wheelhouse the marine guard, the sailing master and his mates, and the midshipman and lieutenant of the watch all looked conspicuously away from Ned and Charlotte. Lovely. His men had heard them arguing.

As soon as they got back to Kingston, Ned would find out what it would take to get their marriage annulled. Because he was not certain it was legal, he hoped it would take nothing more than burning the marriage certificate he and Charlotte had signed.

"You're doing it again." Charlotte yanked her hand from his grasp when they reached the entry port. She turned and put her foot down to find the first slot of the accommodation ladder.

"What?"

"Muttering."

"You do it too."

Charlotte gasped. "I do not!"

Ned rolled his eyes and sighed. After she disappeared down the side, he started down after her.

"Wait! You're going to step on me."

He growled deep in his throat. "Go faster."

"You go slower."

Ned looked down, over his shoulder. In the boat below, Lieutenant Martin and the crewmen stared up at him and Charlotte, wide-eyed.

What must they think of Acting Captain Ned Cochrane now? Doubtless that he could not control his wife or a wayward midshipman, whichever they thought Charlotte to be. Either way, their opinion did not bode well for his continued leadership aboard *Audacious*.

Except to give his men commands, neither he nor Charlotte spoke on the trip across the bay to *Alexandra*. At one point, he thought he saw her eyes drift closed as if she were dozing off, but when she opened them—slowly—and noticed him watching, she turned her face away from him.

He sent her up the side of *Alexandra* first and followed behind. She stood just beyond the entry port when he attained the deck, rubbing the top of her left arm, her brows pinched.

"Welcome aboard, Captain Cochrane. Commodore Ransome is waiting for you in his quarters." Lieutenant Campbell touched the fore point of his hat.

Ned returned the salute. "Thanks, Angus." He settled his hand on her lower back to move her toward William's cabin and leaned close. "Is your arm paining you?"

She dropped her right hand. "Only a little. From climbing the ladders."

"When we return, I could have them use the bosun's—"

"No. I am well enough to make use of the ladders."

Ned smiled to himself. That was the Charlotte he loved—the one with spunk and spirit, not one to give in to a minor injury, such as getting shot.

"William does not need to know of my injury," she whispered as they crossed into the shade of the wheelhouse.

"I fully agree." No need to let his commanding officer know he'd let the man's sister place herself in the path of incoming fire from an enemy vessel.

The marine guard stepped aside for Ned to knock on the door. Dawling let them in and then led them around the dining table and into the day cabin.

"Julia!" Charlotte rushed toward her sister-in-law, who sat, rather stiffly, in one of the straight chairs at the large round worktable. William caught Charlotte with one arm around her waist.

"It is all right, William." Julia reached her left hand out to Charlotte, and William released his sister. "I have several cracked ribs, and William did not want you accidentally hurting me."

Charlotte took Julia's hand and leaned over to kiss her cheek before kneeling by her side. "I was so worried about you. When we found out that Shaw had you…" She pressed Julia's hand to her cheek.

"Captain Cochrane," Julia inclined her head at him; Ned bowed. "It is good to see you again."

"Mrs. Ransome, I am relieved you are safe and well. Except for the cracked ribs, of course."

"Captain Cochrane," William said, "I do not believe you have met my brother, Captain James Ransome."

"James!" Charlotte jumped up, spun around, and flung herself at her brother, who groaned, staggered, and then put his arms around his sister.

"'Tis good to see you too, little sister." The similarity between James and William astonished Ned. He wondered if the third brother resembled them so greatly.

She stepped back and reached up to touch the scars across his cheeks. "How came you to be here?"

James and Julia exchanged a dark look. "It is a long story, Charlotte, that must wait for another time."

"What's wrong with your voice? Are you ill?" Charlotte ran her hand down his waistcoat, as if trying to feel his lungs for sickness.

"A throat malady, but nothing catching." James smiled, but his expression seemed forced.

Julia started to rise. William was instantly at her side to offer his assistance. Charlotte did the same on her other side. Julia smiled at her and Ned. "Dr. Hawthorne gave me some laudanum to take, but I wanted to wait to see you first." She tucked a lock of Charlotte's hair behind her ear. "Your hair is growing back so fast. Perhaps by your wedding it will be long enough that we can do something with it."

Charlotte looked at Ned, William, James, and then back at Julia. "Our wedding?"

"Yes, in the chapel at Tierra Dulce. I believe it will be good to wait for the banns to be read—not that for the two of you it would matter here. It will give us time to plan the wedding breakfast properly and give our neighbors time to plan to attend." Julia pressed her hand to her right side, pain clouding her face, and she leaned into her husband's side. "And until we reach home, Charlotte, you will stay here on *Alexandra* with us."

Charlotte shook her head, but Julia was not looking at her. She looked instead at William, who in turn looked at Ned.

"Captain Cochrane, I will make it an order if I must."

Ned thought back to the half hour past—the way Charlotte's shrill voice rubbed on his nerves like a holystone against the deck, the way she disobeyed and countermanded him, the way she scolded him for doing things she herself did, the way his men heard all of it. Perhaps it would be better if Charlotte traveled back to Kingston aboard *Alexandra*.

He straightened under the stern eye of his commanding officer. "Commodore Ransome, Mrs. Ransome, you must do what you think is necessary, of course. I know you are concerned for her welfare and reputation. I am also."

Charlotte's face fell from expectation to disappointment.

"So Charlotte will stay with me on *Audacious*. She is my wife."

❦

Charlotte Cochrane loved her husband very, very much. She couldn't show him how much with her two eldest brothers standing there staring at her, but she would find a way, somehow, to let Ned know just how much she appreciated how he stood up to William so they could stay together.

"We will discuss this later." William helped Julia into their sleeping cabin.

So that was where Ned had picked up that phrase—from William. She wondered if William liked lecturing Julia as much as Ned liked lecturing her.

With just James left in the room with them, Charlotte crossed to Ned and wrapped her arms around his middle. "Thank you. And I am sorry about our quarrel earlier."

He squeezed her back. "I as well."

They dropped their embrace when William returned moments later. He closed the door to the sleeping quarters and came back to stand in front of the worktable, arms crossed. "Why were you so long in responding to the orders to report to *Alexandra*?"

"That is my fault, William." Charlotte stepped in front of Ned. "I had been down in the sick berth all night attending the sick and injured, and I had to get cleaned up and changed before we could come."

William looked down at her uniform with an arched brow. "Changed?"

"Out of my soiled uniform into this one. They are the only garments I have left. Fortunately, my sea chest remained behind on *Audacious* when I came to *Alexandra* in Barbados, so all of my belongings are still there."

Her brother did not seem to find this news as cheerful as she did. His lips pinched together. "Perhaps Captain Witherington has more women's clothing he would be willing to part with."

"Those gowns are for his fiancée." Charlotte swiped her hair back behind her ears. "Besides, they are far too big on me. You saw how long the blue dress is on Julia, and she is much taller than I. I wore it once when I was Captain Sal—Captain Witherington's guest." So everyone now knew that Salvador was actually Julia's brother. Good. She liked him very much and was glad to now call him family.

"We shall discuss this later." William called for his steward.

Dawling appeared almost immediately. "Aye, Com'dore?"

"Pass word for Dr. Hawthorne."

"Aye, aye, sir." Dawling knuckled his forehead and disappeared again.

Charlotte glanced between her brothers. "Why send for the surgeon? James, are you certain you are well?"

"I did not call him for either of us." William sat at the table and motioned for the others to do so as well. "Something happened with Mr. Kent during the night, and the doctor wanted to talk to you, Ned, about it, since the lad is under your command."

As they waited for the doctor to arrive, Charlotte sat on her hands, swinging her feet, and combing her teeth over her bottom lip. A faint buzzing filled her ears, and William's, James's, and Ned's voices echoed oddly in her head.

Finally, Dawling showed the young doctor in. He nodded at each of them with a tight smile.

"Report, Doctor."

"Yes, Commodore." Hawthorne slid his thumbs into his waistcoat pockets and rocked back on his heels. "During the night, Mr. Kent began having a fit—a seizure—due to the pressure the swelling is putting on his brain. I was able to sedate him, but I need to perform the surgery soon if he is to have any chance at surviving."

Ned stood and paced a tight circle behind the table. "So you are saying there is no chance that he will recover on his own."

"No, sir."

"Surgery is the only option?" Ned stopped and rested his hands on the back of Charlotte's chair.

"Yes, sir."

"Very well, then. Perform the surgery."

"Yes, sir." Hawthorne now turned his attention on William. "Commodore, this is a very tricky procedure. One slip, one mistake, and it will kill him. It would be best done on land, but taking him ashore would jostle him too much and possibly cause another seizure, which could also kill him. Because that is not an option, it would be better done while we are at anchorage here. The water is calm, so there should not be much danger of sudden motion to jostle my hand."

"How long will the surgery last?"

"Hours, sir. First, I must determine exactly where the swelling inside the skull is. Then, I must bore a hole in the skull—"

William raised a hand and closed his eyes. "Please, Doctor, I do not need to know the details." He turned to Ned. "Witherington has just begun the painting work to turn *Vengeance* into *Serenity*, which will take several hours to complete also. Have your master carpenter confer with mine, who has already asked to go ashore for wood for repairs. They could go together and save us time."

"Aye, sir." Ned's fingers brushed against Charlotte's shoulders, sending a shiver of pleasure down her spine.

"Dismissed."

Ned snapped to attention. The doctor gave a half bow and left. Ned picked his hat up from the table. Charlotte rose to leave with him.

"Charlotte, you will stay."

With her back to her brother, she looked up into Ned's beautiful gray eyes.

"I will wait for you in the boat." He touched her cheek and then exited, closing the cabin door behind him.

Charlotte turned to face her brothers. James, though lounging on the sofa in the corner and looking not the least interested in what was about to happen, was still someone who could be either a help or hindrance to her.

"Please sit, Charlotte."

"I would rather stand, thank you." She crossed her arms and held them there despite the burning tightness of the wound.

"Very well." William clasped his hands behind his back. "You may return to *Audacious* to retrieve your dunnage. You will then immediately report yourself back to this cabin, where you are to remain until we dock in Kingston. Do I make myself clear?"

"No."

"In what way was I unclear?"

"Oh, your demand was perfectly understandable, but I am not going to do that, William. Despite the fact I am currently dressed like a midshipman, I am not one of your men whom you can order about and expect to obey your every edict." Her arm hurt too badly to keep them crossed, so she mimicked William's stance instead.

"No, you are my sister. My sister who has not yet reached the age of majority and is therefore still my responsibility and, in the eyes of the law, unable to make decisions of your own."

She had been making decisions of her own for years now, though many of them did not turn out quite as well as she expected. But her decision to marry Ned was different. "Then it is a good thing you gave us your blessing, as that negates any objections to the marriage or to Ned and me living as man and wife."

William stiffened. "Have you...has the marriage been...?" A ruddy flush rose from his neck up into his face.

An answering heat flared in Charlotte's cheeks. "No. Not yet."

"Good. Then your reputation can still be salvaged."

She threw her hands out in front of her. "Why does everyone believe that my marriage to Ned will ruin my reputation?"

"It is the method in which you married that concerns us, not the marriage itself, once it truly takes place." William glanced over at James, who seemed to be more interested in cleaning under his fingernails with a letter opener than in William and Charlotte's argument.

"Jean Baptiste is a minister. He led a church in New Orleans for twelve years before he had to sneak out of town one night to keep from being captured and sold into slavery."

"A minister of what kind of church?"

"A Baptist church, and they even ordained him. So he's as official as any rector Julia would find to wed us."

Although, there was that gorgeous fabric Suresh had sent her. She would love to have that made into a gown and stand to publicly vow her love and devotion to Ned.

She knew one way in which she could appeal to William that he would not be able to resist. "Besides, is it not God who is the ultimate authority in such matters, not men? Ned and I made our vows to God"—or was that *before* God?—"and that makes us just as married as you and Julia because we made the same vows you did."

William gave her an indulgent smile. "It would make Julia and me very happy if you would come aboard *Alexandra*, if you would choose to wait until you can have a real wedding, with your family there to witness it, before you enter into the marriage estate. Julia has her heart set on a wedding in her chapel and then giving you and Ned a fancy wedding breakfast. If you and Ned are known to have... behaved as a married couple before then, Julia is afraid your marriage will be tainted with rumors of impropriety for the rest of your lives. She does not want that for you."

Charlotte groaned. Of all the contemptible, rotten arguments to use. "All right. I will go back to *Audacious*, get my belongings, and then come back to *Alexandra*. But I do this under *extreme* duress."

William crossed the room and kissed her forehead. "I knew you would eventually see reason, Charlotte."

Shaking her head, she left to rejoin her husband. No, she could not think of him as that now. But as soon as she climbed down into the boat, she could tell he read the truth in her expression. He would not talk to her for the entire trip back to *Audacious*.

When Charlotte reached the top of the accommodation ladder, Declan stood there, offering her a hand up. Ned, coming up directly behind her, expressed her own astonishment.

"What are you still doing here, Mr. Declan? I thought you were to return to your vessel as soon as we arrived." Ned started toward the great cabin, as if he did not want to be seen on deck with Charlotte. Not that she blamed him. After he stood up to William and declared he would disobey a direct order if William gave him one, she betrayed him and gave in.

Charlotte trailed along behind Declan and Ned.

"I wanted to make sure I had a chance to say goodbye to you, Cap'n. And to the missus." Declan winked at her over his shoulder.

Missus…but not yet in the eyes of her family. She bumped into Declan, who had stopped just inside the door to the big cabin. She tried to push him out of the way. Finally, with a laugh, he moved. Another time, another place, she might enjoy his teasing nature, but not today.

He turned around and wrapped his arms around her, lifting her high off the floor. "I'm going to miss you, little missus. *Vengeance*—I guess I should get used to saying *Serenity*. *Serenity* isn't going to be the same without you. Everyone thinks so."

"Thank you, Declan." She managed to get her arms around him and patted his shoulders. "You can put me down now."

"Do I have to?"

She caught Ned's accusatory glance over the giant's shoulder. "Yes, Declan. You have to."

He gave her one last squeeze and then set her down.

"Goodbye, Declan. Safe journey."

"And you as well."

She left him and Ned to their farewells and went to the sleeping cabin to retrieve her belongings. There wasn't much, and it was all in her sea chest except for the coat and waistcoat she'd discarded on the floor this morning because one of the sick sailors had missed the bucket and gotten her. She did not want to leave them behind—they were the only spares she had. But she was not going to put them in her sea chest and have everything in it smell like that.

The walls vibrated when the cabin door closed. She went back out into the main room. Ned stood staring out the stern window.

"I am going to go down to the galley to see if Cook has an empty bread sack I can use to pack these soiled things over to *Alexandra* in." There, she'd said it—not in so many words—but she had admitted that she would be leaving *Audacious* for her brother's ship.

"Take a farthing with you," Ned's voice came out flat and uninterested. "Cook does not like to give anything away he can sell."

"I don't have—"

"In the second cubbyhole in the back of the desk. There's a latch that opens a secret compartment."

Charlotte found the small stash of coins and took out a farthing. "Ned, I'm sorry. He...he made a compelling argument."

Ned shook his head but still would not look at her. "Just go and get your sack so that we can get you back over to *Alexandra*. We don't want your family to think I am debauching you."

"That's not what they think."

He did not reply.

Near tears, Charlotte grabbed the doorknob. It turned, but the door would not budge. She pushed and then pulled. No movement.

"Ned? Did you lock the door when Declan left?"

"No." He finally turned away from the windows. "Perhaps it is stuck." But even his greater strength produced no different result. The door was locked, or barred, from the other side. They both pounded on it and called out—for Declan, for the marine guard, for the steward—but no one came.

"I'll go around and see what the problem is." He went into the sleeping cabin.

At his banging on the door that connected to the captain's galley and then to his steward's cabin, Charlotte looked in on him. He turned, confusion, with a hint of amusement, affixed in his expression. "I do believe someone locked us in."

Charlotte scooted past him and tried the door. Her neck tingled along her hairline, though she wasn't certain why. She turned and pressed her back to the door. "Why would anyone do such a thing?"

Ned shrugged and took a step toward her. "No one is answering our calls for help."

Charlotte took a step toward him. "Ned, I told William I know in my heart that, in the eyes of God, we are most definitely and surely married. I only agreed to go to *Alexandra* because Julia did not want any rumors to get started about…what we might have done…" she swallowed hard…"might do before we have a public church wedding."

Ned reached over and tucked her hair behind her ears. "But what do those rumors matter if we are already married?"

"They don't—"

Ned's kiss stopped her words and her thoughts. Oh, yes. She loved her husband very, very much.

Chapter Twenty-Five

Dawling carried a pillow in from the bed and handed it to Julia, who tucked it under her head. William's steward stood there a moment, staring at her, but then, with a shake of his burly body, he turned and left the room, muttering.

William pulled his knees up and wrapped his arms around them. "Is lying on the floor really that much more comfortable than the bed or a chair?" For he found sitting on it highly uncomfortable.

She reached her hand up and patted his elbow. "It is the first time in days I have felt that I could breathe almost normally. There is still a sharp catch here"—she touched a spot halfway around to her back—"but it is not nearly as bad as before."

"And the laudanum?"

"It helped some. I did not dream while I slept." The shadow of memory passed through her eyes, but she blinked and it vanished.

"You only slept an hour. Perhaps you did not take enough."

"I told you, half the amount the doctor ordered is fine. I know how it affects me, and I do not want to find myself in such a state that I cannot tell memory from reality."

So she feared the laudanum would force her to remember what happened on *Sister Elizabeth*. He could not blame her for preferring to live with the pain. He just found it hard to believe that lying flat on her back on the floor could possibly be comfortable.

"Has Charlotte returned?"

He shifted his weight and leaned over her to brace his arm on her other side. "Not yet. But *Audacious* is a good distance from us. And if I know Charlotte, she is going around to say goodbye to everyone on the ship."

"William…what day is today?" She traced his jaw with her fingers. "Sunday."

"You did not lead prayers this morning."

"I held a brief service before the noon meal, while you were sleeping." He captured her hand in his and kissed her fingertips. "The Scripture from the New Testament was the story of the prodigal son."

"Any word from Dr. Hawthorne on how the boy fared surgery?" She twined her fingers through this.

"He survived the procedure. Dr. Hawthorne says that now only time will determine if Kent recovers." On the floor or not, William did not want this time to end.

Julia rolled her head from side to side, causing her unbound hair to fan out into more of a riot of curls. "Where is James?"

"On deck. He said he had his fill of dark rooms, that sunlight and wind would be better restoratives than any of the doctor's cures."

She raised her gaze to the ceiling. "It was so dark in that little place. There were times I despaired of ever seeing the sun or the blue of the sky again. But then Shaw would send for me to taunt me, to play his games, and I actually found myself longing for the solitude and protection that the darkness provided." A tear rolled out of the corner of her eye and down into her hair. "William, will I ever be able to forget? How do you live with the memories of the battles, of the lives you've taken, of the men you've seen die?"

He set them aside, knowing he did his duty for king and country. "Whenever one of those bad memories comes, it helps if you stop it and replace it with a good memory."

"I don't know if I can." She let go of his hand and reached up to wipe away another tear before it could fall.

"Let me see if I can help." He leaned forward and kissed her.

She was smiling a bit dazedly when he raised his head. "I like that kind of good memory."

He spent a few minutes making more good memories with her until his own back and sides started hurting from his awkward position. She had the audacity to laugh at him—which made her side hurt worse again. He stood and stretched and then resumed his place by her side.

She took several shallow breaths until her pain eased. "If we are so infirmed at thirty and five-and-thirty, I do not want to imagine what we will be like in our sixties."

He took her hand and kissed the back of it. "We shall be even more in love than we are today."

"How do you know?"

"Because I love you more today than I did yesterday, and more then than the day before."

"Do you think we will have children?" Julia's right hand moved to her abdomen.

"Of course we will. I have already told you I expect a full complement of lieutenants for a seventy-four." He rested his hand atop hers where someday, soon he hoped, their child might grow.

"What if I am like Susan and cannot bear children?"

"But Susan is with child."

Worry clouded her green eyes. "Or was when we left. It has been two months. She has had so many miscarriages. I pray this will be the child they have so yearned for."

Julia's mention of their friends brought back to the forefront of William's mind something he had been mulling over for the past week, ever since having to leave her at Tierra Dulce, not knowing if she was safe and then learning she hadn't been.

"I am going to resign my commission."

Julia started to laugh, but it ended quickly with a moan. "No, you are not. You cannot be that anxious to have children."

"That is not—I do not want to leave your side, Julia. It is not safe. I will not be able to leave you again, knowing what happened this time." He wanted her to stop smiling, to understand his sincerity.

She rested her hand on his cheek, rubbing the side of his nose with her thumb. "William, you have dispatched the only threat to me. And you know as well as I do that after five weeks on land in Portsmouth, you would have traded everything you have to be back at sea. And that was when you still had the fraternity of naval officers. You would be miserable at Tierra Dulce. There is nothing for you to do there."

He tried to muster offense at the suggestion he could not be of use at the plantation. "I worry too much."

"You worry too much, but I love you for it."

"You lie."

She grinned, the tip of her tongue caught between her teeth. "I do love you."

"Aye, madam, you do." He kissed her. "And now I must go see what is keeping Charlotte from reporting as ordered." He pushed himself up from the floor—not as easy a task as when he was younger. "Shall I send Dawling to you?"

"No, but thank you for the kind offer."

He laughed and shrugged into his coat and grabbed his hat from the table. At the door he turned and took one last look at his wife, spread out on the floor. "I love you."

"Aye, sir, you do."

⚜

Declan crowed with laughter. "You should have heard them pounding on the doors. That didn't last long, though, before all went quiet."

First he flirted with her, and then he came up with a scheme to get her alone with her new husband. Michael shook his head. "Did you have everyone aboard in on this plot to give Captain and Mrs. Cochrane a little private time?"

"Just the officers. And the steward. And the sailing master. Oh, and the marine sergeant and the guard at the door. I think that was all." Declan looked down and started counting on his fingers as if each were a person. "Yes, I do believe that was all."

"How will they get out?"

"Aw, the steward knew to go undo the bolts after an hour, but he's under strict orders not to disturb them."

"Sometimes, I have to wonder…" Michael leaned over the bulwark.

The sailor hanging from the swing waved his paint brush. "All finished, Cap'n."

"Well done." He hoped the man had spelled it correctly.

"How much longer are we staying here, Cap'n?" Declan leaned against the balustrade.

"I believe you and *Serenity* should be able to leave as soon as Commodore Ransome gives permission." Michael checked his pocket watch. A quarter past four. Even if the newly dubbed *Serenity* left now, *Alexandra* and *Audacious* would never make it out of the bay before sunset, and navigating the narrow strait at the mouth of the bay in anything but full daylight was sheer folly. And because he would be aboard one of those ships himself, he did not look forward to such a risk.

"Where's Picaro, Cap'n?"

"He went on to Kingston with the prize crew aboard *Sister Elizabeth*. Commodore Ransome's lieutenant had orders to let Picaro leave as soon as they dock. He never was happy doing things the way we did them. I only hope he does not get involved in something more sinister just to feed his desire for money." Michael braced himself against the gunwale and assisted the carpenter's mate up and over onto the deck.

Michael moved forward on the quarterdeck as the sailor cleared block and tackle and the swing.

"You'll have a lot of recruiting to do in a short time. Commodore Ransome said Lieutenant O'Rourke is a good judge of character, so listen to him. But you'll have Lau, Suresh, and Jean Baptiste to help you once you get underway."

"Not me, sir." Jean Baptiste stepped out from behind the wheel.

"What's that?" Michael stopped and faced the best sailing master he had ever served with.

"I'm not going with you back to America. It isn't safe for me there." He ran his hand over his head, beaded with sweat under the hot sun.

"But Philadelphia is in the north. There's no slavery there. And the

Declans are abolitionists. They are happy to have you work for the company." Michael looked at Declan for support.

"My father was excited when he learned your story—that you'd run away from New Orleans to escape being made a slave only to find yourself sailing on a ship that went around liberating slave ships. He's probably already set up speaking engagements for you so you can tell your story of how you escaped New Orleans in the middle of the night in a sugar barrel—"

"That is a falsehood. I rode out of town in the middle of the morning on my horse. I did have help from some of Jean Lafitte's men and took refuge with them in the bayous while I let my trail grow cold. I learned how to sail and navigate by making my way through those swamps. I'll never forget what they did for me."

"Yes," said Declan, pounding his meaty fist into Jean Baptiste's shoulder. The smaller sailing master staggered back a step. "That's exactly the kind of story that the abolitionist societies love to hear. Adventure, pirates, escaping the slavers—"

"I'm still not going." The set of his expression meant there would be no arguing with him.

"But why?" There had to be more to it that the slavery issue.

"It gets cold in Philadelphia. Snows."

Declan nodded enthusiastically. "That first snow of winter, when it covers the ground and gets about knee-deep, is the best sledding snow."

Jean Baptiste shook his head. "I don't like the cold. Not even Louisiana kind of cold. Here's where I'm meant to be. In the tropics." He ran his hand along one of the wheel cogs. "I'll sail her back to Kingston for you, but that's my last stop."

❦

As long as she stood very still, it was almost as good as lying on the floor.

Or, as Dr. Hawthorne had recommended, being still, exerting herself as little as possible, would help her heal faster than anything. William had laughed and said it was a good thing she'd be stuck on his ship for a few days, then.

William. Her heart filled near to bursting with love for him. She was not quite certain how it worked, but she was happy God knew from the time they were children that she and William were supposed to be together.

She jumped at a knock on the door, but the flash of pain was bearable. Or not unbearable, anyway. "Yes?"

"Mrs. Commodore, a visitor to see you, ma'am."

"Thank you, Dawling." She turned, ready to welcome Michael to *Alexandra,* but she drew another quick breath at the sight of a black man with shaved head and hawklike features.

"Says he's Mr. Buh-*teest*." Dawling lingered at the door.

"Thank you, Dawling. That will be all."

"Missus, I think I should stay." The steward kept his eyes trained on Michael's sailing master.

"It's all right, Dawling. I will call if I need anything."

He didn't look at all happy about it, but Dawling capitulated and left the room. If she knew him at all, he kept his hand on the doorknob and his ear pressed to the jamb.

"Do sit down, Mr. Baptiste." She motioned him to one of the chairs at William's worktable.

"No, ma'am. I won't stay long."

Good, because that meant she did not have to try to be polite and sit down also. "What can I do for you?"

"I would like to come work for you, Mrs. Ransome."

A preacher turned pirate wanted to work for her? "What do you mean, Mr. Baptiste?"

"At the plantation. Salvador—your brother, ma'am—told me all about how you and he worked together to free the slaves at your plantation. And every time we went back so he could check on you, I saw how things were there. People were happy. They have good lives." He stood so still, he could have been an exquisitely carved piece of ebony wood.

"What do you think you could do on the plantation?" The pain in Julia's side fought with the gentle sway of the ship.

"I grew up on a sugar plantation outside New Orleans, ma'am. I can do everything—plant, cultivate, harvest, cure. And I can read and write and calculate."

Julia thought not about the sugar cane and refineries, but about the white clapboard chapel. "And I hear you preach."

"I've been known to do so, yes, ma'am. Had my own congregation for a dozen years."

Jeremiah loved talking about God, but even he admitted he was no preacher. "Mr. Baptiste, I would be happy for you to come work for Tierra Dulce. Will you return to Kingston with us?"

"No, ma'am. I will sail *Serenity* back for Captain Witherington."

Julia crossed to William's desk, eased herself down into the chair, and pulled out stationery, ink, and quill. "I understand *Serenity* is to leave within the hour."

"As soon as I return to pilot her, ma'am."

But with the delays of Kent's surgery and Charlotte's late return, *Alexandra* and *Audacious* would now be stuck here until tomorrow morning. She penned a note to Jeremiah, sealed it, and gave it to Jean Baptiste. "Take this to the overseer at Tierra Dulce. He will find you a place to stay and put you to work until I get there."

The sailor tucked the letter into his waistcoat pocket. "Thank you, ma'am. I promise, you will not be sorry a day that you've hired me."

"I know you will justify my trust in you, Mr. Baptiste."

He let himself out, and Julia cleaned up the writing supplies. Perhaps having one of Michael's former crew working for her at Tierra Dulce would make her long-lost brother feel not quite so far away.

She looked up at another knock on the door. "Yes?"

The door opened and this time it was Michael.

"Don't get up, Julia." He hurried to her side.

"I think I will. I'm not comfortable here." She took the assistance he offered to return to her feet.

"Do you have a place for him?"

"Jean Baptiste? Yes—or, rather, Jeremiah will find a place for him working on the plantation. When I get home I will ask him to preach for us on a Sunday to see if he is the preacher we've been waiting for at the Tierra Dulce chapel. What about Suresh? He isn't looking to make a change like that, is he?" Julia grinned at her brother.

"You will never get my steward from me. Not only will I always outbid you, but he is loyal to me. That's a rare thing in my line of work." Michael wandered around the cabin examining the furniture and fixtures. "Not much for showing off, is he, this husband of yours?"

"No. But that's one of the many reasons why I love him."

Michael flopped onto the sofa in the corner—the one her desk had sat beside on the voyage over from England. He leaned his head back against the high arm and covered his eyes with one arm.

Julia almost laughed at the melodramatic pose. "You're going to miss your ship."

"Yes." Michael's wail reminded her so much of when they were children and would perform theatricals for Mama, Jeremiah, and Jerusha. "England, sister. He's making me go back to *England*. I hate it there."

She ventured a light chuckle. "You haven't been there since you were ten years old. You don't know that you'll hate it."

He lifted his arm and peeked at her with a grin. "I'll hate it."

"You're incorrigible."

Heaving a dramatic sigh, he covered his eyes again. "Don't I know it? But at least I'm not as bad as Declan."

"Declan?"

"Yes, locking Ned and Charlotte in Ned's cabin like that."

Julia gasped, and then gasped again, all humor gone, shock overriding the sharp pain in her side. "What?"

Michael swung his legs around and sat up. "Charlotte did not tell you?"

"William hasn't come back with her yet." Julia pressed her fingertips to her temples. "Oh, this is terrible."

Michael made a face of comic disbelief. "Why is it terrible? They're in love and they're married. That's what young, in-love, married people are supposed to do. Steal away and spend time alone together."

"But they aren't married, not really." She wrung her hands, trying to think of how she could keep this a secret.

"How do you figure that? I was there. I signed the marriage certificate as a witness. I handed the bride over." His chest puffed with pride.

"But they weren't married by a rector or parish priest or bishop."

"You doubt the authenticity of Ned and Charlotte's marriage, but you yourself plan to ask Jean Baptiste to become the preacher at Tierra Dulce's church? So he's good enough for the black folk, but not good enough for us?" Michael lost all traces of humor. "If that's what you think, then you're not the Julia Witherington I remember."

"No, it isn't that..." But maybe, somewhere deep down in a part of her she didn't want to admit existed, that was why she had such a problem accepting that Charlotte and Ned were truly married. Shame bubbled up, and she pressed her hands to her hot cheeks. "You're right. I've been prejudicial against Jean Baptiste—but not because he's black. It's because he's not English. Not someone who would be acceptable by *society's* standards."

She gaped at her brother. "Michael, I've become just like her! I went to England for a year, and they turned me into one of them."

He eased the tension between them by throwing back his head and laughing. "Yes, Mother was a stickler for maintaining everything the way it would have been back in England. So, now, what is your position on Ned and Charlotte?"

Julia swallowed hard around the sting of recognizing her own weakness in allowing everyone in England to shape her into someone for whom appearances were more important than what she knew in her heart to be right. "My position is that Captain and Mrs. Cochrane should be allowed to be together, if that is what they wish."

Her brother bounded up from the sofa and came over to gently hug her. He ended the embrace with a loud kiss on the cheek. "That's the sister I remembered."

"Good. Because now you're going to have to help me explain this to William."

Michael shook his head. "No, ma'am. Husband-and-wife waters are too rough for this pirate to sail. That's between the two of you."

"What good is having my brother back if you're not going to help me?"

He gave her a smacking kiss on the other cheek. "There are times when a brother helps, and then there are times when a brother runs away."

The door opened and William entered. Michael leaned closer. "And this is definitely a time for running away," he whispered.

"Coward," Julia whispered back.

"Good luck." Michael waved, greeted William, and slipped out the door.

Chapter Twenty-Six

"W here is Charlotte?" Julia looked beyond William as he entered and Michael exited.

He shut the cabin door. "I was waylaid by the doctor, who wanted to tell me that Mr. Kent woke up and took a little water."

"So you haven't gone to get her yet?"

He stepped into the quarter gallery. "No."

Julia waited until he came back out to continue the conversation. "Don't bring her back."

William poured water over his hands into the washbasin and then used it to splash his face. The end of the first week of October and still the full heat of summer. "What did you say?"

"Let her stay with Ned if that is what she wants."

He looked at Julia, water still dripping from his chin, to see if she looked feverish or if she, like Mr. Kent, had received a blow to the head, causing her confusion. "Why?"

"Because they're married." She looked at him as if he were the one not thinking straight.

"But you said until they were married in a church, you thought they should be kept apart."

She shrugged, a slight upward movement of her shoulders that brought no grimace of pain. "I was wrong."

"Does this have anything to do with Jean Baptiste's visit to you?"

"Indirectly, yes. I was being too English in my notions. I forgot that I'm more Jamaican than English."

At that outrageous statement, he had to laugh. "I do not know what that means, but whatever it is, I am certain Charlotte will be very thankful for your change of heart." He dried his face and hung the small towel back on its peg. "If you are feeling up to it, I thought you might like to come see *Serenity* off before I head over to *Audacious* to chart routes with Ned."

"Yes, I do believe a walk to the quarterdeck will do me good."

He gave her the support of his arm. In the wheelhouse and on deck, all of the officers and crew were especially solicitous toward her, and she basked in their attentions. William left her with Michael at the starboard side of the quarterdeck and gave orders for a boat to be prepared and for the sailing master to be ready with his charts.

By the time he rejoined them at the bulwark, *Serenity* was moving apace, every man of the scant crew busy with his duty. As the quarterdeck passed, Michael raised his hand in a wave, and Declan and Jean Baptiste raised theirs in a return farewell.

Until now, seeing Julia and Michael standing side by side, William had forgotten that in his initial encounter with Julia twenty years ago, upon first glance he had mistaken her for Michael, an error most of the men aboard her father's ship had made, to Julia's benefit, as it had allowed her to roam freely about the ship dressed in her brother's clothes with her long hair tucked up in a knit cap. Looking upon them now, most would guess they were sister and brother, but not that they were twins.

Three bells marked five thirty in the evening. It would be dark soon—earlier than sunset, as the cliffs would block the sun once it dipped low on the horizon. William bade Julia farewell and descended the accommodation ladder while she and Michael returned to the big cabin for supper.

After a short trip across the water, shorter now that *Serenity* wasn't between them, William, his sailing master, and his new first lieutenant, Campbell, were ushered to Ned's cabin. In the dining cabin, Charlotte helped the steward set out Captain Parker's china for supper. She didn't just blush when she looked up to greet William—her entire head turned red. No need to wonder why she had not returned to *Alexandra* hours ago. His baby sister—

He set that unproductive line of thought aside. Another issue needed to be addressed, and it needed to be addressed before *Audacious* returned to Kingston.

After dining with Ned's five lieutenants, William asked Ned to call a meeting of the officers in the wardroom—lieutenants, midshipmen, and warrant officers. With a question in his gray eyes, Ned made it so.

"Charlotte, you will join us, please." William waved her toward the door.

Wide-eyed, she followed Ned out the door and down one level to the wardroom. More Spartan than the captain's quarters, the main area of the lieutenants' berth provided more room for the number present.

As soon as the last midshipman filed in and closed the door, William spoke.

"As many of you know and many of you have surmised, the midshipman you knew as Charles Lott on the crossing from England was this young woman in disguise, my sister and now your captain's wife."

William marked shock in a few faces, but the rest nodded, smirked, or acted as if they did not care. "Though it was an ill-judged decision on her part, Midshipman Charles Lott served with distinction"—here the two youngest lieutenants nodded emphatically—"and served with as much dedication and honor as a man."

Beside him, Charlotte stared at him, her lips parted, eyes wide, cheeks pink.

"Since being rescued from her abduction by pirates, she has once again stepped in where needed, protecting the members of this crew, including risking her own life to board the frigate *Sister Mary* to rescue Lieutenant Gardiner, Midshipman Jamison, and Midshipman Kent—who is recovering from his surgery, according to Dr. Hawthorne. In fact, she saved Mr. Kent's life twice, even after, I am told, he did everything he could to make her stay on *Audacious* the first time unpleasant."

A frisson of agreement circulated in the room. "Many of you witnessed her courageous act of putting herself between Kent and the incoming fire from the pirate ship *Sister Elizabeth* during this most recent battle, for which she received the thanks of taking grapeshot to her arm, shot that would most likely have killed Mr. Kent had she not intervened."

Now even those midshipmen who had smirked and made quiet scoffing sounds in the beginning looked ready to praise Charlotte for her actions.

"You have all heard the rumors, the legends, that have surfaced through the last thirty years we have been at war of women disguising themselves and serving valiantly in the Royal Navy. I put to you tonight that the legend of Charles Lott will add greatly to the mythos."

Both Charlotte and Ned stared at him now, while the others around them discussed William's proposal amongst themselves.

Moments later Lieutenant Gardiner stepped forward and the room once again grew still. "Commodore Ransome, Captain Cochrane," he smiled at Charlotte, "and Mrs. Cochrane, the officers of His Majesty's Ship *Audacious* are proud to be the bearers of the legend of Charles Lott. He came to us in Portsmouth a green lad with much to learn. He served with honor, led with a kind firmness, and did not retaliate when wrong was done to him. His young life was snuffed by yellow fever at Barbados, but he was not ready to leave us yet, so his ghost remained, reappearing during times of great need to protect the crew of *Audacious* and, especially, her captain."

The first lieutenant turned and scanned the faces around him. "Gentlemen, long live the legend of Charles Lott."

"Long live the legend of Charles Lott!" the others cheered.

Gratitude swelled in William's throat, and from the redness of her eyes, Charlotte struggled hard to keep her own emotions at bay.

Ned stepped forward. "Dismissed!"

Charlotte wrapped her arms around William's middle. "Thank you, William." She craned her head back to look up at him. "How did you know all of that?"

He tweaked her chin and extricated himself from her embrace. "Your husband is my subordinate officer. He must report everything to me." He glanced over his shoulder at a red-faced Ned. "In his own time, of course. And occasionally to my wife before he reports to me. Which will never happen again, will it, Captain Cochrane."

Ned snapped to attention. "No, sir, Commodore."

"Very good. Now, you and I have charts to review." William took Charlotte by the shoulders and turned her toward the door. "And you have a ghostlike legend to maintain, so I suggest it is time you disappear and stay to the big cabin until we reach Kingston."

The back of Charlotte's neck turned bright red, and William had no trouble imagining the thoughts running through her mind. He had more trouble trying to ignore the fact he knew what she was thinking.

He prayed God would give them a happy, fulfilled marriage that matured and grew despite the unusual way in which it began.

CRACO

From his hammock William could see Julia's open eyes staring at the whitewashed decking above her. She seemed afraid even to blink, but eventually, as the night wore on, her eyes grew heavy and closed.

William, however, could not sleep. He could not stop watching her, thanking God she had been restored to him, praying her pain would abate, praying her mind would settle on happy memories, praying his presence would give her the peace she needed to sleep through the night.

She woke up screaming. He jumped out of the hammock and reached for her. She hit and clawed at him, moonlight illuminating the terror in her distant eyes.

He grabbed her wrists to keep her from injuring him or herself. "Julia, wake up. You are safe. You are home."

The word *home* made her blink. She stopped struggling; her body went limp. Tears poured from her eyes. "It was so real. He was there."

"He's dead, Julia. I watched him take his last breath. He can never hurt you again."

Her eyes drifted closed.

William took down his hammock and used the narrow space beside the wide box bed to pace and pray.

Each time she woke up screaming, it took William longer to wake her, to calm her.

The fourth time it happened, Dawling arrived with Dr. Hawthorne while Julia still struggled against William.

When finally she broke through the nightmare and truly awakened, William trembled and dripped with perspiration from the exertion of trying to hold her still.

Dr. Hawthorne leaned over her; she kept tight hold of William's hand.

"I do not understand why the laudanum is not keeping her asleep. Captain Ransome seems to be responding to it much better."

William gazed into her teary eyes and knew he'd have to countermand her choice. "She did not want to take it, afraid it would make the nightmares worse."

"She must take it. She needs to stay as still as possible for the broken ribs to mend. The struggling, the screaming, will only make them worse." Dr. Hawthorne pulled a bottle out of his coat pocket.

"Yes, Doctor, I agree. I will ensure she takes the proper dosage." He took the bottle, as finding the one the doctor had given Julia earlier would be difficult without lighting all the candles in the cabins. He knew she'd probably stashed it somewhere out of sight hoping he would forget about it.

"Good. Send for me if you need me again. I am on the night watch with Mr. Kent and Captain Ransome."

Dawling saw the doctor to the door and returned with a glass of water. William measured out the dosage of the powder and stirred it into the liquid and turned back to Julia, glad James had chosen to stay in the sick berth where the doctor could deal with his nightmares and outbursts, if necessary, and that Michael had hung his hammock in the berth Declan had used in the wardroom, where he did not have to witness his sister's anguish.

He scooped Julia's head and shoulders up with his left arm and held the glass to her lips with his right hand.

Julia pressed her lips together and turned her face away.

William leaned closer. "Do not make me force you to drink this in front of Dawling," he whispered.

She turned her head back. "But I can't fight him. If I drink that, and he takes me again…"

He kissed her forehead, his own heart hammering at the agony in her voice. "I will be here to fight for you. You can stop fighting now and just rest. I will protect you."

"Promise me, William."

"I promise."

"I love you."

"And I love you. I will protect you, now and forever." He pressed the glass to her lips and she drank, wrinkling her nose at the bitter taste.

She slept.

He did not.

Morning came. *Alexandra* and *Audacious* moved back out into open sea and set course for Kingston.

Julia awakened, groggy and disoriented. William stayed with her much of the day, and they both dozed occasionally.

She took the laudanum without resistance that night. "The nightmares are there, but hazier, not as real."

Through the night, William awakened at every bell sounding, checking to make sure Julia slept. A few times he could tell she was in the throes of a nightmare—she clutched at the bedding, kicked her feet, tossed her head. But as quickly as it began, it ended, and she succumbed to the powerful lure of the laudanum.

On Tuesday Midshipman Kennedy had just marked noon when *Alexandra* entered Kingston Harbor. If Declan delivered the message as requested, carriages from Tierra Dulce should be waiting for them.

Sister Elizabeth lay anchored in the harbor and, through his spyglass, William was pleased to see O'Rourke touch the tip of his hat in salute as *Alexandra* came to anchorage nearby.

William's first call of duty was to report himself to Fort Charles to see if the new admiral had arrived and then to begin the work of reporting and claiming the prizes and bounties.

But first he had to see his wife home.

Under normal circumstances he would have bidden Julia farewell at the dock, seen her bundled up into one of the carriages, and gone about his work. But these were not normal circumstances.

Though she mentioned a headache, Julia seemed much more alert today than yesterday. She still had pain in her side, but even that seemed lessened. When the jolly boat reached the dock, she climbed from the boat to the quay with only a hand-up from William.

Jerusha cried out and ran down the dock, Jeremiah close behind. They coddled her like a delicate china vase and ushered her down the dock to the waiting carriages. William waited for the second boat to arrive, this one with Michael and James.

Michael, the man who had spent the past fifteen years as a pirate, walked down the dock toward the carriages. Jerusha turned, looked questioningly at him a moment, and then she screamed, threw her hands in the air, and jumped up and down before smothering him in an embrace.

Jeremiah—

The Tierra Dulce overseer seemed happy to see Michael, but he was nowhere near as surprised as someone who'd believed Michael dead these fifteen years.

"Do you think we will ever have such a reunion with our family, William?" James held his hands out in front of him as the sergeant of the marines locked his shackles.

William rested his hand on his brother's shoulder. "I do, James. Whether it is here or on the other side, where we will be with Father again, I believe one day we will all be together." He looked down at the iron cuffs around his brother's still-raw wrists. "I am sorry for this."

"I am ready to face the court-martial and whatever judgment they pass. You cannot blame yourself for my disobedience."

William cuffed his neck. "Please do not speak that way in front of the court. Be honest but do not put the words of condemnation into their mouths for them."

"Aye, aye, Commodore."

William nodded at the marine guards, who shuffled James away toward the cart that would take them to Fort Charles, where James would remain until his hearing.

O'Rourke arrived from *Sister Elizabeth*. "It is good to see you, Commodore. You are a day later than expected."

"A story that can wait until another time." He looked at each of his lieutenants, now gathered with him on the dock. He reviewed their orders, catching O'Rourke up on what he needed to know. "It will be late tonight or early tomorrow morning before I arrive. If the captain from Fort Charles challenges you, Mr. Campbell, tell him—"

"Tell him Commodore Ransome is called away on urgent business for Admiral Witherington."

"Very good. Now, see to your duties, and we will square everything away when I return."

"Aye, aye, sir."

The boats' oars had all struck the water before William made it to the end of the dock. Charlotte and Michael sat in the seat across from Julia and Jerusha, while Jeremiah sat in the box with the driver. William opened the door—and realized there was no place for him to sit.

Julia raised her head from Jerusha's shoulder. "I should have waited to get in until we said goodbye." She started to push herself up off the seat, but William stayed her with his hand on her knee.

"Goodbye? I was going to take you home, make sure you arrived safely." He looked into her eyes, expecting to see a haze of confusion brought on by the laudanum, but they were as clear as her lagoon.

"William, you have work to do. As you can see, I am quite safe, surrounded by family and friends." She placed her hands on his cheeks and leaned forward, grimacing. "But I do love you for wanting to see me safely home, even if it means shirking your duties."

She kissed him. "But I won't let you do that. I love you too much to let you do something so out of character." She kissed him again. "Go see to your duty and your prize vessel and your bounties. That is what is important now. And then, as soon as you are finished, come home to me." She lingered over a final kiss.

"If you are certain." Her kisses, and her insistence he do his duty, lightened his mood instantly.

She leaned back with a groan, hugging her ribs and making Jerusha cluck over her with concern. "I am certain, William."

He stepped back from the carriage, closed the door, and touched the fore point of his hat. "I will see you in a few days, then."

The carriages—one full, one empty—rolled away, and William rounded, ready to return to duty. It was a long walk from the Kingston docks to Fort Charles, but knowing Julia had recovered sufficiently that she could bid him a cheerful farewell only hours after clinging to him upon awakening from her opium-induced sleep relieved his greatest burden.

After half a mile he stopped and turned to look back down the road toward where the carriages had sat, his mind replaying Julia's farewell. Her sweet kisses. The joy in her face and eyes and voice. Her releasing him from his promise to stay by her side.

She released him from his promise to stay by her side.

No wonder she'd laughed when he'd told her he would resign his commission to stay with her, to watch over her. She'd laughed because she'd known something that he just realized, something he couldn't believe it took him this long to figure out.

Julia didn't need him.

He was either the biggest fool in the world, or he had not yet begun to comprehend how much God had blessed him.

Most men desired wives who needed them—needed their strength, their protection, their wealth, their social status. Julia needed none of those things.

But God had instead blessed William with a wife who loved him. And that was all he needed.

Chapter Twenty-Seven

Everyone raise your glass." William waited for all around the table to comply. Then he said, "Congratulations to the newest post captain on Jamaica station, Ned Cochrane."

"Hear, hear!"

"Congratulations, Ned."

"Well done."

Charlotte took a sip of wine but put the glass down almost immediately. Three weeks. That was all. Three weeks for the banns to be read, the preparations to be made, and James's court-martial to be finished with and James released so that Charlotte and Ned could have their official wedding ceremony and then have four or five glorious weeks alone together aboard *Audacious* as they sailed back to England. Or, as alone as they could be on a ship with more than six hundred others aboard.

In an effort to keep Charlotte busy, Julia had been trying to teach her how to run a household. But Julia's household included everyone who lived and worked at Tierra Dulce, which meant more ledgers and inventories and keys than Charlotte could keep up with. And there were days when all she wanted was to be left on her own, to read a book or to write a letter, but she was never alone. Julia wanted Charlotte by her side at all times.

Here it was, the seventh day of November, and yet still no firm date for the wedding ceremony had been set. Which meant that even though Ned and William were staying at Tierra Dulce tonight before heading back to Fort Charles in the morning, Charlotte and Ned had to sleep in separate bedchambers, again, as they had every other time he and William had traveled out to the plantation.

She'd grown so frustrated with the entire ordeal that she was making herself ill. Being awakened in the middle of the night several times a week by Julia's screams was probably not helpful, either, though the nightmares did not seem to be doing her sister-in-law any harm. And they were happening less often—and never on the nights when William was here.

She and Ned should elope—oh, wait. They were already married. Had already lived together as man and wife, albeit only for two nights before *Audacious* docked in Kingston.

"Any news of James's hearing?"

Every time William came home, Julia asked the same question. And every time, William gave the same answer.

"Until the new admiral arrives, we do not have enough officers of higher rank than James to convene a court."

And then the next question.

"Any news of the admiral's arrival?"

But now, tonight at dinner, William said, "Scouts report that a first-rate ship of the line was spotted docking in Barbados two days ago bearing a flag and pennant of a Vice Admiral of the Blue."

Charlotte's heart leaped. As soon as the admiral arrived they could convene James's court-martial. He could be cleared of the charges against him and returned to duty—and in the meantime come to Tierra Dulce for her wedding—before getting his new ship. It took about a week to sail from Barbados to Jamaica. The admiral could be here by Saturday. They could convene James's hearing Monday… by this time next week, she could be preparing to be a bride. Again.

She glanced across the table at Ned. He winked at her.

Soon, my love.

After supper Charlotte, Julia, and Jerusha retired to the small parlor while William, Ned, Michael, and Jeremiah discussed the latest developments.

Tonight the separation did not last long. Ned stepped into the room. "Charlotte, would you do me the honor of a stroll about the porches?"

Fear twitched in the back of Charlotte's mind. Ned must have sensed it. "It is light yet. We will come in before it grows dark."

She put her embroidery aside, rose, and took his arm.

From the back of the house they had a spectacular view of the sunset. Just under a mile away, beyond the cane fields, the lagoon looked like an enormous sparkling ruby reflecting the red sky.

Ned pulled her in his arms and kissed her. She liked this kind of stroll around the porches. So long as it didn't end with Ned's being knocked unconscious and her being abducted by a pirate, be he good or not.

"How soon do you think we can plan the wedding and then leave for England?" She rested her hands on his chest and her cheek against her hands, looking out at the sunset, wrapped in her husband's arms.

"Once William has confirmation the ship is carrying our admiral, he will dispatch messages to the other commodores with the date the admiral sets for the court-martial."

"When will that be?"

"It is at the admiral's discretion."

"Can William encourage him to make his discretion next week?"

Ned's chuckle rumbled under her hands and cheek. "I am eager to have the matter settled as well, but we must have patience."

Charlotte pushed back so she could look up into his eyes. "You know I have no patience."

He pressed his hand to the back of her head until she rested it on his chest again and then settled his chin atop her head. "I know." He held her silently for a while. "I have other news."

"This is a special day. First your promotion confirmed, then news the admiral is coming, and now even more news. I might die of excitement."

He tightened his squeeze until she laughed. "I'm sorry. What is your news?"

"The final determination of our prize money was made today."

"Will you get your share at a post captain's rank or a lieutenant's?"

"I was only an acting captain, still rated a lieutenant, during the action, so I will draw a lieutenant's share."

"That is not fair. You were a captain. You should—"

He squeezed her again. "Will you let me continue, please?"

She heaved a sigh but smiled and caught the tip of her tongue between her teeth. She loved teasing him.

"Are you listening?"

"You wanted me to stop talking, so I stopped talking." She started to push back from him, but he held her head down.

"Can you take nothing seriously?"

"Other than wanting our wedding to happen soon?"

He sighed.

"I'm listening."

"With the prize money from the payout on *Sister Elizabeth* and her cargo, as well as the bounty on *Sister Mary* and on Shaw, I have made just over ten thousand pounds."

Charlotte did push back this time, studying his face carefully to see if he teased her. But pride, serious and genuine, beamed from his eyes and smile. "Ned, we're rich! With my ten thousand and your ten thousand...we have more than we'll ever need." She pulled his head down to reward him with another kiss.

Ned perched on the edge of the porch railing, holding Charlotte's hands in his. "Commodore Ransome and I talked about it on the way here. We need a home, Charlotte. We need to decide where our home is going to be."

"Home? Why, home is with Mama in Gateacre. We'll visit while we're in England."

He gave her his indulgent smile. "I mean a house for us, you and me and our family someday."

"Oh." Yes, that was the reason she and Ned were having to stay apart until they could have a real wedding ceremony. So that they could have a house of their own in which to raise children. Someday. She hoped not right away. She'd been separated from him so long that she wanted to have time, years perhaps, to spend with him before children interrupted them.

"We need to start thinking about where we want our home to be. I have been attached to William's command here at Fort Charles, which means we could be here for years. But if the war ends with America, as it may soon, there could be changes in the western fleet—reassignments or retirements of entire divisions. We do not need to decide right away, but we need to ask ourselves if we want to live here in Jamaica or in England."

She leaned toward him, craning her head back as she got closer. "I do not care where we live, so long as we can be together."

അപ

Julia ignored the stitch in her side as she hurried back to the main house. "Charlotte! Michael! News from Kingston!"

Her sister-in-law and brother both came out of the study.

Charlotte bounced on her toes. "Is it about James?"

"Yes. The admiral arrived yesterday. William is bringing him and his wife here tonight so we can meet them. Yes, Charlotte, Ned is coming also. James's hearing has been scheduled for Thursday." Though it had only been a week since William and Ned's last visit, Julia's anticipation to see her husband again almost matched Charlotte's excitement.

She pulled another letter from her pocket. "And this came for you, Michael." She only had to see her brother's smile to know the letter came from Serena.

"I must go speak with Cook about supper tonight." Julia started off toward the kitchen. "With the admiral and his wife here, it will be much more formal than family dinner, so please dress appropriately."

After setting Cook in a tizzy, though assuring her that the fillet of beef she already had roasting would be perfectly fine for a Vice Admiral of the Blue, Julia met with Jerusha to discuss the table setting.

"Jeremiah and I will take supper in the kitchen tonight, Miss Julia."

Jerusha unlocked the silver cabinet and began pulling out trays to polish before their guest arrived.

"No, you will have dinner with the family, just like you do every night."

"It might reflect badly on the commodore for the admiral to see us at his dinner table."

"It will reflect badly on the admiral and his wife if either of them has a problem with whom I invite to sit at my table. You will attend us for dinner tonight, Jerusha. If you don't, I'll…I will terminate your employment at Tierra Dulce." She set a fist to her hip and tried to look stern.

"If you think you can make me leave Tierra Dulce by terminating my employment, you don't know me very well." Jerusha bent and pulled out more silver service.

Julia laughed. "I know." She hugged the woman who had been more than a housekeeper, more than a friend for twenty years. "And that's why I love you so much."

Jerusha shooed her away, but not before Julia caught a hint of extra moisture in her brown eyes. "The commodore is going to be here in less than two hours. You'd best go get ready."

Julia pulled a few maids away from their normal duties to take over polishing the silver from Jerusha so that she could get ready also. She sent another to freshen one of the vacant bedrooms for the admiral and his wife to stay in tonight.

She wished she'd had more time to prepare. She and Cook would have planned a special meal, a special dessert. She could have invited some of her neighbors—the ones she would especially want the admiral's wife to know.

But perhaps it was best to introduce them to the intimate family circle first. Let them settle in. Later, she could plan a welcoming reception for them when they could come and stay a few days.

She stood at the wardrobe looking through her gowns for too long. Each one held such memories. The gold and bronze dress she'd worn to the dinner party at Witherington House and again to the dinner at which she'd met William's officers for the first time. The green gown she'd worn to the concert when Sir Drake Pembroke's cologne had given her a migraine—she had not worn it since that night. The ivory silk with the blue velvet overtunic she'd worn the night she asked William to marry her. Her wedding dress, a plain lavender gown with an overdress of ivory lace from Susan Yates's mother's wedding dress. The periwinkle gown with the heavy gold brocading at neck, sleeves, waist, and hem she'd worn to Charlotte's debut ball. Every gown reminding her of William.

She pulled out the ivory and blue dress, running her hands over the luxurious fabrics. The same colors as William's waistcoat and uniform coat, but smooth, cool, and fluid rather than rough, hot, and stiff.

Seated at the vanity, she started pulling the pins from her hair.

"Do you want me to do it again, ma'am?" her maid asked.

"No, I will be leaving it down tonight. My husband prefers it that way." Opening the lacquer box on the table before her, she withdrew two combs with mother-of-pearl inlay and used them to secure her hair back from her face, though a few wispy curls made their way free. She smiled. William liked to let those tiny strands wrap around his fingers as he pushed them back from her cheeks.

Jerusha knocked and entered. "Carriage coming up the drive, Miss Julia."

"You look lovely."

Jerusha smoothed her hand over the burgundy silk dress Julia had brought back from England for her. "I'm afraid I'll ruin it."

"Mmm. Just like you ruin all of your garments." She hooked her arm through Jerusha's. "Come, help me greet our guests."

The housekeeper protested, but Julia did not listen, pulling Jerusha out onto the front porch with her just in time to see the carriage pull up into the circle drive. Julia smiled at William, Ned, and then frowned.

"They made the admiral and his wife ride facing backwards." What must they think of William's manners? The guests of honor were always given the forward facing seat.

The gold braid along the brim of the admiral's hat sparkled in the late afternoon sun. Though the side points of the modified version of an old tricorn swished from side to side as he looked around, he never turned his head far enough so that Julia could see his face. Beside him sat a woman wearing a deep-brimmed bonnet, a veil fluttering from its edges.

The carriage stopped and Ned climbed down first, followed by William. Julia caught herself from calling out the instruction that they were supposed to let their guests descend first.

William smiled up at them as he climbed down from the carriage to the ground at the bottom of the porch steps.

"Mrs. Goodland, Mrs. Ransome. May I have the honor of introducing you to the new admiral of Jamaica station?"

The man climbed down, his head lowered so the hat hid his face. Julia ducked her head, trying to see him. And then he looked up.

She gasped. "Papa?"

His craggy face broke into a grin, and he took the steps two at a time and swept her up into his arms. "Oh, my bonny girl."

"Papa, it's really you! You're here, in Jamaica."

He set her down and tweaked her chin. "You act as though you haven't seen me in years. It has only been about three months, by my calculation."

"Oh, Papa. What a three months, though."

He caressed her cheek. "So William has told me. We shall have time to speak of everything, but not now. Not tonight." He turned to Jerusha. "Mrs. Goodland, a delight to see you again."

"And you, Sir Edward. What a welcome sight you are. I'll go in and make some refreshments ready."

Charlotte came out as Jerusha went in. Her eyes widened at the sight of Julia's father, and after a startled glance at Julia she dropped into a deep curtsey. "Welcome home, Sir Edward."

"Miss Ransome"—he cast a glance over his shoulder at Ned before continuing—"or should I call you Mrs. Cochrane? I am not certain."

She sighed. "I am not certain myself anymore. Everyone around here calls me Miss Charlotte as we don't know what my proper name is."

At the bottom of the steps, Ned's face went from smiling to warning in an instant, but only Julia saw it.

"Come, Julia, Miss Charlotte, there is someone I want you to meet."

Julia's heart suddenly stuttered and then started again with an irregular beat. William's note had said he was bringing the admiral *and his wife*. She swallowed hard. The memories of Mama were still vivid in this house even more than eighteen months after her death.

Admiral Witherington reached up to help down the veil-shrouded lady. "Julia, Miss Charlotte, I have the great honor of introducing you to my wife, Lady Witherington."

The woman reached up and swept her creamy veil back.

Charlotte grabbed Julia's arm with painful intensity. "Mama?"

The woman removed the bonnet, revealing without a doubt that she was indeed Charlotte and William's mother. She opened her arms and her daughter ran to her, sobbing, apologizing, and expressing her astonishment at seeing her in Jamaica.

Julia's head buzzed with questions. She looked up into her father's green eyes and found she could not ask one.

Behind them Charlotte's excited voice began detailing her experiences since the moment she sneaked out of Susan and Collin Yates's townhouse the day before *Audacious* and *Alexandra* set sail from Portsmouth.

Sir Edward took Julia's hand and tucked it under his elbow, leading her to the porch steps. "We shall tell all at supper." He stopped halfway up the steps and pinned her with a worried gaze. "You...you aren't angry with me for remarrying, are you?"

"Papa, I—" Words jumbled in her throat. "Mrs. Ransome?"

He ran his knuckles along her jaw. "That is you now, my dear."

Charlotte's voice stopped suddenly. Julia looked down to see why and saw Charlotte staring, dismayed, up at the porch. Julia turned and looked up. And her stomach lurched.

Her father stiffened. Michael froze.

Julia looked at William, who shook his head at her.

"M-Michael?" Sir Edward stepped back and would have fallen down the steps had not Julia steadied him.

Michael's confused gaze sought Julia's.

"Papa is the new admiral of Jamaica station, Michael. He's come home—and he's remarried." She prayed her brother and father could reconcile, like the father and prodigal son in the book of Luke. She had read the story so many times since Michael returned to her life that she almost had it memorized.

Michael nodded, his expression hardening. "Then I suppose it is good that I will be leaving for Philadelphia just as soon as possible."

Chapter Twenty-Eight

The study door slammed closed. Julia flinched and ushered every-one—everyone but her father and Michael—into the large for-mal sitting room at the front of the house.

William sat in the chair adjacent to the end of the settee where his mother sat, looking for all the world as if this were any other normal day. As if he expected her father to listen to what Michael had to say rationally, calmly, and make his judgments objectively.

Jerusha brought in a tray with two decanters: one of wine and the other of fruit juice. For the first time ever, Julia chose wine over juice. "Mrs. Rans—I am sorry, Lady Witherington. How did you and my father come to be married?"

William's mother tasted the juice and looked up to thank Jerusha, who poured her a full serving. "I know it must be difficult on you, especially, Julia, to know I am married to your father, to hear me called by your mother's title. I do not want to distress you. You must call me Maria. Or, as I have already offered, Mama."

The warmth of emotion from that day, which seemed so long ago but was only a few months back, rushed in. The day William's mother had accepted Julia as her own daughter.

"Thank you…Mama." As soon as she said it, it sounded right.

Not like the raised voices she could just make out coming from the study on the opposite side of the house. She glanced at William. She had been right. There would be yelling.

"Your father and I have known each other for years, ever since my dear George's funeral. Your father and George were close friends, and he promised George he would look after our family. He made certain the boys were well placed and that Charlotte and I had what we needed."

"Nothing I did was ever good enough for you!"

Julia closed her eyes, cleared her throat, and affixed a smile on her face. "And then you saw each other again in Portsmouth this summer."

"Yes. It was the first time since the funeral, but I felt as if I knew him well through his friendship with George and the way he took William under his wing." Maria Witherington smiled at her eldest son.

"You should have had courage enough to tell me you did not want to join the Royal Navy!"

Maria glanced in the direction Michael and Sir Edward had disappeared. "I-I could see your father still grieved for your mother, Julia. I understood his pain, so whenever I had the opportunity I made sure he knew he could talk to me if he ever wanted to."

"...compared me to William Ransome my entire life!"

"I am certain he appreciated that." Julia looked toward the study and then toward William. He squirmed a bit in his chair at his name being brought into it. She'd warned him it would come to this.

Maria smoothed her hand down her skirt. "Your father has such a sensitive soul."

"Now you're being idiotic, Michael!"

Julia burst out into nervous laughter. "Yes, currently on display for all of us to hear."

Her quip and the laughter that followed helped release the tension in the room. "So you helped Father through his grief?"

"Yes. He held on to so much from when Michael die—disappeared that your mother's death was nearly his undoing. If you had not returned to England with him, I do not know what might have happened to him."

"Oh, yes, because a pirate is such a trustworthy sort."

Julia looked at William and could tell he was thinking the same thing as she. If she had not returned to England, none of their lives would have turned out so well.

"As you recall, I returned to Gateacre to prepare for Philip's home-coming before you left for Jamaica. Charlotte was supposed to go with the Fairfaxes to the country the morning before your ships left."

"He made me feel like I was worth something, like I could accomplish whatever I set out to do."

"And you set out to become a pirate? Brilliant idea!"

"Philip had been home but a day when an express arrived from Collin Yates telling me that if Charlotte was at home with me to keep her there until he could arrive to retrieve her. I did not know what was going on, so I waited. Two days later, he came. He'd been to the Fairfaxes' country home looking for her, and they told him they had received a note from Charlotte saying she was staying in Portsmouth to assist with Lady Dalrymple's daughter's new baby. Collin knew that wasn't true, so he figured Charlotte had decided to go home instead."

"How foolish were you to believe such a thing?"

Maria put her arm around Charlotte's shoulder, kissed her temple, and drew her close. "We thought you were dead. Captain Yates went to great expense trying to find you."

William said, "I shall reimburse him, Mother."

She patted her eldest son's knee. "No need. Sir Edward has done so already." She looked at Charlotte again. "And then your note arrived from Madeira. We knew you were safe but thought you were travel-ing with William and Julia, not disguised as a midshipman. Really, Charlotte."

"You never responded to the ransom demand because you never wanted me for a son!"

"THERE WAS NO RANSOM DEMAND! And you ARE my son. Want has nothing to do with it!"

Jerusha came back into the room, and Julia jumped to her feet. "Dinner. Shall we adjourn to the dining room?"

After William said a blessing over the meal, Maria continued her story. "Your father and I really have Charlotte to thank for bringing us together. I was in such a state when we could not discover where you had gone, and he comforted me."

"He was back from London?" Julia speared several pieces of beef from a platter before passing it to Charlotte.

"Yes, fresh from his promotion to vice admiral and with new orders to take over in Jamaica. We had grown so close over those weeks. We thought as friends. But then, when it came time for him to leave, we could not say goodbye. So he asked me to come with him to Jamaica as his wife." She stopped and cocked her head. "Are we farther away from the study in here?"

"No. They are no longer yelling—"

"Julia!" Her father's voice boomed through the house.

Startled, she rose. William started to stand also, but she waved him back down. "If he wanted both of us, he would have called both of us." She left the dining room and headed for the study.

Her father stood in the doorway, expression still stormy.

"Papa?"

"Where is the brandy?"

"What brandy?"

He clenched and unclenched his fists in front of him. "Every man's study has brandy."

"Papa, no man has lived in this house since before you bought the place. None except Jeremiah, and he does not use the study." She looked past him into the room. Michael sat on the sofa, arms stretched out across its back, legs crossed. "Is everything…have you resolved your differences."

"That's what we need the brandy for."

"I see. I will have some brought to you."

"Thank you." He stepped back into the room and closed the door.

Before she could return into the dining room, the butler greeted her at the door. Not so formally trained or utilized as those in England, he looked worried. "Is everything all right, Mrs. Ransome?"

"My father would like a bottle of brandy and two glasses brought to him in the study."

"Yes, ma'am." He marched off toward his pantry, where he must have had a bottle already prepared for the gentlemen for after dinner.

Julia went back into the dining room and took her place at the foot of the table.

No one ate, but all looked down the table at her. "He wanted brandy."

❦

Michael stared down into the amber liquid. He'd never had brandy before. He would probably never have it again.

His father had not touched his glass since pouring it. He read through the small leather-bound ledger line by line. After a long while, he came to the last page, closed it, and pulled off his glasses.

"There are only two people who could have given you an accounting so accurate. And I know Julia believed you to be dead. Explain to me why I should not have Jeremiah Goodland immediately imprisoned for giving aid and comfort to a known pirate."

Michael put his glass down on the low table in front of him. "I had been on my own for a couple of years. I could not keep a crew together because I would not hurt people, so our prizes usually ended up escaping from us. After one especially humiliating defeat, I lost most of my men when we put into port. I had heard rumors of how well Tierra Dulce was doing, so I decided to come back and take what was mine. I wasn't certain what I planned to do except come into the house and take whatever I could while everyone slept.

"Jeremiah caught me and recognized me. I told him everything. He wanted to take me inside right then and tell Mama and Julia, but I knew they would not understand and could never forgive me, so I refused. But I think Jeremiah knew that one day I would become a man and realize how important family is. He told me a story from the Bible, only at first he told me just a portion of it. A story of a son who has everything and goes to his father and says everything is not good enough, that he wants half of the inheritance he is to receive when his father dies."

"The story of the prodigal son." The corner of Sir Edward's mouth twitched.

"He stopped at that point in the story. He said that he would give me a record of Tierra Dulce's income and let me know what portion of it was mine—my birthright, my inheritance. And so long as I took only that amount, and did not hurt anyone on the ships, he would continue giving me the information." Michael snorted and shook his head. "Now that I think of it, he reminded me a lot of a Royal Navy captain. He demanded to see that ledger every time I came to him to get the updated account information. He demanded a full report of my activities. Because I knew I had to report to him, it kept me from doing things that could have gotten me or other people killed. Kept me from doing things I never would have been able to live with."

Michael told him the rest of the story, about liberating slave ships and becoming an American privateer.

"How many slave ships?"

"Seventy-eight, sir. Each carrying more than three hundred souls."

"Did Jeremiah ever tell you the rest of that story?"

"Yes, sir. Each year, he would add a piece until I knew the entire outcome. He tried to convince me I was like that boy and you were like that father, but I didn't believe him. You already know why."

Sir Edward chuckled. "I think the entire household heard why."

"I did not believe a father could forgive a son like that. Because if the father forgave the son for straying so far and making such a mess out of his life, then that would mean the son would also have to forgive the father for making the son feel that he could never live up to his brother—or in my case, to William Ransome."

"What made you change your mind? What made you believe in forgiveness?"

"Serena." The sound of her name coming from his mouth filled him with such longing he could barely keep himself from going to the door and walking to Kingston to find the next ship headed north.

"Ah." Green eyes twinkling, Sir Edward sat back in his chair, elbows propped on the high arms, fingers steepled before his face, index fingers tapping his lips. "A lovely name for, I'm certain, a lovely young woman."

"Yes, sir. Her family has taken me in as one of their own. Her father is making me a partner in his importing business, along with his own son, who happens to be my closest friend in the world. Serena and I plan to be married as soon as I can return to Philadelphia." Which would be much sooner now that Michael did not have to go all the way to England to see his father.

"Philadelphia is such a long way away. I hope you plan to bring your Serena down for a visit so she can see the beauty of the place you grew up."

"I plan to do more than just bring her for one visit, Father. Declan and I will be expanding his father's business to the Caribbean. And I am certain Serena plans to find reasons to come down here with me as often as she can."

Sir Edward clasped his hands together before dropping them into his lap. "Wonderful. The family will be back together again."

Michael could not rejoice with his father. "Not the entire family. It is my fault Mama died. If I had only come back and let her know I was still alive. But I was so afraid that discovering her son had turned pirate would be the death of her. So I stayed away."

"She was ill for a long time, Michael. The doctor believes it was stomach cancer. You could have come back and she still would have died."

"But she would have known I was still alive."

Sir Edward made a noncommittal sound in the back of his throat. "So will you go back to Kingston with us tomorrow to try to find a ship headed north?"

Anticipation leaped in Michael's chest. "Yes, sir. I have waited so long. It seems impossible I am finally going to get to see Serena again."

Sir Edward stood and straightened his uniform coat with a tug at the waist. "They have probably finished the main course, but they may still be at dessert. And I do not know about you, but I have worked up a hunger."

Michael stood, but looked at the two glasses of brandy, untouched. "Sir, the brandy?"

His father looked at the glasses and bottle as if just now realizing they were in the room. "Ah, yes. Julia needed to know we had not murdered each other, and a study should always smell like wood smoke from the fireplace, dusty books, and brandy. At least, that's what my father's study always smelled like." He picked up the glass, sniffed it, and set down again. "Cannot abide the stuff myself."

Shaking his head, Michael headed for the door.

"Son?"

He turned back to face his father. "Yes, sir?"

Sir Edward laid his hands on Michael's shoulders. "You have become a good, strong, capable man. I am proud to call you my son."

All the disappointment Michael had experienced as a child hoping his father would say those words tried to choke him. But he swallowed past it—and it disappeared. "And I am proud to call you my father."

In the dining room, the main course had been taken away and the dessert course laid, but Julia had set aside plates for both of them. Michael looked around the table, wishing Serena could be here to see this. His family.

Only, his family was missing one person. He might never be able to forgive himself for not coming back before Mother died, but watching Father with Maria made Michael wonder if there would ever come a day when he would be able to call her Mother without feeling a pang of guilt.

Over dessert, he announced his intention to return to Kingston tomorrow and find a ship headed north.

Julia looked devastated.

"But I will be coming back often and bringing Serena with me." He explained what he and Declan would be doing.

As he'd hoped it would, this cheered his sister. "Then, of course, Serena must stay here at Tierra Dulce while you search the islands for beautiful pieces to take back to the Americans."

He reached across the corner of the table and squeezed her hand. "That's what I hoped for."

Instead of splitting up after dinner, everyone adjourned to the sitting room, where talk continued until the early hours of the morning.

Charlotte slept, curled up on the sofa between her mother and Ned. And everyone else yawned often and spoke of going to bed until William stood, took Julia by the hand, and said goodnight.

Michael did not want the night to end. He knew he would be coming back, but everything would be different when he did. He shuffled down the hall toward his bedroom, too tired to lift his feet fully from the floor.

"Michael?" Julia came out of her room, wrapping a belt around a dressing gown.

"Yes?" He leaned against the wall across the hall from her.

"Mama's death was hard on me, but I know how much harder it has been for you to accept there is nothing you could have done to change the outcome."

He blinked and swallowed back the guilt.

She handed him a plain, fabric-covered journal. "I found this when I was going through Mama's papers and books. I know she would want you to have it." She smiled tenderly. "She wrote it for you."

He opened the book to the first page. It was dated shortly after his ship was taken by the pirates.

> *Dearest Michael,*
>
> *You are the joy of my life. And though we are now farther apart than the world can imagine, we will always be together, because I carry you in my heart...*

Michael closed the book when the words blurred too much to read them, and he pressed it to his forehead.

Julia wrapped her arms around him, and he melted into the comfort of her embrace. "I like what she wrote in that first letter. Because it is true now that we have found each other. We will never be apart again, no matter how far we go."

"Because I always carry my sister in my heart."

"And I always carry my brother in my heart."

Chapter Twenty-Nine

Dishonorably dismissed from service, along with thirty days' prison time, and accounting for time served. As soon as he completes the paperwork, James will be free to leave." Ned reached for Charlotte to hug her after giving the three waiting women the good news—but he would have to catch her first.

"Mama!" Julia let go of Maria Witherington and reached for Charlotte as she sank toward the floor.

Ned was faster, sliding his hand behind her head just before it hit. The small, airless office where Julia, Maria, and Charlotte had been allowed to wait to hear the outcome of the hearing was not fit for the men who worked in it, much less for three ladies.

One of the officers brought water. Julia dipped a handkerchief in it and started wiping Charlotte's forehead while Maria tried to get her daughter to drink.

Charlotte coughed and sputtered, and her eyes opened. "What— why am I on the floor?"

"You fainted." Maria looked around the room. "You, there, bring that chair over."

The frightened lieutenant did as he was bade.

"Ned, lift her."

He did so, easily. "She's been complaining that with all of the complications that have happened to delay the wedding, along with waiting to find out what would happen to James, she has not been feeling well."

Maria took the handkerchief from Julia and wiped her daughter's face with it. "Nausea? Fatigue? Loss of balance and concentration?"

Fear crept into Ned's throat with each symptom Maria mentioned. "Yes, ma'am. All of those."

"I expected as much." Concern dug lines between his mother-in-law's brows.

"Mama? What is it?" Julia knelt beside her stepmother.

"Nothing another seven and a half or eight months will not cure her of." She turned her frown of concern on Ned.

Ned lifted Charlotte's hand. A disease that would linger for seven or eight months? "What is it, Lady Witherington? What ails her?"

Julia patted his arm, amusement dancing in her green eyes. "Something that has been ailing women since time began, Ned."

"But what is it?" And why did Maria look as if she might yell and Julia as if she might laugh?

Julia leaned forward. "She is with child, Ned," she whispered.

"No. She cannot be. We have been apart since..."

Julia raised her eyebrows and cocked her head.

"We have to get married."

Maria's frown deepened. "I thought you *were* married."

"We are married, Mama." Charlotte tugged her hand out of Ned's. "And I wish you all would not speak of me as if I am not here."

Maria looked around. "Come, we will wait for James outside. Charlotte, do you feel well enough to walk? Take your husband's arm." She did not need so much volume for the three standing near her. Ned looked around. The two officers watched them with open curiosity.

Ned put his arm around Charlotte's waist and whisked her from the building to the waiting carriage.

"I thought we were waiting for James." Charlotte dropped onto the seat, making it bounce. "Julia, do you mind riding backwards? I was getting queasy on the way here."

"I do not mind." Julia climbed up into the open-top barouche and sat in the seat facing Charlotte.

Ned turned to help Maria in also, but she did not step up. "You are certain you were legally wed in the eyes of the church?"

"Their marriage is legal," Julia said, shading her eyes from the warm afternoon sun. "I had my solicitor look at the certificate and he verified it. In the eyes of the law, they have been married for just over six weeks now."

Maria stepped up into the carriage and sat next to her daughter, but she looked at Julia. "If you make them have a wedding ceremony now, people will be able to count back and know that Charlotte was already with child at the time."

Color flooded back into Charlotte's face. "What you are saying is that Ned and I have been kept apart because we were convinced we needed to have a real church wedding, and now I don't get to have a wedding because—" Her face pinched and she turned away from all three of them.

"We can still have the wedding breakfast, though. Put the word out to those who will spread it that we wanted James to be there. People will understand why it was so long delayed after the wedding that way." The creases in Maria's forehead began to ease.

Charlotte sniffed and wiped her eyes on the handkerchief her mother and Julia had used to cool her face. "A wedding breakfast would be lovely, but what is more important to me is to know if Ned and I can stop pretending like we aren't married and start living together as man and wife."

"Yes, Charlotte."

That meant Ned needed to start working on finding them a place to live. There was a little place, not far from Tierra Dulce, but he wanted Charlotte to see it before purchasing it. She would have to live there, so she should have a say in it.

"Oh, there is James."

At the guardhouse ahead of the carriage, a marine guard led James to the door. His indigo coat had been stripped of all insignia of rank. He blinked against the brightness of the sun, holding his arm up to shield his eyes.

"Ned, do be a dear." Maria prodded his shoulder.

"Yes, ma'am." He trotted across the yard and retrieved James, bringing him back to the carriage, where the three ladies made a fuss over him.

Ned bade them farewell and returned to the large building where the court-martial had taken place. Inside the five commodores and Admiral Witherington still conferred. Ned assumed Sir Edward was giving them all their new orders.

Ned hoped William's new orders included getting his three ships out to sea: *Alexandra*, *Audacious*, and *Auspicious*—a former pirate ship now captained by a recently promoted Patrick O'Rourke.

Ned found his favorite place to sit and wait for William whenever they came ashore. The low rock up beside the palm tree tended to be overlooked by everyone else whose ships were laid up in ordinary, coming to the fort hoping for something to do. He settled onto the stone and leaned his back up against the rough trunk.

Charlotte was with child. A baby. A family of their own. Ned had never known his father, also a sailor, who had gone off to war and never returned. Mother still kept the page from the *Naval Gazette* listing Edmund Cochrane among the dead in a little known battle in a little known corner of the world.

The Kingston *Chronicle* reported that the Congress of Vienna was even now hosting settlement talks between Britain and America. If peace was achieved, it would be the first time in Ned's life his country—and thus his navy—would not be at war.

William insisted a country still needed its navy even during peacetime. But the peace with France had brought about a necessity to cut down the number of men and ship at sea. What would happen now with no wars at all?

Ned needed an alternative. While his prize money gave him stability and eliminated worry about the immediate future, it was not enough to support a family forever.

He liked Jamaica. Charlotte did as well. She had been learning from Julia how to run a sugar plantation. Ned had never considered becoming a farmer. Spending several weeks once on his brother-in-law's farm outside Plymouth had nearly been his undoing. But here, in a place so beautiful as Jamaica, with Julia to learn from? How could he go wrong?

William came out into the yard, spotted Ned in his usual spot, and waved him over. Admiral Witherington joined them.

"We're going back out to sea, Ned. The Admiralty is looking to strike a blow that could turn the war in our favor. In three weeks we'll sail northward into the Gulf of Mexico and join with the fleet for an attack on New Orleans."

Going back to sea. Battle. "Charlotte is with child."

William and Sir Edward both gaped at him. Sir Edward recovered first. "Congratulations, Captain. A momentous occasion."

But it was not congratulations he wanted. "What if something happens to me, sir? My child will be fatherless, like I was. I don't want my child to have to live like that."

"Nothing will happen to you. If it does, you know we will all help Charlotte with the child. You cannot let fears of what might happen keep you from doing what you know you should."

William was right, of course. Ned set aside his anxiety over the fate of a child not yet born. "Tell me about this offensive."

❦

Charlotte turned every way she could to see the dress in the mirror. Julia's seamstress had done a wonderful job, working the midnight blue silk with silver swans embroidered throughout into a beautiful gown.

In the week since Mama had diagnosed her, Charlotte's appetite returned. Instead of finding nothing appetizing, she now ate anything Cook would put in front of her. She had especially developed a fondness for roasted goat. And today, she could eat all the roasted goat she wanted to at her wedding breakfast.

Guests had been arriving for almost an hour now. Julia planned to have Ned and Charlotte enter at eleven o'clock. Because of the distances people traveled to attend such an event, unlike a wedding breakfast in England, this would be an all-day occasion.

And other than the family and the officers from *Audacious* who came, she did not know most of the people who would be here today. But Julia knew them. And it was a good way for Mama to meet the neighbors, because she would be living with Julia until the house Admiral Witherington—she still could not think of Sir Edward as *Papa*—had commissioned in Kingston was finished.

Her hair hung in soft waves almost to her shoulders. Ned teased her that some night he would take a pair of shears and cut it all off again, for she did not need long hair to be beautiful the way some other women did. But she noticed how he liked running his fingers through it and imagined once it was long again that he would forget what she'd looked like with short hair.

She yawned. Ned was supposed to come get her when it was time to make their appearance. Maybe she should lie down until then.

Closing her eyes, the warm comfort of sleep drifted in.

But before it could take hold, the door opened. It couldn't be eleven o'clock already. She kept her eyes closed, not wanting to lose the soft tranquility she'd found.

"Ned—"

A hand covered her mouth, pushing her head deep into the pillow. "Make a sound and I'll kill you."

⊶⊰⊱⊷

With the cane harvest about to begin, this might be the last time for several months that Julia would get to see some of her neighbors. And it looked as they had felt the same way, as everyone she'd invited had come.

"You should have had one of these for yourself," several of her neighbors remarked, passing by with a plate piled high with Cook's goodies. More than one of her neighbors had tried to hire the mulatto woman away from Tierra Dulce, but Julia guarded her jealously and awarded her handsomely for her skill in the kitchen.

Yes, Charlotte and Ned's wedding breakfast did serve the additional purpose of formally introducing William to those in the area who had not yet met him. Attired in his dress uniform, he, along with her father, drew quite a bit of interest and appreciation from the women. But they weren't the only ones. Patrick O'Rourke looked quite dashing with his new epaulettes, and the lieutenants from all three ships drew plenty of female admirers.

"Julia, dear." Maria pointed at the hall clock visible through the open doors. A few minutes before eleven. She'd best send Ned for Charlotte.

She looked in the study, where he'd been earlier, but no Ned. Where else would he be? Oh, yes. She went to his second favorite room in the house. He sat at the table eating scraps from the roasted goat Cook was carving.

"If the goat is about ready to go out, do not you think it is time you and Charlotte made your appearance?" Laughing, she shooed him out of the kitchen. "Come out whenever you are ready, and William will make the announcement."

Returning outside, she found William and let him know it was almost time. He went to the top of the porch steps at the back of the house, standing near the door to the bedroom corridor, where Ned had been instructed to bring Charlotte out.

Moments later Ned appeared—alone and panic-stricken.

Julia joined him and William on the porch. "What is it?"

"I cannot find Charlotte anywhere. Things are knocked about in our room, as if there was a struggle." He blanched. "I think Charlotte's been taken."

Chapter Thirty

Charlotte worked at the knot in the silk neckcloth whenever Henry Winchester had his back turned. The office building blocked them from view of the main house and yard, where the guests milled, and the pistol he had tucked under his belt kept her from crying out.

"Your families ruined the Winchesters, and you're all going to pay, starting with you."

Not only did Henry have an edge of insanity in his voice, he looked as though he had been out in the wilderness, chased by animals for months. And the fact he'd had to bring one of Ned's neckcloths to tie her to one of the porch posts while he dug for something in the small garden meant he had not planned this. He was acting on emotion, not intellect.

"I planned everything. My brother did not trust me. He did not believe I could make plans and follow through with them. He believed he was better than everyone else and smarter than everyone else. I'll show him that I can make a plan and follow through with it." He kept muttering to himself as he dug.

She almost had the knot loose.

"What are you doing?" He jumped to his feet and tightened the knot at her wrists, as well as the one around the beam. "I will kill you, Charlotte. You could have married me, but instead you chose to jilt me for who? For a sailor, a nobody."

A biting retort readied itself on Charlotte's tongue, but then she thought of the baby. That one thought was what had made her walk calmly out of the house with Henry, had made her stay quiet and not call out when he led her down to the office and around behind it. She had to do whatever it took to save herself so she could protect her child. And that meant not inciting Henry to do anything worse than he had already done.

He knelt, picked up the spade, and started digging again. "This was my garden. She thought she was so clever, making the steward keep his own garden and cook his own food instead of eating in the big house like Jeremiah. He's not worthy to walk in my footprints. Why should I want to eat at the big house with the likes of him?"

Charlotte started working on the knot again.

This time the more vigorously Henry dug, the more he babbled. About his brother. About Jeremiah. About Julia. About his mother and sisters.

She could move her hand—oh, yes! Her right hand slid free from confinement. The cloth fell away just as Henry's spade hit something hard.

Charlotte wrapped her hands in the cloth to make it look as though she were still tied up. Hopefully he would not notice how loose her binding was now.

He pulled a small iron lockbox out of the hole he'd dug under the corner of the porch. Taking a key from his pocket, he opened the box.

Inside was more money than Charlotte had ever seen in one place.

"Ten thousand pounds," Henry murmured. "All mine. Now I don't have to share with Arthur. He never shared anything with me. Made me look the fool in front of Julia Witherington." He looked around, wild-eyed. "They can't know I have it. They'll keep chasing me. They'll never stop chasing me."

"You should fill up the hole, Henry. Fill it up, and they won't know you came and got the money."

He set the box on the edge of the porch and bent down to push the large pile of soil back in the hole.

She had one chance—only one. Swiftly, she released her hands from the neckcloth, picked up the chest, and dropped it on his head.

Pregnancy may have made her sick, dizzy, tired, and off-balance, but it had done nothing to disturb her aim. She rolled Henry over so he would not suffocate in the dirt—she made sure he was still breathing—and then she took the gun from his belt and ran back to the main house.

Three lieutenants ran toward her. "Mrs. Cochrane, we've been looking for you."

"There's a man behind the office building. Take him into custody. Where is Captain Cochrane?"

"He went down toward the lagoon, ma'am."

Charlotte handed him the gun and then ran through the confused crowd on the lawn and toward the wide path cut between the sugar cane that led to the secluded lagoon.

"Ned!" Her stomach made her sorry for the large breakfast she'd eaten. She slowed and took deep breaths to try to control the nausea. "Ned!"

"Charlotte?"

Relieved to hear his voice, she bent over and braced her hands on her knees, gasping for air. Ned swept her up in his arms and carried her back to the house. He sat on their bed, holding her, rocking her back and forth. "I thought I'd lost you again."

"It was Henry Winchester. I sent some of O'Rourke's lieutenants to arrest him." She told him what had happened.

"Ned, before we buy that little sugar plantation, can we make sure that there are no more Winchester brothers?" She buried her head in the crook of his neck.

"I'll make that my mission. That, and protecting you and our child. I want to make sure we have a very long life together."

"Good. Because I've decided that if we're going to become sugar planters, we're going to need a big family to run the place." She kissed the side of his neck. "A *big* family."

‹✥✥›

Julia Ransome lay in her husband's arms, admiring the pattern the moonlight made through the billowing lace curtains.

"How can I ever leave you again after what happened today?" William's breath tickled the back of her neck.

She pulled his arm farther around her and snuggled her back into his chest. "Henry Winchester has been apprehended. He will be charged with piracy. And then we know what happens after that. There is nothing more to worry about."

"I will resign my commission. Tomorrow. I can tell your father before we go back into Kingston. I never have to leave you again." He pulled her closer and kissed her neck, her shoulder. "If I love you, how can I leave you?"

"I need to show you something." Julia untangled herself from him and the covers and got out of the bed. She lit a candle and crossed to the bookcase beside the fireplace. She pulled two volumes off the shelf and brought them back to the bed with her. Sitting cross-legged, facing him, she handed him the candle and opened the older book.

William looked down at the handwritten page. "What is it?"

"This is a journal my mother kept. I've found dozens of them, going back to when she was a young bride and her dashing Royal Navy captain was called out to sea. She filled book after book with love letters to my father. Love letters that he has given me permission to read so that I can understand who my mother was and how much she loved my father and Michael and me."

She pulled that book from his hand and put the newer one in it, opened to the first page. "I'd like you to read that to me."

He turned the journal so the light shone better on its page and began reading.

My darling William,

To carry on a tradition started by my mother, I am writing these letters not only to recount the daily events at Tierra Dulce but also as an expression of my deep love for you. As a way of holding you near to my heart while duty keeps you far away. As a way of telling you that no matter how far apart we are, we will always be together because we are in each other's hearts...

"I cannot write dozens of journals full of love letters to you if you are here all the time."

"You're daft, woman. Do you realize that?" He closed the book, snuffed the candle, and pulled her back into his arms. "When I became an officer in the Royal Navy, I did it because I wanted to protect my country and fight for my king. But I don't think that's as important now as protecting my family and my home. And I need to be here to do that."

"William, if you were not a naval officer, you would not have been able to protect me—to come after me, to attack Shaw. That threat is over, but there are others out there. Foreign invaders who could attack our country, pirates and privateers who could attack our livelihood. Your mission has not changed. You still fight for king and country. It's only your quest that has changed."

"My quest? So I am now a knight errant on a quest for his lady love?"

"If you like. Before, your quest has been to win battles and fight for promotion and prize money. Now, your mission is the same, but you have only one quest." She twined her fingers through his.

"And what is that, my lady love?"

"Your quest is to return home safely to me at the end of every mission." She turned to look at him, the moonlight bathing his beloved face in a soft glow.

"I love you, Julia Ransome." He kissed her until she could no longer think about pirates and missions and quests but until only one thought formed coherently in her mind.

"I love you, William Ransome."

Tierra Dulce Plantation
St. Catherine's Parish, Jamaica
April 1844

Julia Ransome wiped her tears from her cheeks, hoping none of her friends and neighbors saw her. Most would consider it only natural for a woman to cry at such a time as this, but tears were never natural for Julia.

An embrace from someone wearing a bonnet with an enormous brim almost smothered her.

"It was a beautiful service." Susan Yates stepped back and used her own handkerchief to dab at the trails of moisture on Julia's cheeks.

"Thank you, my lady."

"Would you stop calling me that?"

"It is your rightful title now that Collin is an earl."

Susan turned and gazed at her husband. "His brother's death was quite unexpected. And to have died a bachelor at *his* age…" She shook her head.

A pair of warm hands settled on Julia's shoulders. "Yes, not everyone can be so blessed as to fall in love at a young age and be pursued by that woman until he finally marries her."

Julia rapped her fan against William's knuckles. "He will never let me forget that I proposed to him. Of course, if I'd waited for him to get around to it, we would not be standing here today."

Both Julia and Susan turned to gaze upon the young couple standing at the top of the porch steps receiving congratulations and well-wishes from the wedding attendees.

Susan turned and hugged Julia again. "Now we are truly sisters."

Julia laughed and extricated herself from the embrace of her dearest friend in the world. "You said that twenty-nine years ago when Frederick was born and we came for the christening, and again two years later when you came here for Edward's. Just as becoming godparents to each other's children does not make us sisters, becoming mothers-in-law to each other's children does not make us sisters either."

At fifty-seven years old, Susan Yates could still pout and simper like a debutante. "Will you not even pretend it does for my sake?"

"Is there anything that could make us closer than we already are? You are the sister of my heart, *my lady*." Julia arched a brow at her.

Susan laughed.

"Does that mean I have to call her sister, also?"

A distinguished man with thick silver hair and a neatly trimmed mustache joined them. The only thing that kept him from achieving true perfection was the scar that ran diagonally across his forehead into his left brow.

Julia tilted her head to receive her brother's kiss on the cheek.

Susan narrowed her eyes at him. "I still have not forgiven you for taking my daughter away from me."

"*I*? I do believe you have me confused with someone else named Michael Witherington." He quirked a smile at Susan and leaned closer to Julia. "Namely, my son, the scoundrel, who stole Lady Marianne away and forced her to live in Philadelphia." He straightened. "Besides, you still have a daughter remaining at home."

"And you're getting even with Michael through us, Susan. Your Frederick is taking my Eleanor away." Julia smiled up at William when he gave her shoulders another quick squeeze.

"There were times I never thought it would happen." Susan sighed. "Frederick takes after his godfather." She cast a glance at William around the eight inches of hat brim that stuck out beside her face.

"'Twas your idea to send him here to apprentice to Julia and learn how to run a successful business." William settled his arm around Julia's waist. She leaned into him, enjoying every moment she got to spend with him.

"I only did so because you were still at sea most of the time when he came. I thought, under Julia's influence, he might turn out to be sensible like her rather than taciturn like you." Susan's eyes twinkled.

Oh, how Julia would miss Susan when she and Collin returned to England in a few days. Though steamships made the crossing safer and shorter, she still did not get to see them often enough. Another tear escaped. And Eleanor. Her dear, sweet girl would be leaving also. Sailing with her new husband to New Orleans for their wedding trip before returning to England.

Tenacious as ever, Susan returned to one of her favorite topics—at least, a favorite on this visit to Tierra Dulce once Michael and Serena arrived. "If you do not send Marianne and your son home—to England, I mean—for a visit soon, I shall have to speak with Sir Edward and have him intervene."

Michael pressed his hand to his chest as if experiencing heart pain. "Oh, no! Never that. My father is still finding ways to make me suffer for spending most of my youth as a pirate who took gold from him to subsidize liberating slaves."

"And let us not forget kidnapping innocent young girls." Charlotte Cochrane slipped her small hand through the crook of Michael's elbow and smiled up at him.

"And forcing them to marry the sea captains who rescue them against their brothers' wishes." Michael cast a sidelong glance at William.

As usual, William refused to let Michael rile him. Sometimes Julia thought that if William had known marrying her would result in discovering her brother was still alive and would become part of the family once again, he might not have been so quick to go through with it.

"I am happy that if she had to marry someone against my wishes, it was Ned Cochrane." William inclined his head to his sister. "It seems to have worked out well for her."

Julia stifled a laugh. Yes, with seven children—the eldest, Charles Lott Cochrane, born almost nine months to the day after their wedding—and with a sugar plantation successful enough to rival Tierra Dulce, Julia would agree that the marriage, started on such ill-advised terms, had worked out well.

Charlotte, complaining of hunger pains, cajoled Michael into escorting her to the food table. William excused himself to join Collin and speak to the officers who had driven out from Fort Charles to attend the wedding of Admiral Ransome's daughter.

Due to being under his father's command, Captain Edward Ransome, their oldest son, had come home for his sister's wedding. Nathan, newly made a commander under his uncle Philip's command, was on his way to India, so he could not come home.

Julia dashed the tear away and scanned the groups milling about the lawn. A booming laugh caught her attention and brought a smile to her face. Retired Admiral Sir Edward Witherington, with Maria at his side as always, held court under the arbor near the food table, leaning on his cane and no doubt telling stories of his adventures. And, naturally, there with them, the delight of Julia's life: eighteen-year-old Margaret Jane Ransome. Of their four children, Margaret was most like Julia in looks and in temperament.

At a nudge from Susan, Julia dragged her attention from Margaret's dimpled cheeks and dancing eyes. "Yes?"

"Who is that young man?"

She followed Susan's gaze. A tall young man with dark hair, hooded eyes, and a melancholy air stood in the shadow of the house. "That is Stephen Grayson, our new steward. He arrived yesterday. I invited him to come to the wedding so he could start getting to know the family—the entire Tierra Dulce family."

"It seems there's one family member he seems interested in getting to know." Susan nodded toward the group gathered around Sir Edward.

Julia wished Susan had not talked her out of tucking her spectacles into her reticule. Was it Margaret who drew Stephen's unalterable attention? Concern, followed by joy, fluttered through Julia's chest. It was too soon to hope, but hope bloomed nonetheless.

"I always worried that Margaret was too much like me." Julia hooked her arm through her best friend's. "That she would have to go through the stigma of being called an old maid, of fearing she would never find anyone who loved her and whom she could love in return."

"Do you regret that you did not marry until you were almost thirty years old?"

Julia thought back over the past thirty years of her life. William. Edward. Eleanor. Nathan. Margaret. Tierra Dulce. A husband who loved his vocation—and now was home much more often. Children who loved each other, their parents, and their home, but who had thoughts and ideas of their own.

"No. No matter how much pain and loneliness I experienced in my life before I married, I would not change one thing. I have the best family—including a sister," she squeezed Susan's arm, "the best home, the best life anyone could hope for. And in the end, where we are now is what matters, not fretting over choices made in the past."

Julia watched as Margaret moved away from her grandparents and toward the house. Stephen Grayson stepped forward and then hesitated. Julia willed him to find the courage to speak to Margaret, but he let her go by without taking notice of him, her head no doubt filled with plans for modernizing their harvesting and production equipment to maximize Tierra Dulce's sugar output.

Yes, Margaret was her mother's daughter.

And that was just the way it should be.

Book Group Discussion Questions

1. What expectations did you have when you began reading the book? Were your expectations met? Were you disappointed with anything in the story?

2. What did you learn about the time period that you didn't know before reading this book? What did you learn about how people lived and what life might have been like? Was there anything you didn't understand (terms or social customs)? Was there anything you expected to see but didn't?

3. In this story, there are a lot of hidden agendas and identities. In what ways did you see this happening and with which characters?

4. There is quite a bit of concern over Charlotte's "ruined reputation" in this story—first from her disguising herself as a boy and living with the other midshipmen (in *Ransome's Crossing*) and now from having been abducted by a pirate. Is reputation—what is known or assumed about someone's background—as important today as it was then?

5. Charlotte shows once again that she's willing to go against her family's wishes to be with the man she loves. Would you be willing to do that?

6. Before the modern era, it wasn't unusual for women to find themselves at the mercy of men around them. What were your thoughts on Julia's interactions with Shaw? Could she have done more to protect herself? to protect James?

7. Captain Salvador considers himself a moral man, yet he also claims to be a pirate. In what ways did Salvador live up to the Christian morals of his family? In what ways did he betray those morals? What did you like about Salvador? What did you not like about Salvador? What would you have changed about him?

8. James Ransome reveals to William and Julia his jealousy over William's "easy" rise through the ranks in the Royal Navy. Was James justified in his jealousy?

9. What did you think about the way in which Julia described God's forgiveness to James—by comparing it to the way James's mother loved and forgave him?

10. Read Luke 15:11-32. How is the parable of the prodigal son exemplified in this story?

Crew Manifests

HMS *Alexandra*

Commodore William Ransome

First Lieutenant Patrick O'Rourke

Second Lieutenant Angus Campbell

Third Lieutenant Horatio Eastwick

Fourth Lieutenant Eamon "Jack" Jackson

Fifth Lieutenant Robert Blakeley

Sixth Lieutenant Josiah Gibson

Midshipman Walter Kennedy

Midshipman Christopher Oldroyd

Steward Archibald Dawling

Boatswain (Bosun) Matthews

Surgeon James Hawthorne

Sailing Master Ingleby

Purser Holt

HMS *Audacious*

Captain Ned Cochrane

First Lieutenant Lewis Gardiner

Second Lieutenant Millington Wallis

Third Lieutenant Richard Duncan

Acting Fourth Lieutenant Thomas Hamilton

Acting Fifth Lieutenant Cornelius Martin

Midshipman Harry Kent

Midshipman Louis Jamison

Midshipman Charles Lott

Midshipman Isaac McLellan

Master Carpenter Colberson

Boatswain (Bosun) Parr

Sailing Master Bolger

Purser Harley

Captain of Marines Macarthy

Vengeance

Captain El Salvador de los Esclavos

First Mate Martin Declan

Second Mate Simon "Picaro" Donnelley

Sailing Master Jean Baptiste

Boatswain Hanyu Lau

Steward Suresh Bandopadhyay

Kaye Dacus lives in Nashville, Tennessee, and holds a master of fine arts degree in writing popular fiction from Seton Hill University, is a former vice president of American Christian Fiction Writers, and currently serves as the president of Middle Tennessee Christian Writers. She loves action movies and British costume dramas, and when she's not writing she enjoys knitting scarves and lap blankets (she's a master of the straight-line knit and purl stitches!). To learn more about Kaye and her books, visit her online at kayedacus.com.

Ransome's Honor

Book 1 of The Ransome Trilogy

❧

Once Youthful Sweethearts—
Can Their Love Be Renewed?

When young Julia Witherington doesn't receive the proposal for marriage she expects from William Ransome, she determines to never forgive him. They go their separate ways—she returns to her family's Caribbean plantation, and he returns to the Royal Navy.

Now, twelve years later, Julia is about to receive a substantial inheritance, including her beloved plantation. When unscrupulous relatives try to gain the inheritance by forcing her into a marriage, she turns to the only eligible man to whom her father, Admiral Sir Edward Witherington, will not object—his most trusted captain and the man who broke her heart, William Ransome. Julia offers William her thirty-thousand-pound dowry to feign marriage for one year, but then something she could never have imagined happens: She starts to fall in love with him again.

Can two people overcome their hurt, reconcile their conflicting desires, and find a way to be happy together? Duty and honor, faith and love are intertwined in this intriguing tale from the Regency era.

Ransome's Crossing

BOOK 2 OF THE RANSOME TRILOGY

❦

Danger, Duty, and Deception on the High Seas—
Will True Love Prevail?

In order to get to her secret fiancé in Jamaica, Charlotte Ransome must disguise herself as Charles Lott, a midshipman who joins the crew of one of the ships in a convoy led by her brother—Commodore William Ransome.

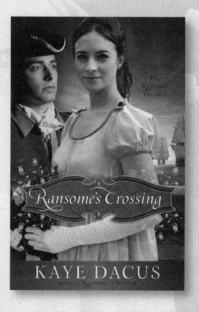

Unknown to her, First Lieutenant Ned Cochrane, also in Ransome's convoy, has set his heart on Charlotte after meeting her briefly in Portsmouth. But because he is about to leave for a year of duty in the Caribbean, he despairs of finding her unmarried when he returns home.

During the transatlantic journey, an attack on the convoy throws Ned and "Midshipman Lott" together. Though unsure as to whether he should let Charlotte know he sees through her ruse, Ned decides to keep her secret for now . . . and hopes to eventually win her love. However, Charlotte soon discovers that losing her heart to the handsome lieutenant is not the only danger she faces on this Atlantic crossing.

Courage, faith, hope, and love shine in this exciting romantic sea adventure from the Regency era.

To learn more about books by Kaye Dacus
or to read sample chapters, log on to our website:

www.harvesthousepublishers.com

HARVEST HOUSE PUBLISHERS

EUGENE, OREGON